Bound in Scales

By Steven De Luca

Prologue

Excerpt from Alduce's Atlas of Dragons.

The Black Dragon: draconis noire and daconis grandus noire.

I have encountered two types of black dragon. The smaller of the species, draconis noire grows to approximately 20 feet in length from snout to tip of tail, and 8 feet in height, talon to head. The larger grandus noire is much bigger by comparison, easily twice that size.

Both varieties of black resemble the mountain species of dragon (see draconis montemous) most closely, but is sleeker and has a more graceful shape. They have long elegant necks, thickening to the trunk of the body, are four legged with equally long tapering tails, balancing the body shape in a perfect symmetry. Their wingspan, when fully extended, is generally twice the length of the body mass, less neck and tail.

It should be noted that black dragons are rare as fully developed adults and I have only come across two confirmed subjects during all my research and travels.

As an embryo, the unhatched foetus of most dragon eggs tends to be black, only developing colour after leaving the shell. Within the first few weeks of hatching, the scales lose the black of new birth and quickly change to their adult colour.

In the rare event of a dragon not developing any colour and remaining black, I suspect a pigment deficiency during developmental growth of the embryo. This results in a genetic trait that prohibits the scales to naturally change colour.

The black scales, while no less resilient than any other colour, are less metallic in appearance and do not reflect light as brightly as their coloured counterparts. On closer inspection, it appears that some light may be absorbed, rather than reflected.

One thing blacks can accomplish better than their coloured counterparts is the ability to fly at altitude, sustaining flight through both the troposphere and into the stratosphere. What they lack in scale pigment, nature has balanced with the ability to reach impressive heights far beyond that of any of the coloured species.

Black dragons are excellent fliers in general and possess high stamina, allowing them to spend long hours airborne.

One of the known black dragons is Nightstar, a male draconis grandus noire, spanning an impressive forty five feet in length. He has short thick horns atop a heavily armoured head ridge. He is pure black except for the silver patch emblazoned on his chest in the shape of a star, that his name derives from. His place of origin is unknown, and he is one of the more unusual examples of the dragon race. While there are little recorded facts about Nightstar, he has been known to display strong magical abilities.

Part One

Transformation

Chapter 1

Alduce dragged himself up the steep mountain path towards his destination. Wind tugged at the thick black cloak wrapping his medium frame, rustling a large sack slung across his shoulder. He approached the mouth of the cave and squeezed behind the thick bushes that disguised the entrance, the wind abating as he entered the rocky shelter.

Pulling back his hood he reached into his cloak and withdrew a small glass orb that flared, illuminating the inside of the cave. In the far corner, built into a recess not visible from the entrance, stood a metal door, no handles, locks or keyholes marring the solid impenetrable surface. Alduce placed a hand upon the door and a panel of light flared to life beneath his palm, scanning up then down. An internal locking mechanism clicked and the door slid back into the rock, magic to some and science to others. Stepping through the darkened recess, Alduce held up his light orb until he located a switch and flicked it on. He palmed the orb, its light dimming as he slipped it back inside his cloak. A generator whirred and bright panels in the cave's ceiling came to life, chasing away the darkness. It had been a big job sourcing and installing the power cells, but it was worth the effort.

A laboratory filled the cave, full of strange apparatus and machinery, some of it technology, some alchemy. This was the workshop of both a scientist and a sorcerer. Alduce dropped the sack and shrugged off his cloak, draping it over a high backed leather bound chair situated in what appeared to be a living area.

He was of average height with black hair and a tanned face and looked to be in his early thirties, but in fact he was much older. He didn't have the kind of face that would stand out in a crowd and he liked it that way.

He rummaged in his sack and brought out eight thin metal rods, silver in colour and approximately the length of a man's index finger. There was a clear area at the rear of the cave where the roof sloped to meet the floor. Alduce carried the rods to that cave wall, where eight holes had been drilled into the rock to accommodate them. They were arranged like the points of a compass and he started at the point where north would be, inserting the first rod, then to the next, the north east position, moving round until each hole had one of the precious rods inserted. They fitted snugly, almost flush with the surface of the stone, only a small part left protruding. Once all the rods had been distributed, he dragged the high backed chair over to the cave wall, his cloak swinging as the legs scraped across the floor, placing it in front of the compass-like formation he'd constructed.

He reached into his robes and removed two further polished metal rods that he fitted together with a click, tugging on each end to test they were locked in place securely. One end was plain and the other was fashioned with a slot. He added a black handle to the end that wasn't slotted. The newly assembled device resembled a dangerous looking weapon roughly the length of his forearm. Sitting himself in the chair facing the cave wall, he removed a small dragon shaped pendant from around his neck. He slid the dragon off the chain and slotted it into the end of the wand, securing it in the tight groove that had been fashioned to hold it steady. He pocketed the chain and held the wand before him, arm outstretched, examining the device.

He had named it the Flairestaff and it was one of his more successful inventions. Thumbing the switch on the base of the handle started a slow stream of blue sparks flickering and jumping along the silvery metal shaft, turning and twisting along its length, drawn to the small dragon fixed at the end. The electrical sparks continued to flow, the pendant absorbing their charge until it glowed like white metal in a blacksmith's forge.

The electricity activated the raw power of the lightning stored within the dragon, a Flaire made artefact, imbued with the natural force of lightning and the magic of alchemy. The metal used to fashion the little dragon was extremely rare, highly valuable, and difficult to source.

Alduce stretched out his arm, pointing the charged dragon artefact at the topmost rod in the circle, before pushing the switch in the Flairestaff's handle all the way down. A streak of blue-white lightning leapt from the artefact straight to the rod, crackling as it touched the metal sunken into the rock. Alduce started to turn his arm in a wide circle and the lightning jumped seamlessly from the top rod to the next in line, joining both with a thin streak of charge that sizzled and sparked. He moved smoothly on round the circle, leading the lightning to the next rod until he completed the circle, then thumbed the switch off.

The rock inside the circle shimmered as if viewed through rippling water, slowly changing until another cavern could be seen through the rock, blurry and out of focus, like a heat haze on a hot day. The effect faded and the view cleared, leaving behind a gateway to another place. Alduce had opened a portal, he didn't know exactly to where, but it wasn't his own world. The view through the opening on the cave wall was like looking through a window, into a cavern much like his own, except this one was empty and dark. Alduce took a deep breath, pocketed the wand and grabbed his cloak and sack. He slipped out his light orb, reactivated it and stepped through the portal into the cave beyond. Holding the orb high to light his way, he followed his own footprints in the sandy floor, left by his previous journeys to this unnamed world.

The portal behind him remained open, powered by the Flaire rods. They held enough natural charge to power the portal for decades but Alduce planned to only spend a few hours on this side of the gateway.

He emerged from the dark cave and looked out across the landscape of the new world he stood upon. Snow covered mountains walled the horizon far to the North and undulating grasslands, scattered between rocky hills, led away from the cave mouth. A few stands of sparse trees grew where they could on the slopes, fighting for nourishment in the stony soil. Alduce strode from the cavern with purpose; he knew where he was going. He'd made multiple trips here previously with a singular purpose in mind. As he walked, he glanced up, observing the skies above him. It would be fatal if he was spotted before he reached his destination.

He was confident that he had arrived at exactly the right time, but there was no harm in being cautious. He walked for half an hour or so, cresting the hill he climbed, crouching down as he neared the skyline. Two large boulders covered with a rock coloured canvas were his destination and he sneaked forward to the shelter he had made, keeping low. Wriggling between the rocks, he looked out from the gap facing the valley below, to observe his quarry.

There in the hollow between the hills sat a female dragon easily 30 feet in length. She was dark green in colour and her scales shone in the daylight, metallic and bright. Alduce settled down to wait pulling a long brass tube bound with bands of dark worn leather from his sack. He had uncovered plans for this device in an old book and while it wasn't his own invention, he was still proud of what he had fashioned. With the addition of specially ground glass lenses, fitted correctly, he assembled a viewing device that made things in the distance appear closer than they actually were. He named it Long Eye and it was an excellent way for observing dragons from the safety of his hide.

He extended the telescopic tube, tripling its length and peered through the eyepiece. He spied on the unsuspecting dragon taking care not to make any sudden movements or unnecessary sound. He was far enough away to feel safe— or at least, as safe as he could hope to be when one observed a dragon. Being so close to the fabled creature, he knew only too well that if she discovered him, his fate would be sealed.

When it came to humans, dragons were dangerous and unpredictable at best. When it came to a mother dragon sitting on a nest of eggs, Alduce was sure that danger would increase tenfold. He scanned around the nest. It wasn't a traditional nest, like a bird, but more a hollow in the rocky ground. He was rewarded when he spotted what he was looking for: cracked shells. Where there were cracked shells, there had to be hatchlings, probably hidden by their mother's bulk. Alduce watched and waited. Finally, the dragon rose and stretched her massive wings, then leapt into the air. In the depression she had vacated, there were three small shapes, craning their necks and beating the air with stumpy wings, not yet fully formed, squawking like hungry chicks.

Newly hatched dragons.

Alduce focused on the majestic green mother as she climbed into the sky and disappeared from sight. His patience had at long last been rewarded. Opportunity presented itself and it was time to seize it. Quickly, before he could change his mind, he scrambled out from his hiding place and half ran, half tumbled down the slope towards the nest. His large sack flapped behind him as he bounced and hopped over the loose gravel and scree, slipping and sliding until he reached the bottom. He scanned the sky in the direction the mother dragon had taken, then all around, alert eyes seeing nothing. Leaning over into the hollow, he peered into the nest. The smell of decaying flesh and faeces assaulted his nostrils, causing him to gag.

The nest was occupied with the female dragon's three offspring, a red and two greens—one a bright emerald and the other a darker forest hue. Bones and skulls cluttered the nest, the unfortunate remains of animals the hungry dragonets had dined upon.

And there, right at the back, the reason for his journey here. The object he desired. The unhatched egg.

It sat to the rear of the three young hatchlings, pushed aside and abandoned by its mother when it failed to hatch. Nature may have denied the unborn dragon inside a life, but Alduce hoped to provide it with a second chance. He jumped over the small heads of the three snapping dragons and carefully picked his way across the bones rolling and cracking beneath his feet. He grasped the unhatched egg with both hands—it was much heavier than he expected—and thrust it into his sack. Crawling quickly from the nest he took one last look at the magnificent creatures and sped off up the slope towards his shelter. By the time he reached the two rocks, sweat was running down his face. The uphill run and the weight of the egg, combined with the urgency to get back safely before the mother returned, had exhausted him. He squirmed back into his familiar sanctuary, breathing raggedly after his exertion and rested his head on his arms, closing his eyes. Relief swept over him and his breathing gradually returned to normal; he had done it, he had rescued the egg.

He had been observing the female dragon for months, watching the nest and waiting for the eggs to hatch. Four eggs had been laid and the one he now had in his sack was the smallest. Alduce wasn't sure what the normal size of a dragon egg should be, it probably depended on how big the dragon laying it was. His egg, as this is how he now saw it, just managed to fit inside his sack, even though it was the smallest of the clutch. When sat on its blunt end, the tapered end of the egg reached halfway between his knee and his waist, when he stood upright. It had failed to crack open with its siblings and been forgotten by its mother, but not by Alduce.

The sound of the mother dragon's wings passing overhead—along with the renewed cacophony of squawking hatchlings—alerted him to her return. He peered out from the gap as the dragon dropped a tawny coloured deer from her blood smeared jaws into the nest. Three ravenous miniature dragons descended on their meal and squabbled over their share, tearing chunks of flesh from the dead animal. The mother dragon watched her young as they fed, neither aware of the missing egg or the presence of its plunderer.

After the young dragons had consumed their meal their mother settled back down into the hollow. Alduce crept from his shelter with his prize, crouching as he descended the other side of the hill. Maintaining a brisk pace he traversed the rocky ground with a practiced ease. He'd made this journey many times while waiting for the dragons to hatch. Soon he came in sight of the cave he had emerged from, his escape almost complete, ready to return to his own world.

A dark shadow passed overhead, the sound of wings disturbing the air above him. Instinctively he crouched, covering his head with his arms and squeezing his eyes shut, not that this would help protect him from an angry mother dragon. If she had discovered her egg was missing and picked up his scent, she would be angry her nest had been violated. Although the egg hadn't hatched, the maternal dragon would still exact vengeance on the perpetrator. Alduce had been over confident and believed his escape had gone unnoticed. Thinking himself smarter than the dragon would be his undoing. The fear of being seared with flame or being torn apart by huge talons terrified him. He had been so close to procuring this vital element for his research.

When his expected demise never came, Alduce cautiously opened his eyes and peered out from between his arms. What he saw wasn't what he expected, there was no vengeful dragon come to flame him in anger. Sitting calmly before him was a large black crow. It wasn't just large, it was massive! At least seven feet tall.

Alduce had never seen anything like it before and stared, mesmerised as its black intelligent eyes watched him from a cocked head. It was as if the crow was studying him. The irony of the situation wasn't lost on Alduce: it was usually himself that was the scholar, not a huge bird. The mannerisms it displayed as it scrutinised its subject made it look almost human. But it wasn't. It was a fully formed giant crow, shiny black feathers, pale yellow legs and a dangerous looking beak.

His relief from his unexpected visitor not being the mother dragon faded. The scholar in him wanted to learn more about the unknown giant bird standing before him, but the practical survivalist in him took over. An encounter with this bird could be just as fatal as one with the dragon. While it may not be as large or as powerful, it was still more than a match for any human being, should it choose to attack. The crow hadn't made any aggressive moves toward him so far and Alduce hoped that was a good sign. He would need to get past the bird to return to the cave, as at present the colossal crow blocked his way entirely. Moving with exaggerated care and keeping his movements slow and steady, he attempted to circle round the crow. Once he was back inside the cave, it was just a short hop to the waiting portal and safety.

The big crow, unfortunately, wasn't having any of it. As Alduce tried to edge his way round the bird, it hopped back in front of him, halting any progress towards the cave. It was as if it understood what he planned to do and was deliberately trying to prevent it.

"Hey now, bird," Alduce soothed, "I just need past." The big crow titled its head, as if listening to his words.

He tried again to circle round the black feathered obstacle, to no avail. The crow hopped once more between him and the cave mouth, cocking its head at a peculiar angle, almost playful, enjoying a new found game.

An idea came to Alduce. This giant crow may be clever, but he was Alduce, sorcerer and scientist. He studied and understood alchemy, science, and sorcery. He would not be outsmarted by a bird no matter how big it was! He reached inside his cloak and withdrew the light orb, holding it above his head and moving his arm from side to side, to attract its attention. The giant crow followed his movement, its head swaying in time to his arm, almost hypnotic. It liked the shiny bauble, just as Alduce hoped it would. He thumbed the orb's surface, slowly illuminating it and bringing the light from dim to bright. The big crow cawed in surprise, never taking its eyes from the now brightly lit orb.

"Oh, you like that, yes," Alduce crooned.

The giant crow squawked, almost in answer to his words, hopping now from one foot to the other, like an excited dog waiting for his master to throw a stick. If he tossed the orb away from the cave, he was sure the crow would be attracted to the shiny bauble. He would be able to make a dash for the cave once the bird was distracted. It would mean the loss of the orb however, which would be disappointing. They weren't difficult to make, but he'd owned this one since he'd graduated to master and it held some sentimental value for him. Regardless, it was a small price to pay to escape with his life and the dragon egg.

Tensed to make a dash for the entranceway, Alduce tossed the orb onto a patch of dense withered grass, reluctant to smash it on the hard rocky ground. After all, once it was broken, no light would be emitted and his plan would cease to work. The big crow watched the orb as it arced through the air and landed safely on target in the grass, glowing brightly. The crow looked at Alduce, then back towards the orb, head moving back and forth, watching the man, but tempted by gleaming glass. The moment stretched and for a second or two, Alduce didn't think it would take the bait. Then it sprang into the air, flapping its powerful wings and dived for the glowing orb.

Alduce didn't stay to watch, although he was intrigued at the bird's actions and would have liked to study it more. Self-preservation won out over scientific interest and he turned and sprinted towards the cave mouth. He reached the entrance and ducked into the dark interior, panting as he skidded to a stop on the sandy floor. Only then did he look back, he could still see the crow from where he stood. It picked the orb up in its beak and turned its head from side to side, eyeing the glowing glass as it strutted back towards the cave entrance. Thankfully it was too big to fit through the slim cave mouth. Safe now, he observed the huge bird as it played with its new toy.

The crow arrived in front of the cave entrance, blocking out the natural daylight as it poked its head into the gap. It was smart enough to realise that it wouldn't fit inside and didn't attempt to squeeze its body any farther than its outstretched neck would allow. The darkness of the cave was illuminated with the brightly glowing orb, held fast in the giant bird's beak, lighting up its head and reflecting in its deep black eyes.

With a quick flick of its head, the crow opened its beak and tossed the orb directly at him. His reaction instinctive, Alduce snatched the orb from the air before it hit the ground and stood open mouthed. The crow had fetched the orb and returned it to him, when he thought it lost.

Not what he expected.

"Thank you very much," he said and on an impulse, bowed to the wonderful creature in gratitude. The crow nodded its head as if it understood, then withdrew from the cave mouth, turned and launched itself into the air. Alduce pocketed the orb and walked back outside as the huge crow climbed higher and higher into the sky. It cawed as it flew off, the sound of its harsh voice forming a word.

Human

Alduce shook his head, convinced the stress of the acquiring the egg and confronting the giant crow were making him hear things. The huge bird climbed higher, its powerful wings carrying it into the distance, until it became a tiny dark speck. He would like to know more about these wondrous giant birds, but not today. A future project perhaps.

He hefted the sack, adjusting the strap on his shoulder. Patting the heavy egg at his side affectionately as he walked back through the cave to the waiting portal. Stepping through the shimmering curtain with his newly acquired prize, he returned to his own world.

Chapter 2

The laboratory was crammed with all manner of weird and wonderful equipment. Cabinets and machines filled the floor, benches and shelves, stacked with jars and bottles, fought for space along the cluttered cave walls. Narrow pathways wound between the machines and devices to a clear well-lit workspace space where Alduce laboured.

Removing the drill from the top of the dragon egg, Alduce grunted from the effort as he turned it upside down. Rotating the egg on the stand, he positioned a glass bowl beneath the hole he'd made. Clear viscous liquid drained from the hole in the tough shell, dripping into the bowl. When the fluid from inside the egg had slowed to a stop, Alduce rotated the egg once more, the hole now back at the top. He transported the fluid from the egg to another apparatus, pouring its contents into the hollowed out centre of a turntable receptacle. Sealing the container with its lid, he stepped back and gripped a handle fixed to a side wheel attached to the apparatus. Cranking the wheel, he built up speed, spinning the turntable holding the precious amniotic fluid that had surrounded the dragon foetus. The faster he turned the side wheel, the faster the liquid spun and centrifugal force caused the fluid to separate, the less viscous part rising to the top.

He released the handle leaving the turntable to spin unaided and reached for a large syringe, set out on a tray on one of the many work benches surrounding the walls of his subterranean laboratory. The turntable slowed to a stop and Alduce quickly opened the lid, syphoning off the top part of the separated fluid. Once he harvested the precious liquid, he stored his syringe in his *cold shelf* cupboard, an invention he had made to keep things from spoiling. The cupboard was cold, but not quite freezing, which would help preserve the fluid inside the syringe until he was ready to use it.

The thick remains left in the receptacle of his spinning device would not be wasted either. This was also something he needed. Scooping out the gluey residue, he deposited it into a glass jar. He screwed on its lid and placed the jar into his cold shelf cupboard, alongside the syringe.

Returning to the now drained egg, he scooped it up and transferred it to a large vice, tightening the custom made jaws securely. He chose a large bone saw from a vast selection of tools hanging on his wall, and proceeded to score the egg with the saw's blade. When he had made a groove in the shell's tough surface, he went to work in earnest, working the saw backwards and forwards, lightly at first, until there was enough depth in the score for him to apply pressure to his cutting. He worked his way around the surface of the shell, deepening the cut, careful to not break through to the inside of the egg.

By the time he had made a deep cut along the egg's surface, sweat was running from his forehead and his arms ached. He opened the vice, rotating the egg, exposing the underside. He rubbed his face on his sleeve, and with tired muscles, began the procedure on the unmarked side of the shell. He worked until he created the same groove along this side. When he was satisfied with the second groove he rotated the egg, firstly the top and then bottom, joining the cuts with the saw until a perfect channel ran completely around the circumference of the shell.

Alduce blew on the saw blade, cleaning the dusty residue from the metal, then wiped it with a cloth. He worked all the excess dust from between the teeth. He didn't know if the dust from the shell would corrode the steel, but it was good practice to clean your tools when you had finished using them.

The resilient shell of the dragon egg had taken the edge from the blade and it would need sharpened, but that was a job for another time. For now, he hung it back in its place, swapping it for a hammer and a cold chisel, remembering a life before he had been a man of science and a practitioner of magic. In his past he had spent some time as an apprentice to a smith, working in a forge, learning how to use tools and craft things from metal. His time there had served him well, it was one of many skills he had mastered, one of many in his unusually long life.

Setting the chisel into the groove, he focused intently as he positioned its handle perpendicular to the shell. He tapped the flat end with the face of the hammer, taking care and gently striking the metal, driving the wedge of the chisel blade down into the shell. He worked methodically from one end of the cut to the other, his progress painstakingly slow. Fearful that one misplaced stroke would damage the unhatched occupant.

He was finally in a position to advance his study of dragons and learn the secrets held within the shell. One careless mistake now could set his lifetime ambition back decades.

He turned the egg over once more, gripping the shell tightly, terrified he might drop his cumbersome burden, carefully repeating the process along the other side. As he reached the middle of the cut, his patience was rewarded with a loud crack, the shell remained intact, but was weakened sufficiently along the groove. Grinning like a small boy, he bit his lip in concentration as he removed the egg from the oversized vice and clasped it to his chest protectively, like a mother with a new born babe. He carried it across to a shiny metal workbench, clean and free from any of the usual clutter that filled the laboratory.

He placed it, wide side down, on the bench and retrieved his hammer. Holding the egg steady with his free hand, he took a large breath and raising his arm, brought the hammer down with precision, striking the top of the shell with a confidence he didn't feel. The hammer's head landed squarely across the hole he'd drilled to drain the fluid.

A sharp resounding crack echoed around the cavern and the egg split neatly into two perfect halves, exposing the unborn dragon it had homed.

Alduce removed the shell halves and stowed them away; these alone would fetch a king's ransom at any reputable apothecary shop. Anxious to examine the foetus the shell had protected, he spread the form of unborn dragonet out across the metal workbench, its miniature black scales glistening, still damp from the amniotic fluid.

Myth and legend stated that all unborn dragons were black until they hatched and gained their true colour. Now Alduce knew it for certain. However, now he knew this to be true, it made him contemplate how this was known. Whoever recorded this information, must have opened more than one dragon egg or witnessed multiple hatchings. Something he would ponder at a later date, along with a great many other mysteries that his particular line of work often posed.

He unfurled the small wings, spreading them out on either side of the body and wondered why this unfortunate little creature had failed to hatch with the rest of its siblings. He carefully examined the front and rear legs, then the head, checking to see each was as it should be, satisfied that the unborn dragon was perfectly formed.

Alduce crossed his laboratory and opened the doors of a large glass cabinet, sat atop a metal box with many dials and switches across the outer panel. He placed the dragon foetus inside and closed the doors, flicking a switch on the panel, the dials springing to life, the gauges lighting up and indicator needles bounced erratically as the apparatus began to hiss. The glass chamber emitted a faint green glow, lighting up the small form of the dragon as a mist began to fill the inside of the machine.

He had accomplished much this day and was physically and mentally drained. Opening a small doorway, near to where he had activated the portal, Alduce retired to his small sleeping area, formed from an extension of the original cavern.

He switched off the lights to the main laboratory, leaving only the eerie green glow behind. Pulling the small door closed on his greatest endeavour to date, he looked forward to some well-deserved sleep.

Chapter 3

Alduce stood outside the cave, the wind that had torn at his cloak yesterday replaced by the warmth of the morning sun. He wiped the sleep from his eyes, the welcome heat reinvigorating after a good night's rest. Travelling through the portals took its toll on the body, and added to that was his trek to the dragon's nest and carrying back the egg, which was a lot heavier than he expected. He ventured further outside to wake fully, enjoying the sunlight. It was difficult to keep a routine when he was working inside the laboratory. With no window to the outside world and no natural light, it was easy to lose himself in his experiments, never knowing if it were night or day.

A screech from high overhead pealed out and he gazed up into the cloudless blue sky of the new morning. An eagle soared above the landscape, gliding on the warm thermals rising from the ground below. Its wingtips outstretched, feathers splayed, like fingers reaching out towards the heated air currents. Alduce contemplated what it would be like to soar like the eagle. His thoughts drifted back to yesterday's encounter with the giant crow, wondering where it had come from.

He hadn't really explored the world where he acquired the egg after discovering dragons thrived there. After his strange confrontation with the giant crow, he entertained the idea that it may be worth an extended visit. But not now, it would have to wait. One thing at a time. The work ahead of him would be difficult and he would need to put all other distractions aside if he wanted to succeed.

He watched the eagle as it grew smaller, disappearing into the blue sky, then like the eagle, he disappeared too, back into the shade of the cave, leaving the morning behind.

The dragon foetus lay splayed out on the metal surface of the workbench, legs and wings pulled tight, fastened with an intricate arrangement of straps and wires. Alduce held the tiny foreleg with one hand as he carefully pushed the razor sharp scalpel between the small black scales of what he thought of as the dragon's wrist. He had commissioned the finest set of blades possible from a swordsmith known for his skills with metal and as the blade pierced the dragon's tough hide, he knew the tools were up to the task.

Ordinarily, even the best steel would be no match against dragonhide. The scales of the unborn dragon hadn't had time to fully develop and they had spent a full night in the glass misting chamber, exposed to his own brew of chemicals, magically enhanced with a softening potion, allowing the scalpel to cut as it should. He would have to be quick, as the temporary effect on the scales wouldn't last the day. He was an accomplished sorcerer, but even his spells wouldn't weaken dragon scales permanently.

Sliding the blade deeper, he sliced the hide from the muscle and flesh beneath, peeling the dragon's skin away from its body, one scale at a time. While he was fully aware his time was limited, he couldn't rush such a delicate procedure. The dragon's skin wouldn't stay softened for long, a mistake now could have a detrimental effect on the overall project. Dragon eggs were rare, he knew only too well how difficult they were to come by and he had been searching an extremely long time for his opportunity. He couldn't afford any errors, not now he had all the ingredients he needed to succeed.

Time rapidly passed as he slowly and methodically removed the hide, carefully cutting and slicing, pulling the freed sections of dragonhide from its small body, working over every inch of the creature. Turning and twisting the dragon's carcass, he grew adept at manipulating the skin and rotating the blade to attain the best cutting angle.

His fingers ached and his vision swam from the precise work as he made the final cut from the dragon's throat all the way over its belly to the base of its stubby little tail. He dropped the scalpel into a tray and wiped his hand clean of the dragon's red blood. It wasn't black or green ichor as he had suspected it might be, but red blood, just like his, which bode well for his future plans.

He peeled the hide from the carcass, like removing a cloak on a hot day, working until he detached it, the small partially developed wings still attached and intact. Taking it back to the misting chamber, he placed it inside, suspending it with rods and hooks. Arranging the hide so that it hung like a cape, he spread it out, to allow the flow of air inside. Setting the dials once more, he flicked the switch and the machine hummed into life, hissing vapour into the glass chamber. This time the process was for cleaning the skin and scales, no magic just steam, designed to remove any blood or stray pieces of flesh from the inside of the hide. The glass clouded as steam pumped through the chamber. There was no green mystical glow this time, just beads of condensation as they trickled down the glass inside the foggy chamber.

Alduce returned to what remained of the dragon's body and with the practice of a seasoned butcher, set about his grizzly task. He cut and chopped, removing everything of value from the remains. Teeth, eyes, heart, tongue, everything from this dragon was worth something to someone. Dragons were not only rare, they were imbued with a natural magic. A magic that permeated every fibre, every part of its body no matter how small; if you knew how to release it and maximise its potential.

He stored the contents in jars and boxes, some suspended in preservation liquid, some to dry out naturally. With this part of his work complete, all that remained were the bones and a small skull the size of a clenched fist. He scooped them up and left the laboratory, it was dark outside now—a whole day had passed while he worked on the dragon. The night sky was clear and he didn't need his light orb to show him the path that lead to the top of the hill. He had walked this path under the starlight many times, often sitting on the hilltop above his underground laboratory, gazing up at the night sky and marvelling at the many stars. He knew the stars he could see were distant suns, surrounded by other worlds, so far away from his own it was difficult to comprehend.

He set the dragon bones on the ground and placed the skull on a flat rock. The wind and sun would bleach them white, the elements cleaning them better than he ever could. He would let nature do her work, saving him the chore.

Staring back up at the sky once more before heading back to his underground abode, he wondered if any of the stars he could see with the naked eye, were worlds he had reached using the portal.

Chapter 4

Excerpt from Alduce's Atlas of Dragons.

The Green Dragon: draconis vertus.

My first encounter with a dragon was with a green, probably the most commonly seen of the whole draconis species. Greens are the most traditionally shaped dragon; as such many stories and myths are based around this variety. They are one of the larger breeds, fully grown adults are in excess of forty feet, and it isn't uncommon for them to grow larger. Their scales, when examined closely, are metallic and polished. When viewed in direct sunlight they appear pearlescent, the nacreous coating resulting in the optical effect of a multi-coloured spectrum beneath the base green, like oil on water.

Greens have a typically triangular head with two widely spaced horns, sweeping back parallel to the protective spikes on the back of the head and neck. The green also displays a small beard of hard spikes underneath its chin - the longer and thicker this is, the older the subject. Rough ridges and small nose horns decorate the top half of the snout and their slit-eyes tend to be yellow or orange, with a narrow black pupil which results in the dragon having near perfect vision. Ears, barely distinguishable and situated to the rear of the heavily armoured head, below the horns, are extremely acute.

Greens are found on many worlds that support dragons and are quick tempered and easy to upset. They will respond to flattery and are quick witted and intelligent. Caution should be employed when engaging any dragons in conversation, however, one should be extra aware when speaking with a green dragon. They can be tricky and devious and are known for their prowess when it comes to leading conversations and their ability of persuasion, which I strongly suspect is linked to their magic.

Galdor the Green is one example of the many greens I have encountered. He is honourable and magnanimous, yet a force to be reckoned with if he believes you to be an adversary. He is particularly patient and his memory is long. I believe Galdor to be in excess of two hundred years old and his life experience has added to his wise outlook. If befriended, Galdor will stand with you as protector and ally, but anger him and he will search you out, his wrath unstoppable, his justice severe.

* * *

Once the dragonhide had been fully cleaned, Alduce removed it from the misting chamber. The perfectly formed scales gleamed under the artificial light of the laboratory like tiny black mirrors. He marvelled at the way the scales flexed on the hide, stronger than metal yet supple enough to move like soft leather. Running his hand across the surface of the scales, he was aware of the magic they contained. Even though the dragon never hatched, it was a creature of magic, born of magic.

Spreading the hide out on the clean surface of his metal workbench, Alduce used the scalpel to cut it until he had one flat piece, stretched out like a fireside rug, scales facing upwards. He measured the length and breadth of the hide, writing the results down in a small notebook and adding them to a formula, scribbling away until he had a final figure.

Taking a needle, a cord and some clear tubing from one of the many storage cupboards, he sat down in front of the device containing the turntable and rolled up his sleeves. He connected one end of the tube to a valve on the machine and inserted the long needle into the other. He tied the cord around his upper arm and made a fist, the veins standing out as he clenched his fingers tightly and then opened them a few times. The vein in the crook of his arm stood out, raised and blue and he slid the needle beneath his skin, tapping the flow of blood.

Red liquid crept into the clear tube as Alduce untied the cord and cranked the handle with his free hand, drawing his blood into the machine. It ran inside the device and was transferred into a glass beaker perched in the turntable recess, dripping onto the clean glass, covering the bottom of the container, steadily filling it with his lifeblood.

When the required amount of blood had been extracted and the container was almost full, he removed the needle from his vein, using his finger to stem the puncture in his skin. After a few minutes he let the pressure off and was pleased to see the blood had stopped flowing. He stood up quickly, eager to get on with his experiment, but his head swam. Reaching out to steady himself, he gripped the back of his chair, catching his balance. He had taken a lot of blood and risen too soon, his body warning him he should recuperate, but he needed to finish the next part of the process with his warm blood before it cooled. He could rest when he was done.

Carefully, he picked up the container holding the lifeblood spilled from his veins and carried it over to his work area. Retrieving the thicker fluid drained from the dragon's egg, stored in his cool cupboard, he sat it alongside the flask. Taking an empty jar from the shelf he poured the gelatinous residue, shaking the jar to dislodge its viscous contents, filling the new jar to a line indicating the half way mark, then added his warm blood. At first nothing happened: the blood sat atop the egg fluid, not mixing, like oil and water. He took the syringe and added its contents, injecting it into the centre of the flask between the blood and the clear thick jelly. And waited. Then, after a moment, a vapour began to creep from the flask, like steam rising from a kettle.

Slowly at first, tendrils of red seeped down into the clear liquid below, like the growing roots of a plant, stretching and lengthening. The clear liquid acted in a similar way, reaching up into the thicker blood, clear shoots penetrating the red. More vapour rose and inside the glass flask the strange reaction continued. Alduce watched as the human blood battled with the clear liquid from the dragon's egg, the unnatural essence of man melding with that of mythical beast, swirling and writhing inside a container of glass as the combining liquid moved ever faster. It seemed that even at this level, human and dragon were foes.

Once the mixture had compounded, the reaction was complete. Alduce picked up the flask, the glass hot to the touch as he blew away the remains of vapour, peering inside at the now pink liquid. He wouldn't have been able to mix it any more thoroughly had he stirred it with a spoon for an hour. Sealing the flask with a lid and making sure it was tightly fastened, he returned the newly created mixture to the cold cupboard, where it would have to sit for at least two weeks until it was ready.

He tidied up his mess, cleaning his apparatus and stowing it back where it belonged. He abhorred an untidy laboratory, everything must be clean and neatly stored, after all, he was a scientist and he needed to behave like one when he wasn't practicing his magic.

When he finished, he retired back to his living quarters, which were completely different inside compared to the laboratory part of his subterranean dwelling. There was his sleeping area, a small kitchen and his study, where he spent most of his waking hours. He had a large number of books and journals displayed in a huge bookcase, carved into the rock wall of the cavern and arranged by his own method of cataloguing.

Reaching up, he pulled down one such journal, bound in green dragonhide, the scales much larger than the small black ones of the newly acquired dragon skin. The hide that covered the journal was magically altered, reducing it enough to bind the book, as even a single fully grown scale from a green dragon would have been too large. Even though the black scales were smaller than the ones that bound the journal, they were no less impressive. Dragonhide, regardless of size and colour was always spectacular.

The journal was one of a large set, all bound in the same green metallic dragonhide, neatly arranged along the top shelf. He place this volume on his desk, sat down and opened it, preparing to record his findings and thoughts so far, regarding the egg. Picking up a quill, he hesitated before dipping the nib into the ink jar. He had seen other tools for getting ink onto paper, but preferred the quill, for his work, it felt right. When writing, he preferred the traditional method over the modern, even if it was a little more effort.

He stared at the blank pages bound into the dragonhide, ready to absorb the ink and the knowledge of his writings, but he didn't start. He closed the book and ran his hand over the surface of the green dragonhide, contemplating what he was about to undertake and any consequences his action might have.

The scales felt cold to his touch as he caressed the cover, reminding him of how he had obtained the dragonhide for these wonderful tomes.

Chapter 5

Alduce had been an apprentice, learning sorcery and magic under the watchful eye of his master, Caltus. He hadn't been educated about science yet—that discovery was to come later when he acquired the dragon artefact and learned of portals and travelling to other worlds. Science was something his master hadn't yet shared with him. The old sorcerer was a traditionalist and told Alduce that once he had mastered sorcery he was free to dabble in the lesser arts.

Caltus had sent him on an errand to find the black cave mushrooms he needed for an enchantment he was preparing. The mushrooms could only be found underground and Caltus had given Alduce his very own light orb. He had told his young apprentice he would need it for searching out his quarry and gruffly thrust the valuable orb into his hands.

His old master was never one to show emotion and this was his way of gifting the orb to his apprentice without appearing to be generous. Alduce still had the light orb somewhere in the laboratory, the magic Caltus had instilled in the glass long exhausted, but precious to him anyway, a nostalgic reminder of days long past.

With this newly acquired gift, the young Alduce had ventured forth, heading north from their home. They had been living in the South, near the city of Learning, named for its many academic buildings and scholarly organisations. Caltus told his young apprentice to search the caves, high up in the foothills of the Pendron mountain range. Caltus needed the cave mushrooms for his spell, that was true, but his old master hadn't just sent him on an errand. It had also been a test, a rite of passage. Alduce knew that if he was successful and returned with the rare mushrooms, Caltus would promote him from apprentice to journeyman.

He learned much from his master and was ready to progress, so he set out well prepared, with all the supplies he might need and a positive frame of mind. He bought a horse and enough provisions for seven days, giving himself three days to travel there, three to return and a full day to search the caves for the precious mushrooms. Little did he know that his adventure was going to be the start of something that would last a lot longer than his initial trip and he would discover mysteries beyond his wildest imagination.

He travelled for the first three days, riding by day, resting at night, encountering few people north of the city as most merchants and visitors arrived from the far south. He studied by firelight, reading the few books he brought along, appreciating the gift of his very own light orb. Alduce never stopped learning, avidly reading whenever there was a spare moment. He once remarked to Caltus when they visited Learning's grand library, there were so many books and never enough time to read them all. Caltus told him he needed to get his nose out of his books every now and then and experience the world around him. Practical experience was just as relevant in his education and training, his old master said. At the time, Alduce doubted his master's words, but now, thinking back, the old man had been wise indeed. He always was.

He arrived at the caves, impressed with the backdrop of the Pendron Mountains, giant snow covered peaks, pushing into the clouds and stretching north, far beyond the distant horizon. The lower foothills were riddled with caves and Alduce had to be careful as he traversed the land, open shafts common amongst the rocky terrain.

On the third night, as the sun dropped below the Pendron peaks, painting the sky in pastel oranges and pinks, he came across a deep cave, the mouth wide enough for him to lead his horse through and take shelter for the night. He was weary from travelling and only took time to feed and water his horse and himself, before building a fire outside the cave mouth and banking it up for the night.

Fire would keep away any Watchers, large feral creatures that were known to inhabit the remote hills. He didn't want to wake in the night to find he had an uninvited guest invading his shelter.

He settled down on the sandy floor, making himself comfortable in the warm dry cave, the sand softer than hard ground outside. Inside the protection of the rocky walls, the chill of the night was kept at bay. He quickly drifted off to sleep, the day's ride and the fresh mountain air contributing to his tiredness. Slipping deeper into his dreams, vivid images surfaced in his subconscious and a feeling of desolation and despair dragged him further down into the depths of an emerging nightmare.

He tossed and turned, restless and in conflict, though he didn't know why. He awoke in the darkness, sitting upright and startling his mount, drenched in sweat, like a man with a fever. His heart pounded, threatening to explode from his chest, his breath came in short rasps and he couldn't shake the feeling of isolation and agitation.

He tried to remember the nightmare and what it was about it that distressed him. But, as with all dreamers who wake, the memory of the dream fades quickly, leaving them unable to recall the details.

Rummaging in his cloak, he pulled out his orb and thumbed the glass surface, concentrating as he willed the light into being, banishing the darkness. All was as it should be, no danger hid in the shadows, nothing lurked in the darkness. Rising from the ground, he stepped out into the night, leaving the orb on his makeshift bed.

His fire had reduced itself to a glowing pile of embers and as he passed, he felt the heat on his clammy skin. Away from the remains of the fire, the night breeze chilled him as his breathing returned to normal. Looking up at the stars in the night sky, he took comfort in the familiar patterns and constellations.

His mind cleared as he focused on the distant stars, so far away it was staggering to even think how far one would need to travel to visit them. And if he ever travelled from his world to one of these heavenly destinations, what would he find there? Men like himself? Animals or plants he would recognise? Air he could breathe? There were so many more questions than answers. That was one of the attractions of studying, searching for the answers and unravelling the mysteries life held.

Alduce returned to his sleeping roll, but he was no longer tired, he was wide awake now. Taking the orb, he decided he might as well enter into the depths of the caves and seek out the mushrooms. It didn't matter if he hunted for them during the day or at night as the caves were permanently dark. His illuminating orb would light the way, but he would need more than the light it provided to avoid becoming lost in the underground labyrinths.

Alduce scouted around the sandy cave floor, picking out small pebbles and stones until he had enough to fill the pockets of his robes. Piling them in a mound on his blanket, he set the orb on top, cupping his hands around the heap. Reaching deep inside for his magic, his hands began to feel the rising heat as it flowed through his fingers and into the orb, cascading down into the stones and pebbles below.

Light flared though the gaps in his fingers, his hands glowed in the darkness, the dark shapes of bones visible through translucent skin. The light flickered and dimmed, then surging one last time returned to its usual brightness.

Alduce scooped up the orb and the pebbles below now glowed like smaller orbs, bright light emitting from each one. It was a simple spell, one which any first year apprentice could easily master with practice. The stones were now infused with light from the orb and shone like miniature suns. While the orb that Caltus had given Alduce would hold the light for over ten years of continuous use, the small pebbles would only last a day, maybe two, before the light faded and they returned to normal.

The secret of making an orb hold the light for any length of time was in the forging of the glass and the preparation of the incantation. Alduce had rushed the spell, as a temporary enchantment was all he needed. He didn't plan to be any more than half a day searching the caverns. The stones infused with light would be used as markers as he descended, making a trail to help him navigate out of the deep underground labyrinth when he was ready to return.

He patted his mare's neck, murmuring soothing sounds. She had a placid nature, was well trained and would remain in the cave without wandering off.

Pocketing the pebbles and holding the orb out to light his way, he proceeded to the rear of the cave. The tunnel burrowed downward and he followed its path, like a giant mole, in search of the black mushrooms.

Chapter 6

Alduce the apprentice scoured the dark caves, seeking out the mushrooms, frequently stopping to place a glowing pebble in a crevice or nook in the rock walls. If none were available, he sat the glowing guide stone in the middle of the path, placing it on top of a larger rock or scooping up the earth to make a mound.

He used the glowing pebbles sparingly, making tactical decisions when and where to leave them, often at a fork or junction, or when the path took a twist or a turn that might be confusing on his return. He did not want Caltus coming to search for him. If his apprentice didn't have the wits to figure out how not to get lost in the dark, he would never hear the end of it. And, if he did end up lost, he wouldn't see a journeyman's sash for at least another year. Caltus could be a cranky master sometimes and Alduce would suffer his temper, especially if the old sorcerer had to make the journey he had entrusted to his apprentice in order to rescue him.

Black mushrooms were rare, but Alduce had already picked at least a dozen, storing them in the small sack he'd brought along. He estimated that he'd been wandering below ground for at least three hours, though it was difficult in the constant dark to measure the passage of time accurately. If he could double his count of mushrooms, Caltus would be happy and he would be able to get back above ground and return to civilisation earlier than planned.

The tunnel he was currently exploring opened out into a wide cavern. He held the orb at arm's length, letting the light reach out into the blackness, illuminating the area. He scanned the floor for more mushrooms reasoning that such a large expanse would surely be home to the rare fungi, when he spotted two pin pricks of light, twinkling in the darkness. Covering the orb, the two points of light vanished. It must be a reflection of his light rather than something giving off its own. Uncovering the orb, Alduce searched for the unusual reflections, wondering what he might discover in the deep underground cave. Holding the orb aloft, he searched the darkness, but there was nothing there.

Perhaps the lack of light was playing tricks on his eyes or maybe it was because he hadn't had a full night's sleep and his eyes were tired and strained. He turned away from where he thought the light had been and came face to face with its source.

Two huge eyes peered directly into his own.

Alduce froze in terror as wave of panic washed over him. He dropped the orb to the sandy cave floor, where it rolled and came to rest, still shining brightly, revealing the head and neck of a dragon!

Green metallic scales reflected in the darkness, its eyes much larger than the pin pricks he had seen before.

Alduce stood frozen to the spot as the beast blew air from its nostrils, the breeze warm as it rolled over his face. He was glad that it was only warm air and not the searing hot flame that the fire breathing creatures where capable of.

He wasn't near enough to the tunnel where he'd entered the cavern and didn't think it wise to turn and run, not with the dragon so close. He drew in a breath, only now aware he hadn't been breathing and squared his shoulders. The dragon hadn't yet burned him to a crisp, so he would take that as a good sign. Dragons were known to be intelligent creatures, some more intelligent than men. If this one intended to kill or eat him, there was nothing he could do to stop it.

He decided he would act. He had nothing to lose if he was going to end up being the dragon's dinner. He reached down and retrieved his fallen orb, holding it high its light ran along the scales of the mighty green beast, decorating the cavern walls with a deep green flickering, each hand sized scale shimmering like a polished mirror of green.

"Greetings, magnificent dragon," he said. His voice small and insignificant before the huge reptilian beast. "I am Alduce and I mean you no harm. I've come in search of black mushrooms and I... er... didn't mean to... you know... disturb you." The words were out of his mouth before his brain had the chance to think what he had said. This was no way to speak to a dragon, but he wasn't sure what the right words were when you came across one face to face in its dark underground lair. The dragon's eyes stared into his own, small bright moons penetrating his soul, hypnotic and strange, but somehow calming too.

And then the dragon spoke. Not at all what Alduce expected.

* * *

Drawing himself back to the present, Alduce opened the great dragonhide tome once more. Dipping his quill into the ink pot, he scratched the sharpened end of the feather across the pages, recording his findings. He wanted to write everything he had discovered so far, regarding his experimentation with the dragon egg.

He hadn't thought of Galdor the Green, the dragon he'd stumbled across while searching the caves of the Pendron Mountain range, in a long time. It was over one hundred years since his encounter with the green dragon, while he was green himself, still an apprentice with a lifetime of studying and learning ahead.

He concentrated on his writing, noting down the events of the last few days while they were still fresh in his mind. Each fact carefully penned, an accurate description of his experiments. When he finished, he left the book open, as he always did, allowing the ink to dry. Tired and weary, his eyelids became heavy and began to close. Tomorrow he would set out on the long journey to the city of Learning and he would pass close to the foothills of the Pendron range. Perhaps this was why he recalled his adventure underground. He left the open tome on the table, crawling into bed, exhausted and ready to sleep.

Chapter 7

A week later, Alduce rode into the city of Learning through the main north gate, leading a pony packed with the remains of the dragon egg that he intended to trade. After seven long and boring days through the empty and mostly barren northern lands, his supplied were nearly depleted. He had deliberately chosen the location of his laboratory to be far from civilisation and sometimes wished he could travel locally using the portals. It was exciting visiting strange new worlds, stepping through the portal and travelling unfathomable distances. Riding on horseback for a week to get to his nearest city was a chore he was never pleased to perform.

He rode his horse through the city, the people and the noise a diverse change from his usual isolation. As he entered the trading district, the city streets grew even more crowded. He weaved his way through the busy throng of people to his destination, dismounting outside the last shop at the end of the road. An old battered sign hung crookedly above the door professing supplies of the magical and arcane.

He tied his animals to the rail and the pony whickered as he removed the packs. Hitching one under each arm, he fumbled for the door handle and pushed his way into the shop, a small bell tinkling pleasantly as he entered.

Inside, shelves lined the walls, crammed with an assortment of containers, jars and boxes in a wide variety of colours and shapes. There was a welcoming aroma of herbs and spices mingling together to create a soothing smell. Alduce took a deep breath, enjoying the heady mixture of scents.

A small grey haired shopkeeper stood behind the long counter, leaning lazily on its polished wooden surface. Rows of bookshelves stretched the length of the shop behind his head, volumes jammed into any available space, like oddly shaped bricks in a poorly built wall.

"What brings Alduce the elusive down from his mountain and into my shop?" the grey haired shopkeeper asked.

"A horse," Alduce answered, swinging the packs up onto the counter, "and highly valuable items to trade."

The shopkeeper grinned, "Your jokes don't get any funnier, you know. Valuable items, you say? I'd better be the judge of that, if you don't mind." He reached for the first sack, pulling open the ties that held it closed.

"I believe I said highly valuable, master Bervus. Go ahead, paw the merchandise before you buy it. Didn't you tell me you hate people coming in here and pawing? Yes I'm sure the phrase you used was, pawing your merchandise like sticky fingered thieves."

"Bah!" Bervus retorted, "You sorcerers take things far too literally." He smiled at Alduce, taking the sting from his words and set the eye glasses hanging from a chain around his neck onto the bridge of his nose.

"How are the spectacles working out for you?" Alduce asked.

"They're wonderful, Alduce, truly wonderful. I can see things a lot more clearly, helps me when I'm trading. I get a good look at things I could barely see before." He looked up, his eyes huge through the thick round lenses captured in the fine wire frames. "You never did say where you got them from. Did you make them yourself? Some kind of lower magic?"

"No, Bervus, I never made them, they came from... a place I know, many months travel from Learning," Bervus would never know just how far Alduce had travelled to find the shopkeepers spectacles and the man wouldn't believe him even if he told him. "It's not magic. It's science."

"Science? Is that some kind of sorcerous word? Honestly, always with the mysteries. Now let's see what you've brought old Bervus. Something special I hope." Delving into the sack, he pulled out the contents, one by one, stacking them neatly along the counter.

There were sealed jars with organs inside, preserved in liquid. Boxes filled with similar items, dried out, the moisture removed to stop them from perishing. He looked up at Alduce when the sack was empty and indicated the second one. Alduce nodded and Bervus set out the contents from the second sack with the same practiced ease onto the now crowded bench. The last things he removed were two halves of the giant shell. He set one half on the counter and examined the other closely, sniffing the inside, peering at it and tapping it with his fingers.

"Tough and thick, and incredibly large. Are these what I think they are?" he said.

"Well that depends on what exactly you think they are," Alduce teased.

"In that case, you won't mind if I test them to see if they're the genuine article? You won't be offended?"

"I would insist upon it, Bervus, our transaction relies on both parties being fully satisfied."

"Very well. Bolt the door and pull the drapes, please." Alduce did as requested while Bervus searched through the drawers built into his side of the counter until he located what he was looking for.

A small glass jar filled with what appeared to be finely grained yellow sand.

The shop dimmed as the light from the window was blocked out by the heavy drapes. Bervus unscrewed the lid and took a pinch of the fine yellow sand between his fingers, rubbing them together. Smoke drifted from the tips of his thumb and forefinger and he moved his hand along the counter above the items. Fine grains drifted slowly down, like suspended motes of dust caught in a beam of sunlight, changing from solid particles to wispy smoke, trailing along in his hand's wake. The smoke slowly enveloped the counter, covering everything set out on the wooden surface, curling around the jars and boxes, swirling along the surface of the egg shells as if drawn to the items. A soft golden light started to radiate from the dragon's remains, steadily getting brighter until everything set out on the bench emanated with a vibrant golden glow.

Alduce touched each jar and box, naming the contents within. "Dragon veal, vital organs, blood, teeth, eyes, heart, tongue."

Bervus stared at each in turn, his jaw dropping a little further with each item Alduce listed.

"And of course, dragon egg shell." He performed a little bow and smiled at the shopkeeper. "Highly valuable, as promised, proven genuine by the authenticity powder, as you've witnessed." He smiled. "Nice spell by the way. Did you prepare the sand yourself?"

"It's the Cole Man's, he owes me a few favours and he's the expert when it comes to sniffing out fakes," Bervus said. "Not," he quickly added, "that I would ever suspect you'd bring me items that weren't genuine."

The golden glow faded and Alduce pulled open the drapes, letting the natural daylight flood back into the shop.

"Truly amazing, Alduce. Did you see how brightly they glowed, the potential magic they hold must be powerful indeed. Where did you acquire such items?"

"That, my dear Bervus, is a trade secret. Be satisfied with the knowledge that each item is authentic."

"Bah! More mystery. Fine, have your secrets if it pleases you. Our deal still stands then?"

"If you have managed to obtain what I want, it certainly does."

"But Alduce, you know the value of this merchandise. You know my clients and how much they would pay for even a small piece of shell alone! Our deal seems unfairly one-sided. Are you sure?"

"Bervus, this is why I chose to deal with you. There are many shops like yours in this city, but you, my friend, are the fairest trader I know. Yes, I know the worth of what I bring. Worry not master apothecary, if you are so concerned, you can owe me a favour or two, next time I need something. Agreed?"

"As long as it's not my eyes in a jar... or my heart!" Bervus said. "Come master sorcerer, I think I'll close up early and you and I can find somewhere to dine and have a drink or three, to celebrate our transaction. My treat." He carefully tided up, taking each item and storing it out of sight below the counter.

"We'll get your animals stabled and get you a room at one of the more reputable inns on the west side. My supplier is due to arrive in the city tomorrow and he has sent word that he brings exactly what you desire." Bervus lifted a hatch in the counter and joined Alduce on the other side. He unbolted the door and held it open.

"After you," he said and followed Alduce out into the street. Pulling the door closed behind them, he produced a large brass key from his pocket and turned it in the lock.

"I know a great tavern on the west side, the owner owes me a favour or two. They do the most fabulous steak you'll ever taste, served with a mouth-watering mushroom sauce."

Mushrooms, Alduce thought...

Chapter 8

"Greetings, Alduce, collector of mushrooms," boomed the dragon. "I am Galdor the Green. It has been many years since anyone has ventured this deep into these caverns and disturbed me."

Alduce stood frozen to the cave floor, his jaw hanging wide, not quite believing his eyes.

The dragon had spoken to him and used his name.

He quickly gathered himself, as Caltus had taught him. It didn't matter that you stumbled or fell, his master often said, but that you got back up and kept going.

"It is my great honour to meet you, mighty Galdor," he said, "I'm terribly sorry I've disturbed you."

Galdor sniffed at Alduce, moving his long snout close to the man and inhaling noisily, wide nostrils flaring. Alduce barely saw the dragon's nose as all he could focus on was the beast's huge mouth and rows of ivory coloured fangs. A forked red tongue flicked out from between the razor sharp teeth, like an angry viper, tasting the air.

"You smell of magic," Galdor rumbled. "Magic and mushrooms. I am hungry little human, I've been trapped here a long time."

"Trapped?" Alduce asked, not wanting to mention the hunger.

"Yessss," the dragon hissed, "trapped. And hungry." Galdor emerged from the shadows, stalking around behind Alduce, putting his considerable bulk between the apprentice and the tunnel he'd used to enter the cavern.

"Well, perhaps I could assist you, magnificent dragon," Alduce said, trying to think of a way out of his predicament. "I could bring you some food, if you wish." He started to move around the dragon, searching past the beast's body for the cave mouth. If he could get into the narrow cave, the huge beast wouldn't be able to follow him.

"Really?" Galdor asked, "You would leave and return with something for me to eat? Most kind little Alduce, most kind."

Alduce stepped slowly towards the cave mouth, nodding, "Yes, that's exactly what I would do, bring you back a feast, a feast fit for a... dragon, yes."

"How stupid do you think I am?" asked Galdor, thrusting his neck past Alduce and turning his head back to face the man, blocking his path to freedom. "Maybe I shall eat you! Better to take what I have in front of me now." Galdor snorted, the heat of his breath wafting over Alduce.

"Nor are you enthralled by my voice. Your magic prevents you from falling under my hypnotic spell." He shook his head, "No, I think if I let you leave, you would not return with food," Galdor's tongue danced along his teeth. "You would return with more magic wielders, foul sorcerers and stinking mages. You would slaughter me after you cast your enchantments."

Alduce could see no way out. The dragon's logic was sound and now he had insulted the creature's intelligence. The beast was smarter than he expected. If he was to be eaten, there was nothing he could do to stop it. The dragon was stronger, faster and much larger than him. Physically, he was Galdor's inferior. He could hear Caltus telling him to use his brain; if you can't solve a problem one way, his old mentor would say, try attacking it from a different angle. It was definitely time to employ another approach.

"Very well," he said, "eat me if you must. But know this mighty Galdor, I am your best chance at freedom, eat me now and you'll never know if I could have freed you."

The dragon drew back his serpentine neck, head swaying from side to side like a cobra preparing to strike. Alduce stood his ground as Galdor roared, lunging forward with his jaws wide open.

Chapter 9

Bervus had been true to his word, he was the perfect host and had made good on their deal. Alduce enjoyed the day he had spent with his old acquaintance immensely; most of the time he was so caught up in his work that he had no time for other things.

A trip to the city of Learning was a welcome break, but whenever he was away from his laboratory, he couldn't help feeling guilty. He was all too aware the hours he passed in the company of others equated to time spent away from his work, a distraction from the advancement of his studies.

He removed the tack from the horse and pony as he returned to his mountain laboratory, letting the animals run free. He stored the equipment in a cave he used as a stable, near the foot of his mountain. Alduce preferred the animals roam the lowlands when he had no need of their services. He could easily catch them, when needed. They were smart enough to realise he supplemented their grazing with grains and vegetables when he could, making them easy to catch when he wished to make a trip. Gathering his belongings, he trudged up the steep incline to his secluded workshop, picking his way over the rough ground, finally reaching his destination.

He palmed the metal door inside the cave entrance and the familiar light swept down the length of his hand, welcoming him back. The door slid open and he stepped inside, depositing the full sacks brought back from the city of Learning, on the nearest workbench.

He strode purposefully across the laboratory to the chilled cupboard, overhead lights flickering to life as he passed beneath them. He reached inside and brought out the jar he had left settling and inspected the contents. It was no longer a pink liquefied mix of blood, but had solidified into a thick clear jelly. Everything was ready. He mentally prepared himself for the next phase of his experiment. He had gathered, stolen, traded, and prepared all the necessary ingredients he needed. It was time to put all his hard work, all his studies and research, to the test.

Setting out all the necessary equipment, he bustled around the laboratory, whistling as he worked. He removed two sealed jars from the sack, leaving the rest of the items he had traded untouched for now. He emptied both jars into a large bowl, mixing the colourless liquids, then added the clear jelly he had made from his own blood and the fluid from the dragon egg.

The jars from Bervus contained two key ingredients necessary for the final stage of his experiment: a magical bonding elixir and a combustible agent. These ingredients were both created by a reputable mage master Bervus knew and trusted. Alduce could have formulated them himself, but they took months to perfect and travelling to the city to trade for them, even though he disliked the journey, was much quicker and convenient.

Taking all the items he had collated and carefully lifting the bowl, he left the laboratory and climbed up to the top of his mountain.

The moment of truth was upon him.

* * *

Alduce sat inside a circle made from the bones of the unborn dragon, pushed into the ground like grotesque monoliths. The night sky was darkening and a crescent moon tilted above the horizon, its dull glow casting an ethereal light across the mountain top.

Alduce removed his clothing and stacked it neatly away from the bone circle. The cold wind chilled his skin and he could feel it tighten as the hairs on his neck stood up. But it wasn't a reaction to the cooling breeze, rather from the excitement and anticipation he felt.

If his experiment proceeded as planned, he would be the first sorcerer to complete the process successfully, as far as he was aware. He grasped the dragon pendant that hung around his neck, the only thing he now wore, and took a deep breath. No point in putting this off any longer, now was the time for action.

He dipped both his hands into the bowl and spread the viscous concoction over his body, the cold mixture making him shiver as he applied it to every inch of his skin, chilling him to the bone. With shaking hands, he picked up the small dragon skull and covered it with the mixture too before applying a generous coating to each vertical bone in the circle. Covered in the cold liquid, he reached for the dragonhide, draping it over his shoulders like a small cloak. Hands trembling, he steadied himself as he placed the dragon skull in the centre of his bone circle, reaching out and summoning his magic.

The black dragonhide shimmered and the scales rippled, creating a sound like tiny bells as their metallic surface moved, scale clinking against scale. Alduce braced himself as he felt the hide begin to grow, sliding over the mixture on his skin as it provided a magical lubricant.

The hide grew as it slipped over his back, encompassing limbs, wrapping them in the expanding cloak of scales. Alduce could feel a heat now, he was no longer cold as magic warmed his skin and the hide closed around his bare flesh. Where the hide covered his arms, it wrapped all the way around, meeting and joining, leaving no exposed skin. His back, legs and torso were all subjected to the same process as the hide magically stretched and engulfed the man beneath.

His face was the last to be covered and once his skin was hidden Alduce looked like a knight in a black armour of dragon scales. He could still breathe through his mouth and nose, see through his eyes and hear with his ears. The dragonhide hadn't grown to cover his sensory organs, for which Alduce was grateful.

Reaching down, he grasped the skull with alien hands that now resembled talons. He raised it above his head, calling forth the magic of the pendant, now hidden beneath the layer of dragon skin. His chest glowed brightly as the pendant, encased in the protective armour of scales, radiated magical light.

Lightning seared down from above, a blue-white flash struck the dragon skull and leapt, like a fiery spider web, to each bone in the circle. The skull's sockets burned white, eyes of lightning staring out before engulfing it fully and running down the upraised arms that held it aloft. Alduce dropped the skull and it struck the ground, empty and hollow, the irradiating lightning gone.

The light from the bones faded too, no longer bright candles of energy, the last of the magic and lightning dissipating. Blue sparks fizzled out, leaving the crescent moon to provide the only source of illumination on the mountaintop.

Alduce swayed, his legs weak and his head dizzy. He had survived the magic and lightning. He was prepared mentally for what was to come next, but unprepared for the searing pain that engulfed him. The conduit between his own skin and the hide of the dragon, was the magical liquid he had prepared, a thin coating that now flowed through the space between the two.

The heat built uncomfortably, growing hotter, a raging inferno scorching the liquid, heating it until it transformed. Thousands of tendrils reached out. Minute creeping roots, digging into flesh and hide. Growing as they burrowed, knitting the coating of scales directly to the flesh of the man. Alduce opened his mouth to scream in pain, and found his voice replaced by a beastly roar, echoing eerily across the mountain top.

He fell forward, arms outstretched as he hit the ground, pushing himself to what he still thought of as his knees. As his own skin and flesh fused with the dragonhide, the pain increased and Alduce could only wait for the unbearable transformation to finish. Limbs stretched taking on the form and shape of a fully grown dragon, the beast that was once a man threw its head back and roared, no longer in pain but in triumph. Wings unfurled, leathery limbs growing in size, completing the final part of the metamorphosis.

The dragon reared up on powerful hind legs and extended its wings, flapping them a few times. The beast was completely black, except for its chest, where silver scales formed the shape of a star. The awareness of Alduce was still present, even though he was no longer a man. He had changed his form into a dragon, but still possessed the mind of a human. He knew there was one last vital step that needed to be taken or he might lose himself completely in the spirit of the dragon. This was unknown territory and he must proceed with caution.

He called on his magic, willing himself to become human once more.

Nothing happened.

Frightened of being trapped in this form forever, Alduce almost lost himself completely to the wave of panic that engulfed him. But then finally, after what felt like a lifetime, the heat returned, burning from the inside, forcing him to forget about the terror. The dragon's magnificent form shimmered, white light glowed beneath the hide. The joints between each scale pulsed with magical energy, bathing it in a cold unearthly luminosity. Slowly the dragon shrank, growing smaller as the shape changed back to that of an armoured man, clad in black scales.

The glowing intensified as the scales reduced and were absorbed into the sorcerer's skin, until no trace of the mythical beast remained.

Alduce stood for a moment as the glowing pendant around his neck faded and the magic ended. He looked down at his naked form, running human hands across his cold skin. He shivered mightily and his head swam as he lost consciousness and sank to the ground.

His last waking thoughts returned him to a time long past.

Back to Galdor's cavern.

Chapter 10

Galdor's mighty head lunged towards Alduce and the apprentice sorcerer screwed his eyes shut and braced himself for the inevitable. Surprisingly, it never came.

He waited, then after a moment opened his eyes to see Galdor's head level with his own. The dragon studied the man, tilting his head this way and that, trying to get a better look at his tiny prey.

"You think you can free me?" Galdor purred like a giant cat, his voice vibrating inside the apprentice sorcerer's ears.

"I don't see why not," Alduce said. "I am a sorcerer, I have magic at my disposal." He desperately tried to prolong his reprieve, perhaps there was a way to leave this cave and survive his encounter with this fearsome beast. "Before I decide on the best approach to your... our predicament, you better tell me how you came to be stuck deep underground."

If he could get the dragon to tell him how he had come to be trapped here, maybe he could buy himself some time to plan an escape. "And, just so you know, mighty Galdor, I would have returned with food for you. I intended no deception. I am a man of my word before anything else. Use your beastly magic, you will know I speak the truth!" Alduce didn't know if the dragon had the ability to detect a lie and he hoped the confidence of his bluff would be enough to convince the creature.

"Very well, little sorcerer with the big heart, Galdor will tell you his tale. We will see what you can do to assist and if after that, you deceive me, you will return to being my next meal. Agreed?"

Alduce had no choice but to concede to Galdor's terms, but he paused before answering, giving the impression he was contemplating the dragon's proposal.

"Agreed," he consented, "however, when I succeed, I shall ask a boon of you and you will grant it. These are my terms, if they are unacceptable, eat me now and be done with it."

Galdor growled and didn't answer. Alduce hoped he hadn't pushed the beast too far. He wanted to appear confident and now he feared he had overplayed his hand. The dragon thrust his face as close to Alduce as possible without touching him, his huge eyes searched the sorcerer's soul, staring menacingly at the man.

"Agreed," he finally said, "but do not test my patience, I warn you. I have become a touch less tolerant since being trapped in this underground prison." Only then did Alduce release his breath, grateful to still be alive, but unsure what he had let himself in for.

"Good. Tell me then, Galdor the Green," Alduce asked, "how you came to be trapped in these caverns. I am intrigued to learn your story. I admit, I'm puzzled as to how such a large creature as yourself was confined here. Especially when the actual tunnels I used to get here are so narrow. I had to squeeze through at places and I'm small compared to you."

"Very well, human, listen well and do not interrupt me, green dragons do not appreciate interruptions. There will be ample time for any questions you may have, after I finish." Galdor drew in a huge breath, took a theatrical pause, like a bard waiting for his audience to settle, then began his tale.

"On another world, in another time I was once the mightiest of dragons, a leader and a king. Dragons were plentiful and we ruled the lands. No force could stand against us when we were united. We were revered and worshipped by humans. Understand, we did not ravage towns or burn villages, nor eat people, this is not generally in our nature. Although, I admit, there are times when some individuals will behave this way." He paused, staring at Alduce as if to impress this fact upon him.

Alduce remained silent, heeding Galdor's warning about being interrupted.

"For thousands of years the balance was maintained. There was enough room on my home world for man and dragon, but as the millennia passed, our species dwindled, while yours bred. Mankind was like a plague across the lands, reaching out into the wilderness, building your towns and roads, cutting down forests and taming the world. Dragons were once a social race, but as time passed, we withdrew and distanced ourselves from the race of man, making our homes in faraway places, unpopulated by humans. Our Lands had a ruling council, the Dragon Moot, eleven of the oldest dragons, selected by their peers for their intelligence and knowledge. I, being their leader, ruled over the council and while everyone had a say, my voice was the final word on any decisions or rulings. I would hope I was a fair and just leader and while I was part of the moot. Even though our numbers lessened, our community was still strong." Galdor paused once more, looking up towards the roof of the cavern as he contemplated his next words.

"We endured."

Alduce nodded, saying nothing, holding his tongue as he was bid. He settled down on the cave floor and sat the light orb on the ground beside him. The light radiated from the glowing globe, shining upwards and reflecting on the underside of Galdor's impressive frame. The scales of the dragon's belly were not green but a golden yellow, like sunlight rippling across water. The dragon was truly a magnificent creature and even though Alduce was terrified, he couldn't help marvelling at Galdor's deadly beauty.

"Anyway, that is all ancient history, a lifetime that once was and is now no more." Alduce was moved by the obvious sorrow in Galdor's voice. "Everything was ruined by my adversary and fellow council member, Blaze. A black dragon, named so because of a flash of white lighting on his chest. We were once friends, or so I thought. Little did I know he plotted against me and would become my bitter enemy. I guided my species and upheld the peace. I advocated our withdrawal from the ever spreading population of mankind, believing our isolation best for all concerned. Blaze had other ideas. He debated that we should take back what was once ours by force. We should burn the cities of man, crush them with our strength and magic. He maintained your species were but an annoyance, insects to be crushed by the might of dragons. I should have foreseen his motives and recognised his deep rooted hatred earlier. Perhaps then I could have taken action and prevented his rise to power... and my downfall. Alas, as ever, we are wiser after the event than before it. I expect we dragons and you men can both relate to that."

Galdor lay down on the cave floor, his wings rustled as he folded them on his back. Settling down beside Alduce, he rested his head on his outstretched front legs, like a dog lying beside its master, his large eyes reflecting in the light from the orb.

"Blaze the Black is why I'm here, Alduce. I learned, much to my dismay, black was his nature and blacker was his heart. Let me tell you of that black dragon's betrayal and how I came to be in my dark foreboding prison."

Alduce leaned forward, spell bound, not by magic but by the dragon's natural ability to tell a tale, captivating his audience with every word.

After all, it wasn't every day a dragon bared his soul to a human.

Chapter 11

Alduce opened his eyes and winced. His head pounded, each thump like a hammer striking an anvil. As he became fully awake, he remembered the events of the previous night.

He had managed the transformation and taken the form of a dragon. All his research and hard work had been successful. He remembered the pain, the fire in his blood and the ripping of limbs and muscles as his shape changed, his bones moving and growing, becoming a beast of myth and magic.

He had actually changed. He had done it!

His throbbing head jerked him back to the here and now, a terrible side effect of his incredible metamorphosis—severe dehydration.

Slowly he rose from the dishevelled bed, his back sore and his neck stiff. He was wearing his robe and he vaguely recalled pulling it on before stumbling down from the mountain top and collapsing into a heap, completely exhausted.

From his research, he had expected this would be a normal part of the process when he first changed shape. The larger the creature the subject changed into, the bigger the physical effect on the body. He also read that he would get used to it, the more he swapped back and forth between forms. He expected his body would acclimatise and adjust until the transition became bearable and the pain lessened.

Or at least, he hoped that this was true. His research had only applied to what other sorcerers had recorded about shape changing. And none of those records mentioned transforming into a dragon.

He had never experienced pain so intensely before, nothing compared to the agony and ecstasy he felt. But even if it didn't improve, didn't get any easier, he knew it wouldn't stop him changing into a dragon. Not now he had the ability to do so.

Not only was he a sorcerer and a scientist, now he was also a shape changer. He examined his body, hands running over skin that felt no different from the day before. There was no physical change to his appearance as a human, no tell tail signs of the beast within. No visible evidence of the absorbed hide.

The feeling he had experienced when he changed back to a human was hard to describe, like shrinking, a diminishing of being and a reduction of his true self. The way the scales and hide had been absorbed into his human body was astounding, and a little terrifying, but he felt and looked normal.

This was a reassuring sign.

Mixed up in the assault of emotions the transformation had wrought, he felt the spirit of the dragon coursing through each fibre of his being, powerful and alien. Was it the unborn spirit of the small unhatched beast he liberated from the egg? Or was it his own self, taking on a new persona, a dragon state of being? He didn't know the answers to these questions, but he needed to remain aware of any potential influence on his own individuality.

He fetched himself a glass of water from his kitchen and drank it down in one long draught, a sharp coldness stabbing the back of his brain. Re-filling the glass, he took smaller mouthfuls, his thirst still not fully quenched. Wandering around his living quarters in a dazed state, he contemplated his incredible accomplishment.

A grumbling from his belly made him realise how ravenous he felt. He grinned to himself: the noise sounding like a tiny dragon inside him, crying out to be fed. No doubt another side effect from the transformation. His body had been through a lot and the ordeal had demanded much more than he could have anticipated.

This was nature's way of telling him to refuel. His resources had been exhausted when he changed shape and now they needed replenished. He would fix himself a hearty morning meal—not a meagre breakfast as usual—a feast, as that was what he desired. Once he attended to his hunger he would record last night's events, writing down the details of his experience and how he felt, both physically and mentally.

His mind raced, he had so much to document and the information he recorded would prove vital in his ongoing research. He should eat first, then sit and write it all down before he forgot anything.

He wanted to plan the next phase as well, as changing into a dragon was only the first step in his research. He wanted to fly, to cast magic in dragon form, to meet and interact with real dragons. The thought of how much he could learn and how much he would be able to accomplish if he was able to study dragons first hand, fuelled his desire. There was so much to try, the possibilities were endless.

He wondered if he would be able to fly naturally. Would this be something his dragon self would know instinctively? Or would he have to learn? Another question without an answer. One he planned to find out soon enough.

His stomach grumbled again, reminding him of another hungry dragon. One he stumbled across, so many years before.

Chapter 12

Alduce listened as Galdor told his story, the dragon's voice conjuring a strong image of a society filled with dragons and their culture. A place where Alduce would truly like to visit and study someday.

The scholar and the dreamer in him recognised that this would be a fantastic opportunity, to visit and learn about a world inhabited by dragons. The realist worried that no matter how wonderful it all sounded, if he couldn't free Galdor, the only thing he would likely be studying was the inside of the beast's stomach.

"So, Blaze formed a pact with the mage," Galdor continued, "and they plotted to get rid of me. Once I was removed from the council, nothing would stand in Blaze's way, and he would be free to assume charge of the moot and convince them to make war on mankind." He snorted his displeasure and hot dragon breath washed over Alduce again, reminding him just how deadly Galdor could be if he chose to end the apprentice's short life with a fiery blast.

"Blaze came to me and at the time, I believed his concern genuine. I was fooled by his supposed friendship and the way lies rolled easily from his foul tongue. He told me he had uncovered a plot, said that some of the council of eleven, my moot, had been collaborating with men. How they plotted to overthrow my rule and remove me from the council, that a revolt was inevitable and that we were the minority, that my kin supported them. I was such a fool, blinded by rage I failed to see what was right under my snout, and instead saw lies and mistruths, enemies where there were none, schemes and skulduggery where it didn't exist. Blaze was clever, he manipulated me and I was unaware that it was he that was the true traitor. It was him that sold his black heart to the mage, sold it for power and control at my expense. Only when I realised how stupid I had been, did I see the real Blaze, the power hungry creature that would bring ruin to my kin and blight our species in the eyes of humanity." Galdor fixed his stare on Alduce, his huge eyes sombre as he told his story.

"Why would dragons trust the mage?" Alduce interrupted. Immediately he shrunk back against the cavern wall, realising what he had done. He had accidentally interrupted the dragon. But Galdor seemed unconcerned, caught up in the telling of his tale.

"A good question," Galdor said. "I believe the mage was extremely powerful and he was able to shield himself from our ability to see his lies. His powers of persuasion must have been enhanced by his magical abilities. He wormed his way into Blaze's confidence with promises of power and wealth and Blaze, consumed with his greed, gave his words credence with the other dragons. No doubt making promises of his own to convince and manipulate them. At the time, it wasn't obvious to me, but being stuck here, with only time to reflect, I have though much about the events and how they transpired that day.

"He must have been powerful indeed," Alduce said.

"I trusted Blaze as he manipulated me into hunting down the mage he said was responsible for the unrest in our kin. My vanity helped fuel his untruths and give credence to his lies. He told me he followed the mage and overheard him conspiring with the moot, convincing them I was a weak leader. That they would prosper under a stronger and smarter king. It angered me that my kin would think so little of me and that anger blinded me to the convincing ruse that Blaze had spun. He said the mage turned their heads with the promise of his hoard and when he mentioned this, I coveted it too. I should have known this was a lie, but I was too obsessed. Everyone knows of our obsession with gold and jewels, and it was once a great addiction with me. Indeed, it is partly why I am trapped in this dark cavern. I trusted Blaze and he promised to lead me to the mage's secret stronghold, where we could not only confront him, but claim his hoard for our own. He told me that it had to be done that night, as this would be the only chance we had before the mage convinced the moot to rebel against me. We must strike now, the chance wouldn't come again. So it was that I set out, unprepared with only Blaze's story and no real evidence. He tricked me into acting before I had time to think. I should have found out more about this mystery mage, who he was and what his powers were, what abilities he was proficient in."

Alduce hung on the dragon's every word in awe. This mighty beast was by no means stupid; in fact, he displayed an intelligence that was so much more than Alduce had ever imagined. This dragon was completely different to his preconceived expectation of the man eating, flame breathing, monsters of legend.

"Blaze led me far from our home, the Lifting Plateau," Galdor continued, shaking Alduce from his reverie, "and we flew for hours into the deep wilderness where no man or beast had made their home. Even the trees and plants were scarce where we travelled, the blighted lands barren and empty. We landed close to a range of caves, deep black holes that ate into the mountainside, foreboding passages that only led to my downfall. Blaze said he had followed the mage here and watched him as he disappeared inside the mountain, where, Blaze had it on good authority, the mage had hidden his lair. And his gold.

"I was eager to end this mage and his plans to undermine my rightful position and barged by Blaze, into the cave he said the mage used. We dragons can see well in the dark, our eyes are no match for most, except probably owls, their eyes and a dragon's have much in common. Alduce stored this snippet of information away. Something else to ponder at a later date... if he survived.

"So, I led and Blaze followed, he guided me this way and that, turn left here, he would say, I think I can smell his scent, or take the middle fork, I see a footprint here or a disturbed stone there. Little did I know he had visited these caves before and this trip wasn't his first time inside the mountain. Fool I was, I took heed of his words, followed his advice without thought or question. We arrived at the mage's lair, quiet and stealthy, but he knew we were coming, he was expecting me and my duplicitous companion. They had prepared a trap and I had fallen foul of their subterfuge. We exited the labyrinth of tunnels and entered a large cavern, lit by globes similar to the one you carry with you now." Both sets of eyes glanced down instinctively at the glowing orb. Galdor was lost in the moment and Alduce waited for his gifted story-teller to continue.

"We could see the mage across the expanse of the cavern, he was through an archway that glistened with light and it looked like a cave within a cave. Blaze said we should enter into his inner cave, confront him and take his gold, he was sure this would be where the mage hid his valuable hoard. I should have suspected something was amiss, but I had been goaded and cajoled by Blaze for weeks and the red mist of my anger distorted my reason and shielded the truth from my eyes.

"I leapt from where we crouched and pounced through the archway into the smaller cave. As I sprang into action, the mage turned and smiled at me, quite unperturbed. He greeted me with contempt as he scorned me for my stupidity, and he told me of their scheme and how I had fallen for the web of lies he concocted with Blaze. As I stood looking back into the main cavern, the archway I had passed under started to reduce. I learned, much too late, that it wasn't another cave I had jumped into, but a passage to another world, this world, this very cave.

"The mage had opened a portal between my home world and yours, and they had tricked me into passing beyond the archway, lured me with false intent and trapped me here. The archway shrank as the mage controlled the portal, making it too small for me to return through. He attempted to jump back across the threshold of the ever shrinking archway and return to Blaze, who remained safely on the other side. A fierce anger welled up inside me, we dragons can often be led by our emotions, and I unleashed my wrath upon the mage. I truly believe he thought me peaceful enough that I would not be a threat to him. Perhaps Blaze had manipulated him too, as the black dragon rumbled his laughter from beyond the portal. I spewed a fiery blast from my jaws and engulfed the mage in a torrent of flame. His hair and clothing ignited and his skin and flesh melted like wax as it slewed from his bones. As he died, his magic died with him. The archway, now reduced to a circle the size of my head, a window on the cave wall, winked out of existence forever. The last sight that I saw of my home world was a gloating black dragon, victorious in his schemes as the rock wall solidified and he disappeared for ever."

Chapter 13

Alduce dipped his quill into the inkpot, his steady hand recording his thoughts as the nib scratched across the pages. He took great care when he wrote in the tomes bound in green dragonhide, not only for their rarity and value, but because the precious hide of scales had been a gift from Galdor.

This particular journal was dedicated solely to his shape changing, the sorcery and the science of how he had transformed, the ingredients and the way in which he had prepared them, and his feelings and observations. He wrote of his experience and how he felt, the intense pain and the unexpected ecstasy that consumed him when he had transformed into the dragon's form.

When he finished documenting his findings in the heavy paper pages, he set the huge book aside, leaving it open once again, allowing the ink to dry. He would hate for his writing to smudge the precious hide bound paper. He reached for and opened another scale bound tome. This new book was one he used specifically to record information about dragons. Galdor's skin had given him enough material to make many such books. He started writing down what he had discovered about the mother and her nest alongside all the other research he had managed to collate. Anything he could find in old books or local myths, gleaning information and talking to people who claimed to have seen or encountered dragons, would be recorded in this volume. That and his own encounters with these wondrous creatures, every detail important. With his new found ability to transform into a dragon himself, he expected to fill the pages with his own experiences too.

He outlined a sketch of a dragon, drawing a human figure to scale, then on a whim, added the giant crow he'd seen upon his return with the stolen egg. He would note down more about that encounter later, he planned to do a little research on the giant bird and find out what it was. It had certainly been unusual, another subject he would eventually get round to learning about.

His head felt better now the pounding had faded to a dull ache, but his buttocks had gone to sleep and his fingers tingled with cramp. How long had he remained in one position, writing? Standing, he stretched and his bones cracked at the movement. He had sat longer than planned, lost in his writing and his musings. Something Caltus had often chided him for when he was an apprentice.

He was eager to test the transformation again, but first he would eat and drink again, his body craved more sustenance. Transformation, he was to learn, took a lot out of a person.

He bustled round his kitchen, whistling tunelessly to himself. Putting together a huge meal of bread, cheese, and cold meats, he added dried fruit, mainly peaches, of which he always had a large store. They were his favourites. He drew a jug of cold water from his well, staying clear of ale or cider, imagining with slight amusement the havoc a drunk dragon could cause. Alcohol was best avoided when you practiced magical transformations.

The well water was fresh and cold, and he drank it down greedily. Alduce had bored through the rock when he first discovered the cave, tapping into a natural subterranean spring. It would have taken a year's solid labour, carving and drilling through the tough bedrock, without a little help from his magic.

He sat and ate, wolfing down his meal until his grumbling stomach was silenced and his hunger sated. He also emptied the water jug, drinking more than he needed in an attempt to combat the after effects of future dehydration.

He was subconsciously preparing for his next transformation and had already decided that he was going to attempt it again.

Making up his mind, he decided he couldn't wait. If he thought about the pain he might put it off.

He left his laboratory once more, still wearing yesterday's clothes. He would need to wash and change soon, it didn't pay to neglect the smaller comforts of being civilized, even when he lived on his own.

Exiting the cave he was surprised to see it was dark and much later than he expected. The black blanket of sky above was decorated with a million distant stars. Climbing the steep path to the mountain top, he sat next to the bones and skull used for the initial metamorphosis. He wouldn't need them now and should gather them up and take them inside. The bones would fetch a good price with master Bervus. Perhaps he would keep the skull, small though it was. He felt a strange connection to the unborn dragon and decided that he would hold on to it. It was an unusual feeling and he wondered where it had sprung from. Sentiment wasn't something he usually suffered from. Being a man of science he was normally extremely practical.

Alduce removed his clothes, folding them neatly and placed the small skull on top, piling the bones from the spell circle next to them. The Dragon pendant swung forward as he bent down with the bones, the artefact had played an integral part in the shape changing: the power and magic it possessed were almost limitless and he wouldn't be able to change without it.

He considered himself lucky to have acquired the dragon pendant, Flaire artefacts were hard to come by and he had certainly earned his.

Chapter 14

"Come, Alduce," Galdor said, "come and meet the mage who trapped me here." The dragon turned and retreated into the darkness of the cavern looking back over his shoulder, "And bring your light with you, there is something I believe you should examine."

Alduce stood and brushed away the dust from the cavern floor. Picking up the light orb, he followed the dragon, mindful of Galdor's tail as it flicked from side to side a few feet off the floor. He imagined with some trepidation the damage a tail like that could cause if he were struck by accident, far less deliberately.

"Meet the nameless mage," Galdor said, a hint of humour in his voice. "He lies where he fell, no gold or treasures did he have. Even though he was in league with Blaze, I do not think my black hearted adversary ever intended for him to survive, but instead to be trapped on this side of the portal with an angry dragon. Circumstances dictated he die with me, but had he survived and made it back through the archway to my own world, I suspect his life expectancy would have been short. He served his purpose and would have no further use to Blaze, of that I am sure. I do not know what lies he was fed or what promises were made to him. He surely must have believed it was worth the risk, meddling with our kind. He was no match for the black dragon's treachery."

Galdor sniffed the corpse that lay at his feet, blackened like an overcooked roast, ancient and mummified. What remained of the skin was stretched tightly over the skull, its lipless mouth preserved in a deathly grimace.

"He looks like he's grinning," Alduce remarked, "although I doubt his thoughts were pleasant while you seared his living body to charcoal."

"He deserved his fate," Galdor snapped, "I fought for my freedom when I realised their game. He wouldn't be this way had he not intended me harm!"

"I'm sorry Galdor, truly I am," Alduce replied, realising he had a new found respect for the imprisoned dragon. "This man made a choice to oppose you, I am only here by chance and do not intend you any harm. I gave you my word that I would do everything I could to help you." Waving his hand at the charred corpse of the mage, he continued. "You will have to excuse my comments, it's my way of dealing with a difficult situation. I don't wish to end up like the mage," adding a lot more quietly, "or in your belly."

The cavern was thick with tension, Alduce and the dragon faced each other with only the orb to light the scene. He was afraid for his life, could see no means of escape and Galdor was too clever for him to talk his way to freedom. If he had overstepped the mark and angered the dragon, then so be it. He had managed to put on a brave face and keep himself going on sheer nerves alone. But those nerves were wearing thin and turning to hysteria. He could see no solution to his problem. He straightened his back and stared at Galdor. Two terrifying dragon eyes stared back unblinking and Alduce didn't know what to expect. He was shocked when Galdor started to chuckle, a deep rumbling sound that was quite infectious.

"Forgive me, Alduce. I am not use to dealing with men. Seeing the mage after telling you my story has opened old wounds. I was angry at being deceived, reliving the events is unpleasant for me. You show a spirit that is worthy of a dragon and I have been rude to the only intelligent guest I have had in over a century."

"A century! You've been trapped in this darkness all this time? One hundred years of imprisonment without seeing the sun. Galdor, that's terrible." Alduce was genuinely sympathetic to Galdor's plight, the thought of being trapped in an underground cavern for days was bad enough in his mind. Years would be unbearable; one hundred years was unimaginable.

"I too would be angry and bitter if our positions were reversed. There is no need for forgiveness, I was flippant because I was scared. I didn't stop to think. I didn't know. How have you survived so long? What do you... eat?" Alduce asked the second question before thinking it through. He was now deeply entangled in Galdor's predicament and he hoped apprentice sorcerers wasn't the answer to his stupid question.

"I can see we have both formed pre-conceived ideas regarding one another. I believe I have misjudged you too, Alduce. Despite my predicament, I was once a good judge of character and my stay here has undermined that. What say we start anew? A fresh beginning is what is needed here." Galdor reared up and spread his wings.

"Greetings Alduce, I am Galdor the Green and I am pleased to make your acquaintance. I have been trapped in this underground cavern for over one hundred years and I am not my usual self. I'm sure you can appreciate why, after hearing my tale. I would be eternally grateful if you could help me with my plight, however, should you wish to leave, I will not stand in your way, nor will I eat you or burn you to death, like the unfortunate stinking mage," he snorted.

"I am able to sleep for long periods of time," Galdor explained, "decades or longer, it's something dragons can do. I can preserve my strength that way without the need for food, which I admit, is incredibly scarce down here. I've managed to scavenge a few meals over the years, but only when something wanders into my prison." He didn't mention what that *something* was and Alduce didn't feel the urge for him to elaborate.

He was stunned, he had no words to express the relief he felt. Galdor had offered him his freedom with no repercussions or fear of death and yet all he could think to say was, "Stinking mage?"

"Yes, he stinks, but not of charred flesh. He stinks of a strong magic. I can smell it from his corpse even after all these years, like an acrid taste, bitter and foul."

Alduce stepped forward and inhaled deeply but could smell nothing. Galdor gave another rumbling chuckle as Alduce sniffed.

"Can humans smell magic?" he asked Alduce. "Tell me you can, tell me he stinks of it."

"No, Galdor, I smell nothing. The mage is totally free from any odour I can detect, be it magic or decay. However," Alduce crouched down and stretched out his hand, "I can *feel* it," he looked back to find Galdor's huge snout crowding in behind him. "And you are correct, it's strong!"

Running his hand along the prone form of the dead mage, he pulled it back as if burned, causing Galdor to withdraw his head.

"Sorry, Galdor, I didn't mean to make you jump." He smiled at the thought of someone his size startling such a huge beast.

"I was taken unawares by the power I feel emanating from the dead mage. After one hundred years any residual magic he may have held on to should long have dissipated." He waved his hand, as if shaking off a cramp. "My hand is tingling from the magic I feel, as if the body is charged, like the air before a thunder storm." He rubbed his hands together. "Interesting," he murmured almost to himself, "very interesting." Galdor leaned back in, observing the man.

"If he died over one hundred years ago, why is his body still whole? He should be naught but dust and bone," Alduce mused, more to himself than his large acquaintance.

He ran his hands back over the dead mage and as he reached the man's neck he slowed down, fumbling through the folds of what remained of his robe. He pulled out a chain and untangled it from the remains, looping it over what was left of the charred head. As he did so, the corpse disintegrated before his very eyes, the rags crumbling and the remains of the mage withering until there was nothing left but dust and old bones, stained and pitted as if they had been exposed to the elements and eroded by time.

"Strong magic," Galdor said in Alduce's ear. "That is what I have been smelling. That is the answer to why he remained whole. You have removed what preserved his body and he perished before our eyes."

Alduce held up the chain and a small shape dangled down, a beautifully crafted pendant, fashioned in the image of a dragon. It appeared to be made of metal and shone as it caught the light from the orb. "I've never seen anything like this. The metal is light and hasn't tainted, even though the mage was engulfed in flames. There's no sign of any soot or tarnish. It must be substantially strong too, as it didn't melt."

Stepping away from the remains, he instructed the dragon, "Sniff the mage now Galdor, can you still smell magic from his bones?"

Galdor sniffed, drawing air in through his huge nostrils, making a sound like a strong wind on a blustery day.

Nudging the skull with the tip of his snout, he answered Alduce's question. "I can smell no magic. It smells as it should. Dead. Very old and very dead, that is all."

"And what if you smell the pendant?" Alduce asked. Galdor leaned in, eyeing the small talisman hanging from the chain in the sorcerer's fist and repeated his sniffing. "Strong magic, stinks like all human magic, yes, potent and powerful. Do you know what it is Alduce? I believe this might be how the portal from your world to mine was controlled. It stands to reason, powerful magic would be required for a spell of that magnitude. I remember when I flamed the mage," he stopped eyeing the tiny dragon pendant and looked directly at Alduce. If a dragon could look sheepish, Alduce guessed, this was as close as it got. "That is when the portal started to shrink." The dragon concluded.

"You may just have something there, Galdor. I suspect the pendant is some kind of focal charm that can store magic. It certainly feels powerful, extremely powerful. If the mage was using this to assist in a bridge between our two worlds, when his life was ended," Alduce didn't belabour that point, "his hold on the magic would have ended and his control over it too, causing the spell to end."

Galdor was enthralled, hanging on each word Alduce spoke. "Alduce," he purred, "do you think it would be possible, since you now possess this magical charm, that you could use it to re-open the way home for me?"

Alduce held the chain at arm's length, studying the spinning dragon charm as it twirled at the end of the chain, the excited dragon waiting for his answer.

"Galdor," he replied, "Why don't we see? As my master is fond of telling me, you never know until you try!"

Chapter 15

Alduce stood on the mountain top, the cold wind chilling his naked body, the hairs on his skin standing on end once again. He reached for his magic, touching its source and drawing it into the Flaire pendant around his neck. The same dragon pendant he had lifted from the body of the dead mage so many years ago.

The sky brightened as a flash of lightning streaked down and Alduce focused the power at his command, using it as a catalyst for the transformation. This time he would only need to concentrate on changing from his human form to that of the dragon hidden inside, no other ingredients necessary after the initial spell.

He released the magic, letting it flood out from the artefact and into his body. Willing the change and fixing the image of the dragon in his mind's eye.

His skin burned as he felt the transformation take hold for the second time, human skin changing to black metallic scales, blood pounding through his veins, liquid fire coursing through his very being. The pain intensified to an unbearable level and only when he was close to losing consciousness, did it begin to fade. He fell forward onto his knees, arms outstretched. Where his hands had been, long claws sprang forth, black talons bursting from what had moments before been his fingertips.

His whole body stretched, growing larger in both length and height. His arms and legs metamorphosed into a dragon's limbs and wings emerged from his back, increasing in size until they were fully formed. Alduce didn't feel any more pain after the burning sensation subsided. As his form changed he experienced a stretching sensation and imagined if he were a tree growing this quickly, this is what it would feel like.

Throwing his head back, he opened his newly acquired jaws and roared into the night sky. Powerful dragon lungs sounded out across the mountainside as the transformation finished. Where he had stood as a man, now a huge black dragon with a star of silver on its chest, took his place.

He extended his wings, and the leathery hide snapped like a mainsail as they unfurled to their full span. He flapped them experimentally, feeling the power and knowing how easily they would lift him skyward. Muscles rippled under the scaly hide that cloaked his back, their strength incredible.

He was ready, he knew he could fly, instinct had taken over and he crouched low to the ground and sprang upwards, huge back legs propelling him skyward.

He felt invincible. Nothing could stop him.

He was a dragon.

As he leapt from solid ground into the air, his wings took over, using minimal effort as they propelled him higher with each muscular stroke. It was as easy as breathing, with no conscious thought required, just a natural and instinctual process.

Alduce rose, higher and higher, climbing from the mountain top as his wings pushed him into the sky. The ground receded and he basked in the euphoria of flight as it washed through his entire body.

He was flying. No effort needed, no practice, no fear of falling. No learning was necessary, his dragon form knew what to do. Even though his mind was still human, his body was all dragon, from the tip of his snout to the point of his tail, and he relished it.

Roaring, he felt pleasure at the sound of his new voice. Setting his wings to glide, he sped through the darkness. His dragon eyes allowed him to see clearly, even though daylight had long since faded. Like an owl, the ability came naturally to him. He remembered Galdor's words and the comparison the green dragon had made. Instinct took over.

As he dropped back towards the ground, he tilted his wings, angling them to catch the air, stopping him from crashing back into the mountainside and propelling himself level with the land, wings set, gliding a few dragon widths above the rocks. His night vision picked out the form of a deer, warm blooded and scared as it fled before him. He could smell it, taste its fear as it scrabbled across the rocky ground, terror clouding its ability to flee from the massive predator above.

Alduce tipped a wing, banking around as the deer veered to his left. Extending his talons, he prepared to strike. Then, at the last second he retracted his claws and skimmed over the deer, leaving it to run free. He would not kill for pleasure in his dragon form. He trumpeted a salute to the reprieved animal and pumped his wings once more towards the heavens. He gained height with ease, this time flying down to the lowlands and meadows until he reached inhabited lands. Small villages and hamlets stood out in the darkness—their windows shone brightly making them easily seen from above.

Alduce flew on, testing his abilities, climbing high then diving as fast as he could, pulling up at the last second and skimming treetops, down draughts from his huge wings disturbing the leaves like the wildest of gales. He twisted and pivoted, his manoeuvres agile and skilful despite his size, pushing his abilities and revelling in the thrill of the flight.

After a few hours, he realised his flight had taken him much farther than he believed possible. He had become so engrossed in the act of flying that he hadn't noticed how far he had travelled. Before him glowed the lights of the city of Learning. A journey which had taken him days on horseback had taken only one night of flying.

He was sorely tempted to fly over the city and examine it from above, perhaps land on a rooftop of one of the larger buildings, but he decided against it. The buildings may not support his weight and Learning's residents might be afraid at the sudden appearance of a dragon, a creature that hadn't been seen in this part of the world for countless years.

A solitary figure stared up from the city walls, peering into the darkness. With keen dragon sight, Alduce was able to witness an astonished expression on the guardsman's face. The man peered out into the darkness in disbelief. Alduce wondered if anyone would believe him if he told the tale of a dragon materialising out of the night sky.

Turning around, he veered away from the warm lights of humanity, departing the city with a renewed vigour. Beating powerful wings, he rose majestically, disappearing silently into the darkness. He knew exactly which direction he needed to head, his internal dragon sense like a compass pointing the way home, back to his laboratory in the mountains.

Chapter 16

Alduce was aware of Galdor's intent stare as he focused on the power of the dragon pendant. He opened himself to the magic, drawing on the energy he could feel stored inside it. He had used magical artefacts before and was aware of how they worked, storing latent energy that a sorcerer could access to enhance their power.

What he didn't expect when he reached for the source of the magic was the incredible reservoir of power stored within such a small charm. He felt the magic brimming within the small metal dragon, much more than should be possible for its size and recalled Galdor's words.

Strong magic, stinks like all human magic, yes, potent and powerful.

The green dragon wasn't wrong and Alduce flinched as lightning crackled inside the dark cavern and surged into the pendant dangling from the chain he grasped in his fist. Galdor's breath whistled as he exhaled and Alduce knew he wasn't the only one who felt the strength of the magic called forth. He wasn't sure what to do next, as the power was magnified through the swinging form of the small metal dragon. Before he had any time to decide how to contain such an abundance of magic, eight small trails of what appeared to be lightning leapt from the metal dragon towards the cavern wall.

Each individual streak of the magical lightning spread out like points on a compass and struck the rock, north, north east, east and so on until eight glowing metal shafts were illuminated on the cave wall.

The magical lightning travelled from each point, joining and creating a circle which gathered speed, energy and magic, moving faster and faster until it was so fast that it blurred into one. The cave wall swirled before his eyes and inside the circle a point of light formed. Alduce was in control and felt that at any time he could stop the magic, by closing the opening he had created, even though it was new to him. Something special was happening and he wanted to see what this unknown magic could do. The metal rods had been set in the cavern wall deliberately and must somehow be connected to the mage's original spell. The spell that had opened a passageway between Galdor's world and his own.

The light at the centre expanded, rippling like the reflection of sunlight on water, blurred shapes came into focus and Galdor gasped as the image expanded and steadied.

"Alduce," the dragon crooned, "you have done it! You have restored the archway. You are truly a sorcerer of great knowledge and power. You have opened the way home for me after more than one hundred years."

The gratitude in Galdor's voice was like a cold drink on a hot day and Alduce drank it down. The feeling from this proud and powerful creature, paying a lowly apprentice such a magnanimous compliment, was overwhelming.

"Galdor," he whispered, "I am but an apprentice and you pay me a great compliment for accidentally stumbling across the answer you so desperately desired."

"Well then. Apprentice you may be now, I can only believe when you become a master, you will be the most powerful human who ever practiced magic! I would dearly love to stay and discuss the how and the why, Alduce, my rescuer, but I fear to waste another second stuck in this dank prison. I must return and see how the years and that black hearted dragon have changed the home I once knew." The dragon pushed his long neck through the window the portal had created, as if testing it. He withdrew his neck and shook his head then turned to face Alduce.

"You asked me a boon when we made our deal, sorcerer. Name it now and I will grant it."

Alduce slowly nodded, "My boon, mighty Galdor, was not to meet my end in this cave," he grinned. "And remaining on the outside of your belly is reward enough for me."

Galdor roared a rumbling dragon laugh.

"I desire no more," Alduce continued, "to see you gain your freedom is more than enough payment. It's not every day I'm given the opportunity to meet a dragon."

"You are a humble man, Alduce, I doubt there are many among your race that would turn down such an offer. It gives me hope for the human race."

The dragon tucked one leg under his chest and bent the other in an imitation of a bow.

"I will remember this and the lesson you have taught me here today, that dragon kind and human beings can become friends." The dragon stood and raised himself up onto his hind legs, extending his wings. A gold shimmering light emanated from around him, growing brighter and like a snake shedding its skin, Galdor did the same with his. Dragon scales and hide slid from his body and the new scales beneath gleamed like a rainbow as multiple colours washed over his body then settled on the green that was Galdor's colour.

"I leave you my hide of skin and scales. A sorcerer such as yourself will find many uses for it, I am sure," the reborn dragon said. Stepping from his discarded skin, Galdor leapt through the portal. Alduce watched in amazement as the dragon turned and pushed his head back through the cave wall. He spoke, as if talking through an open window, this time from his own world.

"Galdor the Green owes you much more than the hide he has shed and the magical necklace you hold. Remember this Alduce, for I shall not forget. If you ever chance to visit this world, seek me out." Galdor pulled his head back through the portal and called from the other side.

"Quick now, close the archway behind me... "

Alduce let go the magic he held and the window between worlds started to recede, slowly closing. Just before the light on the cave wall winked out, he heard Galdor's voice, muffled and distant, "Thank you."

The portal and his voice faded, leaving the young apprentice sorcerer alone in the now empty cavern. The light orb pierced the darkness, shining over the dead mage's bones. All that remained of the dragon was his magnificent hide and an unimaginably tall tale that no-one would ever believe.

Chapter 17

Alduce finished recording the night's events in the green scaled tome, bound with Galdor's hide. His fingers were numb from writing, cramming everything he remembered onto the pages. As soon as he had returned to his laboratory, he started writing so he would remember each little detail of the transformation and the flight.

The wonderful flight.

Even the smallest detail or feeling might be vital to his ongoing research. Shape changing wasn't unheard of amongst sorcerers, mages or even witches. As far as he was aware, however, no-one had managed to become one of the rarest and mythical creatures ever to exist: a dragon.

Alduce had been fascinated by dragons and their lore even before his unexpected meeting with Galdor. After the green dragon escaped his imprisonment, Alduce returned to his master. Caltus was pleased with the amount of black mushrooms he'd gathered.

When he told Caltus of his encounter with Galdor, his master accused him of eating some of the mushrooms and hallucinating everything, scolding him for getting high when he should be working and learning.

Alduce protested his innocence and eventually convinced his master the dragon was real and so was his part in assisting with Galdor's release. There was a dragonhide waiting to be retrieved, deep within the safety of the caves. Incontrovertible proof that Alduce's tale was true. Caltus hummed and hawed, trying to pick holes in his telling of the story. He wasn't going to journey to the Pendron Mountains on a fool's errand, he wanted to be positive Galdor and his gifted hide existed. But he relented when Alduce produced the small dragon pendant and showed it to the old sorcerer.

Caltus recognised the metal at once and made Alduce tell him everything again, then a third time for good measure, nodding here and there as the young apprentice repeated each and every event. He rigorously questioned his apprentice, making Alduce elaborate when he required more information.

This was where Alduce had learned his attention to detail. His old master had often emphasised the importance of recording all the information, however insignificant it may appear. Hidden gems, the old man had told him on many an occasion. You never know what hidden gems the details can hold.

Caltus told Alduce about the Flaire, the metal his dragon artefact, as he called it, was made of. The metal was able to hold great quantities of magic and could be used as a conduit to amplify sorcery. He had given his apprentice access to many books and scrolls, collected over the years. While there wasn't much information about the Flaire or its properties, between them they had pieced together a working knowledge of the potential of the small dragon on the chain. Alduce had tried to give the Flaire artefact to Caltus, he was his master after all and it was only right that the old man should take charge of such a valuable and powerful charm.

Master Caltus had refused, quite vehemently, telling his apprentice that while the temptation to own such a piece was great, everything he knew about such artefacts suggested that they did not just happen to be found by accident. He told Alduce that the Flaire dragon had sought him out for a reason. If Galdor's passage of time had been correct, and there was no reason to doubt a dragon as they were known to be extremely accurate time keepers, then the pendant had waited for over one hundred years for a new neck to hang round and it wasn't his. The respect Alduce already held for his master had increased tenfold that day. Even now, he still missed the old man and his infinite wisdom.

Leaving the newly penned page open to dry, he contemplated his next move. He wanted to learn more about dragons, their behaviours and their culture. From the information Galdor had shared with him, he now knew they weren't the beasts from a bard's tales, all fire breathing and gold hoarding. They were intelligent and social creatures, with their own society, laws and rulers. He wanted to study them, speak with them and learn all about dragons first hand and he was now able to do so, as one himself. If he could travel to Galdor's world he would be able to live with the dragons there and study them, if they accepted him for one of their own. Perhaps it would be prudent to find somewhere else to practice being a dragon first, before he ventured into the unknown.

He didn't know what to expect and wondered if a real dragon would be able to sniff out a shape changer. If they learned his secret, how would they react? Would they punish him for stealing the unhatched egg? How would they view his actions and what he had done to complete the transformation?

He hoped if dragons knew what he was, they wouldn't be offended and seek to punish him. He did feel a little uncharacteristically guilty about the unhatched egg, but didn't know why.

Yet more questions that his scholarly mind begged answers to.

There was only one way to find out. As Caltus often liked to remind him, he would never know until he tried.

Part Two

Discovery

Chapter 1

Excerpt from Alduce's Atlas of Dragons.

The Yellow Dragon: draconis flavinium.

The yellow dragon is one of the more spectacular breeds, not that all dragons are not highly spectacular, however yellows shine like the sun. Their scales are not truly yellow and never uniform in pigment and shade. Study of the yellow's scales has allowed me to reach the following conclusions. The top layer of the scales are an opaque yellow, and while this allows the overall colour to appear a base yellow from afar, on closer inspection, the scales hold a myriad of shades, ranging from a bright golden to a deep burnished orange.

Viewing a yellow dragon in the morning sunrise, the midday sun or an evening sunset will make the same dragon look like three different specimens.

Yellows are closely related to their larger cousins, the greens and their characteristics and shape are similar, if not smaller. Their physical shape and distinctive swept back wings make them the perfect candidates for flight. Their competitive nature and confidence in the air make them one of the best fliers, when it comes to aerial prowess.

One distinctive feature of the yellow, that no other dragon I have encountered so far displays, is the darker 'shark fin' spines. These start behind the horns and grow larger as they run down the length of the neck. Other species neck decoration stops before the wing ridges, but with the yellow, they continue across the back and between the wings, growing largest at the shoulders then decreasing in size as they run along the spine to the tip of the tail, the last fin sitting upright on the tail point, forming a three bladed arrow head.

Note: I believe that during the evolution of the yellow dragon, while it is one of the smaller species of all draconis, nature has equipped it with an extremely lethal weapon in the form of its unusual tail. The tail itself is all muscle and the three hard tail fins are, by design, tough as steel, incredibly sharp and hold a poison with effects similar to that of a scorpion sting.

Sunburst the Yellow. (Subspecies: mountus, hill or mountain dragon.)

I encountered Sunburst early into my dragon studies, or rather he encountered me. He was curious, but also hesitant at the same time. Once my relationship was established, Sunburst grew friendly and I earned his trust. Only then was he happy to converse for long periods, educating me and becoming a great font of dragon lore and behaviour.

Sunburst displays the typical competitive nature of all yellows and is at his happiest when flying or hunting alongside a friendly adversary.

Sunburst excels in low flight and his aerial expertise and ability to change direction quickly, make him one of the most competent fliers I have encountered in all the dragon types I have studied. He was also able to outfly Nightstar when flying through forested areas, on the hunt.

It should also be noted that yellow dragons have green eyes and an acute sense of smell.

Other dragons will eat out of necessity while yellows will also eat for pleasure and are the gourmets of the dragon world. They love their food with a passion and a yellow will fly for miles in an effort to find a tastier buck or a particular species of fish.

It is my opinion, that while dragons could never be described as innocent or childlike, the yellow can sometimes feel like the younger sibling of the dragon family.

Note: Sunburst can appear placid and non-confrontational and is mostly even tempered. However, if he is wronged, slighted or feels he has been taken advantage of, be warned, this dragon has a dark side.

* * *

Alduce flew above the land, his black scales gleaming like polished metal in the morning sunlight. The patch of silver scales blazed on his chest like a bright star against the night sky. The star appeared when he transformed, the Flaire artefact melding from rare metal into scales of silver, standing out against the black ones.

As he flew, Alduce was amazed at how exceptional the sight of a dragon was. Not only could he see admirably in the dark, during the daylight hours his vision was remarkable. Scouring the terrain below his wings, he drifted lazily on the warm air thermals, instinctually catching the heated updrafts rising from the ground.

He set his wings, holding them outstretched to maximise the lift and rode the air currents as if he had been flying all his life. Alduce created a new portal to travel here and the ground beneath was unfamiliar. This was a new world and he hoped it would be inhabited with real dragons. His main reason for coming here was to practice living as a dragon, flying, hunting, and learning what it was to be the beast he now had the ability to change into.

He arrived through the portal he created using newly fashioned Flaire spikes. Each set of eight he manufactured took him to a new world. He learned how to fashion the rare metal but, so far wasn't able to influence which world the newly made portal would take him to. He had also discovered other portals that could be used to travel through. But they were static and difficult to locate and he couldn't find much about who had created them or how.

He now owned three sets of spikes, one set that allowed him passage to the world where he had acquired the egg.

The set from the underground cavern on the slopes of the Pendron Mountains, which opened a portal to Galdor's home world.

And his newest set, which brought him here. Wherever here was.

Alduce wasn't ready to venture to either of the other worlds. He wanted to get familiar with his new form, somewhere new, where he knew no-one and no-one knew him.

He had made a new set of rods especially for this journey, using the raw Flaire metal Bervus acquired and traded for the dragon remains. Bervus thought he had the best part of their deal, and that might be true as in terms of income the apothecary would generate. Being able to fashion the raw Flaire into rods allowed Alduce the ability to travel to other worlds. That was worth more to him than any profit.

As he drifted above the countryside he noticed a lake in the distance reflecting in the sunlight. Tilting his wings, he adjusted his course towards the lake, descending towards the grassy hillside, relishing in the speed as he hurtled towards his destination. The lake nestled in a small valley and Alduce followed the undulating land as he came to the water's edge.

Tipping his wings, he trailed them in the water as he crossed the shoreline and glided out over surface of the lake, rippling the calm surface. He watched his reflection as it kept pace with him, speeding over the watery mirror below.

An unexpected realisation came to him, this was the first time he was actually able to see what he looked like in dragon form. He crossed to the far shore and pulled up, turning his huge black wings to catch the air and slow himself down, timing it perfectly and landing gracefully, the pebbles on the beach crunching beneath his talons.

Standing at the water's edge, he peered at his reflection. A huge black dragon with a silver star emblazoned on his chest stared back.

An impressive sight.

No mirror would have been large enough for him to appreciate how impressive, in his current form. Examining his image he marvelled at what he had become, coming to the conclusion he was a perfect dragon. Science and sorcery had allowed him to transform, but he never imagined how imposing he would look. He titled his head, it was long and horse shaped, tapering to a snout with protruding nose holes, ridged and slightly upturned. He pulled back his gums in parody of a smile, jaws lined with ivory teeth, each one the size of a man's forearm. The man inside, remembered his encounter with Galdor, how terrified he had been when the green dragon flashed his razor sharp teeth at him.

Piercing yellow eyes, part way between that of cat and snake, glowered from a flat face. Hard boned ridges curved around the contours of his eye sockets, like solid eye brows Alduce tried twitching, almost hypnotised by the effect. Small pointed ears and curved horns sat atop his head and a long serpentine neck thickened as it joined to his body.

Leathery wings jutted out from either side of his spine ridge. Five wicked talons, black and shiny, protruded from each of his claws, each one a weapon, sharp and deadly. His front legs were shorter than the sturdy rear ones and when his talons were retracted, he could use his claws like hands. His larger back legs give him his stability when on land and provided power enough to propel his heavy mass into the air, even from a standing take off.

His scales were like overlapping shields, providing the legendary protection that made dragons so difficult to harm, black except where the silver ones formed the five pointed star on his chest.

All in all, he was an impressive sight. A black dragon, a beast of legend, appearing perfect in every way, full of power and truly magnificent.

A sound from behind caused him to jump and he felt foolish as he turned to see a smaller, yellow dragon observing him from the embankment above the lake shore. Magnificent dragons, such as himself should not get startled, but he was only a dragon in shape—he reminded himself—he still possessed the mind of the man.

He wasn't sure what to do as the yellow dragon eyed him from where he perched on the ridge.

Was there a protocol when dragons encountered one another?

This is why he was here, to learn, but he wasn't sure what to do, now that he had finally found another of his adopted kin.

The yellow dragon surprised him for a second time as he dropped his foreleg underneath the front of his body and bent his neck forward and showed deference to the larger black dragon, bowing like a courtier before his liege.

"Greetings, cousin black," he said. "What do you seek in my lake?" Alduce could understand the words the dragon spoke, the power of the Flaire artefact, even while manifested as scales, allowed him to understand any language and in turn, be understood.

The yellow dragon was half his size, but no less spectacular and showed no sign of subservience as he first suspected, speaking clearly as an equal. His bow wasn't from deference but a show of respect.

He remembered when he had helped Galdor escape. The mighty green had given him the same bow.

"Greetings yellow cousin," Alduce spoke back, his voice gruff and unused, but pleasant sounding to his ears. "I seek nought, merely caught by my own refection, a moment of vanity, I confess." He instinctually knew the yellow dragon was a male, he didn't know how, he just knew, a dragon sense.

"We dragons can be vain, it is surely in our nature. I need not warn you of the pitfalls of continued indulgence along that path, it will only lead to one's own ruin." The yellow dragon's words held a message that Alduce was unable to interpret, but he maintained the appearance of understanding and intelligence before his smaller *cousin.*

"Wise words indeed, my friend," he replied. He could sense the magic from the yellow dragon, it wasn't as powerful as his own, but it was there, part of its being, crucial for its existence. He imitated the bow, dipping his own head as the yellow had done. "May I enquire as to whom I address?" he asked, keeping his tone formal.

"I am known as Sunburst, my yellow scales are the colour of the sun. When I take flight I burn across the sky like a celestial fire," the yellow replied. "A little dramatic, I know." Then he grumbled, the sound like distant thunder, almost like a chuckle.

"Your words are as radiant as your yellow scales, friend Sunburst. I suspect when you take flight, two suns light the heavens," he mimicked the yellow's chuckle and was happy at the way the grumbling sound made him feel. He would have to record this feeling in his journal as this was something new and unexpected.

"You flatter me cousin black. I thank you for your kind words."

Alduce took an instant liking to Sunburst, his manner was friendly and speaking dragon to dragon was exciting and fun.

"Now you know my name and have paid me praise," the yellow dragon said, "I would enquire to know yours and perhaps return the compliment."

Alduce hadn't considered a dragon name and he could hardly tell Sunburst his human one. He quickly thought of a suitable title that would sound right to a fellow dragon.

"I am Nightstar the Black," he improvised, copying the way Sunburst spoke, "the star on my chest, silvery and bright, illuminates the darkness." He wasn't quite sure were the name had come from, but it felt right.

"Impressive introduction," the yellow dragon chuckled. "We are a pair of opposites, you and I. You represent the qualities of night, black scales and silver starlight, while I am the day time, golden sunlight, bright and radiant. A balance, I think." Alduce liked the comparison. His new yellow acquaintance was right, they were as opposite as day and night. As opposite as dragon and man.

He wondered at the dragon mind and made a mental note to explore this further. Sunburst was not only intelligent, he was articulate and quick witted with an elegant prose Alduce had not expected from a dragon. He had hoped to learn more about dragons and this chance meeting was providing his first lesson.

"Cousin Sunburst, I am a stranger to your lands. I have travelled a great distance to meet new kin. It is fortuitous that we have met here on the shores of your lake. Would you share your knowledge of the land with me and educate me in your ways?" Sunburst remained silent as he appeared to consider the request, contemplating his words.

"I propose we acquaint ourselves first, I think better on a full stomach and I would like to see how the mighty Nightstar carries himself in flight and on the hunt."

The yellow dragon crouched and then sprung into the air, unfurling his wings as he launched himself skyward. Alduce, now Nightstar, watched the yellow dragon, marvelling at the ease of his movements. The draft from his wings washed over, him causing the long grass on the embankment to ripple like waves upon the water.

The smaller yellow dragon presented him with a challenge of sorts and the beast within, Nightstar by name, accepted it. He felt he was being tested, given a rite of passage to prove himself worthy. Sunburst wanted to see how well he flew, how good a hunter he was. His dragon sense took over and he leapt into the sky behind the yellow dragon with a determination to prove himself worthy, not only to Sunburst, but also to himself.

Sunlight reflected off Sunburst's yellow body, causing him to glow, intense golden rays so bright Nightstar squinted from the glare. The yellow dragon wasn't wrong with his introduction, he was indeed a celestial fire lighting the sky. He was predominantly yellow, the colour deeper on his back and wings, gradually turning lighter as it reached his flanks. His chest was burnished orange and when his scales caught the sunlight a certain way, they glowed pearlescent gold.

Nightstar beat powerful wings, climbing above Sunburst and positioning himself where he wouldn't need to squint when he looked at the yellow dragon. The black dragon's wingspan was impressive and a lot wider than that of the yellow. Making the most of his size advantage, Nightstar climbed, higher and higher pulling his body into the air, farther and farther from the ground. Sunburst stayed with him, remaining below the mighty black, never faltering as they ascended. Nightstar turned as he rose, spinning his body in a lazy corkscrew manoeuvre as he pumped his wings. The dark shadow on the ground below diminished, growing smaller the higher he climbed. Even with the ability of his dragon sight, it wasn't long before he wasn't able to see it.

As they climbed, the air grew colder and the man inside the dragon knew that the atmosphere changed the higher you rose. He looked for Sunburst and was surprised to see he had dropped the smaller dragon and was now alone. Sunburst had levelled off and was gliding, maintaining his height and Nightstar suspected that he had pushed the yellow to his limit, the smaller dragon unable to follow any higher.

Breathing became laboured as Nightstar pushed himself higher, testing his own limits. It became difficult to draw precious oxygen into his lungs, he too, had reached his zenith. He could see the glowing yellow dragon, now far below. Golden sunlight gleaming from his yellow scales make him easy to find in the vast expanse of infinite sky. If Sunburst's sight was half as good as his own, he was sure the yellow would be watching him and would be impressed by his ability to rise so high into the atmosphere.

He levelled off and set his wings wide, dipping the tip in a salute to Sunburst and was happy to see that the yellow dragon mimicked this action acknowledging him. Breath grew shorter and Nightstar couldn't sustain flight this high any longer. Taking a dragon sized lungful of thin air he rolled his wings and flipped himself upside down, his head now looking beyond the sky and out into the darkness that was the stratosphere.

His vision swam and he felt light-headed, he was as high as he had ever been and the light-headedness he was feeling was part excitement, part lack of oxygen. It was time to leave this wonderful place before he passed out. A sudden thought panicked him. If he lost consciousness, he didn't know if he would revert back to his human form. Not something he wished to contemplate, given his current location.

Tipping his neck backward he spiralled into a dive, folding his black leathery wings tight into his flanks. He gathered momentum, slowly at first, then picked up pace, getting faster and faster. He was aware of Sunburst's position below him and as he dropped, he adjusted his decent to speed past the smaller dragon as he plummeted towards the ground.

Sunburst peeled out of his glide and dropped into a dive, following Nightstar as he passed, tucking his yellow body into the slipstream created by the larger beast. The yellow dragon roared in joy and they both hurtled downward together. Sunrise following night.

White mists of thin cloud scattered as the two dragons raced through them, streaking ever downward. Nightstar experienced a rush of elation, he never thought being a dragon would be like this. He was more than just a mythical creature and he was more than a man, more than a combination of the two, he was Alduce-Nightstar, creation of science and sorcery, he was...

The ground loomed before him and all sense of euphoria vanished, his moment of epiphany replaced by the realisation he needed to stop before he collided with the ground. He pulled out of the dive and attempted to open his wings but the air pressure and the speed fought against him.

He altered his descent reducing his downward angle and tried again. Wind caught in the huge black wings, cracking like a whip as they filled with air, slowing him down. He levelled his flight just in time, pulling up with seconds to spare. He flew low over the lake, talons dragged across the water disturbing the calm surface, pushing up frothy waves. He glided to the far shore and landed feeling his huge dragon heart pound beneath silver scales. Sunburst followed him from his place in the sky and lazily drifted across the lake's surface in a gentle descent, a lot more relaxed and controlled than Nightstar's near fatal plunge. He dropped onto the lake shore and landed gracefully beside the larger black, tilting his triangular head and eyeing the larger dragon.

"Nightstar, you are well named," he said. "I never saw a dragon fly so high! When I reached my limit, you continued upward, fading into the darkness beyond the sky. Your black scales blended with the darkness, but the silver on your chest blazed fiercely, like a star in the night." He slowly shook his head, "A night star indeed."

Alduce, now thinking of himself as Nightstar, grinned inside, his chance choice of name had worked out better than he could have imagined. "Thank you Sunburst, you flatter me, I think."

"Not at all, cousin black. Not only did you rise into the night that hides above the clouds, you dropped like a shooting star. I thought you were going to crash into the ground! Had you waited a heartbeat longer, you surely would have."

Inside Alduce glowed with pride, his stupid stunt earned him the respect of a real dragon. He wouldn't tell the yellow how close it had really been, not now that Sunburst believed his near miss to be deliberate and timed to perfection. He impressed the yellow dragon with his antics and was in a good position to use the situation to gather more information.

"I have been practicing my prowess in the air, I admit," Nightstar replied, "I am happy to see it was worthwhile."

Here he was, a human shape shifter who had been flying less than three weeks, getting praise from a dragon who had been flying all his life. His dragon sense and his natural instinct were responsible, he knew, but he felt a huge sense of achievement to have been given this praise. He decided he would take control of this conversation and show Sunburst he was a dragon worth his scales.

Worth his scales? Where did that come from? When he was in dragon form, he noticed he thought like a dragon. Was Sunburst having an influence on his dragon self too? He would be sure to record this in his journal when he returned to being human. Much later. He was enjoying his new found dragon sense too much to think about going home just now.

"You said we would hunt, friend Sunburst. I am ready."

"As am I, Nightstar. Come, follow me. See if you can keep up." He grumbled his chuckling sound as he hopped into the air, looking back to see if Nightstar was with him.

"Your flight to the heavens was impressive, I grant you. Flying high and flying low are two different things, mighty black. Low valleys and forest trees are more suited to a yellow dragon's skills." He blew a trumpeting challenge and sped off, wings beating in a golden blur.

Nightstar leapt from the lakeshore in pursuit, the smaller dragon weaving this way and that as he undulated across the ground, flying fast and low. He swept down into a valley and flew along the inclines of the embankments, turning and twisting as he followed the contours and the hills.

Cresting a rise, Nightstar chased the nimble yellow as he approached a vast forest. The woodlands were populated with mighty oaks, tall elms and unknown varieties of trees that were new to Alduce. The scholar inside the dragon body made a mental note to return here and examine the leaves of these new and unknown woody giants.

Sunburst's statement hadn't been a boast. The smaller yellow flitted through the dense forest like a sparrow in a hedgerow, his size allowed him to pass through gaps in the foliage and branches where the larger Nightstar couldn't fit.

Sometimes, when Nightstar was faced with hitting a tree, he would rise above the forest canopy to avoid it and would hear Sunburst rumble his chuckle. The yellow dragon was having fun besting his larger companion, it seemed.

They carried on through the trees. Sometimes Nightstar was able to follow the twisting yellow shape of Sunburst as he wove through impossibly small gaps, but often needed to seek an alternative path that allowed his larger body to pass. Taking the less direct route meant that Sunburst pulled ahead and even though this wasn't a race, Nightstar was clearly a poor second to the more agile of the two dragons.

The forest started to thin and the ground beneath dropped away into a huge meadow, stretching off into the distance. Nightstar caught up with Sunburst as the yellow slowed, his frantic wingbeats forgotten as he glided to a halt in the long grass. Nightstar landed next to his new friend and Sunburst turned, as if noticing him for the first time.

"Ah, there you are," he chuckled. "I feared you had been lost in the trees mighty Nightstar."

"You had me at a disadvantage, Sunburst," he said allowing the yellow dragon his victory. "It was a good flight and you are the better dragon when it comes to low flying through dense forests."

"And you when it comes to reaching impossible heights. It appears we both have our strengths and weaknesses. As it is with dragons."

"Wise words," Nightstar agreed. The same logic applied not only to dragons, but also to men, if only they would realise it.

"Now we will hunt. All this flying makes me hungry," the yellow dragon announced.

Nightstar hadn't eaten since he transformed. His last meal had been as Alduce, consuming human food. Until now he hadn't given much thought to eating while in dragon form. He had been too occupied with his flying and exploring since his arrival on this world. He wondered why that might be, was it something to do with the shape changing? Or could it be, as his research indicated, dragons would eat when hungry and not need to feed again for days or sometimes weeks? He suspected it was probably the latter, everything so far with his new form appeared to follow a natural pattern. It didn't matter to his physical dragon body there was a man inside. His stomach growled at the thought of food and a wave of ravenous hunger washed through him. Nostrils flared as he picked up the sweet scent of something on the wind.

"You smell them too? Your sense of smell is almost as keen as a yellow!" Sunburst said, breaking his train of thought. He could certainly smell something, something appetising but he didn't know what it was. The scent was new to him, his dragon senses were different from his human ones and he was still adapting to these new sensations.

"They smell wonderful," he answered, not alerting Sunburst to the fact that he had no idea what it was they were talking about. "I will follow your lead, yellow cousin. This is your hunting ground and I am your guest." Sunburst tipped his head, nodding his understanding, then swayed his short yellow neck from side to side, inhaling through his nostrils and flicking a light blue forked tongue this way and that, tasting the air.

"Our feast awaits," he stated, "there is no ceremony in the hunt, Nightstar, though I appreciate the respect you have shown me. Eat your fill." He sprang from the grass and flapped his wings, keeping just above the ground, the long grasses bent and swayed as the downward strokes raked air over the meadow.

Nightstar felt himself salivate as the hunger took hold and he hopped into the air, drawn along by the scent that grew stronger and more pleasant.

The drumming of hooves was accompanied by a thin cloud of dust as Sunburst suddenly veered skyward and twisted in the air, changing direction. As Nightstar climbed he was able to see the animals spooked by the yellow dragon... and smell them!

Dragon senses took over completely as the four legged feast scattered about the meadow. He could sense the heartbeats of the strange animals, feel their terror as they attempted to cheat death. Sunburst chased what could only be described as a large woolly deer, somewhere between a sheep and a stag, its antlered head, barrel body and long legs were covered in a light brown mass of curly wool. It ran, changing direction often, in an attempt to evade pursuit. Sunburst roared as he missed the beast with a desperate lunge, travelling past where the beast had been just a moment before, his talons snatching at empty air.

Nightstar soared above the herd, the beast froze as his ominous shadow blocked out the sunlight, casting a patch of darkness over the meadow, startling the creature. That was all the time Sunburst needed to change direction and sink his wicked claws into the beast's back. The dying woolly deer screamed and Nightstar smelled its warm, appetising blood, as its flesh tore open.

Instinct took over and he lost himself in the thrill of the chase. He was distantly aware of Sunburst as he started to devour his kill, but a more pressing need took hold as he singled out a beast for himself. He swooped down, talons facing forward, wings bent back as he went in for the kill. Rage and frustration vented from his mouth, his roar causing the herd to scatter everywhere as he missed his target.

These creatures were fast!

He spun, bloodlust coursing through his dragon form and roared once more, a challenge or a warning, he wasn't sure. He needed to make a kill and he needed it now. Looking for the beast that had escaped his first attempt, he banked round and made a second pass.

This time he was smarter, following the animal as it pivoted and darted in an effort to survive. Nightstar made a lunge and the deer stopped and turned, springing away from where it had expected the dragon to be. This time he was ready for the sudden change in direction and had faked the attack, pulling up short and using his left wing like a sail, he turned sharply into the oncoming path of the terrified animal. His talons sank into the animal, ripping skin and flesh, bones shattered beneath the crushing grip of his talons and warm blood sprayed in a fine mist, tantalising his senses.

Using his weight, he dragged the surprisingly robust animal to the ground, biting into its succulent neck. His teeth ripped through delicious tasting meat and warm blood filled his mouth, igniting his taste buds. The human part of him, deeply buried in the dragon at present, was a little shocked at the violent way in which he devoured his prey, but he also knew it was the natural order of things. Nature was a harsh mistress and dragons needed to eat.

He tore flesh from the bones of the dead deer, swallowing down great pieces of divine tasting meat and savouring the raw flavour. This animal grazed on grassy plains, fresh and wild, and the taste filled his senses. A lean dish of sweet meat, its blood and skin fuelling his appetite. Stripping flesh from beast was easy work, using a combination of talons and jaws, he soon reduced the deer to little more than a pile of bones.

The power a dragon had in its bite combined with the effective use of talons made it a killing machine. Nightstar was a force to be reckoned with, his size and strength coupled with the physical power of his body and the armour of his scales made him feel invincible. The sorcerer inside the dragon wondered if the kill was causing this feeling of power, he would have to catalogue this in his journals too and make a comparison the next time he fed.

His forked tongue rolled around blood stained teeth, licking them clean and enjoying the lingering flavour.

Sunburst swayed across the grass towards him, it was almost funny to watch the way he moved, his belly distended after feeding. But the red blood smeared on his yellow scales was a vivid reminder of the violent kill he had made.

"Curly bucks, difficult to catch but definitely worth the effort," he said. "My stomach is filled to bursting."

Nightstar belched, "Very tasty!" he could easily devour a second buck. Sunburst may be full, but he was half his size. He peered out across the grasslands in hope of spotting another. "The herd are long gone," Sunburst chuckled. "They will have fled the plain and found hiding places among the trees. The can hide in the forest and are difficult to spot, their coats help them blend into the undergrowth. We were lucky to catch them in the open, they will be wary for a few days now," he chuckled again, "but they soon forget."

"I didn't realise I was so hungry," Nightstar admitted.

"There's still plenty meat left on my kill," Sunburst offered. "I couldn't eat another mouthful. I think my curly was bigger than yours too."

"But mine was faster and didn't freeze in terror like yours."

"A kill's a kill and mine was definitely the larger of the two," Sunburst stated with pride, his competitive nature obvious. "I am ready for a rest and I always feel drowsy after I gorge." He yawned, flashing bloodstained fangs. Witnessing a dragon yawn was an imposing sight. However, Nightstar felt its infectious tug, not sure if it was a human reaction, but unconsciously copying the yellow dragon with a yawn of his own.

"Now we have flown together and hunted," Sunburst said, "we are more than just acquaintances. You have proven yourself a worthy companion, Nightstar. I would gladly call you friend. You asked about these lands and said you were a stranger. I admit, I have never met a black dragon before, it is rare indeed for a hatchling to remain the colour we are inside the egg, rare and impressive."

"I am what I am," Nightstar said, not knowing until now, how rare his colouring was. It would be prudent to avoid having any conversations about his hatching, unsure how to answer any awkward questions that might arise. He attempted to change the subject. "I'm not completely black, I have my silver scales too."

"Yes you do. I noticed the blood from the curly bucks doesn't stand out on your black scales as it does on my yellow. I need a bath," Sunburst yawned again. "I need a nap first, though."

The yellow dragon turned round and round, like a dog before it settled, lying on the trampled grass with a satisfied sigh.

Nightstar felt tiredness descend as he watched his yellow companion lay his head on outstretched front legs and close his eyes. He copied the smaller dragon's actions and turned a few times himself before lying alongside the already snoring Sunburst.

The black dragon was content. Letting his mind drift, he welcomed sleep.

Chapter 2

Excerpt from Alduce's Atlas of Dragons.

The Red Dragon: draconis rubaria.

The red dragon comes in many shades, males tend to be a flat solid red and females can range from a fiery scarlet to deep crimson.

Red, along with green is the more common of the dragon pigments and where greens are known to have the more traditional dragon shape, the red is less squat, thinner and sleeker.

As one would expect, the red dragon is an elemental fire dragon and is capable of producing flame with little effort. Red females are extremely attractive to any male varieties and have an almost hypnotic effect. I have learned that female dragons secrete a hormone designed to attract males when they are in season. When they are ready to clutch, the red female can cause most males to feel a strong attraction towards her. The red female is renowned for producing the strongest scent and this may be why reds are one of the most common colours.

Other traits that are more common in reds than other colours are that they are fond of riddles and have a great love of precious stones, rather than the usual metals such as gold and silver.

The red is of average size and normally get no larger than forty feet in length. They have wide wings, are robust and resilient and their scales are known to be one of the toughest amongst dragons. Their bodies are heavily armoured even though the adornments look decorative, they are incredibly practical in matters of defence.

Subject: Blood Rose (female, crimson.)

Rose (also known as Blood Rose) is practical, friendly and loyal. Life mate to the yellow, Sunburst. She has high eye ridges that make her appear more feminine, if *a dragon could be described as such. Her voice is soothing and her manner relaxed and informal. It is my opinion that Sunburst is the envy of many males that inhabit the White Mountains, as his mate is a perfect example of the draconis female.*

* * *

Nightstar lazily opened one eye and cocked an ear in the direction of the sound that pulled him from his slumber. Sunburst still lay where he was, gently snoring like an old man in his favourite chair. Nightstar heard the noise again, a wet thudding sound that stopped and started with no discernible pattern. Opening his other eye, he slowly raised his head above the long grass and thick bushes that partially obscured him, peering in the direction of the noise.

A large dark shape straddled the carcass of Sunburst's woolly buck, scavenging off the remains. The wet thudding sound was the beak of the biggest bird he had ever seen, pecking flesh from the bones of the dead animal. He remembered the man sized raven outside the cave when he retrieved the dragon egg. This wasn't the same one, obviously, as this was a different world, but it was surely the same species, just larger.

Alduce hadn't come across these birds in any books when he was studying. Master Caltus hadn't mentioned any creatures like these when he had tutored his apprentice. These giant birds must be extremely rare if there were no written records or knowledge of them.

His second encounter with this species rekindled his interest. He had been too absorbed with his transformation to spend time pondering his first meeting, but now, as he lay there, sleepily observing through the eyes of a dragon, Alduce the scholar awoke.

He studied the huge black bird, its feathers like dark satin. It fed on the remains of the curly buck, distracted by its feast. He should try and get a little closer and get a better look.

It was strange how his human brain thought. His dragon eyes saw perfectly, but the man inside the tough hide and scales wanted to creep forward for a better look. Slowly and as quietly as he could, he lifted his bulk from the ground, keeping himself as low as possible so he wouldn't be seen and startle the bird. He crawled like a lizard, crouching with his legs splayed out and wings folded flat, edging closer.

The bird stopped pecking and looked up to see a dragon bearing down on it. The panic in its black intelligent eyes was plain as it launched into the air, flapping black feathery wings frantically in an effort to evade the dragon. It let out a long caw.

Danger! It squawked, *Drake!* And Nightstar understood what it had said!

How could this be? He could understand many languages when he wore the Flaire artefact. Even when it was part of the silver scales that formed the star on his chest, it still performed this function.

But crows didn't speak, at least not as far as humans were aware. Perhaps when he was a dragon the artefact let him understand other creatures. Did it have new abilities when in its scale form? More mysteries to ponder.

Another black shape rose from behind the carcass and followed the first into the air, it was smaller and slower and appeared to be a youngster, judging by its size. Alduce now thought that the large bird that had returned his light orb had been a youngster too. Nightstar stood and watched the huge birds disappear into the sky, a mother and its offspring in all likelihood, making their escape.

"What's all the fuss?" Sunburst asked as he joined Nightstar.

"Big birds eating your kill," Nightstar replied. "I've seen... " he hesitated. He was about to say he had seen their kind before, but that was on another world and might not be easily explained. "I've seen big birds before, but never that large." Sunburst didn't notice the correction, or if he did, he failed to remark on it.

"Larcrowe," Sunburst stated, not surprised at all. "They scavenge. As is their nature. Scrounging for a free meal." The yellow dragon had a way of stating the obvious, plainly speaking and straight to the point. The scholar that listened with Nightstar's ears liked that. And he found Sunburst likeable.

"Are they common here?" Nightstar continued, not wanting to seem excited about this species. Would a dragon ask questions a scholar might? He didn't know. Sunburst didn't think it unusual as his answer was matter of fact.

"Not really. They sometime come across from the eastern lands, they live near the coast in the cooler parts. I think they prefer it, I've never seen them in the far south where it's warmer. I have flown near to their colonies once or twice, but they tend to stay away from dragons and our lands. They are good fliers, not as good as dragons, but good enough. They tend to be hard to catch in the air and not worth the effort. They don't make for good eating, tough and tasteless."

"I would like to see their colonies," Nightstar said.

"Not worth the trip, it's cold and windy in the east and you can smell the salty sea. The salt makes my snout itch. It isn't pleasant there and I don't like it. I prefer the grasslands, much kinder on the snout. And they are noisy! All that squawking and chattering. Mindless noise, just stupid birds."

Nightstar concluded that Sunburst couldn't understand what the Larcrowe had said when it flew off. But he had. Another interesting discovery he would have to write down in his journals. He was going to be extremely busy when he transformed back to his human self. He decided to change the subject as he sensed, this time from his human side, that there was nothing more to learn from Sunburst about these giant crows other than he had named them Larcrowe.

"So, Sunburst, you said you would tell me about your land. What is there that a stranger may find of interest?"

"You are an odd dragon, Nightstar, you ask many questions."

"It is the way of my kind," he improvised. "Black dragons are born curious and we like to travel. I have journeyed far from my own lands and wish to know what lies beyond their borders."

"And where is it you have come from?" Sunburst asked. Nightstar needed to come up with an answer to the yellow dragon's question. He quickly scrabbled for a response the yellow dragon would find believable.

"My home is far to the east, beyond the salty sea you spoke of. An extremely long way from here." He hoped it sounded credible. If Sunburst didn't like the east, there was a fair chance he didn't know much about what lay beyond.

"There is only the vast ocean to the east. You have journeyed from the lands of men beyond the great waters?"

"That is correct, my home is across the ocean, far beyond the lands of men."

"Strange, I thought all dragons left those shores in the times of the Great Exodus," Sunburst mused. "It would appear not every dragon came west."

Alduce quickly stored this information away. He would have to find out more about this exodus, there was a tale here that was worth hearing.

"Do the humans not hunt you?" Sunburst continued, "Their sorcerers with their foul magic, their warriors with their enchanted blades and magical staffs? Do they not drive you from your lands, take your skin and scales as trophies?"

"No. My kin are few and live far from men, in places where only dragons can fly, safe from their reach and their cursed kind." He hoped Sunburst would accept this.

"It is told that the dragons of this land once came from across the great ocean to escape from the clutches of humans. They hunted our kind relentlessly, killing without reason and driving our kin from their homes. In our legends it is known as the Great Exodus. Many died before the crossing and only the strongest managed to traverse the great ocean. Not all our brothers and sisters, it would seem, left to make that crossing. The humans sometimes come here, but this is our land and any that arrive on our shores are chased away, turned back. If they resist, their wooden boats are flamed and they perish. Never again will we tolerate their cruelty."

Nightstar was surprised to hear the venom in Sunburst's words, furthermore, on his home word, people feared dragons and no man would deliberately seek to confront such powerful creatures. The men from the east must be powerful indeed, if dragons felt it necessary to flee from them.

"I need to bathe," Sunburst declared, changing the subject. "The blood from the curly buck has dried all over my beautiful scales. Let us return to the lake and clean our hides."

He leapt into the early evening sky, the low sun turning his yellow hide a deep burning orange. Nightstar followed, his black hide paled in comparison to the yellow dragon. He felt he had more in common with the large black crow than the magnificent dragon that had befriended him, unaware he was really a despised human.

Both Dragons bathed in Sunburst's lake, cleaning their hides in the warm shallow waters until they gleamed. Alduce was enjoying living the life of Nightstar and was thankful the yellow dragon he had met was friendly. He had already pointed out that he thought Nightstar was odd, but he was content to answer his questions. They had flown and hunted together and a bond had been forged. This appeared to be the dragon way.

The evening sun weakened as it started to drop in the sky. Sunburst took advantage of what was left of the fading heat, sunning himself dry on the grassy shore while Nightstar chased the silvery fish that inhabited the lake. He eventually caught one and snapped it down, the raw fish tasting divine. His dragon taste buds were something else he would have to note, when he finally held a quill in his claw... No, his hand. The more time he spent as a dragon, the more his mind thought that way. *Skin and scales, I'll have to keep on top of that,* he thought.

He strode out of the lake, shaking the excess water from his body. It ran off the black waterproof scales easily, some of the drips splashing onto Sunburst.

"Have a care, Nightstar, you're wetting me. I cannot believe you're still hungry, eating fish now, after you feasted on curly buck." He snorted a noise that was as close to laughing as a dragon could manage. "That will be why you're so large, I suspect, always eating."

"You think me large?"

"Indeed, you are one of the largest dragons I have met. You are at least twice my size. Are all dragons across the eastern ocean as big as the mighty Nightstar?"

"No, I am larger than most," Nightstar told Sunburst not wanting to lie to his new friend anymore that he had to. It did not sit well with him. "Most dragons are a similar size to yourself. My colour and size are unusual among my community. I'm a bit of a loner, I suppose."

Nightstar had unconsciously described himself as Alduce. When he thought about it, he had closed himself off from society, living in his remote underground location, locked in his studies. Yes, he had friends, or perhaps they were professional acquaintances. His obsession with his work and constant thirst for knowledge had led to his isolation, living in a cave tunnelled into the side of a mountain. A laboratory he called home. Was it a coincidence that dragons also lived in caves? Perhaps it was the dragon mind that allowed him to see things differently. He had never dwelt on it before, never needed human company, content on his own. It wasn't until he became Nightstar that he realised he liked having a friend, especially a friend who was a yellow dragon. Yes, he was content as a human, but he was happier being a dragon.

"Well then," Sunburst said, "you need not be alone in these lands. I understand that they are foreign to you and I've been pondering what it is that I find unusual about you. It has been like an itch under my scales since we met. Now I know."

Nightstar froze. Did the yellow dragon know his secret? Had he worked out the mighty Nightstar wasn't what he pretended to be? Could he smell the human beneath the armour of his scales? What would the yellow dragon do if he knew the truth?

"Don't look so worried," Sunburst rumbled, "you are a stranger in a new land and our ways must be different from yours. You have travelled far and I understand now. Had I arrived on your shores I would feel the same. Relax and be at peace, friend. You are welcome here. Sunburst the Yellow will be your guide, should you wish it."

He extended his short yellow neck in the now familiar respectful bow and Nightstar was at a loss for words. This creature, this intelligent being had shown him, a stranger and an imposter, kindness and compassion. The dragons of myth burned homes, stole livestock, hoarded gold and breathed fire down on terrified villagers. They were heartless and cruel and not expected to show mercy. *How wrong our human perceptions have been*, the Alduce part of his awareness thought. He stood up and bowed low to Sunburst.

"Thank you, Sunburst. Your warm welcome and acceptance are more than I would have expected or deserve. I am truly fortunate to have made your acquaintance."

"You're not really, you know," Sunburst chuckled. "It took me all my courage to approach you when I first saw you. I wasn't sure how a large black dragon, twice my size, would react to an impudent little yellow sneaking up on him. I believe you are not alone in being fortunate." Sunburst stood up and spread his now dry wings. "Come, let us retire for the evening. I know of a cavern that isn't far and it is comfortable and large enough for oversized guests."

He sprang into the air, pivoted mid flap and flew towards the setting sun. Nightstar, relieved that the yellow dragon accepted him at face value, took off after his new friend. His first encounter in this new land, with a real dragon, had gone better than he expected.

He hoped his good fortune would continue.

Chapter 3

Excerpt from Alduce's Atlas of Dragons.

The Frost Drake: draco glacius.

Winterfang, male: Elder of the White Mountains Moot.

White Dragons come in many forms, one of which is the Frost Drake. The drake is one of the larger species, draco rather than draconis and is easily distinguished from the other varieties of whites by their smaller front legs. Their hind legs are larger and their wingspan is the most impressive across all dragon types.

Their scales differ in appearance, where most other dragons have a metallic look, a frost drakes scales are unique in their own way. On closer inspection, the scales resemble polished ice, smooth on the surface but multifaceted underneath the clear top coating. This allows light to reflect, creating an effect similar to the sun reflecting on frozen snow crystals.

Frost drakes are on the whole, a pure brilliant white, while their horns, talons and bony ridges are the colour of worn ivory. Spikes grow from beneath the chin forming a long beard that resembles frozen icicles. As it is with other species, the longer the beard the older the dragon. Their eyes are a cold blue, however, there are some instances where this species have hatched with red eyes. At first, I believed the red eyes were that of an albino, but the subjects are not afflicted with the usual traits of albinism or hypopigmentation (see dracus albino) and I have concluded that eye colouration is genetic.

Frost Drakes are highly intelligent and difficult to befriend. They have a preponderance to be loners and can often appear aloof when compared to the friendlier yellows and blues. As their name suggests, they are mostly found in the far northern regions and favour the higher altitudes. Their white scales are the perfect camouflage and allow them to become almost invisible on snow, when stationary. This species tend to have longer graceful necks and tails, compared to the squat thicker bodied species. They are fair flyers, but tend to lack stamina over distance. Note: possibly due to cold air and altitude.

Frost Drakes are also known for their excellent swimming abilities and enjoy bathing.

As well as being able to breathe fire, the frost drake can produce an icy vapour of sub-zero temperature, freezing anything it touches.

I encountered some frost drakes in the higher regions of the White Mountains, but the most memorable of them all was Winterfang.

Winterfang: Male, Frost Drake, Elder of the White Mountain Moot.

Winterfang is easily seventy five feet in length with an estimated wingspan of over eighty feet.

He has piercing blue eyes that are hypnotic when stared into. He is slim and sleek and is graceful in both the air and on land. He is highly respected throughout the White Mountain community and regarded as wise and just.

I believe that his age is in excess of two hundred years. His experience and the loyalty he shows to his peers has resulted in him being chosen to lead the moot for many decades.

He is a true leader and an impressive creature who has the best interests of his community at heart.

* * *

Sunburst flew high over the plains and Nightstar followed. He had lived with the smaller yellow dragon for five days, sharing a cave that Sunburst called his temporary home. They had spent their time hunting and flying and Nightstar questioned his newly appointed guide about many dragon related topics, taking care not to be too obvious in his interrogations.

Sunburst was happy to tell Nightstar all about his world, its inhabitants and their lives. The part of his mind that was Alduce thought the dragon community didn't sound too different from the cities of humans. He would never have thought dragons would live and act as men did, but from what Sunburst had described, this was exactly the impression the yellow dragon had given.

They were flying to the yellow dragon's main dwelling place, the White Mountains, and at present the plains they flew over were all that filled Nightstar's vision.

The rolling grasslands were scattered with lakes, rivers and forests as far as his dragon eye could see. These lands would be an ideal place for men to settle, they were fertile and green with ample resources and fresh water in abundance. But he knew now that Sunburst's kin would never tolerate humans on their land. As they progressed across the plains, Nightstar could see giant herds of beasts traversing the ground below, many different species, a lot of them resembling cattle in appearance and behaviour.

He realised that in this land of plenty, the animals of the plains were more than enough to provide sustenance for more dragons than he could imagine. No wonder dragons thrived here.

As the two airborne companions passed over the herds, the animals scattered from the danger above, kicking up dust clouds in their panic. They might be easy pickings, but they still ran for their lives when dragons passed overhead.

On and on they flew, Nightstar strong now after days of flying practice. His dragon self was much more confident with the body he had created. He was more relaxed in his transformed skin and scales, more accepting and less concerned he would give his true self away. However, he still remained cautious, it would be a mistake to let his guard down fully. After his initial reservations he would trust his dragon instinct, allowing it to guide him on behaving as a dragon should.

He studied Sunburst and learned a lot from observing his mannerisms and actions. The more he mimicked the yellow dragon's behaviours, the more naturally they came to him. Sunburst was only one dragon though and Nightstar was still apprehensive at being immersed in the colony of dragons that made their home on the slopes of the White Mountains.

He learned from Sunburst that over one hundred dragons lived there, dragons of all colours and shapes. Forest dragons, sea dragons, mountain dragons, hill dragons, snow dragons, Sunburst's list went on forever. According to his stories, there were dragons named after each geographical feature. He even talked about dragons that lived in swamps. The Alduce part of him thought these sounded like alligators with wings.

Sunburst was a yellow hill dragon, he told Nightstar proudly, from a long line of yellows, and any clutch fathered by him stood a high chance of having yellow scales.

Alduce wanted to meet as many different varieties of dragon as he could, wanting to catalogue them all in his journals, naming each one, their colour and size, their characteristics, each little difference that made them unique from their peers.

He could live among dragons for years and not have enough time to study them all. He was aware he would need to apply a certain carefulness to his research. He was an unknown dragon, a stranger in an even stranger land, a place that was not his home. He couldn't afford to ask too many questions that would make him stand out even more.

He was pleased he covered the basics with Sunburst. His yellow host chatted continuously and grew much more relaxed in the company of his large black friend. Nightstar had grown to like the yellow dragon and forged a fine friendship with him. Sunburst had a pleasing personality and was easy company—easier than most humans he knew. He hoped that the other dragons of his colony were half as accommodating.

Nightstar lifted his head from the plains, pulling his vision from the tempting beasts below. He had been flying for hours, marvelling at the pleasant lands below his wings, studying the flora and fauna as he passed. It was easy to get lost in wondrous act of flying and relish soaring through the skies. Stamina and strength came naturally to him the more he flew and being airborne was now as instinctual as breathing. Long distance flying was something he could accomplish as his mind wandered, without thought of the actions. They had flown far today and he looked north to the horizon, he could see the distant peaks of their destination: the White Mountains.

Just as the plains and grasslands had spanned below him for miles without end, so too did the impressive mountain range that now filled his vision. Snowy white peaks rising into the clouds, stretched across the horizon, pushing higher and higher into the sky. An awe inspiring wall of frost white monoliths that made Nightstar wonder—or perhaps it was the scholar deep inside—what lay beyond.

As Alduce, he would never be able to even consider such an incredible journey over the vast peaks. But as Nightstar, he would be able to soar above them and revel in their snowy beauty, bright white beneath his night black scales. When it came to travelling, flying over terrain humans found impossible to traverse, was just one advantage dragons possessed over mankind.

Onward they flew, yellow and black, Sunburst leading, Nightstar content to follow. The air grew colder, not unpleasantly, the chill breeze refreshingly cool on his scales, like a bright autumn morning with a snap in the air. Upwards they climbed, flight undulating as the land rose and fell through the foothills and valleys of the nearing mountain range. Ascending gradually.

Nightstar climbed out of the last valley, sticking close to Sunburst's tail as they crested another range of low hills, leaving the plains and rivers behind. He drew in a breath, stunned at the sight before him. The vastness of the White Mountains filled his vision, stretching from east to west and ever north, vanishing into the distant snowy horizon.

Before him the slope dropped away, rolling scrub land descended, filled with rocky scree and stunted trees. After about half a mile the ground rose sharply, forming a cliff face, rising straight up from the lowest part of the valley floor, the huge rock wall riddled with caves. The air was busy with dozens of flying dragons, a multitude of colours and shapes, some dodged and spun, others glided, a constant flow as each dragon traversed the air to an unknown destination.

The cliff face was slate grey, devoid of any weeds or grass and was a warren of dark cave mouths, some occupied with dragons perched on ledges, others empty. Alduce was reminded of the busy main thoroughfare that clamoured with the human traffic conducting their business in the city of Learning. This wasn't just a few random caves in a cliff side, this was a dragon city, populated with every kind of dragon imaginable.

The vast rock wall stretched upward and where it stopped, the slopes of the mountains and the snows began. Alduce thought it looked as if a giant blade had cleaved straight through the mountainside, slicing away the lower slopes and exposing the grey rock. All along the top ridge, before the snowline started, dragons sat, lay and perched in the warm sun.

"Welcome to the White Mountains," Sunburst trumpeted, bending his neck backward. "These are the snow spire cliffs where many of us make our home." He set his wings and plummeted downwards, descending towards the foot of the sheer cliff and a large gaping cave, the largest in the whole cliff face.

Nightstar dropped with him and they neared, he realised that the cave was much larger than he had first thought. The mouth formed an arch in the mountain's side, taller than the highest building in Learning. It was wide, a half circle that formed a perfect entranceway, reaching deep inside the mountain.

Sunburst plunged down and flew into the cave entrance, bright yellow scales catching the sunlight, his hide blazing a radiant gold, before disappearing into the darkness of the cave mouth. Nightstar had little choice but to follow and he entered into the vast cavern mouth for the first time. His eyes adjusted from the brightness of the snow covered slopes to the gloom inside the mountain and for the second time today day he was left breathless. His slit-eyes widened instinctually, reacting to the darkness inside the dim cave. Although the only source of light was from outside, his keen dragon eyes adjusted to the gloom and saw everything.

He entered a huge chamber that stretched back, deeper and deeper into the mountain. The hollow inside of the snow covered pyramid had to be at least a quarter of the entire mountain above. There were ledges and caves of all sizes, some at ground level and others scattered throughout the inner dome, a giant honeycomb alive with dragons, instead of bees.

Sunburst landed on the sandy floor of the cave and was rubbing necks with a red—no a crimson dragon—a little larger than the yellow. Nightstar approached and dropped down alongside his friend, folding his black wings and waiting for Sunburst to finish what appeared to be an intimate reunion.

The crimson dragon was sleek and graceful, vibrant even in the dim light. The scales that covered its body were more oval shaped and rounded, compared to his own, which were sharper and pointed. The elegant red neck and tapered head wound its way around the yellow neck of Sunburst, two primary colours clashing brightly. And, Nightstar noticed, his nostrils widening as he inhaled the scent of this intoxicating crimson dragon, it smelled wonderful. Realisation came to him as his sense of smell, coupled with his dragon sense, reinforced what he now understood.

The crimson dragon was a female, and she was beautiful.

Chapter 4

Excerpt from Alduce's Atlas of Dragons.

The White Mountain Moot.

The Dragon Moot is the ruling body in any community. The members of a moot can number as little as three or as high as eleven. Their number is always odd, with one elder or lead dragon who hosts the moot. If anything is undecided by the ruling council the elder has the final decision. To be the elder dragon in any moot is a huge undertaking. Elders are chosen by their peers and can remain in their position for many years. It is not unheard of for respected and wise ruling elders to hold their position for decades.

The elder of the moot is the highest honour that can be bestowed on any individual and commands the utmost respect from each dragon under their wing. They are responsible for all major decisions involving their society and need to be morally just and intelligent.

The moot is made up of two wings, the left and right. Depending on the community traditions and beliefs, each wing is responsible for any number of duties.

A moot can often result in differences of opinion, arguments and hissing, a dragon's way of showing displeasure without resorting to physical violence.

Another noteworthy fact regarding the White Mountain Moot is the pearl of wisdom that is on display. This rare and precious treasure is rumoured to have come from across the vast ocean to the east, at the time of the Great Exodus (see information on G.E.)

I suspect a strong magic is harnessed within the pearl and it is not at all what it appears to be on the surface.

Note: The etiquette of a moot is organised and traditional and any fire breathing, biting, clawing or fighting is regarded as highly unsavoury. Members of the moot who break this tradition, regardless of the instigator, will be ousted from their position. In severe cases, dragons who have been de-mooted have been banished from the community.

The White Mountain Moot members.

Leader: Winterfang, frost drake. Elder. Note of interest: Symbolic spreading of wings over left and right contingents at start and finish of moot. Tradition showing protection for all dragons under elder's protection? Research ongoing.

Left Wing: Spring contingent.

Aurelian the Golden, Female. Blue-cap (the Blue?) Male, Sea Dragon. Amethyst the Purple, Female.

Right Wing: Autumn contingent. Little Wing, Copper Female. Galvon, Forest Green, Male. Raynar the Russet, Male. (For more information on moot members, see index notes/individual bios.)

Note: The White Mountain dragons use the collective noun as follows: A Wing or Flight of dragons.

* * *

"This is my mate, Blood Rose," Sunburst introduced the crimson dragon. "Her scales are the colour of blood and her beauty is like that of a rose, a flower protected by thorns."

"I cannot argue with that," Nightstar said. Folding his right leg beneath his body, he dipped his neck forward in greeting. "I am pleased to meet you, Blood Rose. I am Nightstar."

"Well met, Nightstar," the crimson dragon said, her feminine voice full of welcome. "You'll have to forgive Sunburst, he's always been a little protective of me. Even though he has no reason to be," she butted the yellow dragon's side playfully with her head. "There's no need for formality, Nightstar. You may call me Rose. Blood Rose is so dramatic, don't you think?"

Nightstar felt an attraction to the alluring crimson female and was unsure of the arousal she had awoken in him. He wondered if this was normal or if these feeling were something the human part of him would need to keep in check. Sunburst was his friend, he had grown to like the yellow dragon and did not want to upset him by showing anything other than the appropriate respect for his mate. He hardly believed that as a dragon, he would have to face the same issues that had plagued him as a human: women, or in this case, a female dragon.

He had lived a secluded life and chosen the path of scholar and sorcerer. The discipline he needed to employ to achieve his goals left very little time for the opposite sex.

He was never opposed to spending time with a woman, but he hadn't had much practice and his work didn't allow for many opportunities.

A sudden realisation occurred to him. He wanted more from his life than sorcery and science, from the learning and the magic. He wanted a mate. A mate as attractive as Rose. He was unsure if this was the dragon inside him that made him feel this way or because he could look at his human self from a dragon's perspective.

He would never have thought the challenges he faced from shape changing would have been anything but physical.

"I think the mighty Nightstar has been blinded by your beauty," Sunburst said, chuckling.

"Nonsense," said Rose, "he follows the formal ways. He shows respect in his greeting, unlike some, twisting necks in plain sight." Although Rose scolded Sunburst, Nightstar could tell she wasn't annoyed.

"And you'd not have me any other way," Sunburst said. "I have been absent too long to waste time with formal greetings. You are my mate, we are partnered for life and I miss your companionship."

"Ah, you miss my companionship. Is that so? You disappear for days at a time. Don't think I don't know what you miss." Turning her head towards Nightstar so Sunburst couldn't see, she winked a huge yellow eye.

"I think you also miss the curly bucks. I think you miss them more than me! I can smell them on you, skin and scales. Why do yellows think more of their stomachs than they do of their... "

"I am a free spirit, Blood Rose," Sunburst interrupted. "All yellows are the same. You know it, Nightstar knows it," he chuckled, "and curly bucks are my favourites. It's not my fault their herds don't come this far north."

"I have been instrumental in distracting Sunburst," Nightstar added. "I am new to your lands and he kindly agreed to show me around. It is my fault he was delayed."

"Forgive me, Nightstar. I am broody and I want my mate close by. I wish to clutch and produce many fine eggs," she looked at her yellow mate, "and would prefer if the yellow dragon I chose to father them was there to participate when it is time."

Sunburst puffed air, his nostrils flaring as he made a sighing sound, the dragon equivalent of exasperation. "Our bond is for life, you would consider another to take my place if you came into season and I wasn't there with you?"

"No, I would not," Rose said, "but I do like to tease you." This crimson female had sense of humour.

Alduce had researched everything he could find out about dragons after his encounter with Galdor, but had never come across anything resembling dragon humour. He had acquired many books, visited libraries near and far and even listened to folk tales, myths and tavern stories in his quest for knowledge about these creatures. While his research hadn't fully prepared him for living and acting as a dragon, there were many facts that he had uncovered that turned out to be beneficial.

He had visited the great library of Learning, they had extensive records on many mythical beasts and were renowned for their vast collection of dragon related literature. One thing he learned was dragons often mate for life. When they feel they are mature enough, they choose a partner and remain with them. If one dragon dies, the surviving other rarely seeks a new mate.

"You show Nightstar around the cavern and introduce him to some of the curious onlookers. It would seem they can't keep their eyes of his black hide,"

Rose said. "You can both join me later, there is an empty roost next to my cave, Nightstar. You are welcome to use it while you stay with us."

The black dragon looked around, Rose was right. He was attracting attention from a variety of onlookers, younger dragons, not fully grown, some with black scales of their own scattered through their coloured hides.

"Thank you Rose, I would enjoy spending time here with your community." Nightstar bowed once again, dipping his head and pulling his leg beneath his body. Silver scales stood out against his black chest when he bowed and he could hear whispers from the small group of juvenile dragons that gathered to stare at the unknown black.

He straightened up and turned to face the curious youngsters, just as fascinated at their presence as they were with his. Once more he dipped his head, less formal than he had been with Rose and was rewarded for his actions with a collective gasp of surprise.

"I am... " he had almost introduced himself as Alduce. Where had that come from? He needed to focus, he couldn't afford to slip up, especially in the midst of all these dragons. "I am a... visitor from afar." The young dragons made a noise that was similar to children giggling, they had failed to notice he had almost made a mistake. "I am called Nightstar."

As he finished introducing himself, some unseen sign caused all the young dragons to rush in and show their affection towards the newcomer. A dozen or so juveniles clamoured to get close to him, blues, greens, reds, yellows and a variety of other shades and colours. A rainbow of scales against his midnight black hide. They jostled and bumped him affectionately, as Rose had done with Sunburst, pushing under his wings, twining around his legs and nestling under his wings. Nightstar was overcome with a strong feeling of acceptance and welcome.

"He's black."

"He's so big!"

"Where is he from?"

"Look at the star."

Their chattering filled his ears and he felt like grinning, not something a dragon was able to do with ease, but in his heart, he knew the part of him that was Alduce was overwhelmingly happy at this reception.

"Enough!" A voice boomed out across the cavern floor and a huge white dragon, all ice and snow with wings and horns, startled the young dragons into silence.

Nightstar was impressed and also a little bit intimidated. The white dragon was even larger than he was and had an air of authority about him. His scales glistened like the sunrise on morning frost and while he was all white, his horns, talons and ridges were the colour of ancient ivory, creating an impression of age and distinction. A long white beard hung down from his chin, the spines looked like icicles, frozen in place. This dragon was regal, a king among his kind and his demeanour reminded Alduce of Galdor.

"Ah, Winterfang, we were just coming to see you," Sunburst said. "I have someone I would like you to meet."

"I can see that, Sunburst the Yellow," he intoned formally, addressing Sunburst with his full name. "He's hard to miss." The imposing white dragon reared up and spread his wings, "Dragonets, leave our guest. Your elders wish to speak. Uninterrupted!"

His command was obeyed immediately and the young dragons scuttled free of Nightstar, taking flight, some faster, some more graceful, but all hurried to comply with the white dragon's bidding.

"Can we visit Nightstar again?" a small copper coloured dragonet asked as she skipped across the cavern floor. "He speaks with us and introduced himself, we like him."

"I am sure, if Nightstar wishes it, you can," Winterfang replied, less harshly. "Now, off with you, copper menace!" The dragonet hopped into the air, small wings blurring like a hummingbird.

"I am Winterfang the White, leader of the Dragon Moot, first elder of the White Mountains," he bowed formally. "I gather you are named Nightstar. Welcome to the inner mountain."

Nightstar bowed low and tucked his leg underneath his body, holding his position for a little longer than was usual as a show of respect. This dragon was the leader of their community, not just another dragon. He was older and wiser, the elder that led the moot. He would have to be extremely careful. If any dragon could sniff out his verisimilitude, it would be Winterfang.

"Thank you, Elder Winterfang." Nightstar said, hoping he had addressed the white dragon with enough deference. "I am Nightstar and I humbled by the warm welcome. The White Mountains might be a cold place, but the dragons who make their home here are nothing like the frost and snow."

The white dragon's ice blue eyes studied him and the seconds stretched out as he waited, concerned that Winterfang would see him for what he really was. A charlatan, a human in dragon's skin, a fake. An imposter. He looked nervously at Sunburst, who had sidled up to Rose. They too, waited for their leader to speak.

"Eloquently put," rumbled Winterfang, chuckling and Nightstar relaxed. "Your tongue is as silver as the star you bear upon your chest. When you tire of Sunburst's constant chattering and tall stories, seek me out. I would enjoy talking with you and learning your story. Our youngsters appear to be fascinated with a black adult. It is rare colour and they haven't lived long enough to see someone like you. My years, however, are vastly greater than the sum of all those dragonets added together. I have known a few blacks over the centuries, but none as large as you. And, the star upon your chest is nothing I have encountered before." He dipped his head, "Be welcome, Nightstar. I look forward to speaking with you soon." Winterfang took off, huge white wings powered the snow coloured elder up into the domed cavern of the inner mountain.

"Come on then," Sunburst said, "we have a lot of ground to cover and it doesn't do to keep the elder of the moot waiting. His words may have sounded like a casual invitation, but when Winterfang requests an audience, you don't miss it."

"He's right," Rose said, "Winterfang only wants what's best for the moot and I'm sure he just wishes to know you a little better. The frost drake is a wise and just leader, but you would be smart not to anger him. His wrath is something no dragon wishes to face."

Her warning words shocked him. Winterfang appeared friendly enough, but it would be a grave mistake to underestimate him. Nightstar would have to tread carefully.

"After all, it isn't every day we meet a new dragon," Rose continued, softening her words, "especially one with black scales."

Nightstar followed after Sunburst, the yellow had already forgotten about his summons from Winterfang and was chattering about who was allowed to roost in the higher caves, how there were tunnels connecting this cave with that one and which dragon they would expect to see on their flight around the inner mountain.

Alduce had not expected that interacting with dragons would be as challenging. He had hoped to just meet a few dragons and study them. He wasn't expecting them to live in groups, like humans in cities or towns. He was surprised they followed a political structure, with their own leaders and laws.

He had been foolish to underestimate dragons. His transformation into one of their own had gently eroded his usual caution. His dragon self was more relaxed that the human part of him. He couldn't let Nightstar's persona reveal his true self.

Everything he read, each story, each tale, warned that if you made the mistake of underestimating a dragon, it would be fatal. Of course the rulers of the White Mountains would wish to question him. He was an outsider and unusually black. These dragons had lived here for centuries, they must know each other and be familiar with everyone. A new comer, a black scaled new comer with a distinct silver star, would stand out and be noticed.

He told Sunburst he came from the lands of the east, across the vast ocean. He couldn't change his story now and tell Winterfang something different. He should have prepared a back story before he rushed in and decided to wing it.

Wing it. As a dragon, the irony wasn't lost on him. Master Caltus had a saying when things didn't work out: *never mind,* he would say, *you're only human.* Alduce, the man, understood what his old master had meant. However, now he was quite sure the wisdom Caltus shared with him all those years ago, wasn't as relevant to him anymore. Now he was more than *only human.* Thinking of Caltus calmed his mind and his rising panic subsided. His old mentor's rationality reached out across the years, urging him to think.

What would Caltus have advised him in this situation? He would have laughed at me for getting myself into this predicament in the first place. Then, he would have told me, don't worry about things you can't change, focus on what you can do.

Alduce was creative, he was educated and smart. He would have to make sure that Winterfang believed his story and the reason why he had travelled here.

All he needed to do now was come up with a convincing tale and hope that Winterfang had never crossed the vast ocean and visited the lands in the east.

Chapter 5

Nightstar entered the cavern of the moot alone. Sunburst was denied entry by the moot guard, two stocky greens that could have been twins. The cavern of the moot was guarded, Sunburst told him, and the pearl of wisdom was housed in the moot chamber. The yellow dragon was proud, informing Nightstar the pearl was a rare and valuable treasure.

The moot guard escorted their ward from the landing ledge, through a tunnel of solid rock, reaching deep into the centre of the mountain. Deep into the heart of the dragon council.

Nightstar could feel a rise in temperature as the tunnel widened. Sunburst told him the chamber was heated by fissures in the rock and the mountain sat atop a deep river of magma, the Earth Mothers gift to dragons. He had blown a little flame from his nostrils when he spoke of the Earth Mother. This was the first time he witnessed a dragon producing fire.

He was curious about the dragon fire, but more so about his friend's reference to the Earth Mother. Was this a metaphorical reference to the actual molten rock or did the dragons believed in a deity? He would have to question him about it later, if an opportunity presented itself, but for now, he needed to focus on his summons.

The tunnel ended and he entered into a substantial chamber, occupied by the seven most important dragons of the White Mountains: the Dragon Moot.

The seven were arranged in a circle, their backs to the cavern wall, leaving an empty space for their visitor to enter into their midst. There was no turning back now and Alduce remembered another saying that Caltus had been fond of. *Fortune favours the brave.*

This was the bravest thing he had ever done... or maybe the stupidest. Fortune wouldn't favour the stupid.

Leaving his escort, he strode into the centre of the circle with what he hoped looked like confidence. A confidence he certainly didn't feel.

Bending his neck, he bowed, showing his respect to the ruling body of dragons before him.

"Elders of the White Mountains, my name is Nightstar." Recalling how Sunburst had spoken when they had first met, he imitated his style, "The silver scales upon my black chest, light the night sky like a blazing star." If his language sounded like Sunburst, like a real dragon, his hope was that the moot would be more likely to accept him as one of their kin.

Winterfang was flanked by three dragons on each side and in front of the frost drake, nestled in the hollow of a large slab of rock, sat a huge opaque globe of white. It resembled a giant white pearl, a muted ghostly sheen radiated across its surface, alluring and hypnotic.

The dragon opened his wings and stretched them over the dragons to his left and right, encompassing them beneath his impressive wingspan. The protective symbolism in the gesture said more than his words ever could.

"The moot is now open," he declared, "all are welcome and are under my protection." He folded his wings and gripped the giant white orb in one clawed talon, "Pearl of enlightenment, moonstone of white, grant me the wisdom and the strength to guide our moot wisely." Nightstar's dragon sense recognised the words were steeped in tradition. Winterfang unfurled his claw and the surface of the white pearl radiated and swirled, alive to his touch.

"Welcome Nightstar. We of the moot wish to learn more about you and your visit to our lands. Let me introduce my council."

Nightstar hadn't noticed when he first entered the chamber, but each of the seven assemble members were different. All representatives equal, regardless of type or colour. Humans could learn from the wisdom of the dragon moot.

Winterfang turned to his right, this first dragon of the three was a small copper coloured female. "This is Little Wing." The copper dragon bowed her head, acknowledging Nightstar, her deep golden eyes friendly and warm, scales gleaming like the metal of her colouring.

"Welcome Nightstar," she said.

"And Galvon, the forest green." Galvon's stare was cold. His scales the dark green of pine needles, his yellow eyes hateful as a viper. He barely tipped his head, his manner aloof and uninviting. It was obvious Galvon didn't like him.

"And Raynar the Brown," Winterfang said.

"Raynar the Russet! Not brown!" Raynar protested.

"I'm sorry, my russet friend. Raynar the *Russet,*" Winterfang corrected himself.

"Thank you. Bah, brown indeed. Greetings Nightstar, be welcome." Raynar gave a deep bow and Nightstar knew at once he liked this dragon. He was a deeper colour than plain brown, his scales glowing with a burnished reddish orange and Nightstar understood why he preferred to be called russet.

Little wing was the smallest of the three, Raynar and Galvon were what Nightstar now thought of as an average size, forty feet or so.

"These three dragons make up my right wing, they are the colours of autumn and are a balance to my winter. Nightstar bowed to the three dragons of the right wing, "I am honoured to meet you."

Galvon puffed under his breath and received a glower from Winterfang.

"My left wing is made up of Aurelian the Golden, Blue-cap and Amethyst the purple." Each dragon acknowledged Nightstar as Winterfang introduced them, each one spectacular in their own way. "These three represent the spring, another perspective to my winter and balance to the right wing of autumn."

Aurelian glowed, her warm golden scales on a par with the metallic copper of Little Wing. Blue-cap was the colour of an azure sky with a royal blue patch that covered the top half of his snout and head, giving the impression he was wearing a dark blue hat. Amethyst's scales looked like the gem stones she took her name from and she winked one dark blue eye mischievously at Nightstar as he bowed to the members of the left wing.

"I am honoured to meet you all, too," Nightstar said and meant it. Each dragon was magnificent.

Alduce surfaced in Nightstar's mind and scrutinized the seven dragons assembled. While he was still nervous, only Galvon displayed an unfriendliness. The others had been polite enough and Amethyst and Raynar had been openly friendly. None had given him cause to feel threatened or fear they knew he was a shape changing human.

The more he thought about it, the more he believed while he was in the form of Nightstar, he was undetectable as an imposter. These dragons were old and wise, if anyone could sniff out his secret, surely the seven most powerful dragons of the White Mountains would be able to. He remained careful, it would do no harm to stay alert and exercise caution, his theory wasn't proven, even if he felt he was correct.

"We have asked you to join us," Winterfang said, "as we are interested in where you have travelled from. Perhaps you could tell us more about where you have journeyed from to be here." Nightstar understood the implied question was more than a request.

"Of course, Elder Winterfang," Nightstar answered formally. He had been working on a story while Sunburst had shown him around the inner mountain earlier. "I have travelled far from the east, across the vast ocean in search of new lands. My kin are few and our numbers dwindle. The eastern lands are populated with men, their numbers grow, as do their cities. The never stop breeding and expanding."

Galvon snorted, his dislike of humans even greater than his unfriendliness towards Nightstar. "Why do you not stop them, crush their puny bodies and teach them who truly rules the lands?" he sneered. "Are the eastern dragons so weak? By fang and claw, have they forgotten the fire in their bellies? What... "

"Galvon, let him speak," Amethyst cut in, thrusting her head towards the dark green dragon. "He is one of us, I'm sure there is more to his story." She turned her head back to Nightstar, "Continue, please. I am sure Galvon is only concerned for your kin."

Galvon snorted again. Nightstar was starting to dislike this arrogant green. He bowed his head to Amethyst in thanks, she named him one of their own and that was a good sign. He carried on.

"To answer your questions, Galvon, no. My kin are far from weak, however, we are few while the humans are many. You are all aware of the Great Exodus," he said. He remembered the story Sunburst shared with him when they first met. "Not all the dragons left my shores, some were forgotten, some chose to stay, some were too old to cross the vast ocean." He figured this was a viable assumption to make. "The dragons who remained were spread far and wide, they didn't have a community or the numbers you have. Over the years, the amount of dragons in the east has dwindled. We have become solitary creatures."

He paused for effect, the moot now caught up in his tale. "Your ancestors fled from my home land, they too were hunted and persecuted by the humans of the east. Some dragons stayed. I am a descendant of those ancestors. I never chose to stay. I was born there."

The moot remained silent, even Galvon made no comment this time and Nightstar was relieved they had accepted his story so far. He decided to carry on while his luck held.

"Dragons are now scarce in the eastern lands, my kin are all but extinct. I decided not to retreat into the wilderness and await the ever advancing cities of the humans. Each decade, the humans spread, forging deeper into what was once our home and our refuge. Dragons vanish from the land, some are hunted and slain and others succumb to the long sleep." He also recalled what Galdor told him, weaving it into his narrative, hoping it added credibility to his story.

"I chose to fly west into the great unknown and follow my ancestors. The crossing I undertook was arduous, even for a flier of my calibre. This is how I arrived on your shores. I have come in search of my long departed kin, I have lived most of my life alone and I was the only survivor of my clutch. I never knew my mother or father. I know some of you find me strange." He stared directly at Galvon to emphasise the point and to show he wouldn't be intimidated. He was a dragon and he should act like one. "I know nothing of your ways and am ignorant of your customs." This was a good reason to explain why he was different, why he asked so many questions of the dragons of the White Mountains.

"I wish to learn more about my long lost relations. I would have withered and died had I remained in the land of my hatching. I hope the moot will accept me for who I am," *or for who Nightstar is,* he thought, "and forgive any indiscretions in my behaviour. I wanted more, I want to be a better dragon, worthy of my kin and hope I can learn from you, my distant cousins." He bowed his head to the moot and waited on their reaction.

"It's a sad tale, Nightstar," Blue-cap said. "To hear our distant kin have dwindled to near extinction. I am a sea dragon and have swam in the vast ocean to the east. I have never ventured as far as the distant shores of your land, but know they are indeed a great distance. You have travelled far to reach our mountain, Sunburst speaks true when he names you an exceptional flier. Only a dragon of great stamina and strength would be able to make such a journey."

The moot had already spoken to Sunburst about him and he was glad he stuck with his original story.

"Indeed," Winterfang agreed. "I could not have made the trip Nightstar managed. Frost drakes are fine fliers, but my stamina for such a distance would not be enough." There were murmurs of agreement from the assemble dragons. Galvon treated his peers to a snort and it was Winterfang's turn to thrust his head out towards the cantankerous pine green dragon.

"You have something to add, Galvon? You wish to congratulate Nightstar on his brave adventure into the unknown?"

"I don't think such a flight is... " he said.

"No, you don't think," Amethyst snapped. "A flight of that magnitude is beyond you. Just because *you* are unable to comprehend it, doesn't mean it can't be done. I don't know why Winterfang keeps you in the moot!" she hissed, spitting her forked tongue at the green, who returned the gesture.

"Enough!" Winterfang said. "I keep Galvon in the moot, as I value his words, as I value yours, Amethyst. I can count on him to give me his honest opinion. Six dragons that agreed with everything I say would be of no benefit to our community. However, it would certainly be something my ears could learn to live with. I wouldn't miss the egg speak of squabbling hatchlings at all!"

Amethyst bowed her head to their leader, then in a gesture that Nightstar found surprising, she stretched out to Galvon and rubbed her neck on his.

"I will remember Nightstar's words and include them in our records. They are worthy of note." Galvon conceded, sounding a little less grumpy.

"Good," Winterfang said. "You are free to depart the moot, friend Nightstar. You are only a stranger the first time you visit the White Mountains. I'm sure that Sunburst is desperate to speak with you. Heed his advice, he may be small, but he has a large heart and is a good judge of character. He spoke on your behalf and vouched for you and the moot have listened."

"Indeed we have," Amethyst added. "You are welcome to stay with us for as long as you wish."

The other dragons, including Galvon, all welcomed Nightstar. Winterfang spread his wings out over the three dragons on his left and the three on his right. "The moot is now ended," he announced.

Nightstar was relieved at the conclusion. The protective gesture of the frost drake's wings, this time, curved inwards to the centre of the circle, including the black dragon underneath them, too.

Nightstar bowed to the moot and when he raised his head, looked into the dark blue eyes of Amethyst and felt welcome.

Chapter 6

Excerpt from Alduce's Atlas of Dragons.

Aurora and Grand Moot.

Every seven years the aurora fills the skies above the White Mountains with purples and greens, heralding the time of the Grand Moot. Dragons come from far and wide, those living in isolation or small groups and other communities and colonies.

The summer dragons are the largest community to attend the moot. They are not from the White Mountains, but are an independent colony that make their home in the far south of the western continent of Aurentania.

The aurora, a fantastic display of polar lights, signals the migration of dragons to the White Mountain Grand Moot. Because of the high northern latitude, this natural phenomenon is highly spectacular and creates an atmosphere of celebration. Intensely vivid greens, purples, reds, yellows, and pinks ripple across the sky, lighting the moot with an impressive display of colours.

There doesn't appear to be any reason why this aurora only occurs in a seven year cycle or why dragons flock to the area to observe it and bask under its light. After much investigation, I have concluded that dragons, much like some birds, or even whales, have some inborn instinct to migrate and gather at the time of the aurora.

This coming together is a time of celebration and the Grand Moot allows dragons to socialise, story tell and mate. One theory might be that the allure of the aurora, while purely a natural phenomenon, has some magical properties that dragons are attracted to. Dragons from all over the continent congregate under the aurora's captivating lights. This gathering allows breeding lines to mix and stay strong, as dragons far removed from each other can cross breed, maintaining a strong genetic pool.

The Grand Moot and the aurora are quite something to behold, not only are the skies filled with dragons of all colours and varieties, the aurora itself is a spectacular sight. The two events together are an occurrence that is beyond anything I have ever witnessed.

* * *

Nightstar sat in the meadow south of the White Mountains. The morning sun climbed above the peaks and chased away the shadows, pleasantly warming his scales. Sunburst and Rose were curled together beside him, their three heads craned upward as they watched the arriving dragons. The sky was filled with an assortment of colourful creatures from every corner of the continent, all travelling to the White Mountains for the Grand Moot.

Nightstar had woken earlier that morning and noticed a difference in the dragons he had spent the last four months with. There was an air of expectation, full of charged energy and life, and he felt it too. Sunburst had rushed into his temporary home inside the great cavern, chattering wildly about it being time. At first he thought Rose was ready to clutch, as she was heavily pregnant. Nightstar imagined if she didn't lay her eggs soon, she might burst. When he was able to get some sense from his yellow companion, it wasn't that the expectant father's mate was ready to lay, but that there was to be a Grand Moot this evening.

"This will be your first Grand Moot!" Sunburst told him, barley able to contain his excitement. "Dragons come from the far flung corners of our lands to attend."

Nightstar wondered what the Grand Moot was and why he hadn't heard about such a large and obviously momentous event until this morning.

"Flaxe has woken!" Sunburst told him, by way of explanation.

"Flaxe?" Nightstar asked, unfamiliar with the name.

"Yes, he was once a summer dragon. When he wakes from the long sleep, it signals the Grand Moot. Everyone knows this!"

"I can tell you are excited, Sunburst, but could you explain it to me, a stranger in your community, as I do not know."

"I'm sorry Nightstar, I forget you are from beyond the eastern ocean. You've been here long enough that you've become one of us. You are a dragon of the White Mountain. You will never be a stranger anymore." He repeated the phrase Winterfang used when he was summoned to the moot chamber. "You are only a stranger the first time you visit the White Mountains."

"Thank you Sunburst, I am humbled by your acceptance and honoured that you think of me that way."

"Pah!" The yellow dragon snorted and Nightstar thought he spotted a red flush on the yellow face of his friend.

"You are here, we are friends. It is simple. Besides, Amethyst likes having you around." Now it was Nightstar's turn to feel embarrassed. Sunburst had an uncanny knack of taking a situation and throwing it right back at him.

Nightstar liked Amethyst and was sure—his dragon sense confirmed it—she felt the same way towards him. However, Alduce, the human inside the dragon, was confused by the attraction. The dragon part of him was drawn to the female with scales the colour of the precious stones she was named after. She made him feel welcome and her deep blue eyes hinted at more. The man inside him was not practiced at reading such signs, but the dragon had a much better understanding of the dance she wove.

"Flaxe awoke from his long sleep this morning. He is old," Sunburst paused. "So old. And incredibly wise. He only wakes from his slumber for important events. He has declared there will be a Grand Moot and has woken to celebrate the great gathering of our kin. He was once leader of the White Mountain dragons and is loved and respected by everyone." Sunburst then hurried Nightstar from his roosting cavern and had insisted they watch for new arrivals.

They quickly stopped to gather Rose, who was only too pleased to accompany them to the low meadow in which they now waited.

Nightstar watched Sunburst and his mate as they lay together. Rose was spectacular, her vermillion scales glowed brightly, the final stages of pregnancy making her radiant. He understood Sunburst's excitement when the yellow dragon explained that she was close to laying. He told Nightstar she would clutch tonight, the night of the Grand Moot. It would be seen as incredibly fortuitous. Eggs laid during a Grand Moot were seen as a good omen and hatched strong and healthy. Other dragons with this accolade had gone on to achieve great things, Winterfang himself had been a Grand Moot egg.

The yellow dragon had calmed down considerably since this morning. When he was with the red female she had that effect on him. Nightstar put it down to the soothing influence the red dragon projected. That and Sunburst didn't want to appear nervous around his mate, especially in her condition.

He hadn't been able to quiz Sunburst any more about Flaxe, the long sleep, or the Grand Moot, as his friend had been too excitable this morning. Now he had relaxed a little, Nightstar thought it a good time to approach the subject and see if he could get a better explanation.

"Tell me more of Flaxe, Sunburst," Nightstar asked. "You spoke of him earlier before we rushed here and I was hoping to learn more about him."

"Of course, of course," Sunburst said, "I forget you weren't hatched here."

"You would forget your tail if it wasn't attached to your behind," Rose said sleepily, closing one eye and winking at Nightstar."

"My tail, I'll have you know... " started Sunburst.

"...is long and yellow, oh, I know. You've wrapped it round me and my belly bulges as a result!"

"I'm sure Nightstar doesn't need... "

"Just tell him about Flaxe, or would you prefer I tell him for you?"

"No, my Blood Rose, you rest and I will tell this story." Sunburst rolled his eyes, an unusual and human thing for a dragon to do and Nightstar gave a little snort that was almost a laugh.

"Flaxe is old, an ancient dragon. He led our moot before Winterfang." Sunburst started.

"For over one hundred years," Rose added, and looked up observing a large blue sea dragon as she passed overhead. "Look! Belle Cinder of the sandy shore, Blue-cap will be pleased to see her."

"Yes, Belle the Blue, I see her. Now can I continue?" Sunburst cocked his head towards his mate, flicking his tongue at her.

"Do go on, please," Rose teased him, rubbing her head along his serpentine yellow neck affectionately.

"Flaxe led the moot for over one hundred years," and he nodded at Rose, "he was a wise leader and loved by all. When Winterfang became his successor, Flaxe decided he was ready for the long sleep. He chose a deep cave, far back from the central cavern and rests there, only emerging when he sees fit."

"I see," Nightstar said, wondering about the long sleep, he remembered Galdor had spoken to him of something similar, but he was hesitant to ask Sunburst outright. "I'm afraid that the long sleep isn't something I have had much experience with or encountered much in the east. Is it something all western dragons do?"

"Only the most powerful dragons can enter the long sleep, they have to be strong in magic and very wise to attain it," Rose supplied.

"Indeed," Sunburst said, "and Flaxe is both. When a dragon such as Flaxe gets old and tired, if they are able, rather than passing on, they can enter the long sleep. They find a suitable place to retire, a quiet and secluded cave or an underground burrow or cavern, then seal themselves inside. They can use their magic to sleep for many years, slowing down their breathing until aging all but stops."

Nightstar touched the mind of Alduce as he thought about the great bears of his home world. They would hibernate during the long winter months in a similar way. This long sleep sounded like a magically enhanced hibernation. Alduce would have to make sure and record this in his journals, as this was something he wanted to learn more about.

"So what wakens a dragon from the long sleep?" he asked.

"No-one knows," Sunburst answered. "Until dragons are older and wiser, we never know if we can attain the long sleep and if we do, only then would we be able to say what wakens us."

Nightstar couldn't argue with that logic but he would be keen to speak with Flaxe, now his scholarly interest had been whetted. Perhaps Flaxe would be able to explain the process.

"I would very much like to speak with Flaxe, he sounds so interesting."

"Nightstar, you are an inquisitive one, but not all dragons respond well to questions. I know you are unfamiliar with our ways, and I do not mind answering you... "

"Really?" Rose purred, "Who would have known."

"...as I have grown to understand your ways and your past," Sunburst continued, choosing to ignore his mate. "Flaxe will not tell you about the long sleep. It is forbidden."

"Or you can learn the secrets from the pearl of wisdom," Rose said.

Nightstar had wondered about the mysterious pearl. When Winterfang had gripped it at the moot he had detected magic coming from the white orb.

"The pearl of wisdom? Only the leader of the moot is allowed to consult the pearl!" Sunburst chastised his mate. "If you are able to follow the path Flaxe has taken, your magic will provide the answer. If you are not, you will pass on to the next life, as is the fate of most dragons when they grow old and tired."

"But that is a long way off yet," Rose stated. "Let us not dwell on this. I for one, am more interested in starting new lives, not pondering old ones."

"Indeed," said Sunburst, flicking his tail gently over the swollen belly of his mate. She snapped playfully as it came close and Sunburst pulled it out of reach, her teeth clacking loudly on empty air.

Sunburst chuckled and Rose snorted, puffing some smoke from her nostrils. Nightstar joined in, enjoying the moment, happy in the company of his friends. But, as with all scholars, his curiosity returned and his thoughts were pulled back to the mysterious pearl.

Chapter 7

Excerpt from Alduce's Atlas of Dragons.

The Long Sleep.

Some dragons are able to enter what they refer to as The Long Sleep. It is unclear exactly how they accomplish this, but the information I have gathered thus far, points to the following contributing factors.

The long sleep, while magical in origin is not unlike the hibernation cycle of animals, except that where an animal usually hibernates for the winter months to conserve energy and food, a dragon can choose to enter the long sleep and can stay this way indefinitely.

Dragons are not born with this ability and it is said to only be accessible to those who are extremely intelligent or wise.

The life cycle of a dragon is greater than most creatures; anywhere from 200 to 400 years normally (see: lifespan of the dragon) and when they die, or pass on to the next life as they call it, if there are able, they can prevent this by entering the long sleep.

Side note: the next life is believed to be re-incarnation back to the egg to start their life cycle once again, the dragon spirit never dying and being reborn anew, with no recollection of a past life.

The long sleep, once the secret is known, allows the dragon to enter a state similar to hibernation. The dragon will seek out a secluded location, such as remote cave or underground tunnel where it is quiet. They will seal themselves inside and lower their breathing, heart rate, metabolic rate, and body temperature. Once in the dormant sleep like stage, they can bypass time without the need for sustenance.

Their magic slows the physical ageing process while they sleep and prolongs their life.

Observation: I believe that Galdor, when trapped in the caverns of the Pendron Mountains, although not yet near the final years of his lifespan, relied on an ability similar to the long sleep to survive until he was freed.

A wakeful state from the long sleep can be imposed and I have yet to determine how this is achieved. It is short lived, lasting a few days or as much as a week or two, depending on the subject's size, age, type, colour and magical ability. The wakened dragon can function as normal for this period but must return to the long sleep or face death if it does not.

The dragon must feast, replenishing energy prior to returning to its sleeping cavern.

Note: dragons will take any accumulated treasure with them when they enter the long sleep. This hoard can be plentiful, as these ancients can gather many valuable gemstones and precious metals over an extremely long life time.

Warning: fortune hunters beware. If you are lucky enough to find a dragon hoard and a sleeping dragon, know they have the ability to sense intrusions to their domain and will react aggressively to any violation or disturbance of their privacy.

* * *

Evening descended on the White Mountains and with the dusk came the Aurora.

Nightstar, who had spent most of his day sitting with Sunburst and Rose watching the visiting dragons fly in for the Grand Moot, was in awe of this natural spectacle.

As the sky darkened, so the lights of the aurora increased in brightness. Vast waves of green rippled across the starry expanse, intense blues and reds swirled and circulated creating a kaleidoscope of colour, ethereal and alive.

The meadow filled with dragons of all varieties and colours, the aurora bathing them all in its mystical light.

The snow covered slopes, high upon the mountainside reflected the sky, the mountains changed from their usual icy white to the greens, purples and reds of the aurora, the huge snow fields a glowing canvas for the astral phenomenon.

Nightstar understood why the dragons of the White Mountains had been excited when Flaxe had woken to announce the impending Grand Moot. Not only was there a gathering of dragons from all over the continent, but this spectacular light show was also part of the celebrations. Sunburst, as usual, hadn't told him everything about the Grand Moot. This time Nightstar believed it wasn't because he had forgotten or only told part of the tale, as was his habit, but that he wanted it to be a surprise—which it most certainly was.

Nightstar was content to sit and stare at the hypnotic sky, the mountainside and the gathered meadow of dragons, enjoying the feeling of happiness and companionship. There were dragons still arriving and as they sailed through the night sky, it was hard to tell what colour they were, the aurora painting them all the same.

The black scales on his body had taken on the colours of the aurora too, even a black dragon wasn't immune to the effects of the natural lights, making his appearance the same as any other dragon assembled. Nightstar was happy at this, as usually his black scales marked him as different, but tonight he was the same as everyone else, camouflaged in the colours of the aurora, another multi-coloured dragon, indistinguishably normal.

Four dragons passed close by as they wandered through the meadow and the two males nodded in unison to Nightstar. He was now able to distinguish between male and female dragons and recognise individuals with ease. Even though the two males of the group appeared different, painted in the colours of the aurora, Nightstar knew them both. Verdune and Verdante, the two identical green dragons of the moot guard.

The two greens had shown Nightstar respect, but they were normally taciturn and serious. Tonight however, the atmosphere of the moot and the two females that accompanied them, gave them cause to relax and enjoy the event.

Nightstar nodded back and as he observed the throngs of dragons, he noticed that a lot of male and females were pairing up. Sunburst and Rose were happy to include him in their company but a sudden realisation made him feel like a third wing. His thoughts turned to Amethyst and he wished that she were here with him.

"I think I will take a flight through the skies of the aurora," he told his friends. "There is something special about this evening and I would like to feel the magic of the lights as I fly."

"Don't go too far," Rose said. "We would like it if you were present at the laying and I don't think it will be too long now."

"Rose feels her time is soon," Sunburst beamed. "She will lay tonight, I am sure of it."

"I am... " Nightstar was filled with an emotion so strong he was unable to express himself. Never would Alduce have been lost for words, but never would Alduce have been choked with this foreign emotion either. "I would be privileged to attend. I have never been witness to something so personal."

"We would share this with our friend," Rose said. "You have led a life of solitude and loneliness before coming to our shores. We would see this changed, if you so want it."

"I would," Nightstar replied softly.

"Fly high and fly free," Sunburst spoke the traditional words. "And find that purple temptress and bring her too." He cocked one of his eye ridges like a quizzical eyebrow, implying more by leaving it unsaid.

Nightstar bowed to Sunburst and Rose, it was the best way he knew to show respect and thanks without speaking, as he feared he wouldn't be able to say the words. He launched himself into the air, powerful wings pushing him higher into the aurora filled sky, taking care to avoid the other flying dragons.

As he gained height he looked down over the meadow filled with dragons and marvelled at the sight. There were dragons everywhere, in small groups and in large crowds, the largest of which was a giant circle around a huge dragon. Flaxe. So many dragons had come to pay their respects to the ancient former leader. Nightstar wanted to speak with the old dragon, he would be uniquely interesting to study, but he would need to be careful in his approach. If Flaxe was old and clever, he would surely be curious about a black dragon from outside the White Mountains.

He pushed higher and the ground diminished along with the meadow and the mountains until he was so high that he almost reached the aurora itself, feeling like he was chasing a rainbow.

He understood the science of how the charged particles from the sun emitted flares of light as they collided with the atmosphere, forming the colours of the aurora—but it didn't make it any less spectacular. Tonight the air was alive with magic and he basked in the wash of colours as he flew. Green ripples of light formed patterns that reminded him of the colour of the two dragons of the moot guard.

The two dragons he had seen in the meadow, occupied by the two visiting females, were not standing guard tonight outside the chamber of the moot. If the chamber was unguarded, and was likely to remain that way for the time being, what was to stop him investigating the pearl of wisdom?

Nothing!

He began a slow spiral, setting his wings and relishing in the downward glide, enjoying the moment and losing himself in the flight. All dragons looked similar under the colours of the aurora and no-one would notice his black scales as he returned to the inner mountain. Once he was inside, he would take care not to be noticed. It was unlikely there would be anyone occupying the cavern, everyone should be out and about, enjoying the moot. He needed to remain vigilant, just in case. He knew what he was about to do was wrong and he mustn't get caught.

Once he studied the pearl he would go in search of Amethyst.

He hoped the pearl of wisdom might enlighten him as to what it was a female dragon looked for in a mate.

Chapter 8

Excerpt from Alduce's Atlas of Dragons.

Flaxe: Yellow Dragon: draconis flavinium.

Ancient Elder, former Moot Leader and Long Sleeper.

Flaxe is thought to be over four hundred years old. Before entering the long sleep he was leader of the White Mountain Moot for over one hundred years. Old age and tiredness were the main reason he retired from this position. He also wanted to give Winterfang, his replacement, the opportunity to lead his community, stating that new blood and fresh perspectives maintain strength and objectivity within the moot. He is known to be extremely wise and knowledgeable and is loved and respected by all dragons.

Although his scales are faded and hardly any pigment remains (a result of old age) he is of the species draconis flavinium and is unusually large for a yellow dragon. His colouring is that of ancient parchment and little remains of his vibrant yellow when compared to younger specimens of his species.

No-one knows what triggers the awakening from the long sleep and dragons who are able to partake in this extended form of stasis, will not discuss the process and guard their secret closely.

Flaxe, although extremely old, does not display any signs of tiredness when he is awake. His powerful magic continually sustains him while sleeping and allows him to remain active for a short period of time when awake.

Young dragons flock to his side and follow the ancient dragon, fascinated by the historic stories he tells and his knowledge of past times. The mature dragons will often chastise their young for bothering the ancient dragon, but Flaxe has indicated that their attention and enthusiasm is welcomed and he enjoys the constant companionship.

There is a hidden mystery to this dragon equivalent of an old and respected gentleman. He is still a force to be reckoned with and will wake, not only in times of celebration, but in times of need, when his wisdom may be called upon.

The sleeping chamber Flaxe has chosen is deep within the inner dome of the White Mountain, far back from the central cavern. There is only one tunnel that leads in and out of his chamber. It is secluded and warm, heated by the magma below the mountain and rumoured to be filled with a horde of precious metals and gems accumulated over almost four hundred years.

* * *

Nightstar dropped from an empty ledge high up in the inner dome and glided silently through the darkness. Not many dragons occupied the high levels in the honeycomb of caves and the ones that did weren't at home tonight. Everyone was outside under the magical light of the aurora celebrating the Grand Moot. No guards stood watch at the entrance to the chamber of the pearl.

Nightstar landed quietly in the cave entrance, his talons lightly scraping the rock and echoing in the silence. He folded his wings and crept to the stone wall, crouching low. He scanned the inner tunnel, but as far as he could see, there were no signs of life. He took a last quick glance behind, making sure he hadn't been observed, then moved deeper inside, staying close to the cover of the wall.

When the tunnel ended and opened out into the chamber of the moot, he stopped, suddenly aware of what he was doing. He had been so caught up in the excitement of the Grand Moot and the atmosphere the aurora brought, that he'd failed to consider his actions fully.

He was about to betray the trust of his friends. Friends that had taken him in, welcomed him and shown only kindness to a stranger. This wasn't the feelings of Alduce, this was all Nightstar. He wasn't just one person, or dragon, anymore, even though he knew he was.

Nightstar's persona had grown. He was both dragon and sorcerer and sometimes it was difficult to separate the two.

Alduce's mind was unsure whether Nightstar was influencing the thoughts of the man, but he knew that when he interacted with other dragons, Nightstar's will and instinct became stronger. He never forgot he was human, but it was only when he was alone that Alduce surfaced fully to remind him.

He found it easier now, after months of learning, how to be a dragon and he believed that the dragon within him found it easier not to be a human. He was travelling in uncharted waters of the mind and the scholarly part of his being sailed through them headlong. The cautious man scoured these waters for dangerous reefs, but the dragon soul joined with that scholar and delighted in the journey, sails open to the wind that carried them both into the unknown.

Focus! He scolded himself. This wasn't a time to let his mind ponder such things, he was here for a reason. He shook his head trying to clear his thoughts, he felt a little inebriated under the aurora and wondered if it was effecting his judgement. Nightstar could feel the presence of the pearl and wondered if being so close to what was most surely a magical object was also influencing his thoughts.

Perhaps the pearl was protected by a glamour and this was what was making him feel conflicted. Alduce was more than an adept sorcerer and no charm, no matter how strong, would deter him from his objective.

It felt like the power of the spell was designed to keep dragons, that shouldn't have access to the pearl, at bay. It wasn't able to ward off the strength of Alduce the sorcerer, even in dragon form.

Still, he should be cautious, the pearl was more than it seemed. Anything magical must be treated with respect. A lesson all apprentices must learn early, Caltus had often reminded Alduce, especially something unknown.

Nightstar crept closer to the pearl, it sat on the rock Winterfang had stood behind when he opened the moot. He breathed in, smelling the air and his forked tongue flicked from between his teeth, tasting it. The grassy smell of summer meadows and a taste, almost like sweet honey, filled his senses.

Dragon magic!

His suspicions were correct, the pearl was wrought with a subtle hidden charm.

He leaned in closer, large eyes dilating in the dim cave light, slit-eyed pupils widening to see as much as they could of the mysterious pearl before his snout.

The polished milky surface, like white veined marble, started to swirl. The spiky quills on Nightstar's neck stood to attention like the hackles of an angry wolf.

He wanted to touch it. He wanted to learn the secrets only ancient dragons were privy to. He wanted to steal it, take it back to his laboratory and study it. He wanted it for his own, to lock it away and covet it.

No! It was the pearl of wisdom, it should be respected by all dragons, and humans, Nightstar reminded Alduce. The magic of the pearl was stronger than he expected. He reached out his claw and the light from the pearl's surface reflected on his shiny black talons as he slowly closed them around the glowing orb. He braced himself in preparation, not knowing what to expect.

The magic of the pearl tingled on his talons and a pleasant sensation, warm and calming, enveloped his grip. He could feel the magical power inside and knew why it was named the pearl of wisdom. It held so many ancient secrets, it was crammed full of myths and stories, it had knowledge of a magic he never knew existed. It was everything a dragon should know and so much more.

He probed deeper into the white swirling mist of its secrets, spiralling down through a thousand million white threads, each one different and each one precious, unknown yet somehow familiar. It was far too much for one mind to absorb. It was too much for two minds, for both Alduce and Nightstar, to fully comprehend.

The power of the pearl swallowed him down and he was defenceless to resist its temptation as it pulled him deeper.

Chapter 9

Excerpt from Alduce's Atlas of Dragons.

The Great Exodus.

Note: As told by dragons.

There were once no dragons on the western continent of Aurentania, so named from an ancient dragon word which translates to Land of the Aurora. Dragons originally thrived in the east, indigenous to the continent of Eusavus, over five hundred years previous.

These continents are the two largest land masses on the world of Salverta.

The story the dragons tell is that the land they once inhabited, over the ages, began to fill with more and more humans. Man arrived from the south, spreading across the lands, breeding and building, turning the wilderness into their cities and towns.

The dragons moved north, into less fertile lands, not wishing any contact with humans and everything was peaceful for a few centuries. But the march of humanity was unending and eventually men began to encroach once again, into the new lands the dragons now called home.

Humans grew stronger and as their race advanced and their weapons and magic evolved with them. A time came when they were not content to share the land with dragons any longer and war parties pushed farther and farther north hunting and killing dragon kind.

The scales and hide of dragons were sought after for many reasons and sorcerers, mages and practitioners of the arcane coveted any piece of a dragon as they were imbued with powerful magic and could be used for a number of barbaric human spells. Flesh, bone, horns, blood, and even eggs were the prizes these slayers hunted for. Anything that was part of a dragon was of value to them.

The humans were clever, and through strength of numbers and the power of their own unique magic, learned how to fight and conquer dragons, singling out targets and binding them with spells. They forged sorcerous metal that was hard and lethal, creating fatal weapons and armour that was impervious to dragon attacks. They continued to steal dragon land, century after century, their numbers were limitless and their attacks relentless, until a once mighty race was reduced to near extinction.

Dragons became isolated from each other and searched for more distant and remote places to live. They sought out regions and areas where humans found it difficult to reach and took them a long time to travel to. But they knew, that if they didn't act, their kind would be hunted down until they were only a myth. No more dragons would exist and they would vanish from history completely.

The oldest and wisest of the dragons gathered and formed their first Dragon Moot out of a necessity for their survival. Their choices were limited and their continuing struggle over the centuries was a war they were destined to lose. The only outcome would be the slow annihilation of their species. For each human that was slain, and there were many, two more took their place.

The more scarce dragons became, the more their value to humans grew. Man was fuelled by an ever increasing greed to hunt and slay them. Dragons would have to do more than retreat and hide on this continent, if they wanted to survive.

The moot decided that the only course of action was to leave the land that was once their home and seek out a new place to live, unhampered by the constant threat of humanity.

The north was a barren waste, filled with snow and ice, that stretched on and on without end. While dragons could survive the harsh frosts and the constant cold, this was not a land most of them would be comfortable living in.

The south and east were no longer the wilderness they had once been, mankind had spoiled the beautiful forests, cutting down the trees for their wood. They had destroyed the hillsides, quarrying the stone and leaving their ugly mark upon the desecrated land. They had built their foul cities on the plains, filling the grasslands and meadows with their towns and villages, polluting the rivers and lakes with their waste. The wildlife, once plentiful, had been consumed by the ravenous hordes of mankind as their number sprawled and expanded, year after year, century after century.

This land was no longer beautiful, no longer the unspoiled wilderness it had once been and there was nothing left for dragons here anymore. Everything they had known, everything they loved, had been ravaged and destroyed by humans. They were a plague on nature. A disease with no cure, consuming the wilderness until there was nothing left to take.

Dragons no longer wanted part of their world, they lived in harmony with the nature, never taking more than they needed and the rise of man made them weep with great sadness and loss.

It was time to leave and the only direction to go was west, across the vast ocean, far away from humans and the spoiled lands.

The moot sent out their strongest flyers, four dragons representing earth, water, sky and spirit, to fly west and discover what, if anything, lay beyond the great body of water.

Weeks crept slowly by as the moot waited and when the four returned, they gathered to hear the news they brought.

There was a new land, far to the west, unspoiled and best of all, empty of man. It was ideal place for dragons to settle and make into their new home.

Word was passed to all the remaining dragons that were found, they were told to spread the news to any of their kin they could find. The moot proposed they would fly west to the shores of the ocean, gather there and wait for seven days for all who wished to embark to the new land.

It would be a long and difficult flight. They were to cross an ocean larger than the continent they currently lived on. The dragons gorged themselves before they departed and then rested to conserve their strength for the flight ahead. Not all would see the shores of the new land, only the strongest would survive the arduous Journey.

But dragons were creatures of legend, their strength and perseverance was part of what they were. The constant centuries of struggle with man had whittled out the weak and the slow, the dragons that remained were the last of their kind. They were the strongest, the fastest, and the smartest. They were the survivors, *forged through adversity and they would succeed and they would prevail.*

They were prepared to take the risk as the reward was great, and if they did not, they would fade from existence.

Never again would dragons be driven from their home, their new world was far enough across the vast ocean, the wild untameable sea, that humans in their small pathetic boats would struggle to breach the gap between continents.

And, if one day they ever did, dragons would flame their boats, destroy any men that dared set foot on their shores. They would not allow man to walk on their new land and take it from them.

They had once valued all life, even the tiny men. Allowing them to multiply and thrive had been a grave mistake. Gone was their conscience for human life. Their new world would be different and mankind would be subjected to the full wrath of dragons, should they ever make the mistake of coming to these shores.

* * *

Nightstar drifted through the pearl of wisdom, following threads of knowledge and meandering through the secrets it held. He latched on to a long white thread, awash with multiple colours dappled all along its length. As he examined the information within, he learned about the Great Exodus and experienced first-hand recollections of dragons long past.

He was able to relive the story of their first moot and witness the gathering on the shores of the ocean to the west. He travelled with the dragons, flying forever over an endless expanse of unchanging ocean, golden sunlight bright and glaring during the day, silver moonlight turning the sea to liquid metal at night. He felt the joy of their arrival on new shores and shared the tiredness of their wings. He knew the hunger of empty bellies and the thirst of parched throats after their arduous flight. But he also experienced their excitement of a new beginning in a new land.

The pearl shared the knowledge.

A new thread caught his attention and a black scale filled his vision, dark as night, one scale among many, hard unyielding armour. Then it was gone, replaced by a dark smoke, potent and deadly dragon magic, swirling and drifting, filled with death and destruction.

He jumped to another thread, spinning and weaving, his thoughts reached out and instinct took over, his mind turning to the long sleep. He was rewarded with how to change his body, using magic stored within him to slow down his metabolism and rest. Resting, dreaming and sleeping. It was something that he could easily access, but not until he was much older.

The pearl provided the answer.

His thoughts changed again, searching through the random strands that manifested inside the heart of the pearl.

His vision returned to the black scale, this time it was being probed by a sharp pointed talon. It lifted the scale exposing the skin below, vulnerable and unprotected now the armour shielding it was pried aside. The vision of the scale faded, replaced by black wings, spread wide. The dark smoke emanating from them was denser than air, its weight causing it to sink, swirling to the ground, venomous and threatening.

He skipped once more, jumping to a new thread and discovered the ability to look into the eyes of another, see deep into their soul and learn how to tell if they spoke the truth. He knew at once how to separate lies from truth, to see inside the heart of someone, to stare into their eyes and use the hypnotic vision to search for falsehoods and deception.

The pearl provided the knowledge and showed him the way.

His vison returned to the sharp talon as it opened the skin beneath the scale and drops of blood pooled from the cut to gather on a claw. The vision shifted again.

Thick smoke coalesced, covering the ground, swirling and alive with power, created from deep inside the spell caster, born from the wings of a dragon.

He jumped one last time, uncontrolled and unasked for, latching onto another random thread, opaque and insubstantial, it circulated and swirled within the pearl.

He would have to stop, this was too much to absorb and his mind was pushing him back to the cavern of the moot.

The last thread contained the secret of invisibility, how to change his scales like a chameleon, to blend in to his surroundings, not truly invisible but a clever trick that now appeared simple, once he had been shown the way.

The pearl gifted him with forbidden knowledge. Was it somehow aware of what he wished to learn? He had contemplated some of the subjects it revealed, was it...

Snap!

His claw unfurled and his connection with the pearl was broken. He was back in the gloomy cave, the bright threads of knowledge gone from his reach and the gossamer web of secrets vanished.

He knew so much more than he had before. The pearl exposed him to secrets a sorcerer could only dream of.

Strangely, no time had passed, his journey into the memories of the pearl had only taken an instant, but even that short time was all he could endure.

It wasn't painful, he experienced no discomfort, but it had been difficult to maintain a connection with so much knowledge willing to flow freely and fill his brain. The pearl was eager to feed his hunger and drown him in its knowledge.

The secrets he discovered hadn't been random, these were some of the subjects he'd been thinking about, subconscious questions that he desired answers to.

The pearl had guided him, shown him the correct path among the millions of threads swirling in its secret sea. Just how many more infinite secrets the pearl stored in the swirling threads was unfathomable.

He had wondered about the Great Exodus, heard dragons speaking about it. The pearl had guided him to the correct thread, finding it with simple ease and shared the knowledge of the historic event.

He was intrigued with the long sleep, wanted to learn more about it. Again the pearl had shown him how to attain it and make it a reality, if he chose to enter into its indefinite slumber.

His mind often pondered how dragons could detect a lie, ever since his meeting with Galdor all those years ago. Now he knew how it was achieved and he had the ability to do so himself.

He wondered about the strange visions in between the threads he had explored, the black scale and the dark smoke. They nagged at his subconscious like forgotten memories, just out of reach, stored so deeply the knowledge was too distant to recall or make sense of.

All but the last secret he uncovered had been questions he wished answers to, and the pearl had provided them. Everything but the trick to change his scales to mimic the chameleon, to appear invisible and blend with the environment. This had been a random thread that he'd latched onto at the last minute.

He now understood how powerful the pearl of wisdom was and how wrong it was to use it for his own gain. Winterfang was leader of the moot and had the right to consult the pearl's knowledge for the good of his community. Nightstar was neither a leader nor a natural dragon. He felt guilty stealing the secrets of the pearl and betraying the trust of a community that welcomed him.

Guilt and wonder, shame and excitement, a mix of dragon and human feelings creating conflict, warring emotions from two separate entities occupying his conscious at the same time. The part of him that was Nightstar might not be what Alduce thought of as a true dragon, but Nightstar was real. The part of him that had become Nightstar knew he was a true dragon, his origin might not be that of his brothers and sisters. He wasn't born from the shell like them but he was still a dragon, whether created by sorcery and scientific means, he was still Nightstar, he had the heart and soul of a White Mountain dragon, he was alive and as real as Alduce.

Maybe it was the charm within the pearl effecting his reasoning, maybe it was something more. He wasn't entirely sure, he had searched deep within the pearl and perhaps this was influencing his decisions.

Claws scrabbled on the landing and Nightstar froze as the sound echoed along the tunnel, breaking the silence and his train of thought. He strained to listen, sensitive ears alert for any sound and then he heard it a second time, followed by the rustle of leathery wings folding. This could only mean one thing, the moot guard had returned to their post, trapping him somewhere he shouldn't be. With no visible way out.

Verdune and Verdante, the two green dragons had returned to their positions, safeguarding the chamber of the moot and the pearl within. Nightstar listened to their quiet rumbling voices as they discussed the females they had spent time with. The acoustics of the chamber made it easy to hear each word, even though they kept their voices low.

"I wish we had been able to sneak a little more time away from our duties," Verdante said. "The aurora provides the perfect camouflage. All dragons look the same under its light. The pearl is safe, and it *is* Grand Moot."

"I agree brother," Verdune said. "There will be time later when our relief comes to take over, then we will be free to bask under the aurora and chase any females we want."

"If old Winterfang hasn't forgotten to arrange our replacements, that is," his brother retorted.

"*Old* Winterfang forgets nothing!" boomed a new voice. The leader of the White Mountain Moot had arrived on the ledge and Nightstar now feared he would soon be discovered.

"And *old* Winterfang can see everything too," he said. "He sees that his trusted guards sneak away from their posts to chase the tails of summer females."

"We thought…" Verdune said.

"Relax," Winterfang said, "I'm not so old that I can't remember what it's like to feel my blood rush at a red in heat."

"Or a glowing green with scales like emeralds and a…" Verdante began.

"I can see that you are both preoccupied and I have come to make you a proposal," Winterfang said. "I understand that standing guard on one of the most eventful nights of the year…"

"The decade!" Verdante said.

"…can be difficult," Winterfang continued, "especially when the aurora is in the sky, spreading its influence among us, and far distant females visit our home.

148

I have come to check the pearl and relieve you of your duties until tomorrow. No-one need stand guard tonight. But be warned," and his voice took on a serious tone. "If you ever leave the pearl unattended without my permission, when you are supposed to be guarding it—our most valuable treasure—you will know my wrath." Silence filled the cavern and neither Verdante nor his twin, Verdune, spoke.

"Do you understand?" Winterfang prompted.

"Yes, mighty Winterfang," they replied in unison.

"Well, go then, enjoy the moot," Winterfang chuckled, taking the sting from his words.

The noise of claws scrabbling on rock and wings unfurling, filtered down into the chamber. Nightstar began to panic. Winterfang was here to check the pearl. He would come through the tunnel and into the chamber and there was nowhere for him to go, nowhere to hide and Winterfang would discover a black dragon somewhere he shouldn't be.

Nightstar was worried for Verdante and Verdune, they would be in so much trouble. Winterfang's wrath would be fierce and it would be his fault the two guards would suffer.

Strange that he should worry about the two greens when his own predicament was even worse.

"Wait!" Winterfang called out and the scrabbling claws of the guards silenced immediately. "I would advise when you refer to the leader of the White Mountain Moot, the word *old*," and he drew it out, slowly exaggerating the syllable, "would be best omitted." A silenced followed his words and Nightstar imagined cold blue eyes holding their attention. The moment stretched, before he continued. "And remember, my wrath is something you should wish you never have the misfortune to experience."

Two sets of wings cracked as they caught the air and the green dragons departed the ledge.

"Wise Winterfang from now on, moot leader," a voice floated back through the tunnel. Nightstar thought it was Verdune that had spoken.

Winterfang rumbled and Nightstar was sure it was more of a chuckle. The frost drake wasn't as cold as he pretended.

Claws clicked on the tunnel floor as the moot leader neared, echoing like a ticking clock, counting down the seconds to his discovery.

Nightstar pushed himself back, pressing his body hard against the rock as he waited for Winterfang to appear, and wished he was invisible.

He shivered unexpectedly, even though the cavern wasn't cold, his scales shimmering like a heat haze. The chameleon effect encountered on the last thread of knowledge, began to change his appearance. He didn't vanish or turn invisible, but instead took on the appearance of the solid rock wall of the chamber. Where only seconds before a large black dragon had stood, fearful of discovery, now there was nothing but the illusion of plain old rock.

Nightstar had to look closely at his scales to tell if they were still there. He was amazed at just how hard it was to make out any of his form, and he knew where to look! He remained as still as the rock he clung to, not daring to breathe lest the air from his lungs disturbed the seemingly empty cavern and give him away.

Winterfang entered the chamber and moved directly to the pearl of wisdom, sitting undisturbed upon its traditional resting place. He sniffed the air and bent his snout to the pearl, then walked around behind the slab rock it sat upon, staring back to where Nightstar crouched, camouflaged and still.

Nightstar fixed his gaze blankly looking forward, deliberately avoiding eye contact with the frost drake, sure that if he did catch his eye, Winterfang would notice him and see through the disguise. His nervousness at being discovered almost caused him to snigger hysterically at the poor term of phrase, *see through his disguise.* He was see-through, like the glass pane in a window. No-one looked at the glass, only what was beyond. The chameleon effect, as he named it, acted in exactly the same way. Winterfang looked through him and only saw the cavern wall. And the amazing and terrifying thing was, he was less than twenty feet away.

The frost coloured dragon cocked his head left then right, listening intently to the silence. His cold blue eyes alert as he scoured the inner chamber, prying into the darkness. Nightstar could only wait, fearing he would be caught, sensing Winterfang knew he wasn't alone, even though he couldn't see or hear anything.

Winterfang sniffed the air, pointing his snout to the ceiling then the floor, like a hound on the trail of hidden game. He flicked out his tongue as if tasting the cavern air, then sharply turned his head, facing back towards the entrance, staring behind himself. He was acting spooked, as if he sensed another presence but was unable to detect where it was. He spun his head back round, facing the wall where Nightstar stood, staring and sniffing. Nightstar waited, the tension in the chamber unbearable, then, Winterfang puffed out his breath, sighing huffily and shook his head.

He stayed for a few more moments, long stretched out moments that felt like hours to the anxious Nightstar, then he turned and left the chamber, his snow coloured tail flicking back and forth in the air like the tail of an angry cat. The pearl responded to the movement as his tail passed over the milky globe. The surface patterns swirling gently then slowing to a stop, returning to its veined marble state as Winterfang left the chamber and Nightstar was alone once more.

He listened as the clacking of talons on stone receded down the tunnel, tracking the retreating dragon's departure. He remained motionless, never daring to move, still holding his breath. When he heard Winterfang's wings unfurl and was sure his wingbeats had taken him away from the landing ledge, he expelled air quietly and the only sound that remained was the thundering of his heart.

Exercising extreme caution, Nightstar stepped away from the wall and his skin and scales rippled back into view, the deep dark black they had always been.

The encounter was far too close for comfort and he was sure he would have been discovered. Just as the pearl of wisdom supplied the answers to his question and gave him the knowledge he had been searching for, it had also provided a solution to a problem he didn't even know he needed, until it arose. It was almost like the pearl predicted the future and anticipated his needs before they happened. This gave the sorcerer inside him a great deal to ponder, the mysteries and the power of the pearl were even greater that he believed. This was an ancient magic, ancient even by dragon standards, and that was old indeed. But now wasn't the time to wonder about such things, now he needed to get out of this chamber while the opportunity presented itself.

Creeping as silently as he could, talons retracted and stepping on the hard pads of his feet, he made his way stealthily to the outside ledge. The landing area was empty and freedom was only a few wing beats away, but he stopped, keeping to the shadows, remembering something Winterfang had said to the green guards. *Old Winterfang can see everything.*

Nightstar didn't doubt it for a second.

Eager to leave but sensing the time wasn't right yet, he waited. His heartbeat slowed, but he was still on high alert. He had an itching feeling his exploits this evening weren't quite done yet. Intuition told him to wait, or perhaps it was his dragon sense. Trusting his instinct, he remained still, hugging the shadows of the cave wall. Waiting, but not knowing why.

A large white shape glided by the entrance. The air from Winterfang's wings creating little dust eddies that swirled around the cave mouth as he passed. The moot leader was taking the opportunity for one last look into the cavern as he flew by on his way back outside. He had sensed there was something amiss and hadn't left, attempting to catch the suspected intruder off guard.

And somehow Nightstar had understood that his way wasn't clear, the danger of discovery hadn't yet passed. He had been right to wait, even though he was desperate to escape. He had learned something valuable, a trait all dragons were born with.

Patience.

As a scholar, he was always in a hurry to learn and to discover that which he didn't know. Sorcerers were no strangers to patience, and Alduce, while he could wait for experiments to react or spells to formulate, through necessity, wasn't the most patient person.

He never thought being a dragon could teach him qualities he could apply as a human, but he had been wrong. Caltus, once again, had been right. It wasn't the first time that his old master still managed to educate him, even though his days of being an apprentice were long gone. He had a wise saying for every situation, and *we learn something new every day,* was one of his favourites. It was still appropriate now, so many years later. Today, Nightstar had taken his old master's place and become the teacher and Alduce, the willing pupil.

Winterfang descended towards the entrance, his white scales easily seen in the semi-darkness of the inner dome. He glowed like green ice as he exited into the outside light, the aurora reflecting on his body. He vanished from sight signalling to Nightstar that this time, the cautious old, no, *wise* leader, had truly gone. It was now safe for him to leave.

Taking one last look behind, he hopped from the ledge and glided silently around the inner dome, wondering why Winterfang would chose to leave the pearl unattended. Perhaps the aurora was having the same intoxicating effect on the frost drake as it was on him, impairing his judgement. Aware of Alduce's presence, a memory the sorcerer recalled, came to mind.

Never look a gift horse in the mouth. Another aphorism from Master Caltus. It was time to leave, while he could still do so, undetected. The honeycomb of cave mouths was thankfully empty of dragons, but he took his time getting to the exit of the huge inner cavern, making sure no-one was there to observe his furtive escape.

His mind returned to Amethyst, he should find her and join Sunburst and Rose. If he didn't return with the purple female, his inquisitive yellow friend would wonder why and want to know what he had been up to all this time. Funny how Sunburst heartedly scolded him for asking so many question, when the curious yellow dragon was full of questions himself.

* * *

The gem like scales of Amethyst caught the purples of the aurora, making them appear crystalline and highlighted her natural colour, rather than disguising it. This made it easy for Nightstar to spot her as he flew across the meadow where a great number of dragons had assembled.

He had searched for the purple female, cruising the skies above the meadows, observing the wonders of the Grand Moot. Before he had located Amethyst, he had flown over a large group, mostly dragonets, gathered around Flaxe as he entertained them with his stories. It was true, the ancient dragon attracted the youngsters like iron to a magnet. It was by far the largest assembly of quiet and subdued dragons he'd come across. They hung on his every word, unusually silent and rarely interrupting with questions.

Nightstar had stopped, the scholar inside taking over for a while, he hung on the periphery of Flaxe's group, desperate to meet the ancient yellow and converse with him, but not in front of such a huge audience. The opportunity to listen to the great dragon speak and get to know him through his words was enough for now.

Flaxe's voice captivated his listeners, but it wasn't loud or booming. He had a natural storyteller's voice and when he spoke, you were compelled to listen, his melodious words drew you in and submerged you in the narrative.

Nightstar recognised some of the smaller dragonets that had greeted him when he first arrived, sitting as close as they could get to Flaxe, quiet and attentive now, so different from when they had met him. He was seeing dragons as individuals now, able to pick out faces from a group, if he had met them before. The shape of a snout, the ridges on a head and the angle of horns, all were recognisable features to him now.

His perspectives were changing, previously they had all looked similar and he was only able to identify people by their colours. People? What other way could he think of them? Although they weren't really people, each dragon had a personality. Even personality wasn't the best word to describe dragons. Individuality, that was better, they were all individuals to him now. Nightstar thought more like an individual himself, but it was still difficult to fully distance himself from Alduce and his human side.

He found himself caught up in the story of the Great Exodus, as Flaxe wove a tale of desperate times and the hardship of the long flight across an endless sea. The ancient dragon then rewarded his audience with the finale of their huge achievement and a new beginning filled with hope. He was a master storyteller and he delivered the tale with sadness, adventure and excitement, all in equal measure.

Having experienced the exodus from the shared memories within the pearl of knowledge, Nightstar was amazed at how historically accurate Flaxe's rendition was. He had embellished some of the happenings, making them more exciting for his younger audience, but he hadn't detracted from the events or the actual facts.

Nightstar had stayed to listen to a few more stories, some of them funny, some sad, but always entertaining. He laughed along with the young dragons when Flaxe told them the exploits of the dragonet who couldn't fly. Finding humour at the amusing situation she found herself in, until eventually, she managed to take flight, revelling in the experience. Although the tale was similar to a children's bedtime story human mothers would tell their sleepy offspring, Nightstar enjoyed it immensely, soaring along with the triumphant dragonet on her first flight and relating it to the first time he had taken to the air.

He could have happily sat and listened to all of Faxe's tales, but the pull of another attraction worked its magic as he remembered the beauty of Amethyst purple scales, the curves of her neck and the mischief dancing in her dark blue eyes. Reluctant though he was to leave Flaxe and his mesmerising stories, he had set off in search of the object of his desires.

The aurora was having the same effect on all the adult dragons and as he flew above the meadow, he witnessed many dragons closely pressed together, their necks entwined intimately. Perhaps it was good that Flaxe kept the dragonets entertained, giving the mature dragons time to themselves.

He dropped down neatly, landing perfectly beside Amethyst, who was in the company of two male dragons, obviously vying to be suitable mates for the radiant purple female. Nightstar felt his quills rise and the spikes on his neck stand up, these males were his adversaries and he would see off any challengers for Amethyst's affections. All three heads turned to stare at the black dragon and he quickly reigned in his feelings, conscious that he had made some terrible mistake in etiquette.

The two interloping males backed away, dipping their heads in acknowledgement of the newly arrived suitor. Nightstar quickly realised that his display had been a declaration of his intent towards Amethyst and the two males had seen this and gracefully withdrew, leaving Amethyst exclusively to his company.

Amethyst seemed pleased at his dramatic entrance. "Nightstar," she purred, her voice like silk, "you've chased off the competition it appears." Her eyes met his and he could tell she was happy at his arrival.

"I wanted to see you," Nightstar said, thinking how obviously stupid it sounded, a human reaction.

"And do you like what you look upon?" she teased.

The dragon pushed aside the idiot human and took control, he was Nightstar and he wanted to be with this beautiful female, she was perfect for him. Her purple scales complimented his black and silver, they would be regal and magnificent together. "I like what I see," he replied, "very much. Purple is my favourite colour."

"That is well then, as I find myself drawn to the unusual black of your scales and the silver upon your chest." She gently stretched out her head and tentatively brushed his neck, lightly at first, then with more vigour when he didn't resist. A feeling of pure contentment washed over him, the sensation of Amethyst's head caressing his neck was intensely pleasing and a quiet gurgling purr escaped his throat.

"I was impressed with your display," she crooned. "Those two were beginning to bore me and I was hoping you would find me."

"My display?"

"The way your neck quills signalled your intent," she met his eyes, holding his gaze, waiting for a response.

"Ah, my intent, yes, I'm happy it pleases you." Nightstar wasn't exactly sure what his intent was, but now that he had made a show of displaying it, he suspected the two departed dragons were not as impressed as Amethyst.

"Now that you have declared for me, made it plain that you desire a coupling and will lay challenge to any who attempt to court me, I am content," she huffed a small laugh. "I only wish you had raised your quills for me earlier."

Nightstar was dumfounded and barely managed a response, "I wish to couple with you?"

"And I with you," Amethyst mistook his question for a statement, "and so we shall, but let us take time to enjoy the Grand Moot and the aurora first." She entwined her neck around his and wove her graceful tail along the length of his own. He remembered what Rose had said to Sunburst about their tails and rather than the shock he expected, he tightened the grip of his tail on hers.

"The aurora certainly has made you brazen," she said, "I like this side of you, Nightstar, it is long since I took a mate that I found desirable." Nightstar was surprised how forward Amethyst was. Alduce had never been confident around women and they had posed something of a mystery to him. He should be nervous courting a female dragon, but he wasn't, even though he had no idea what came next. Well, he knew in theory, but this would be another first for the human turned dragon, and he didn't just want to experience this for research purposes, this was different. He felt comfortable with Amethyst and she seemed to feel the same way about him, which made him happy.

"Nightstar!" called a voice from above. Looking up from where they sat, Nightstar saw the familiar yellow underbelly of Sunburst as he plunged towards them.

"Sunburst, you've found us," Nightstar replied.

"Where have you been? I've been looking all over for you!"

"He's been busy," Amethyst announced proudly, "declaring for me. Quills and spikes!"

"Oh, I'm sorry, I didn't notice..." he stopped and looked at the intertwined tails of black and purple. "I, eh, that's good. I can see you've eventually come to your senses Nightstar."

"I'm glad you approve," Nightstar puffed. "You were looking for us?"

"Yes! You distracted me. It's Rose. Its time!"

"Time?" Amethyst asked.

"Rose is going to clutch," Nightstar told her, "and we are invited!" Sunburst's infectious enthusiasm had him just as excited as the flustered yellow.

"She's ready to lay? During the aurora?" Amethyst said, "Why didn't you say? Skin and scales, Sunburst, take us to her." The yellow dragon had what Nightstar could only describe as an idiotic grin on his face. Any other dragon would find it difficult, but for Sunburst, right now, he was pulling it off admirably.

"Now!" Amethyst shouted, shocking Sunburst into movement.

He leapt into the air, wings frantically beating. "Follow me!" He called back. Both Nightstar and Amethyst launched themselves after him, pounding the air to catch up with the aurora tinged yellow blur, as he darted through the busy sky to his waiting mate.

Chapter 10

Blood Rose gleamed under the light of the aurora, her ruby red scales bright and vibrant as she squatted for a third time and pushed out another egg. The glistening wet ovum rocked gently as it came to rest beside the first two. Its mottled surface rippled green then purple, mirroring the aurora above.

"Look! A third and your belly's still full!" Sunburst declared. Nightstar received another blow to his side. Each time Rose laid an egg, Sunburst would head-butt him to emphasise the event.

"Believe me, I know," Rose replied, sounding weary, "that was the biggest yet, my tail end..."

"It's strong and heathy," Sunburst interrupted purposely. Nightstar suspected Rose's comments embarrassed his yellow friend more than he admitted. She did have a certain way with expressing things with a crude descriptive accuracy.

"Just as an aurora lay should be," Amethyst said. She was pushed up snugly against Nightstar's flank and was enjoying herself immensely. "You're doing fine, Rose. Clutching during the aurora will make for a healthy hatching and strong offspring."

Sunburst had led them back to where Rose waited and they had all escorted her to the secluded place where she had prepared her nest.

Nightstar wondered if the large crows he had seen made huge nests of branches, as this nest was disappointingly just a hollowed out piece of ground. Rose had chosen a spot between some large rocks, a few minutes flight from the meadow. She used her claws to scrape out the centre and pile the earth around the outside, creating a protective mound that would encircle her eggs, giving them no opportunity to roll away.

"Here comes another!" Sunburst said and Nightstar tried to minimise the oncoming head-butt and absorb the blow by pulling back. He was too slow. He still managed to get hit. When he moved the other way he pressed firmly into Amethyst's side, which was more pleasant.

Being stuck between an overly enthusiastic father and a potentially enthusiastic mate wasn't the worst place to be, he was with his friends and was witnessing the actual laying of eggs. He was an onlooker in the first stage in the birth of dragons and suspected that he was the only human—all be it as Nightstar—ever to see such an incredible event.

He was conflicted with many emotions. The laying reminded him of the shame and sorrow he now felt over the unhatched egg he had stolen to become Nightstar. Troubled at the way he used the embryo to change shape, but also pleased he had given the spirit of the little unborn dragon a second chance. He now truly believed that some of that spirit lived on in his dragon persona.

He was also fascinated as a scholar, experiencing the act of laying. Being invited to attend such a personal event, filled him with happiness. But he also felt an acceptance. His friends wanted him there.

And he felt a burning desire for the female dragon that pressed warmly to his side.

Being a dragon wasn't as simple as he had thought, but it was a much better adventure than he had expected. When he returned to his laboratory he would be able to fill his journals with so many eye witness facts and observations it would take him long months, if not years, to record them all.

Rose added two more eggs to her clutch, each one an exact replica of the first in size and shape, but the shells were a unique mixture of pastel colours. The first two were pale yellow, mottled with light brown patches, the third was light blue, surprisingly, and the last two were a light orange shade with a faint marble pattern.

Sunburst lay down beside his exhausted mate, fussing over her and helping to rearrange the eggs until she was satisfied. Nightstar wasn't sure if this would have any physical effect on the dragonets inside, but he was sure Rose new best.

"Five eggs is a fine number," he said to the soon to be parents, "thank you for allowing us to be present tonight." Sunburst inclined his head slightly and he could see that Rose had closed her eyes.

"I think we should let them have some time alone," he said to Amethyst, "Rose is asleep."

"I'm resting," Rose said, cocking open one eye at them, then closing it again.

"And so you should," Amethyst said. "You've had a busy night. If the dragonets are as spectacular as their eggshells, when they hatch, they will be magnificent." It was true and was something that Alduce never considered when he had procured the unhatched egg. The shells were like works of art, their patterns and shades similar, yet each one different. As a scientist, he had been more concerned with the contents inside the shell. Now he looked at the dragon eggs with a different eye.

"I need to stretch my wings, come Nightstar and show me the aurora." She took one last peek at the five new eggs gathered together and launched into the air.

"Fly high and fly free." Sunburst said, dipping his head.

Nightstar bowed low to his friend and took off after the purple dragon as she climbed into the shimmering sky. She was taking her time, lazily flapping her wings as Nightstar caught up to her.

"I want to fly for a while, feel the wind under my wings and see the aurora on my scales," she said.

Nightstar was ready to fly, he needed some space and clean clear flying was just what he desired. He didn't mind the huge gathering of dragons, he actually enjoyed being part of the event. As a human he had been a solitary man, often spending long periods of his life alone. He was still tense after his encounter with Winterfang in the moot chamber and a flight would chase that tension away.

He revelled in the act of flying, a natural thing for any normal dragon, accepted without question. But for him, even after travelling hundreds of miles by wing, he still looked forward to each time he was in the air.

And, he was exceptionally good at it.

"After all the excitement tonight, I would enjoy a simple flight," he said.

"I hope you've not had too much excitement," Amethyst called back. "See if you can keep up!" Her wings became a purple haze as she increased her speed, trying to put some distance between herself and Nightstar.

He suspected this was part of the game she played, he could quite easily catch her, but he let her stay ahead, chasing closely behind as they distanced themselves from the other dragons. They danced through the sky, undulating over low ground, soaring high then plummeting, Amethyst led and he followed.

They travelled south, caught up in the thrill of the chase, leaving the White Mountain behind. Nightstar crested a low hill, his snout almost touching Amethyst's sleek tail. He matched her aerobatics move for move, captivated by her graceful lines, the curve of her neck, the beauty she radiated. It wasn't until she dropped suddenly, so intently was he focused on the dragon in front of him, that he realised they were flying through a deep valley filled with a lake. Nightstar recognised the area as one of the many palaces Sunburst came to catch fish. She plunged downward, twisting like a corkscrew, wings spread wide, spiralling towards the water, Nightstar close behind and gaining. When Amethyst reached the surface of the lake, she levelled off, skimming above the waves, her tail trailing through the water's surface and creating a wake, flicking up a spray of droplets. He flew through the spray, each droplet of water caught the light of the aurora like a sparkling jewel, before it returned to the lake, disturbing the surface and creating whole new patterns.

Amethyst landed on the sandy shore and Nightstar followed her lead, his claws sinking into the soft beach as he came to a halt beside her.

"You fly well," she said, "I could feel you in my wake, unshakable."

"You were quick and agile, I didn't want to lose you."

"And you have not. I am strong and fast in the air, purples are good fliers, but blacks are just as good it would seem."

She moved close and wrapped her tail around his, her powerful grip alive like a snake constricting its prey, but not as deadly. Leaning into her embrace he rubbed her neck with his head, mimicking the action she had performed earlier. Amethyst tilted her head back and crooned in delight. "We are alone now Nightstar. The thrill of the chase is over and I claim my prize."

He had followed her to the lake and realised he had fallen under her alluring spell, the chase she referred to was not the flight of tonight. He surrendered fully to her touch and instinct took over as their passion rose, fuelled by the intoxicating influence of the mystical aurora.

Part Three

Betrayal

Chapter 1

Sunburst flew through the storm and Nightstar followed. Rain and wind buffeted both dragons, they were still far from home and the shelter it offered.

It had been over five months since Nightstar had attended the moot and the black dragon had lived with—and learned from—the White Mountain community. He should really return to his own home soon and record everything he had discovered in his journals. But he also wanted to stay and spend more time with the dragons. There was much to write and he probably should to do it while his memories were fresh.

Black storm clouds darkened the day as the rain grew heavier, huge drops battered his black scales and small rivulets flicked from his wings as he flew through the relentless downpour.

Sunburst was a bright beacon of yellow, easily seen, standing out in stark contrast to the darkening sky. Nightstar was thankful his smaller yellow friend had chosen to lead today, especially as the storm worsened. Sunburst knew the lowlands better than any other dragon, it was his favourite place for feeding and he took the opportunity to come here whenever he could.

Nightstar suspected that this particular trip was a good excuse for the yellow to take some time away from the demands of Rose and his new family. He was now sire to five dragonets, all starting to turn yellow like him, and Nightstar had been there to witness their hatching.

It had been an emotional time especially after the last nest of dragon eggs he had seen. Up until then, the only egg he had cared about was filled with a dead dragonet he had stolen and butchered. His perspective had shifted when he witnessed Rose and Sunburst's clutch emerge naturally from their shells.

His feelings were mixed. He regretted that the small life inside the shell had never come to anything, but he was also glad that he had taken the egg and used it for his transformation. The scientist in him, the part of his personality that was Alduce, was clinical and objective. If he had never taken the egg, he wouldn't have been able to experience life as a dragon. Never would have been able to fly or to hunt, to make friends and live among these magnificent beasts. His studies and research would still be confined to dusty old books. This kind of field work was invaluable and as far as he was aware, unheard of.

The dragon part of his mind and the living breathing entity that had evolved into Nightstar was ashamed and saddened at the act of theft and the loss of one small life that would never experience all the things he had. He knew, deep down, this hadn't been his fault. The egg hadn't hatched, this was a natural occurrence and he wasn't to blame. Had Alduce exploited the situation? Was he morally wrong to do so? He was literally in two minds about the whole process, his human and dragon minds, both part of the same being, but both individuals in their own right. This wasn't something Alduce had anticipated, there was no guide book to follow, no instructions on how to become a shape changer. He decided thoughts of this nature were probably best conducted in his human form, back in the safety of his laboratory and he would need to decide soon when he was going to return there.

A rumble of distant thunder rolled through the rainclouds and muffled the unending noise of the downpour. Nightstar was pulled back from his daydreaming by the noise and peered through the storm, unable to see Sunburst. He scanned from side to side, searching the sky in front, but the yellow dragon had disappeared. The constant rain and the droning of the wind had a hypnotic effect when you flew through its midst. The sound eventually became secondary and his mind wandered, causing him to lose sight of his friend and guide.

Panic isn't something a dragon is prone to. However, Alduce was all too familiar with the concept as it started to build. The dragon inside kept him level-headed, he was Nightstar, the mighty black dragon, wind and rain were nothing to be concerned about, his wings were strong and his scales were tough.

He squinted against the rain, scanning the storm clouds, flying blindly, but with more confidence now, looking below for land or anything visible that would help him. As he craned his neck towards the ground, the mystery of where Sunburst had gone was solved. The yellow dragon was flying directly below him, using the larger black as shelter from the worst of the torrential rain.

Thunder rumbled again, this time it was louder and accompanied by a flash of lightning a few seconds later. Nightstar felt a strange sensation in his chest, anxiety building as the tingling feeling grew. He folded his wings and dropped through the rain until he was alongside Sunburst, then levelled out. Rain bounced off the yellow dragon as his make shift shelter no longer offered protection from above.

The wind suddenly gusted, buffeting both dragons across the stormy sky and the driving rain drummed off their wings, adding to the already deafening noise of the elements. Thunder roared again, drowning out every other sound. Nightstar's ears throbbed and he could feel the thunder resonate throughout his body.

They were now directly in the path of the thunder and lightning and there was no calm at the heart of this storm. Electricity charged the air and Nightstar's scales tingled as he anticipated the impending strike.

It came with a terrifying crack that lit up the dark sky. A blinding flash left a jagged afterimage across his eyes. He blinked and raindrops ran like giant dragon tears as he tried to clear his vison. The human mind inside the dragon body could stand it no more, small claws of doubt and fear had burrowed their way deep into the man and he was no longer the powerful, fearless dragon.

The silver scales upon his chest thrummed now, there was no pain, but Alduce knew that something was wrong. He sensed the charged magic and could smell the overpowering stench of ozone all around. The last lightning strike had been so close it had almost hit him. Rising through the panic, the practical scientist buried deep within Alduce surfaced. The Flaire pendant was a vital part of the transformation process and it was forged by lightning, harnessing its natural power. It was attracting the lightning like a giant magnet!

The dragon pendant, an artefact forged from Flaire metal, had transformed into a silver star on his chest when he changed shape. It was still there, part of his scales, part of the spell, its fundamental structure unchanged and still the rare metal activated by lightning. He had to escape from the storm before it was too late, before whatever was happening to his body happened.

He screamed through the storm at Sunburst, "We need to... ", but his words were obliterated by another ear splitting crescendo of thunder. It was no good trying to communicate, he had to act now. He folded his wings and started to dive. Lightning cracked, a jagged electric spear of intense blue-white, finally found what it was seeking. The bright star that blazed on his chest.

* * *

Sunburst watched as Nightstar sailed past, his pace quickening. It was too noisy to shout to the black dragon and ask him why he had taken the lead. It was getting harder to maintain course as the storm worsened. The wind buffeted him angrily and the rain assisted, violently rattling off his scales. He pushed harder against the invisible barrier of wind in an effort to catch up to Nightstar, but was unable to regain the lead. He could only hope the black dragon had spotted a break in the clouds, found a better path for them to follow, a better way through the turbulent sky.

Diving to gain speed, he folded his wings, his body like a yellow arrow as it cut through the storm in an effort to keep up with Nightstar. He found himself underneath the black dragon, and to his surprise, the driving rain lessened as Nightstar bore the brunt of the downpour. Tucking himself tightly below Nightstar's belly and taking advantage of his smaller size, he used his friend to break the worst of the rain, making his flight easier.

They were unlucky to get caught in the storm, especially as they were maintaining such a high altitude. He had hoped they would have been able to pass through the dark clouds, suffer the wind and rain for a short time, then emerge into calmer weather. This storm was proving to be larger than normal for this time of year. Usually a few minutes enduring the elements was enough if you met it head on. The storm swept past as you flew directly through it, travelling in the opposite direction. It was as if this storm was drawn to them.

Thunder rumbled distantly and Sunburst was glad he was no longer flying in front. Surely they would exit the storm clouds soon. If flying conditions got any worse, they were at risk of something dangerous happening. Collision with the unseen peak of a mountain or wing snapping gales. It was late in the summer season and the violent autumn weather had arrived earlier than normal.

Sunburst decided that it was time to admit defeat and seek out a dry cave or even a sheltered valley and wait out the abnormal weather.

Thunder sounded again, this time closer and a few moments after his ears stopped ringing the lighting followed. A crisp flash illuminated his surroundings and the star of silver scales above his head started to flicker, oddly alive against the black of his friend's chest. Small sparks flittered and flicked across Nightstar's silver scales and Sunburst was reminded of the flight on the day they had first met. He had told Nightstar that his chest blazed fiercely, like a star in the night. It blazed now, but not with the serenity of a heavenly body, it blazed like the lightning itself, accompanied by the strong smell of magic, potent magic, detectible even through the howling wind and driving rain.

The elements intensified, resuming their attack, his tired wings exposed to the full force of the storm, the black dragon no longer sheltering him from above. Nightstar appeared at his side, not looking his usual robust self. Sunburst doubted he looked that good himself, but Nightstar actually looked pale, if a black dragon could ever look pallid.

He shouted something through the din of the storm, his words stolen by a peal of thunder, drowning out every other sound in the sky. It must be directly on top of them now. The air felt charged and alive, the thunder resonating through his wing membranes, his very bones.

Nightstar closed his wings and plummeted downwards, his glowing silver scales left a trail across the black sky like the tail of a comet. The inevitable lightning strike followed the thunderclap, streaking past Sunburst's head, so close he could taste the ozone, as the crackling bolt chased after the black dragon.

An explosion of blinding white erupted in a silver corona, rain water sizzled and evaporated. Sunburst blinked, his head pounded and his vision swam.

He peered through the storm in search of his friend, but Nightstar was gone!

A small pale shape occupied the space where the huge black dragon had been, limp and falling fast. Sunburst closed his wings and fell into a dive, cutting through the stormy sky in pursuit of the lifeless object that dropped like a stone.

Chapter 2

Alduce slowly surfaced into awareness. His head throbbed and his limbs ached. He tried to move and pain lanced through the inside of his skull. The noise of wind and rain still persisted, muted and distant and he was no longer wet, no longer a dragon battling through a storm torn sky. He tentatively reached out his talon—no, his hand—his human hand, groping in the darkness at the solid ground his naked human form rested on. Prying open gritty eyes was painful and difficult. They didn't want to open but he forced them anyway.

Oppressive darkness surrounded him, pressing in from all sides and for a moment he feared he was blind. He breathed in deeply and exhaled slowly a few times, a trick Caltus had employed when he needed to relax. Gradually his vision returned. He was inside a cave, its entrance dimly visible as a lighter arch in the blackness. The wind and rain still raged outside and he was thankful of the shelter the cave provided.

Why was he here, shivering and naked? His memory was fuzzy and he struggled to stay conscious. Black mushrooms, he thought, I was looking for black mushrooms. No, that wasn't right, he had been a black dragon, flying through the sky, a wonderful black dragon with... Lightning!

He sat up and instantly regretted moving. How was it possible to feel so much pain? He breathed deeply once more, trying to push the worst of it away. Pain was the least of his concerns just now, his body was intact, even though he was sore. He ran his hands slowly over his chilled scales—no, chilled skin—and was satisfied that no limbs were broken. He was badly bruised and pretty roughed up, but nothing that wouldn't heal in time. Then he explored his chest, it smelled scorched. He could feel the tender flesh, his skin broken and weeping and he was grateful he couldn't see it. Agony flared as he examined the wound and his hand came away damp and sticky.

He still wore the amulet around his neck, at least he hadn't lost it and that was something to be positive about. The Flaire had drawn the lightning from the storm and it had grounded on the silver scales of his dragon chest. The toughness of the Flaire scales had protected him. Dragon's armour was renowned for being almost impenetrable. That, coupled with the resilience of the Flaire metal and the powerful magic of his transformation spell, were all contributing factors in his survival.

He had weathered the storm in more ways than one, had been struck by a lightning bolt and still lived.

Which was a miracle.

What he didn't understand was how he survived the fall.

His last waking memory after the lightning crashed into his scaled chest, was losing hold of his dragon form. The charge from the bolt had reversed his transformation spell and he experienced a mid-air metamorphosis from winged flying dragon to naked falling human. The pain, combined with the shock, had been too much for his frail human body to endure. All he could remember before he lost consciousness was gravity pulling him towards the ground and impending death.

The cave darkened slightly as a huge shape pushed noisily through the entrance, blocking out the faint light from outside as it moved inside. Alduce shuffled backwards, still in a sitting position. He wasn't ready to attempt standing on two legs, he was too weak and out of practice.

There was an almighty clatter from the opposite side of the cave and Alduce winced at the noise, his lightning hangover far worse than anything alcohol could inflict. Just as the pain started to fade to a bearable level, a blinding light illuminated the cave. Searing flame caused stabbing pains in his eyeballs, intense heat washed over his skin and his ruined chest, reminding him how burns react when exposed to more heat. It was too much pain for his already weakened body to bear. As he fainted, Alduce saw the source of his agony, a yellow dragon, fire spouting from its widely stretched jaws.

* * *

Sunburst sped downward cutting through the storm. Rain washed off his scales, trailing behind him, a wave of spray flying from his body as he ploughed through the black clouds. The sky had turned darker now with the approach of night and made it difficult to see anything, even with his powerful dragon eyes. Searching for a black dragon in a sky of rain filled storm clouds was an impossible task. The lightning struck his friend and Nightstar had vanished, his silver scaled star radiant for a second, then it was gone.

He wished he could pick out that beacon of light now as he scoured the turbulent sky. He fixed on a shape, pale and trivial as it tumbled and flailed, buffeted by the winds. It wasn't Nightstar, it was too small and insignificant, but it was all he could see. He pulled his wings tight to his flanks and increased his speed, gaining on the falling shape. As he neared he was able to identify what he was chasing.

It was a man!

Men do not fly. Why would a man be dropping through the middle of a storm? There were no men on these shores, this was the land of dragons and no humans were welcome. Did this puny creature have something to do with Nightstar's disappearance? Surely not. How could such a small creature be a threat to a mighty dragon?

Sorcery! He could smell it now, a whiff of strong magic emanated from the pale human. If Sunburst could smell his magic, the man must still be alive, it was too strong to be otherwise. This man would answer for his foul deeds, he would tell Sunburst what he wanted to know. What he had done to Nightstar, what sorcerous wickedness had he wrought upon his friend? He would answer for his actions before Sunburst killed him.

The yellow dragon opened his wings and thrust out his hind legs, talons opened and wrapped around the human, careful not to crush the weak flesh. He needed the man alive. Once his prize was secure, Sunburst controlled his descent, the ground was somewhere beneath him and he didn't want it to rush up unexpectedly to meet him. He continued down, knowing that he must be close to landing. The storm abated slightly, a sign the ground was near, and as he passed

172

through the low clouds he could see the dark landmass below.

He was far across the grasslands, somewhere near the plains where the curly bucks roamed. As he flew, he looked for landmarks he would recognise and soon he knew exactly where he was. There were caves not far from here. A good place to shelter and wait out the storm. He flew close to the ground where the wind was less severe, clutching the human, careful not to drop him. When he reached the forest where he had flown with Nightstar, he knew he was close to his destination. The trees swayed and their leaves rustled as they clung to the branches, too early in the season for them to let go.

Sunburst veered away from the forest as he passed the huge clearing, the caves he sought were just south of here. Soon, he came upon the entrance he was looking for, a tight arch with a large spacious cavern behind. A good place to shelter and the small entrance would keep out the worst of the storm.

He dropped the human body to the ground and it let out a groan, barely audible above the wind. He picked it up with his front legs, cradling it to his chest. Pushing into the cave, he set his burden down on the sandy floor, sniffing at the prone shape. It stank of sorcery, acrid and bitter, but he wasn't afraid, he was a dragon and he had his own magic, protection against sorcery.

Sunburst pushed back through the entrance, leaving the shelter of the cave. He would search for some fallen branches. If he made a fire inside the cavern, his captive would see him for what he was. A large intimidating yellow dragon. Better still, there would be enough light to look into the man's eyes and snare him with his hypnotic stare. He would get the answers he desired and would see any lies the man told. The man would know his life was in danger and he would tremble before the might of a White Mountain dragon.

Sunburst hopped into the air and flew back over the forest. He looked up as thunder, now far distant, rumbled and lightning flickered high up in the clouds. He scanned the night sky with keen eyes, and thought, *where are you, Nightstar?*

* * *

Alduce groaned as he awoke for a second time, his skin slick with sweat. He felt fevered. A fire burned on the opposite side of the cavern, thick boughs crackled and popped as they blazed. A large yellow dragon was curled up beside the flames, their flickering reflection dancing across his scales and casting a warm pattern across the dark rock. A fire burned in the sorcerer's chest and it throbbed like a beating heart.

The yellow dragon looked magnificent... and huge. You forgot just how large dragons were when you had been one yourself. One eyelid slid open and Sunburst glared at him, a deep green eye pierced his existence as the dragon looked deep inside his soul.

"What do you have to say for yourself, human?" Sunburst hissed. "What have you done with the black dragon?"

Alduce understood what Sunburst said and he felt the magic in the dragon's voice. Even without the Flaire artefact's help, he believed he would have known Sunburst's words.

"I have done nothing with Nightstar, mighty Sunburst," he croaked, his throat painful and dry.

"You speak my true name and his, sorcerer. Who has betrayed our trust to you?"

"No-one has been betrayed. You know the power a sorcerer has over someone if he knows their true name. I will not share them with anyone, believe me."

"That I do believe, but you are still a liar! You are correct when you say no-one else will know our true names as you will not leave this cavern alive. Our secret will die with you," Sunburst growled.

"You remind me of Galdor the Green, he was an angry dragon when I first met him. Oh, he would threaten to eat me, try and terrify me with his awesome power, but I saved his live, I helped him escape his captivity, me, only me, a mere human and he named me friend." Alduce swayed, dizzy with fever. His mind wandered as his thoughts swam. He was sick, his ruined chest was infected and his open wound was red and inflamed. Heat prickled his skin, his body damp with sweat.

"Nightstar lives," Alduce raved, "he is inside me! Yet I feel I am dying, he is dying." Images of black mushrooms and green dragons filled his head. "If I die,

Nightstar will be no more, all gone and no record." He staggered towards Sunburst and thrust out his arms. "Can you not see me, Sunburst? Do you not understand?" He lurched forward and grabbed the yellow dragon by the snout.

"Look into my eyes, see if I lie! I know you can tell." Alduce thrust his face at the dragon, staring into his green hypnotic eyes.

"What trickery is this?" Sunburst said as he peered back. Alduce could feel the dragon's penetrating stare push deep inside his being, searching for the truth of his words. The magic that all dragons possessed. The power to detect when a lie was told or a truth spoken, probed his mind, desperate for the answer.

"You speak true, human," Sunburst said, pulling away. "How is it so? Your words are nonsense, but they are true! Who is Galdor? You babble, you're words make no sense."

"I will tell you my tale, friend Sunburst, cousin and guide, lover of curly bucks, mate of Blood Rose... "

"Enough!" Sunburst roared, deafening Alduce.

"You sound just like old Winterfang. *Wise* Winterfang," he said. He laughed, putting his palms over his ears. Losing his balance, he stumbled, hands outstretched as he fell, attempting to use the cave wall to support himself. His hands touched the stone and he felt a flash of memory from the rock. Crude pictures adorned the cave wall, faded by time and barely visible, making them difficult to see.

Small men with spears and a great flying beast were scratched on to the stone. Alduce, fever fully ablaze, steadied himself on the cave wall and brushed his fingers gently across the images.

He was standing in the long grass, a spear tipped with sharpened flint, grasped tightly in his hands. A warm wind blew across the savannah and the scent of sweet grass filled his nostrils. The clear blue sky was dotted with a few white clouds and the midday sun warmed his body.

He was surrounded by other men, primitive and ancient. Their brown skin decorated with dark mud, applied in patterns and lines, different from man to man. They bent low, using the swaying grass for cover as they crept silently forward. Alduce looked through the eyes of the body he inhabited, beyond the men of his tribe. How did he know that?

Tall animals, long legged and long necked, grazed not far from their position, unaware they were being hunted. His fellow tribesmen stalked this herd and he was with them, he was a hunter.

Animal heads whipped up in unison, spooked as something alerted them to the stalking tribesmen. No-one had made a noise, they were camouflaged in the long grass and unable to be seen by the beasts. What had started them?

The sky above him darkened as a huge shadow blocked out the sunlight, then was gone. Wind whipped at his long straggly hair and the grasslands swayed around him, an ocean of green waves.

Frantic braying shattered the peaceful silence and the herd beasts scattered in all directions as a huge green dragon banked above the panicking herd, wings spread wide, rear talons reaching forward as it dropped from the air. The braying was now accompanied with screaming as the dragon caught one of the long legged animals with sharp deadly claws, the pitiful screams were cut short as claws tore through the poor beast's body, crushing life and breath from the animal.

Alduce, or rather the body that played host to the sorcerer, was thrown from his feet as a charging herd beast knocked into him as it fled from the dragon and its dying herd mate. Roars of rage filled the air as the angered tribesmen were denied their quarry and vented their anger on the dragon. A brown skinned warrior leapt over his fallen tribe mate, brandishing his own crudely made spear. Alduce watched, amazed, as these primitive men ran towards the green dragon, their long spears flew at the green scaled giant, bouncing off its natural amour like raindrops off leaves. He could only lie and watch as the green dragon turned on the source of its annoyance.

Bright gouts of flame spouted from the dragon's mouth and it roared at the small men that attacked it. Fire ignited the grass, dry and combustible and the world around Alduce was transformed into smoke and fire. His eyes stung and his lungs burned, the stench of scorched flesh assaulted his nose and the screaming of dying humans filled his ears. He rolled onto his belly and crawled, keeping low, away from the carnage.

Alduce pulled his hand back from the cave drawings, as if his flesh had been scolded. Man and dragon opposed in battle, ancient enemies since the dawn of time.

Sunburst's roar was the last thing he remembered before he blacked out again, the images of his fellow tribesmen dying and the stink of their flesh burning, vivid in his fevered mind.

* * *

Sunburst listened as the naked human ranted and raved, his voice slurred and his step unsteady. He fell against the cave wall and babbled something about hunting, a green dragon and fire, before finally falling over and rolling on to his back.

He sniffed the still body and could smell magic, death and decaying flesh. The frail body of the small human was fevered and weak. He didn't think that he would survive much longer. The man had said he knew where Nightstar was and he spoke their true names. What did he mean when he said Nightstar was inside him? He even knew of Winterfang. This was extremely bewildering. Was the man's delirium contributing to his perplexing babble? He said he was dying and Sunburst, as much as he didn't want to, agreed with him. The man wouldn't last another day unless...

No! He couldn't do that. It was against everything he believed in. Humans were the enemy, they were known for their deceit. They weren't friends to dragon kind. Fang and Claw! This is the land of dragons and men shouldn't be here.

But, the man said if he died, Nightstar would die too. The human knew something about his friend and Sunburst was sure he hadn't lied. The man spoke the truth, any dragon could sniff out a lie. His *perception,* his dragon sense, informed him this man held the answers. Answers to the disappearance of Nightstar.

Men don't fall from the sky and they don't learn a dragon's true name. And they do not grab a dragon by the snout!

He needed more time, needed the man to live long enough to tell him where Nightstar had gone. He couldn't — wouldn't — give up until he found his friend.

Something was desperately wrong and the black dragon he had accepted as his brother, needed his help.

The wound on the human's chest wept, the charred flesh stank and he could feel the heat from the man's skin as the fever gripped him and burned through his dying body. If this man was the key to saving his friend, and Sunburst strongly believed this was true, he couldn't let him die until he had given up his secret. He needed to understand what had happened inside the storm and what had happened to Nightstar.

If he was going to do this, he needed to do it soon.

Sunburst sat back on his haunches, extended a talon and flicked at a scale on his chest. Sliding the tapered point of his talon under the yellow scale, he flipped it away from his body and drew the razor sharp tip of his talon across the unprotected skin beneath. The lighter yellow flesh opened and beads of dragon blood dripped from the cut. They clung like red pearls to his talon as he carefully withdrew it and held it upright, making sure not to drop any on the cavern floor.

Before he could change his mind, he held the claw above the chest of the prone man and turned it over, allowing the blood to run back down. Beads pooled at the point of the talon, growing heavier until they were too heavy to hold on.

Drip. A small droplet of dragon blood fell.

Drip. Another followed.

Drip. A third and final drop of blood was released and followed the first two into the open wound.

Sunburst quickly withdrew his claw, holding it up to his mouth as his tongue flicked out and cleaned the remaining blood away. All dragon blood was precious and should never be wasted, the smallest drop held magic so powerful, it should never be unleashed without serious consideration. For Sunburst, that moment had passed and he could contemplate it all day, wasting time while the man died. He needed to act now, his decision may be rash, but the small human before him was only one breath away from his last, whether it be from his own failing body or Sunburst's cleansing fire.

Three drops were all he would risk. He patted the open scale flat on his chest and tapped it with his claw. His yellow armour sealed shut, protecting the scratch below, his skin already starting to heal, the magic in the dragon's blood closing the cut and setting the scale securely in place.

The man groaned quietly, the sound barely above a whisper, pathetic and weak. Sunburst waited, not knowing what to expect, he had never used his blood in this way before. He supposed there would only be two outcomes to his blood sharing. The man would live or the man would die. If he lived, he would make the man tell him what he wanted to know. Dragon blood magic was strong, it might extend the human's life long enough for him to be questioned, to give the answers Sunburst sought, but ultimately he would die from the effects. It would be too potent for the man to withstand for any length of time and would burn through his body, eventually turning his blood to poison.

Only dragons could withstand dragon blood.

If he was wrong and the man survived, Sunburst would have no choice but to kill him. If the moot found out what he had done, he would incur their wrath. Winterfang was a just leader, but he could be ruthless when it came to tradition and the protection of their community. Sunburst imagined sharing his blood with a human would be something that severely displeased the ruler of the White Mountain dragons.

If he was found out, he would be banished or worse. Once he had what he needed, he would make sure the man never left the cave, he would burn the body and no-one would even know what he had done. That was *if* the man survived.

A hissing sound from the man's chest alerted Sunburst something had started to happen. He peered closely at the foul wound and noticed something metallic reflecting in the light from the fire. The man started to writhe, his arms and legs, slowly at first, scrabbled on the dirt floor and he mumbled. Not words that Sunburst understood, another tongue, foreign and arcane.

The silver object embedded in the tangle of torn flesh and blood, was more visible now. The drops of dragon blood had mixed into the mess, pushing away the man's own blood and skin and had exposed a small, perfectly crafted dragon!

The dragon blood hissed as it touched the small silver dragon and wisps of steam rose from the wound. The man groaned louder, his legs thrashed and his arms flapped and flailed like wings that would never fly, but were determined to try.

An odour of magic filled the cave, foreign and acrid, and nothing like the pleasant scent of dragon magic. Sunburst didn't know what he had expected to happen, but this certainly wasn't it. He could only stare as his own blood mingled with the blood of the exposed wound. It moved of its own accord, slowly creeping over the damaged flesh, swirling and mixing, an amalgamation of human magic and dragon magic... and something else.

The wound began to heal, imperceptible at first, but the more Sunburst stared, the more he was able to see the outer damage knit and repair, human skin, paltry and thin formed, the ragged edges of the infected flesh regenerating. As the patch he was watching grew and new skin replaced the ruined old, he saw a shadow of something else below the surface of the new flesh. Black scales!

"NO!" the man screamed out and his eyes flew open, staring sightlessly into Sunburst's own. "Don't beat me!" he whispered, "please... " His eyes closed and Sunburst was thankful. The intense look and the pain was more than he could stand. He had peered into the man's soul and relived an old hurt, a great suffering that this man had endured and it was not a pleasant sensation. The man mumbled again and Sunburst craned his head, moving closer, straining to hear the man's fading voice.

"Don't eat me, mighty Galdor," the man softly murmured. Sunburst was repulsed by the thought of eating this man. He stank of death, and of human magic. "I'm looking for... looking for... black... " his voice faded to a whisper.

What was he looking for? A black dragon? It could only be Nightstar. This was the answer he was waiting for. He leaned in, positioning his ear as close as possible to the man's mouth so he didn't miss a single word.

"Mushrooms!" Screamed the man. His back arched and his chest thrust out, slamming forcefully into Sunburst's snout. The yellow dragon pulled back, human blood covering his nostrils and lips. His forked tongue flicked out instinctually, cleaning away the damp red stain.

His universe exploded as the taste of blood, magic, pain and humanity dragged him from the waking world.

* * *

The yellow dragon and the naked human lay side by side on the cave floor. One dreamed of places and times long past. The other slowly healed. Human blood mixing with the blood of the dragon, repairing the damage the lightning had wrought.

Neither man nor dragon aware the unconventional mix would change their lives forever.

Chapter 3

Alduce cringed as the orphanage overseer brought the leather strap down across his bare shoulders. The tough leather sang out like a drover's whip as it lashed his skin, leaving a third mark, an angry duplicate of the other two.

"Put on your shirt, boy," he snarled. "If I catch you slacking again, next time it'll be six lashes and you'll get no supper. See how you like going hungry."

Alduce pulled on his threadbare work shirt, wincing as the rough material rubbed painfully across his newly inflicted welts. It was bad enough that Bandel hated him, but if the fat overseer deprived him of his supper, watery gruel with lumps in it, he would never grow strong enough to escape.

"Move it!" Bandel shouted and the fat overseer planted a cruel boot on his backside and pushed.

Alduce sprawled forward, arms only partway inside his shirt sleeves, unable to reach out and protect himself. His face broke his fall as it ploughed into the ground and his mouth tasted dirt.

Bandel's sickening laugh rang in his ears as he pushed his arms through his sleeves and scrabbled out of the overseers reach...

* * *

A jagged piece of metal, pointed and sharp like a row of dragon teeth, rasped over the surface of the egg. The tough shell resisted, but little by little, the constant movement of the sharp metal scored a groove across its surface. Each time the metal gouged the egg's surface, fine powdered shell drifted from the foul cut. Backwards and forwards, cutting deeper, a vile unthinkable violation of the unhatched dragon inside...

* * *

Alduce ran towards the outside kitchen and joined the line of sorry looking boys from his work crew. Hot tears streaked through the dirt on his face as he remembered his parents and his loving home.

They were dead. The orphanage was his home now.

His life was harsh and cruel, filled with beatings, hard work and constant hunger. Desolation and anguish were all that he knew, and every day he was reminded of his worth. Self-pity and doubt were his constant companions. This was no life for a young boy and he wished the plague that had taken his mother and father had taken his life too...

* * *

Sunburst experienced the pain of the orphaned boy who had grown to be the dying human, through the magic of their mixed blood. The yellow dragon felt an overwhelming pity as he relived the poor boy's life, drowning in his misery. Human emotions filled with the anguish of losing his family saddened him and he could imagine how difficult his life would have been if he had hatched without his dragon kin.

Sunburst hated humans, an instinct he had been born with, but he would not have wished this torment on anyone, be it man or dragon. A small groan escaped from the dragon, his vivid dream delirium pulled him deeper into the man's miserable life. And Alduce was his true name.

* * *

"I'm sorry lad," Master Caltus said, "I can't be taking on any apprentices without patrons or support."

"Please," a teenage Alduce begged. "I'll work hard. I'm a keen study and I learn fast."

"No!" Caltus raised his voice, "I've told you before. I have to convince the guild before I take on a pupil and I've no reason to stick my neck out for a beggar." He tossed an old loaf from the doorway. Alduce deftly snatched it from the air before it landed in the gutter and someone or something else stole his next meal away. "I'm sorry." Caltus said and closed the door in his face...

* * *

The sharp metal teeth cut open the surface of the dragon egg. Two halves fell away and the unborn dragonet inside was exposed, tiny, black, still, and lifeless. Human hands reached in and pulled the pitiful creature free of the violated shell, invading the dead dragonet's resting place. Remorse and sadness filled Alduce as he cradled the magnificent unborn dragon, showing reverence and respect for the lifeless thing, but he also felt something else, satisfaction. Up until this moment, Sunburst had not experienced anything like this in the man's life, this was something new, Alduce had finally attained a dragon egg, and this heralded a new beginning for the human...

* * *

Alduce was filled with disappointment, he had hoped the sorcerer would take him in this time and his perseverance would be rewarded. The master sorcerer had shown him more kindness than he was used to and built his hopes up, only to have them dashed on the rocky shores of despair.

He pulled a mouldy corner from the stale loaf and threw it violently away. A skinny rat darted from beneath some rubbish and grabbed the unintended offering and scuttled off in search of a safe place to consume its feast.

The rich sons of merchants and city officials, this year's intake of apprentices, sniggered at Alduce as they watched their new master reject him. Their contempt and scorn cut deeper than he expected. He felt like the rat everyone hated, but was grateful for the charity of the unasked for bread. He was destined to dine on the cast offs of his betters, but proud enough to know he could be so much more...

* * *

Sunburst felt the disdain and despair that Alduce had known. Humans were so cruel. Dragons would never subject their peers to this cruelty, to be treated like that rat and not as an equal was unforgivable. Dragons argued, sometimes they fought, but the moot saw to it that everyone was taken care of. He almost felt sorry for the young man as he relived his miserable existence. This was no way to live. It was no life at all being rejected by one's own community. Feeling like vermin, unwanted and unloved. The yellow dragon wondered if he would have managed to survived such hardships and nearly felt respect for this human who had endured such a pitiful reality.

* * *

Thus it continued, Sunburst experienced the life of Alduce, sharing the lows of his life and feeling his pain. The young boy had grown into a man and each step in his miserable life was filled with hardship and struggle. The one redeeming factor that he came to grudgingly admire was that whatever his life threw at him, no matter how low the human was brought, he stood back up and kept going. To do so on his own, with no support from his uncaring community was a sign of great strength, endurance to carry on, no matter how tough life became.

Slowly, as he relived parts of his life, Sunburst came to appreciate and understand the man that was Alduce. His natural instinct led him to believe all humans were evil. Through a combination of fevered dreams, the yellow dragon came to learn just what the human, now sorcerer, had strived to achieve.

The scenes that unfolded and were communicated through the magic of the shared blood, were punctuated with strange visions of something else, the sorcerer conducting his experiments with a dragon's egg. Cutting and draining, scraping and stretching, strange devices that were used to perform unnatural actions that repulsed Sunburst to his very core.

What this human had done to the poor egg was a total mystery to the dreaming dragon. Why he had done these thing was even harder to understand. Unhatched dragon eggs should be left for nature to dispose of. When an egg failed to open they were abandoned and forgotten, not mutilated by humans.

He was forced to witness these sorcerous activities, revealed through the fevered visions of this human's life, but was unable to understand them. They made him sad, Alduce made him sad. He knew he was dreaming and he also knew the dreams were real, memories of the human he had rescued from the storm.

He wished an end to these visions, he had seen more than enough, infected with human emotions and experiences, alien and wondrous, disgusting and yet somehow captivating. He wanted the visions to stop and wished he had never shared his blood. He knew it was wrong and yet he had carried on in hope of learning Nightstar's fate. He wanted them to stop but he also wanted to see more, he was confused at the feelings he experienced but he thirsted for answers. The need for knowledge burned inside his body like the legendary fire his kind could breathe.

A vivid story came to Sunburst, it was an early memory the man clung to, a time before his suffering, a time of joy and of being loved. A cherished memory deep in his past.

* * *

Alduce sat in bed, covers pulled up to his chin, the flickering candle on his bedside table cast a warm glow upon the walls.

"What story would you like to hear tonight, son?" Reytran asked.

"Tell me about the dragon, father!" the young boy exclaimed. "I love dragons!"

"How did I know you were going to ask for that one? Young boys should be wary of dragons, lest they eat you all up!" He leaned in close to Alduce holding his hands up like claws and roaring, then snapped his teeth together.

Alduce giggled, drawing away from his father and pulling the covers over his head.

"Because it's your best story," he replied, the bed covers muffling his voice.

"Then you'll go to sleep, like a good boy?" Reytran asked, pulling the covers back down and tucking them in neatly.

"Yes, father. I'll sleep like a log," he grinned.

"A good way for a woodcutter's son to sleep," his father smiled back.

"It was early in the morning and I had risen to the sound of birds singing. Mother was asleep with our new baby son..."

"That was me!" Alduce squealed.

"...yes it was. Anyway, I had to leave my warm bed to go to work. My task for this day was to hike all the way up to the north forest and fell some of the old giant oaks. The rest of my workmates were camping out there, but I had decided to come home, even though it was a long walk, to help mother look after our new son." He waited, but Alduce didn't interrupt him this time.

"I didn't have to take any tools or drive the wagon, as I had walked back through the trees and it was quicker that taking the old north trail."

"A short... cut, you called it," Alduce said, leaning back on his huge pillow.

"That's right, I was taking a shortcut. The trail swings around, taking the long way there. If I cut through the woods, I wouldn't have to walk as far, it would take me less time, and?"

"You could have longer in bed!" Alduce supplied. He knew the story, having heard it many times before.

"Yes," Reytran said. "You are a smart lad. Anyway, off I set, trudging through the forest on my way to work. It was early and the birds were singing as I marched below the trees. Squirrels leapt from branch to branch, rabbits scuttled through the undergrowth... "

"And you saw a bear!" Alduce added, captivated by the tale.

"I was nearly knocked over by a bear. It came lopping down the path I followed and I don't think it even noticed me as I jumped into the bushes. I didn't know what had startled the bear at the time, but I would soon find out."

"It was the dragon, father. It scared the bear, that's why it was running along the trail."

"I suspect you are right again, son. Even something as large and fierce as a bear is no match for a dragon. So, I picked myself up and removed the leaves from my hair," Alduce giggled, "and trudged north. As I continued through the forest, I noticed how quiet it had become. All the forest creatures had stopped their chatter, the birds no longer whistled and chirped, the were no squirrels jumping in the branches overhead and all the rabbits had gone into hiding.

"I thought it was a little unusual, but since a brown bear had passed this way a few moments before, I suspected this was why they were all quiet. The path grew steeper as I headed farther north, into the higher part of the forest. At last I came to the clearing and the only sound in the whole forest was the twigs snapping and the leaves rustling as I stepped on them. I was wondering to myself why it should be so quiet, now the bear had gone. The forest is usually filled with lots of sounds. And then I saw him... "

"In the clearing? Right in front of you?"

"Yes, he was in the clearing, but was quite a bit away. I crouched down, hiding behind a chestnut tree... "

"The big one where we collect the conkers?"

"The very same. Anyway, I peeked round the tree, I couldn't believe my eyes. There, in the middle of the clearing was the largest, greenest, fiercest dragon I had ever seen."

"But you've only ever seen one dragon! How could you know he was the largest greenest fiercest?"

"Because he was! I could tell you a story of dolls and dresses if you'd prefer?"

"No! That's for girls, I want to hear about the dragon."

"Are you sure?" Reytran teased, and Alduce nodded eagerly. "Well, as I was saying, there in the clearing sat a *huge* green dragon. The sun shone down and reflected off his scales, like green mirrors. Its head was the size of our front door, with big yellow horns the size of my arms," and he held his arms high, stretching them out behind his own head, "and white fangs just as long. A giant tail flicked left and right, the grass and bushes flattened in its path.

"As you can imagine, coming across such a terrifying creature wasn't something I was expecting and I was too scared to move from my hiding place. I watched the dragon as it devoured a deer it had caught for breakfast. Its mighty jaws crunched bones as it ate everything, even the hooves and antlers. I thought, if it's that hungry, I'd better not let it see me, I didn't want to end up in a dragon's belly.

"Once it had finished its meal, it spread huge wings the size of a barn roof and leapt into the air, flapping. The draught from its wings rustled the leaves, like a storm blasting through the treetops, as it took off. I watched it fly high into the sky until it was just a tiny speck, then it was gone, as if it had never been."

"Do you think it will come back?" Alduce asked, his eyes drowsy with sleep.

"I don't think so, Alduce," Reytran said. "Dragons are rarely seen these days. You don't have to worry."

"I'm not worried, father," he murmured. "One day I *will* see a dragon and I won't be frightened."

"Maybe you will," Reytran said, standing and fixing the covers, tucking them in around his son.

"I wish I was a dragon," Alduce said as Reytran bent and kissed the small boy on the forehead.

"I'm glad you're not, Alduce. You'd need a bigger bed." Alduce closed his eyes, surrendering to sleep. Green dragons filled his dreams.

* * *

The man continued to heal, aided by the power of the living dragon blood as it flowed through his veins and regenerated the damage the lightning had inflicted. His fever broke and the dragon blood worked its magic.

As the dragon's blood circulated through the man's body, it allowed his yellow saviour to experience his life and his emotions, both confusing and human, but it also changed his view on what a human was.

One last segment of the sorcerer's strange existence was yet to be revealed, exposing the sought after answers he so desperately wanted. The answer to the question he desired would not be the revelation he expected.

Chapter 4

Sunburst's dreams swirled and merged with the fevered mind of Alduce. The man's body was healing, he could sense the magic and feel the power of his blood and knew this would end soon. A final vision swam up to meet him and he could feel the anticipation, the expectation of something long awaited by the sorcerer.

It was night and a crescent moon hung at a strange angle in a sky full of unfamiliar stars. Alduce was high on a hilltop, but nowhere as high as the White Mountains.

He was naked and alone, sitting inside a circle of bones, pushed into the ground. The bones of a small dragon! The skull of the unborn dragonet, torn from the egg in his previous visions, was placed at his feet. Sunburst didn't know how he knew this, he just did. He could feel the cold night wind as it brushed over the tense skin of the sorcerer. The feeling was nothing like the wind on his own scales. Hairs stood out on his human neck and he was filled with excitement. His heart beat and Sunburst could feel the thudding pulse as it pounded in his ears. Alduce was filled with anticipation... and fear.

He grasped the small silver dragon that hung around his neck and Sunburst could feel the thrum of intense magic from the tiny object. He dipped his fingers into the bowl that sat on the ground before him and began to rub the contents over his naked skin. The skin felt strange, smooth and soft, yielding and weak, so different from the tough protective feel of scales.

Alduce shivered as the cold thick liquid made contact with his body and the yellow dragon shuddered as if an icy wind had chilled his very being. His body began to shake, there was something wrong, the liquid felt alive. He could sense another dragon's blood as it touched the flesh of the man, chilling him to the bone.

Alduce positioned the small skull in the centre of the bone circle and Sunburst smelled blood, human and dragon. He placed a small coating of something dark upon his shoulders. Tiny dragon scales! Black and hard, cold and dead.

Skin and scales! It was the hide of the unborn dragon!

He felt the thrum of magic as it started to build, his own scales prickled as it coursed through his body. A flood of magic unlike anything he had ever experienced before. The power was intense and was filled with the stolen life force of the dead dragonet.

The scales and skin enveloped Alduce, crawling across his pale human flesh, wrapping his limbs, sliding over the cold liquid, tinkling metallically as it moved.

Heat blasted through him, burning the chill away, like molten magma over ice. The small black dragonhide grew, stretching and expanding, wrapping round limbs and hiding human skin as it fully covered the body of the man, sealing him inside. He picked up the small skull with fingers that had taken on the shape of talons and held it aloft. The silver scales that formed a star shape on the chest of the man-dragon glowed with an ethereal light. The night star! The sorcerer inside the dragon's skin used a lifetime of knowledge and understanding to call forth the magic that now begged for release.

Lightning erupted from above, blinding and bright as it lanced into the pitiful skull of his unborn kin. Jumping from the skull, the discharge of energy sparked and spat, connecting with the bones forming the circle. Sunburst felt the electricity course through his body, the body that was Alduce, now one and the same.

Alduce dropped the skull and it bounced off the hard ground, the brightness from the lightning flash faded, pale moonlight the only source of illumination on the mountain.

The thing that was neither man nor dragon swayed and its legs buckled as it dropped to the ground. Heat burned as super charged magic flowed beneath his scales, beneath the human skin, it was difficult to separate the two, as everything was mixed together. Spears of pain probed through the burning heat and

Sunburst's agonising roar echoed around the cavern where his body lay. His mind, he knew, was a world away upon a distant darkened hill top.

Just when he thought the pain was as much as he could withstand, his limbs began to change, making it worse. Never had he imagined a pain so excruciating and so terribly intense. Unbearable and unstoppable.

Slowly the thing that was a human-dragon hybrid started to grow, stretching and filling, flesh no longer human, transformed into the black scales of a dragon. Talons bulged, wings sprouted and a spiked tail thrashed out, a giant whip, tipped with a razor sharp point, the tail of a real dragon.

This new creature reared up on powerful dragon legs, the pain abruptly gone, and roared once more. Sunburst roared too. The first time his roar had been a sound of agony and pain, now it was one of triumphant success, exhilaration at finally completing the transformation.

Nightstar—there was no doubt now in his mind that this was him—stretched his wings fully and Sunburst knew he had witnessed the birth of his missing friend. Not from an egg, but from sorcery, lightning, human secrets, and lies.

Adrenaline suddenly turned to panic, as Alduce, trapped in the form of this new dragon, feared he would never be able to change back. Why would he want to change back? This black dragon was perfect, magnificent and invincible. Scales of deepest night gleamed like black diamonds, a silver star upon his chest shone in vibrant contrast. Would such a puny human really be fearful of not being able to revert back to his former self when he could live as something more? Something so much better!

The will of the man asserted itself, taking control of the magic and slowly the dragon began to shrink. White light shimmered over his body, highlighting each scale as a reversal of the transformation reduced the huge form to a naked human. Scales shrank and were absorbed into the man's skin until no trace of the dragon remained.

Alduce ran his hands over his skin and Sunburst could feel smooth cold flesh where the hard scales had been. The night breeze cooled his body and he shuddered, icy shivers wracking his tiny human frame. The trauma of the transformation took its toll and the man fell as he lost consciousness.

The connection between man and beast severed and the yellow dragon drifted deep into a restless slumber, thankful that he was no longer part of the man's memories.

Chapter 5

Sunburst was miserable when he awoke. The blood healing had let him experience the negative events in the human's life. A human he had saved for the second time.

The connection to Alduce and his fevered dreams had been made when the man was dying, at the lowest point of his existence and he lived through the human's misery, tasted his pain and felt the anguish the man had endured. His usual happy demeanour had been influenced by the sadness and misery and he actually felt sympathy for Alduce, which was unexpected, as dragons did not empathise with humans, they loathed and despised them. They were untrustworthy.

But, he also felt the joy, the pure exhilaration of shape changing, transforming into something new and different and becoming a dragon. And the excruciating pain that had accompanied that transformation. How could such a small creature, so weak and seemingly fragile, endure so much agony? The man, Alduce, was stronger than he appeared, even on the brink of death he wouldn't give up and clung to life.

The drops of blood Sunburst had administered hadn't just postponed inevitable death, it appeared they were repairing the damage to his chest. His blood should not have cured the dying man. It should have sustained him for a short while, then burned through his body, consuming him. Sunburst now knew the reason why.

Alduce was Nightstar. He used human sorcery, the charm he wore around his neck and the machines he had seen in their shared visions. Somehow he had used these to change from man to dragon.

This was not right! It should never be allowed. But who could have stopped it? No-one knew but him and it had already happened. It was an abomination, unnatural and... wrong?

Everything screamed inside Sunburst that this shouldn't be, but this was Nightstar, his friend. They had become like egg brothers, he was everything a dragon should be. Everything a real dragon should be.

Now he understood why the black dragon had acted so unusually. It wasn't that he came from beyond the eastern ocean or that he hadn't any traditional upbringing.

He had lied. He had made it all up, fiction to trick a stupid yellow, a gullible fool that believed any cruel lie fed to him.

Yet... he had come from somewhere and it was beyond the ocean and he hadn't been raised by dragons. Sunburst would have—should have—detected these untruths, but he hadn't. Was it because Nightstar... Alduce, he was called Alduce, could mask the truth? From a dragon? Impossible! Sunburst had been fooled, surely older wiser dragons would detect his secret and see him for what he really was. Winterfang has missed it too! And Amethyst. How could she have been fooled? They had grown close, why hadn't she found out what he really was?

But what was he? Nightstar was real, he was a dragon. This was all very confusing. Sunburst had never heard of anything like this, ever. In all the myths and tales of his kind, no-one had ever encountered a situation like this. He was the only dragon in existence to face this dilemma and he didn't have the first idea of what he should do.

Should he flame Alduce where he lay? Burn him to a charred pile of bones? Finish this now and keep everything he had learned to himself? He couldn't bring himself to kill what was locked inside the human, he couldn't kill Nightstar. He didn't have the right to murder the black dragon like that. He didn't know if Alduce would still be able to change back to Nightstar. He had sustained near fatal injuries and had some of Sunburst's blood in his veins now, this might have altered him, altered his magic. Dragon and human magic shouldn't mix, should be incompatible. Sunburst had no idea if adding his live blood to the sorcerer's would change the balance, ruin the spell or kill the man.

There was only one thing he could do, repulsive as it sounded, he would have to wake Alduce and converse with him. This time he would ask the right questions now he knew Alduce was Nightstar. The man would answer and be held accountable. And if he didn't tell him everything he wanted to know and his blood didn't kill him. Well, then he would decide what action to take next.

Chapter 6

Alduce stirred, groaning as he opened his eyes. He was soaked in sweat but his fever had broken and he was still alive. He gently probed at the wound in his chest and was amazed to feel tenderness rather than the expected pain. The flesh had actually repaired itself. Tight pink skin replaced the charred and weeping mess that had been there before. Outside the cave, last night's storm had been replaced by the dull light of day. The embers of a vaguely remembered fire had all but burned out and lying beside it, the green-eyed yellow dragon stared at him, cold and unwelcoming. The face of his former friend bore an expression between disgust and hatred. The good natured Sunburst had vanished. This was the look of a dragon of legend, foreboding and fierce, no friend of mankind.

Alduce understood his resentment. He had deliberately deceived Sunburst, told him lies, misled him, abused his trust and his friendship. He didn't blame the yellow dragon one bit, if their roles had been reversed, he would feel the same.

However, he was still alive and that had to count for something. He couldn't remember much after the lightning had struck and reversed the transformation. All he could recall was falling through the storm, the terror of plummeting and the agony in his chest. He had been in a fevered state and dredged up unpleasant memories, bad times in his life he would rather forget, times of misery and hopelessness.

He met Sunburst's eyes and was lost for words, he wished the dragon would speak, rather than the unflinching stare he fixed on him. He should wait to be addressed and show respect but an idea came to him. He stood on shaking legs, weak from his ordeal and bowed deeply, as if presenting himself to a king. The dragon's eyes followed his movements, but his head was like a yellow statue, rigid as stone. Alduce held his bow for what seemed an eternity, naked and cold, his limbs trembled with fatigue as he waited for a reaction.

"Enough, Alduce," Sunburst spat. He hadn't revealed his true name, yet the dragon knew it.

"You know who I am?" Alduce croaked, sitting down before his legs gave way.

"I know everything about you, sorcerer. I've tasted your vile blood and seen inside your soul, black as the scales you hid behind. You can deceive me no longer." Sunburst was a different dragon, he was angry and Alduce felt an implied threat behind his words. He could offer an apology, tell the dragon he was sorry but it wasn't enough. An apology felt trivial, a friend deserved more. He would try a different tactic. He needed to rescue this situation before Sunburst decided there were one too many humans present for his liking.

"If you know all about me, Sunburst, you will know that we were friends, true friends," Alduce spoke from the heart and a dragon would know this was no lie.

"I don't have the words to tell you how deeply shamed I am to stand here like this." There was no reaction from Sunburst, he had resumed his staring silence, but Alduce knew that he was listening. He was alive at Sunburst's indulgence when he should either be smashed and broken on the ground or burned so badly from the lightning it should have destroyed him.

He needed to get Sunburst talking. If he didn't, he could see in the dragon's eyes how this would end. He recalled the way Galdor had looked at him when they first met. A cold hatred towards humans and a murderous look in his eyes. The same look Sunburst fixed on him now. He remembered the terror of the young apprentice who feared for his life. He didn't want Sunburst to look on him like that. He didn't want to be afraid of his friend. The only difference between Galdor when he first encountered him—and Sunburst now—was the colour of their scales.

"I am alive because you rescued me and I don't know why." He let the statement hang between them, careful to phrase it so it didn't sound like a question, but hopeful Sunburst would supply an answer. He waited and was rewarded with a response, just not the one he wanted to hear.

"Clever, Alduce. You have posed me yet another question without asking it

199

directly. However, I will answer it, but know you try my patience. Surely you must know how patient a dragon can be," he thrust his snout forward, scant inches between them, "and how much you test mine." The yellow dragon pulled his head back, shaking it from side to side, his mannerism oddly human.

"I do not know the *why* either. Why I rescued you from falling through the storm or why I did what I had to do to keep you alive. What you should have asked is *how*." Now Sunburst waited, turning the situation and throwing it back at Alduce. A familiar trait the yellow dragon often employed. Alduce remembered the last time he had done this. They had been friends then.

He remembered when Sunburst had told Nightstar, that after his first visit to the White Mountain, he would never be a stranger again. The loss of that friendship pained him deeply, much more than he thought it would.

Sunburst's words confused him. The dragon couldn't give him a reason for saving him, only how he had done so. But would he tell that to the despised human?

"I think I understand. You don't know why you actually saved me, you did it, but you are unable to say what drove you to do so."

"I rescued a pitiful human who was dropping through the storm as the dragon who was my friend vanished, leaving strong traces of magic behind. I snatched you from the air before you fell to the ground because I wanted answers from you. You were all that was left in the sky after Nightstar had gone. I suspected you had something to do with his disappearance and I brought you here to find out what you knew. To see if there was something I could do to find Nightstar, help him if he needed it. What I discovered was, there is no Nightstar anymore, only Alduce the deceiver."

"Thank you for saving me." Alduce whispered.

"Do not give me your thanks. Your life hangs in the balance and the scales are tipped against you. I will tell you how you survived, as it makes no difference, your crime is punishable by death and you look upon your executioner."

"Nightstar isn't gone, you're wrong!"

Sunburst started to growl, but Alduce needed to tell him the truth. "At first, I thought I was Nightstar and he was me, but now he is more than just a shape I take. I'm still there, inside, but Nightstar has grown, become a dragon in his own right. A real dragon, not the black cloak of scales I donned. Nightstar has shown me things I could never have imagined. I, Alduce, am a scholar, a scientist, and a sorcerer, it is true. But I tell you this, Sunburst of the White Mountain, your kin have taught me that which I could not learn. Nightstar has shown me a new life, changed how I look at things and made the man into much more than just skin and scales. I *know* the dragon I brought forth isn't just a sorcerous conjuration, an illusion of life, he is Nightstar in his own right and always will be."

It felt like a confession as the words poured from him, the explanation said more than an apology ever could. He was glad he had finally told the yellow dragon what he was, how he felt and hoped his former friend would understand the turmoil inside him.

"Look into my eyes and tell me if I lie! You can see I speak the truth. Why do you think no-one saw Nightstar for anything other than what he was?"

"Human sorcery and magic, you used it to trick everyone!"

"I thought so too, I really did, but think about it for a minute. There's no magic a dragon can't sniff out, no matter how strong the spell, you said it yourself, you can smell it, taste it."

"But, you could have…"

"No, I couldn't, you know it! You named yourself my executioner, if you don't believe what I say, flame me, right now, end my miserable human life. I won't stop you. Even though I know your true name, I would never use it against you to protect myself."

Alduce took a risk, if Sunburst meant to end his life, he could have simply let him drop through the storm.

But he didn't.

If he changed his mind after saving him, he could have easily left him to die in this cave.

But he didn't.

Instead he had done something to heal him, something he was reluctant to tell him about. Yet another question to ask.

Alduce spread out his arms, he would remain defenceless against any action Sunburst took against him. He could call on the magic of the Flaire pedant he wore, but he wouldn't. He would take a chance and put his fate into the hands, or claws, of the yellow dragon. He would accept any judgement Sunburst would make. He hoped Nightstar's friendship with Sunburst was enough to save him. He knew the yellow dragon, his heart was good and he didn't have the capacity to be a cold blooded murderer.

"If you wish to end my life, go ahead. I am ready to be judged and will accept any sentence you believe fit."

Sunburst began to grumble, wisps of smoke escaped from his nostrils and Alduce was close enough he could feel the heat from the fire in the dragon's throat. He had pushed the dragon too far and he was going to burn for his arrogance. He braced himself for the end, at least he had shared the experiences of Nightstar, had known other dragons and lived among them, even if only for a short while. His one regret was he never had the chance to record anything in his journals. Even if no-one ever read his life's work, he would always be a scholar.

The yellow dragon leaned forward and looked straight into his eyes. And stopped. Alduce could feel the hypnotic pull of Sunburst's gaze as he searched the truth of his words. Then, to his surprise, the yellow dragon sat back on his haunches like a faithful dog and swallowed down the flames he had summoned with a gulp.

"I can't kill you Alduce and I know I shouldn't let you live. Yet you speak the truth, I can see it plainly. What have you done? What have I done? What will we do now?"

Alduce breathed a sigh of relief. He had counted on the humanity of the yellow dragon to save him. He didn't know if humanity was the right word, but his day was confusing enough already to debate the use of the word. It worked for his brain, he just wouldn't dare put it that way to Sunburst.

Alduce understood Sunburst's confusion, he had lived with the same conundrum for months and it still troubled him. But, he had an idea. He didn't only want to escape his fate, he wanted to save Nightstar.

"I will tell you what I think you have done. You have saved Nightstar, just as you wanted. Your friendship for him was once great, as his was for you. And still is. What I have done is more complicated. I have created a life, brought a dragon into being when all I expected was to take the shape of a creature I admired. I wanted to know more about dragons after my encounter with Galdor the Green, a wise an ancient dragon that showed me a kindness long ago. He took a chance and trusted me beyond our mutual prejudice."

Sunburst listened intently and Alduce could see some spark of Nightstar's friend in his eyes. It would be unfair to say that his expression softened, as he would never describe a dragon as soft, but with Sunburst, he was the exception to the rule.

"If I was given the chance to go back, knowing what I know now, would I do it again? No. I can see how I have hurt you, lied and deceived you and your kin. I would miss Nightstar, but I would miss his friendship with Sunburst even more. I cannot truly tell you what I have done, as I don't know myself. But, I have a suggestion to put to you. You asked what *we* will do now. I will leave your world, travel back to my own and you will never see me again and Nightstar will no longer fly in your skies. Alduce will never set foot on your world again. We will be gone, you won't have to kill me and I will take your true name to my grave."

Silence returned to the cave as Alduce gave Sunburst time to consider his words. The yellow dragon had much to contemplate.

"I gave you my blood," Sunburst said. "I saw it all, I lived your life through your eyes as you writhed in fever. I saw the orphanage, felt the whippings. How can one human do that to another? I felt the misery, the sorrow, and the shame. I saw Caltus, I saw Galdor. I felt the agony you endured when you become Nightstar, the pleasure of your first flight. I know your mind and your heart, I've seen what you were and what you've become. I saw you cut open the egg. The egg you stole and I hate you for it. I admire you for all you have accomplished, your strength, your thirst for knowledge and your tenacity. You never give up. You wouldn't lie down and die, even when the lighting burned a hole in you! I healed you with three drops of my blood, I thought it would revive you for a short while. I never knew it would save you, but it has." Sunburst faced him and Alduce was humbled by his next words.

"We are brothers of the blood. It should never have been, but it is done."

"You gave me your blood! You've seen my life?"

"Not all of your life, but enough to know the man that you were and the man you have become. You are right, the differences between man and dragon are prejudices learned, and it is difficult to change them. Know this Alduce the sorcerer, Nightstar the Black, you are free to leave and return to your world. My blood will extend your life and give you good health, it is an unintentional gift I have bestowed upon you. I trust you to tell no-one of the magical properties of living dragon blood. You know we would be captured and bled, kept like cattle to cure human illness if this secret were ever known. It is fortunate that when we die, our blood magic dies with us."

"You have my word, Sunburst. I will need a few more days before I can travel to the place where I entered your world. It is too far for me to go on foot and I will need my strength before I attempt to summon Nightstar and fly again," he paused. "If I can."

"There are fruit trees and water not far from the cave. Be careful you are not seen, as any other dragon would flame you to the bone should they see a human on our shores." Sunburst stood and turned his back, his tail flicking from side to side in agitation.

"Sunburst," Alduce called after him. "Thank you, my friend."

"I have already told you, I don't want your thanks, your word will suffice. And we are not friends, Nightstar *was* my friend. We are at best adversaries, trussed together by a secret we should never know, by blood we should never have shared and a lie that should never be spoken."

He turned his back on the man, never looking behind as he left the cave. Once he was clear, Alduce stumbled to the entrance and watched as the yellow dragon climbed into the sombre morning sky. Sunburst breathed a gout of fire into the air, expelling the flame he had called forth to burn Alduce before he changed his mind. The sky was filled with a mighty roar as the yellow dragon vented his anger.

Alduce dropped to his knees and wept.

Chapter 7

Nightstar flew south. It had been four days since Sunburst had abandoned his former friend and left the cave where he recuperated. He had rested, sleeping long into the mornings, gathering fruit to eat and branches to burn at night to ward off the cold. He was still naked and had nothing to wear, with only the cave to provide shelter, he was glad it wasn't winter.

Alduce waited four days before attempting to change back into Nightstar, his human form was weak and he needed to gather his strength. Concerned the lighting strike or the blood from Sunburst would somehow effect the transformation, he was relieved when he successfully changed back into the black dragon.

After close examination, he was happy to find that nothing had changed, Nightstar was undamaged and fit for flight. The dull pain in his newly healed chest was to be expected, the magic from Sunburst's blood had performed a minor miracle, but as both Alduce and Nightstar, it would be a while until the pain faded and they were both fully healed.

He was alive and on reflection, he was lucky to have survived, and even luckier that Sunburst had chosen to save him and decided to let him live.

Any hope that their friendship could be repaired, as his chest had been, was gone. No magical ingredient could have been added to change the hurt the yellow dragon felt. He had left Alduce, torn between a myriad of emotions, confused and angry. Alduce suspected that Sunburst understood more than he admitted. The dragon had seen inside his mind and touched his feelings. It may have been alien and new to him, but dragons were intelligent creatures and the complexity of the Alduce-Nightstar relationship hadn't been lost on the yellow dragon.

Was that why he was so upset? He had told Alduce he admired him, then said he hated him. He had seen through human eyes and understood what Alduce had accomplished.

The scholar would have plenty of time to contemplate the last few months when he returned home. Home... it was a hollow lifeless place after living with the White Mountain dragons. It was a workplace, a laboratory, and a study. A place to work and a little room with a bed to sleep in. As Nightstar he had friends to share his life with. He would miss that. His studies and experiments would always be there for him, it was what his life as a human was. It had been fine before his experiences in Sunburst's world and he had been content with his life. It would be fine again. He had a lot of work to catch up with and that would keep him busy. But after the last few months he wasn't sure *fine* was good enough anymore.

Nightstar searched the hillside below for the cave he had used to enter this world. The portal he opened would still be hidden safely inside, out of sight. It was his way back.

A metallic blur sped past his snout as he focused on the land below.

"Nightstar!" the copper coloured dragon cried out, "I have found you."

"Little Wing, you're far from home. Why are you looking for me?" Nightstar was worried. What if Sunburst had changed his mind? Had he returned to Winterfang and told him about Alduce, about the imposter within their midst that he had set free? Surely the moot leader would have sent more than just one dragon to find him? Little Wing was of the autumn contingent, they tended to have more to do with upholding tradition and making sure everything ran smoothly. Something was amiss. At least it hadn't been Galvon that had found him, Nightstar was sure the green dragon was suspicious of everything and did not like him. Forest greens, he had discovered, were like that.

"I've been searching for you for days. Winterfang asked my wing to come south to find you. Galvon and Raynar are with me," she scanned the sky, "somewhere."

"What does the moot leader want with me that's so important he sends you this far from your duties?" There were only two reasons why the frost drake would be searching for him. Had Winterfang discovered Nightstar had trespassed in the moot chamber and interacted with the pearl? Or did he know the black dragon's secret? Either option was something he would rather avoid. He peered across the hillside searching for the cave that would grant his escape. He would easily be able to escape from Little Wing, but if Galvon and Raynar joined her, he would be in trouble with three dragons to outfly. He readied himself to flee, there was no sign of the other two dragons. He should lose Little Wing now, shake her off before her reinforcements arrived and return to his world, closing the portal behind him forever.

"Winterfang needs your help," Little Wing said. "He thinks you might know why Sunburst left and where he has gone. Rose is worried. She said he was acting strange."

"Strange?" Nightstar hesitated, this wasn't what he had expected.

"Well, stranger than that yellow normally behaves. You are his friend, you know what I mean. He returned to the mountain four nights ago. Rose told us he was agitated and she questioned him about you and why he returned alone. He told her you were lost."

"Let's land," he called to the copper dragon, "and continue our conversation on the ground." He was curious to find out what Sunburst had said, what he'd done, and why Winterfang needed his help. He descended to a grassy hillock and Little Wing followed, landing beside him. He would still be able to evade her if necessary, but he didn't want to risk flying any farther as she might be able to sense the portal's energy if they flew any closer to the cave.

"Sunburst has left the White Mountain. No-one has seen him in three days. Rose knows his behaviours, he often disappears for longer, but he usually flies south or west, sometimes north. This time he flew east."

"There is nothing to the east," Nightstar said, "the best hunting is south or west. The east has nothing Sunburst likes, just the ocean and he hates the smell of salt."

"Exactly!" Little Wing said, "Winterfang was right to have us search for you, out of all the White Mountain dragons, with the exception of Blood Rose, you know him best." Even the dragons of the moot thought of him as one of their own, it seemed.

"She was concerned with his mood, he spoke as if he would not be returning. I know she would have followed him if she could, but she has her hatchlings to tend to."

"That's not like him, she has five dragonets to look after. He wouldn't just leave. What more did he say?"

"I do not know, Nightstar. Winterfang felt it was important that we find you soon. He consulted the pearl of wisdom and hopes you will help us, after all, you are one of us now. We were concerned for you both. Do you know why Sunburst would act like this? And why did he leave you here?"

Nightstar considered what Little Wing had said. Could he really contemplate leaving without helping? Could he abandon Sunburst? It was his fault the yellow dragon was angry and upset. It was Alduce and his deceit that were to blame for Sunburst acting out of character. He had returned to Rose and then left her. Nightstar knew how much his mate and their clutch meant to the yellow dragon. Why had he abandoned them? Sunburst had been conflicted when they parted, upset with what he had discovered and at using his blood to save a human. It was Alduce who was responsible for this, he had driven Sunburst away and it was up to Nightstar to fix things. At first he thought Little Wing's story might be a ruse, to keep him occupied while her companions found them. That they knew his secret and this was all a trick to lure him back to Winterfang and the justice of the moot. Now his suspicion turned to concern. She was genuinely worried for Sunburst, his dragon sense confirmed it. He was too.

"I'm sorry Little Wing, I don't know why he would leave like that." He hadn't directly answered the first question she asked, he knew what had upset Sunburst but couldn't tell the copper dragon. "We encountered a huge storm, five nights ago, we were far to the south. It was one of the worst storms I have ever experienced." That at least wasn't a lie.

The more he thought about how intense the storm was, the more he was convinced the Flaire artefact had acted as a catalyst, amplifying the unusually violent storm. They had hoped to fly through the worst of the weather, but the heart of the storm was wherever Nightstar flew. He had been at its centre and the Flaire had attracted the lightning.

"The sky was black and we were caught off guard, we tried to fly through it, but it was unending. Once the thunder and lightning were upon us, we became separated. We couldn't see each other, the wind and rain buffeted me, battered my wings so hard. I had to land, it was impossible to fly in such conditions."

"The storm passed over the mountain," Little Wing said. "It was bad when it reached us and I can only imagine how wild it must have been for you to stop flying. Everyone knows how skilled you are in the air."

"Not skilled enough. I couldn't see Sunburst. I searched as best I could but the conditions were just too severe. That must be what he meant when he said I was lost." He had no choice but to tell another lie and hoped it would protect Sunburst as well as himself. "I couldn't see him and when the storm subsided, I realised I had been driven a lot farther south than I expected. I spent a few days flying round in circles, looking for Sunburst, but if he returned to the White Mountain four days ago, he must have ended up north of where I was. I suspect he was carried by the winds, rather than landing, his smaller wingspan would have allowed him to keep flying. He's a better shape and size to navigate through such adverse weather."

"No-one doubts your loyalty to him, you were not to know where he was, or he you. It is commendable that you have taken these days to seek him out, others may not have done so."

They were distracted by the sound of wings in the sky above as Galvon and Raynar dropped down to land beside them.

"Well done 'Wing," Galvon said, "you've found him."

"We are glad to see you safe, Nightstar," Raynar said. "Aren't we Galvon?

"Yes. If it means we can return home, yes we are! If Winterfang thinks you can help, then yes. I know that dammed yellow is a nuisance but the moot leader is rarely wrong. The pearl has warned him. *We* need your help."

"Thank you, Galvon. Raynar," Nightstar replied. Even the crusty old green was asking for his aid. What had Winterfang foreseen? The pearl of wisdom must have shown the frost drake something to put the dragons on edge.

All thought of escape vanished. Alduce believed the best course of action was to return through the portal.

Nightstar decided otherwise.

"If the moot needs my help, then let us return."

He leapt into the air, the pain in his chest forgotten. If his former friend was in trouble, he couldn't leave.

And if there were consequences, then so be it.

Chapter 8

Excerpt from Alduce's Atlas of Dragons.

Dragon Twins.

When a fertile dragon egg is laid it usually takes four to six weeks to hatch. Eggs come in a variety of shapes and colours and their size is generally in proportion to their parents. Larger dragons producing bigger eggs than smaller dragons.

The only exception to this rule, I have discovered, is what I have named the twin egg. This occurrence is extremely rare and there is no direct bearing to the dragons involved and appears to be random.

A twin egg can be detected as soon as it has been laid and is noticeably larger than the rest of the clutch by approximately one and a half times their size. The shell colour is a shade of mottled light green.

With mammals, twins are created by a division of the embryo. When it comes to dragons, two embryos occupy the same shell. As far as I am aware, this doesn't happen with any other egg laying creatures and is a result of the magic contained within these mythical creatures.

Dragon Twins are not to be confused with egg brothers or sisters, dragons hatched from the same clutch. Clutch mates can often be similar in colour and appearance, but they are not true twins.

The healthy hatching of an oversized twin egg is an event within the dragon community. It is regarded as a favourable omen and twins are believed to have enhanced magical abilities.

Inside the egg the developing embryos can mature in three different ways.

The first scenario is that the strongest and largest embryo will develop normally, taking all the sustenance from the weaker twin. Upon hatching, the weaker dragon will be still born, or live for a short while before dying.

The second is both dragons will hatch and one will be large and one small and under developed, a runt. This is considered a bad omen.

And lastly, both hatchlings will be identical and grow to become true twins.

Additional note: The two green dragons of the White Mountain moot guard, Verdune and Verdante, are true identical twins.

Newly hatched dragonets are usually black in colour when they emerge from the shell. Sometimes they are a darker shade of their adult colour, appearing almost black. The black fades as their colour develops. Dragon twins are born green and their pigment has already fully developed. After considerable research, green is one of the two strongest genetic strains (red being the other) in dragons and I believe that this is why twins are born this colour.

Note: There has been no record of a red twin egg ever being laid.

* * *

Winterfang called the moot to order, spreading his wings over the dragons to his left and right. The seven members were joined by Nightstar and Blood Rose. They had all assembled in the chamber of the moot after Nightstar's return to the White Mountain.

"The moot is now open," Winterfang spoke, reciting the traditional words, "all are welcome and are under my protection." His talon gripping the pearl of wisdom, "Pearl of enlightenment, Moonstone of white, grant me the wisdom and the strength to guide our moot wisely."

Nightstar tried not to look at the swirling surface of the pearl, he didn't know if it would react to his proximity, now that he had touched it. He didn't want the moot to know he had made an illicit connection with the pearl and hoped his nervousness wasn't as obvious as he thought it was.

"The moot are concerned with the unusual disappearance of Sunburst the Yellow. Especially as his mate," the frost drake nodded to Rose, "has informed us of his uncharacteristic behaviour prior to his departure."

"Rose, will you tell us what Sunburst said to you before he left?" Aurelian the Golden asked.

"I want to thank you all," Rose said. "I am lost without my mate, our dragonets need their sire to teach them, to help me provide and nurture them."

Nightstar looked down at his talons, ashamed his terrible secret had driven Sunburst from his home and family.

"We will give any help needed," Aurelian said. "The moot will see to it."

"Indeed we will," Winterfang assured her, "until Sunburst is found and returns home to take care of them himself. Now, tell us what he said, what upset him so, that he felt he had to leave?"

The frost drake stared directly at Nightstar, his icy blue eyes devouring the black dragon, looking for an answer. Everyone knew that the black and yellow were close friends. It wasn't unreasonable for Winterfang to look to him for clues. Who other than his mate would have any idea of what ailed Sunburst?

"He was upset when he returned," she replied, "he said Nightstar was lost." All eyes turned towards Nightstar. It was uncomfortable being the centre of attention and bearing the scrutiny of everyone assembled. The cavern felt like a much smaller space.

"We were separated during the storm," Nightstar said, feeling he was expected to speak.

"Little Wing has informed the moot of your conversation," Winterfang said, "and now that you are found, we need to locate Sunburst. Please continue Rose."

"He wasn't himself, he was agitated and not making any sense... "

"He's a yellow," Galvon muttered. Winterfang glowered at him and it was enough to silence the forest green.

"...and kept apologising, saying he was sorry for his bad judgement," Rose continued, ignoring Galvon's comment. "He said he didn't know what he had done. He was confused. When he left, he said he was going to make amends, fix things. He left and flew east, I watched him as he vanished into the horizon and that was the last I saw of him." She paused, looking around the chamber. "I know he can be unpredictable and other dragons," she looked towards Galvon, "think him strange. But something is wrong, I know it is, call it *perception* if you will, but Sunburst needs help." She turned to Nightstar, "Will you help find him, Nightstar? If anyone can track him, it's you. He has never had such a close friend. You have developed a bond with him and he respects you. I sense a connection between you both, you are my best hope."

"I will do everything I can," Nightstar said, wondering at the way she had emphasised the word—perception. He understood this was how she referred to what he had thought of as his dragon sense, what he had come to interpret as a sixth sense, unique to dragons. He knew this was true as his own *perception* informed him.

"I would see your mate return home to the White Mountain." He knew Rose referred to their friendship, but now he had Sunburst's blood, there was another connection that tied him to the yellow dragon.

"Can you tell us anything more?" Winterfang asked Nightstar. "You spent some time with him when you flew south." He let the question hang and eight heads turned to Nightstar, looking for answers he couldn't give.

"I'm sorry moot leader," he replied, using his title and showing respect. "I wish I could tell you more." He deliberately hadn't answered the question, he knew Winterfang would sniff out any untruths and hoped that his statement was accepted. He truly did wish he could tell them, but knew he would never be allowed to leave the chamber of the moot if they knew his secret. "Everything was fine until the storm hit." Again, it was technically true, until he had been struck by the lightning, his friendship with Sunburst had been more than fine.

Alduce had dug a deep hole and the black dragon felt himself slipping into the abyss. He cursed the storm and the lightning, it had changed everything when it struck him.

The power of the Flaire pendant was unpredictable, created by a race who could understand and control it. Alduce was an amateur compared to them. Yes, he had succeeded in using the power of the pendant to call down the lightning and combine it with the science and sorcery he practiced. He had opened portals and travelled to other worlds. He had used the elemental power of the lightning, bending it to his will.

But did he really know what he was doing? Was the great Alduce so conceited he couldn't admit he didn't know everything? Was it just an unfortunate coincidence that the lightning had struck him and changed him back? Or could it be some outside force, some unknown entity telling him what he had done was wrong? Dropping him to his death in the storm would certainly end his experiment.

This dragon life was no longer an experiment, Nightstar was more than science, more than just sorcery. Ever since Sunburst had shared his blood, the dragon within was stronger. His thoughts and his decisions were his own, he was still Alduce, but the man was becoming more like a passenger, an observer, carried along by a will that was still his, but was Nightstar's too.

"Nightstar?" Winterfang said, "You are deep in thought. Is there something else you know that might help?"

"I was thinking where he would go. Why he felt he needed to make amends. What could lie to the east that would take him away from Rose and the dragonets?" Nightstar replied.

"You would know better than any, what lies east," Galvon challenged, "since it's where you came from."

"There's nothing east but the coast," said Blue-cap, "and the sea."

"Mysteries and the unknown," Raynar said. "Sunburst can be spontaneous, it's part of a yellow's nature, but this sounds as if something troubles him."

Nightstar knew the moot were concerned for Sunburst, just as he was. Alduce wished to leave and return to his laboratory but Nightstar couldn't abandon his friend. He knew it wasn't the wisest choice, but it was the right one.

"I shall fly east," he said. "I will find Sunburst, I owe it to him as a friend. With the moot's permission I would leave and seek him out." Sunburst might not want to see Nightstar again, but his guilt wouldn't let him leave without knowing what had become of the yellow dragon.

There was a rumbling of consent from the assembled dragons.

"Bring him home, Nightstar," Rose said.

"I will not return to the White Mountain without him."

"I will accompany Nightstar," Amethyst said. Nightstar didn't want that, this was between Sunburst and himself. He tried to think of a reason to dissuade the purple.

"No," Winterfang said, saving him from fabricating another lie. "Nightstar will go alone. I have consulted the pearl and this is how it must be."

He spread his wings over the dragons to his left and right, stretching his neck forward. "Nightstar will search to the east and he will find Sunburst and bring him home. I will have no more White Mountain dragons involved, for now. The moot is now closed, my words are final. Aurelian, see to Blood Rose, make sure she is provided for. Go now, return to your duties."

He folded his wings and the dragons started to leave the chamber. It was plain to all assembled that Winterfang had made up his mind and he would tolerate no arguments on the matter.

Amethyst caught Nightstar's eye and raised her eye ridge like a questioning human eyebrow. If he could have shrugged his shoulders, he would have. Instead he shook his head from side to side, a universal gesture understood by both humans and dragons. He pushed forward through the departing dragons, trying to catch up with her but stopped as his name was spoken.

"Nightstar," Winterfang commanded, "I would speak with you."

"Come and find me when you're done, I'll be in the meadow," Amethyst softly spoke, then disappeared into the tunnel with her peers.

Galvon was last to leave and he turned his head back, looking to Winterfang then to Nightstar, he was displeased at being dismissed, but he unexpectedly bobbed his head towards Nightstar. Did he know why Winterfang had held him back?

Winterfang waited until the chamber was empty and Galvon had finally exited.

"What I have to say to you isn't for the ears of the moot. Some of its members might question you about what we have spoken of, but you will not discuss our conversation with them. Any of them. Is that clear?"

Nightstar was unsure if Winterfang was angry with him, his tone was one of authority and he was used to being obeyed.

"I understand," he said and waited for him to continue.

Winterfang craned his neck, making sure the tunnel was empty. "I feel this isn't the first time we have faced each other across this chamber, just the two of us, alone." Nightstar didn't respond, it wasn't a question and he was positive he shouldn't be volunteering anything like a confirmation. If Winterfang suspected something about the night of the aurora, he wouldn't trick Nightstar into confessing.

"I have consulted the pearl," and he scrutinized Nightstar before continuing, "and I have sensed Sunburst is in danger."

"Danger? What kind of danger?" This wasn't something he expected to hear.

"That I cannot say, it is only a feeling, but it is a strong one. The pearl of wisdom can sometimes indicate what is to be, well, perhaps possibilities of what might come to pass. Something happened between you and Sunburst. That much I do know. What it was is a mystery to me. I know you would not see your friend come to harm and I suspect whatever the rift between you, you do not wish to speak of it."

"We had a falling out, a difference of opinion. One which I now truly regret."

"I see it eats at you, weighs heavy on your spirit. Listen to me Nightstar, if you wish to make this right, you need to find that yellow spike in my scales, make your peace and bring him home. Sunburst might enjoy playing the part, but he is no fool. The White Mountain would be a less interesting place without him. The wisdom of the pearl is seldom wrong, but it does not provide all the answers I seek, it only guides me. Reveals small clues, shows me hints and suggestions. It is difficult to explain. I don't expect you to understand, unless you had touched the pearl and felt its presence for yourself." He paused, then said, "Or perhaps you understand everything." The implication was obvious.

Nightstar felt like a mouse and Winterfang was the cat, toying with him. It wasn't just the pearl that was supplying hints, the frost drake was telling him he knew he had been inside the chamber and touched the pearl. Was he giving him the opportunity to come clean? If he confessed what would the penalty for his violation of trust be? He had consulted the pearl and seen secrets he shouldn't.

Winterfang watched, his icy blue eyes once more searching deep inside his consciousness and this time there were no chameleon scales to hide behind.

"I am sorry, Winterfang," Nightstar blurted before the screaming sorcerer inside his mind stopped him.

"What are you sorry for, black dragon? What do you want to tell me?" Cold blue eyes bored into his own, vivid and bright against the frost white scales, willing him to tell the truth. Alduce knew what was happening and surfaced in Nightstar's conscience to break the hypnotic gaze before he revealed his deepest secret. He was sure Winterfang's reaction would not be as lenient as Sunburst's.

The turmoil within caused Nightstar to shake his head and Winterfang's spell was broken, but the damage was done.

"I touched the pearl," Nightstar confessed. If he gave Winterfang this, deflected his probing, hopefully it would save him.

"I know," Winterfang said. "I have known since you touched it. I felt your presence in the chamber on the night of the aurora. I wanted to see if you would confess, tell me what you had done. Know that since you have, there is still hope for you."

"Hope? There is no hope for me, Winterfang, I fear all is lost."

"You sound like Sunburst. He said you were lost and I believe he didn't mean that he couldn't find you. You are a lost soul Nightstar, an enigma to me. Something inside you is wrong, something is missing. You are a lost dragon. Sunburst knew it, he is more perceptive than some give him credit for. Did he know you touched the pearl?"

His deception was beginning to unravel, Winterfang knew there was something different about him. Of course he wasn't like other dragons. Winterfang said he was lost but it was Alduce that was lost. Nightstar was only just finding himself.

"No!" Nightstar didn't want the yellow dragon to be accused of collusion, he had caused his friend enough suffering already. Winterfang mustn't think Sunburst had known he had touched the pearl, he didn't know anything about it.

Had Sunburst seen anything when he shared some of Alduce's memories? He would have surely said if he had. Perhaps he was too angry to mention it. He must not find out, it would only make matters between them worse. Nightstar would make sure the yellow dragon was spared any further pain of betrayal, if he could.

"He didn't know, he mustn't know, my shame is something I would spare him from if I could."

"No-one will ever know, Nightstar," Winterfang said. "I am angry you sneaked into the moot chamber and you will be punished, however, I said there is hope. I know the pull the pearl has on minds not wise or strong enough to resist. I should have made sure the twins didn't leave without replacing the guard. While I am disappointed in your actions, I must take some of the responsibility, I am, after all, responsible for all the dragons at White Mountain."

"Punishment?" Nightstar asked, "Please don't stop me from searching for Sunburst, I need... "

"Silence! You will listen when your elder speaks, do not interrupt me again. If you mistake my understanding for leniency, you are sadly mistaken. I will get to your punishment, but first, you need to understand why. The pearl of wisdom should only be consulted by those who know its secret. I, being moot leader, am privy to this, you, being an immature fledgling, are not!"

Nightstar was at the mercy of the frost drake, he felt like an apprentice once more, being chastised by Caltus for some misdeed or mistake he had made. When his master had been angry or annoyed, Alduce had stood and listened, taken the berating and held his tongue.

Ears open, mouth shut, another saying Caltus was fond of repeating to him. It seemed like exceptionally good advice to Nightstar. This was one thing both he and Alduce agreed on.

"While I blame myself for not taking the necessary precautions and leaving the pearl unattended, I am angry and disappointed at your actions. My *perception* told me you were in the chamber. Do you think me such an incompetent leader? That I do not know *everything* that occurs in the White Mountains?

Nightstar remained silent, hoping Winterfang's question was rhetorical. The silence stretched uncomfortably until Winterfang continued.

"I wanted to see what you would do. I gave you the freedom to fail, and you did. We took you in and made you welcome, Sunburst showed you our ways. You could not have had a better friend, believe me. Know this Nightstar; Sunburst recognised you were special. Your black scales are unusual. You are different. I see a potential in you for greatness, but there is something about you that is a mystery to me, to the pearl, and to Flaxe. Yes, we have discussed you, and the pearl bares your mark now." He waved his talon across the white orb and streaks of black and silver swirled across its surface.

"Like a talon print in the snow, I can follow your journey, I can see what you were shown, see what wisdom the pearl revealed to your eager mind. The power of invisibility is now yours and the secret of the long sleep. These are things you are not ready for. I forbid you from using this knowledge, you are not mature enough for it." He pushed his snout close to Nightstar. "If you don't follow my requests, you *will* incur the wrath of every dragon here. Do you understand?"

Nightstar bowed his head, "I understand, moot leader. I am truly sorry and will do anything I can to make amends."

"That is good. The pearl not only imparts wisdom to those who are ready to receive it, but can corrupt too. I want you to understand why the pearl attracted you. If you realise, it will be easier to resist. The aurora can effect dragons in many different ways, it causes euphoria and impairs judgement." Nightstar thought back to the when the sky had intoxicated him with its magnificent lights, like alcohol to a human. Perhaps his judgement had been impaired, his inhibitions certainly had. He thought of Amethyst and the time they had shared at the lake.

"I believe it was a combination of the excitement of the Grand Moot and the aurora," Winterfang said, "that and the draw of the pearl on your mind, which drew you to the chamber. Once you were alone with the pearl, you were too weak to resist. The pearl is an unusual object, it has an unknown past, even though it has been with us since before the Great Exodus. You are an intelligent dragon, Nightstar, I see this. I said you have a potential for greatness and the pearl senses this too. You are too young, too immature, to handle its power. Its attraction will become addiction if you are unprepared. Given another hundred years, you might have matured enough to learn, but you are a long way from that at present." He huffed out a sigh and continued.

"Here is what is going to happen. No-one must know you have touched the pearl and broken our trust. It would cause unrest in our community if they learned an outsider had accessed something they are deprived of. Dragons can be volatile and easy to anger in situations such as this. The knowledge of the pearl is forbidden to all but a select few. You will not use the knowledge the pearl has shared with you until I decide you are mature enough. You will be allowed to search for Sunburst." He drew in a breath that could only be a sigh, then continued.

"I want you to leave today, the quicker you depart the better it will be for you. I charge you with finding Sunburst and bringing him home. If you give me your promise that you will do as I command, I will let you fly from the White Mountain and bring your friend home. When you return, you will be banished for a year and a day." He waited, offering Nightstar the opportunity to fully understand his words.

"This is your only choice. If you wish to return after your banishment, you will be welcome. I think this will help you find what is missing inside, Nightstar the Black. If this is unacceptable to you, fly from here, right now. But look behind you as you leave, the moot of the White Mountain will be close behind and the justice we deliver will be much different from the terms I've offered."

"Your words hold great wisdom, moot leader," Nightstar said. "You are correct, something is lost, but I'm not sure what it is. I think I can find it, deep inside, I feel it's just beyond my reach." Alduce was part of Nightstar, but Nightstar did not want to be part of Alduce. The dragon wanted to break free of his human side. It was his dragon soul he needed to find, the spirit that had departed the unhatched dragonet Alduce had stolen from its shell.

But it wasn't a dead ghost, it was something more, the dragon essence. It wasn't lost, he could feel it, below his human conscience, stronger now since Sunburst had given him the gift of his blood. If he could embrace it, join it with the physical body of Nightstar, he would be whole. Winterfang made him see this, he had shown him what he needed to seek. Sunburst provided the catalyst with three drops of his blood and that unexpected ingredient had awakened something new inside him.

"I will find Sunburst and bring him home, where he belongs. Perhaps it will help me find myself." He had a purpose now. His friend was in danger and he would repay the yellow dragon for all he had given, all he had sacrificed.

"I am pleased at your decision, Nightstar. I would expect nothing less from a White Mountain dragon. When you return we will discuss this further. I expect you to succeed, failure to do so will void our agreement and the terms for your survival will be renegotiated, by claw and fang. Do we have an understanding?"

"We do. I accept your terms." Winterfang had given him purpose, the means to find redemption, a second chance. If he was successful he would get that chance. If he failed, the moot leader would show no mercy.

"Go now, say your farewells and fulfil your quest." Winterfang inclined his head. "Our moot of two is ended." He stepped aside making space for Nightstar to depart the chamber. As he entered the tunnel, Winterfang's voice echoed from the stone walls. "Fly high and fly free."

Nightstar had found something else, something other than a purpose. He now had direction and that direction was east.

Chapter 9

Excerpt from Alduce's Atlas of Dragons.

Eggs and nests

After conception, females can clutch as little as one egg or much as seven. The amount of eggs laid follows no pattern and is not determined by the size of the parents. The eggs will gestate in the female from three to six weeks, prior to laying. The female dragon becomes gravid, finding it difficult to fly with the extra bulk and weight and will prepare a nest while she is waiting to clutch.

Note: Females can chose if they wish to produce a clutch after mating and are able to manage their level of fertility, giving them the ability to control colony population.

Nests can range from a natural hollow in the ground or a dragon made depression, scraped out with their talons. Dragons have also been known to arrange a loose circle of rocks to keep the eggs together. There are no predators large or dangerous enough to be a threat to a clutch of unattended eggs, however females will remain instinctually protective. Few dragons will even build structures similar to a birds nest, located on flat areas of cliffs or mountains. These are more for privacy that any necessity to keep the eggs safe. The nest, and where it is located, must be strong and secure enough to support the weight of mother and hatchlings, resulting in a large structure. In an established colony, ancient nests are re-used and repaired, if available, rather than constructed from new.

The laying process can be painful and difficult, resulting in physical exhaustion. After a successful clutching, the female will sit on her eggs and the male partner will attend her, often brining food until she recuperates. It is worth mentioning, that after the eggs have been laid, they need no further attention and generally hatch after another four weeks. The thickness of the shell and the magic contained within the embryos are enough to sustain the egg through the final weeks of development.

Most hatchlings will emerge with black scales, however, sometimes they appear black, but are, in fact, a darker shade of their developing colour. As they mature, their scales will progressively take on the pigment of their adult colour.

* * *

Amethyst waited for Nightstar in the meadow, the purple of her scales stood out against the green grass like a gem on satin pillow, gleaming in the afternoon sunlight. He dropped from the sky, gliding towards her, wings fixed, then twisted sharply, spilling air from his leathery sails like a falling leaf. His skilful manoeuvre landing him close by her side, near enough to cover her with his wingspan.

"There's no need to impress me," Amethyst said. "You know I think you are an expert flier. After all, you managed to catch me."

"I thank you for the compliment," Nightstar said. He wished he could share his secret with her, but suspected it would only cause her pain, as it had Sunburst. And he didn't want her to react like the yellow dragon, he didn't think he could stand the loss of her companionship.

"What was so important that old Winterfang asked you to stay?"

"Please, Amethyst, I am not at liberty to discuss our conversation, I wish I could."

"Winterfang does what is best for the White Mountain. He is moot leader and I will respect his decisions, but I don't have to like them."

"My advice, for what it's worth, don't let him hear you calling him old."

Amethyst snorted, small curls of smoke drifting from her nostrils, the sound somewhere between a chuckle and a laugh. "Good advice," she said, "I shall make sure and follow it. Now what *can* you tell me? When are you leaving on your search?"

"I am to depart today, but I didn't want to leave without speaking with you."

Nightstar wasn't comfortable saying goodbye to friends. He had messed up his final conversation with Sunburst and wanted to ensure he didn't repeat that with Amethyst. He was unsure of what exactly to say next, he was hardly an expert when it came to females of any species, and Alduce was no help either.

"That is good, Nightstar, I would have been disappointed if you left without seeking me out. I have grown to enjoy your company."

"It is something I shall miss too," he said. "I wish things could be different, that we could go back to the night of the aurora." The memory of their time together at the lake, under magical green skies, brought him joy, but also great sadness at having to give it up.

"There will be time when you return, if that is what you want," her eyes met his and said more than words could.

"It is, but I need to find Sunburst first. I cannot return until I find him and he is safe."

"There is more to this than you are telling me," Amethyst said, "but I understand if you can't talk about it. I have been part of the moot long enough to know Winterfang acts in the best interest of everyone. I will be here when you return."

"Even if it takes more than... a year?" Nightstar didn't want to hear the answer, he was sure it would not be the one he wanted. "There are things I must do, I have given my word to Winterfang and I owe it to Sunburst."

"If another black dragon comes along, I can't promise anything. Black *is* my favourite colour." She snorted again, trying to make light of her words, but Nightstar could sense she was hiding her emotions.

Before the metamorphosis, when he was Alduce, he could not have imagined the complexity of being a dragon. He had spent months at the White Mountain and learned that these creatures of legend were much more than anything he had ever read about. He wanted to record all he had learned, all he experienced, everything they had shown him, gather everything in his scale bound ledgers.

Humans should know dragons were not as they believed, there was so much more to discover about these wonderful creatures. The blood from Sunburst pumped through his veins, opening his eyes to what was important to dragons, it

225

made him feel strongly about telling their true story. He was now their voice, his discoveries would set the record straight. He knew the blood was effecting the dragon side of him, making Nightstar's essence stronger and he embraced the change. He welcomed it.

"I hope I am the only black you meet," he said, "and if I'm not, I have already displayed for you. You know my intent."

"Return to me when you can then," she stepped in close and coiled her neck round his. "I have chosen not to produce any eggs from our mating, this time. But perhaps when you are ready to settle... " She left the sentence unfinished.

Nightstar wished he could stay, but the longer he spent with Amethyst, the more difficult it would be to leave.

"I can think of no place better to be. I would like to spend more time here. The White Mountains and the dragons who live here mean more to me than I can explain."

He had lost his family and home when he was a boy. He realised that he had found a place that filled the void, a place where he had made friends. A place he wished to be. As Nightstar, this was an easy choice to make. Alduce was quiet and offered no resistance, his awareness remained in the dragon's conscious mind, but he was more of an observer since Sunburst's blood repaired his damaged chest.

A shadow passed overhead as the frost white moot leader glided by, his message clear to Nightstar.

"It is time," he told Amethyst as he unravelled his neck from hers.

"You are a loyal friend, Nightstar. Bring Sunburst home, find our lost brother and see him returned safely. I sense the path ahead will be difficult. The whole moot could feel Winterfang's concern."

"I will do what I can, what I must." He didn't feel like a loyal friend, he still felt like a deceiver. If he could find Sunburst and get him to return to Rose, then maybe he could find what was missing inside and repair what he had broken.

He stepped a small distance away from the purple dragon, the weight of separation heavy on his heart. Looking west, the afternoon sky was blue and

226

cloudless. He launched himself into the air, the sun at his tail.

He didn't look behind as he left the White Mountains, he flew east towards grey skies that mirrored his mood.

Part Four

Redemption

Chapter 1

Excerpt from Alduce's lost journals.

The Larcrowe.

The Larcrowe are a species of huge bird, standing over seven feet tall when fully grown, distantly related to the crow family. They closely resemble the physical attributes of the raven and are highly intelligent.

Larcrowe have the ability to communicate and converse with man and believe in what they refer to as a Listener. A human who has the ability to understand the squawking and cawing of their own tongue and converse with them.

Their feathers are black with a sheen of blues and greens when viewed in direct sunlight. They have sharp yellow beaks, black eyes, pale yellow legs and shiny black talons.

I have encountered Larcrowe on a few rare occasions, coincidently on worlds that are also inhabited by dragons. I have not found any records, journals, books or scrolls that hold any mention of these creatures and find it strange, that after extensive research, no information about them exists.

They appear to be friendly and curious and live in large communities, favouring the companionship of their species.

Collective name: A Colony of Larcrowe.

* * *

Nightstar departed the White Mountain and flew east, maintaining an altitude that allowed him enough height to see a good distance in front, but not too high that he wasn't able to see the details of the landscape below. Scouring earth and air in search of a yellow dragon, his senses constantly alert, he forged on until the dimming light of twilight forced him to seek out somewhere to rest.

He spent the remainder of the first afternoon fruitlessly searching for any clue that would reveal if Sunburst had passed this way.

He set off at first light on the second day, stopping only to drink from a stream and snatch a scrawny beast that reminded him of a mountain goat. The meat from the beast wasn't unpleasant, but it was stringy and lean with an earthy taste. He longed for the succulent curly bucks of the south, tender and juicy, their flesh sweetened by the lush meadow grass they grazed on.

The curly bucks were Sunburst's favourite and Nightstar understood why. The smaller yellow dragon maintained that once you had eaten them, anything else was bland and tasteless. He now knew why Sunburst spent a lot of his time in the west and south of the White Mountains. The eastern lands were mostly featureless, hundreds of miles of rocky hills and scrub grass. There was life here, but nothing that would interest a dragon. Compared to the forest and lakes, the meadows and the mountains, the land he flew over was as dull and boring as his meal.

Water glimmered on the horizon and Nightstar saw the eastern ocean for the first time. Even though the huge body of water was hazy and distant, as he flew closer, he could see that the coastline was unending, spanning far to the north and south. The ocean disappeared into the distant eastern horizon, nothing but waves and water. He continued east getting closer to where the land ended and the sea began. Surely if Sunburst had flown this way, there would be some sign of his passing.

A murmuring sound drifted on the wind like voices from a distant crowd, reaching his sharp ears and peaking his interest. The sound was coming from south of his position and he deviated from his eastern heading to investigate. His flight so far had been uneventful and this was the first time he was presented with the opportunity to investigate anything other than hills and rocks.

Tilting his wings, Nightstar adjusted his direction, homing in on the noise, steadily increasing from a gentle murmur to a busy chattering. He flew low as he neared the location of the mysterious sound, following the undulations of the ground below until he reached the top of a steep incline. Cresting the ridge, the land beneath dropped away and a vast forest, populated with thousands of giant trees, stretched out across the valley below. The source of the noise was housed in the branches of the giant trees.

The Larcrowe.

The trees were occupied with the oversized crows, each adult easily the height of a man, black against the green foliage they perched amongst.

Interest sparked inside the mind of Alduce as he looked out through Nightstar's eyes, curiosity had captured the mind of the scholar within, eager to learn more about these magnificent birds. The part of him that was Nightstar was more practical. In a colony of this size there was a good chance one of the birds may have noticed if a yellow dragon had passed this way.

Nightstar banked over the forest and the noise from below erupted as the Larcrowe spotted the dragon. Sounds of panic filled the air, chattering changed to a crescendo of squawking voices. The birds took to the air, startled by the sudden appearance of the black dragon above their roosting grounds, their beating wings adding to the din.

As they crowed and cawed, Nightstar was surprised to learn that he could pick out words amongst the increasing cacophony, *Firedrake! Flee! Danger!*

As he listened he recognised some of what the Larcrowe said. The Flaire artefact providing a partial translation of the Larcrowe squawking.

He knew when he was in his human form the pendant allowed him to understand and communicate in other tongues. It still worked when it was part of the transformed silver scales on Nightstar's chest, but just not as well. He was only understanding some of words the Larcrowe said and he needed to know more.

The Larcrowe filled the sky, large black wings clapped and flapped while their cries and screeches added to the thunderous sound. They circled around the flying dragon, voicing their indignation and fear, the message clear to Nightstar. His large bulk caught in the centre of a black whirlpool, hundreds, maybe thousands of Larcrowe, swirling around the dragon but keeping their distance, never getting too close.

Nightstar wanted to speak with these birds, they had fascinated him ever since he had encountered them on the plains.

Alduce was equally intrigued, he had encountered a Larcrowe before and he wanted to know more about these creatures. He was a scholar and his compulsion to find out more about these unusually giant crows was strong.

The Larcrowe were intimidated by the large dragon in their midst, they darted in close, then swerved quickly out of reach. Alduce had seen this behaviour with normal sized crows when a bird of prey flew close to their roosting grounds. They would swoop and dive at the larger bird, attempting to draw it away from their home. Their larger cousins were attempting the same tactic, harrying him in the hope of steering him away from their colony.

These Larcrowe were obviously afraid of the dragon and he would need to adopt another tactic if he were to convince them otherwise. He closed his wings and dropped towards the ground, plummeting through the centre of the circling birds that surrounded him, aiming for a clear area in the forest. The Larcrowe followed him down, keeping a respectful distance. A huge black dragon trailed by a wake of oversized black crows.

Alduce had an idea and Nightstar understood it and agreed, there was no debate, both man and dragon were decided on the next step they must take. He distanced himself from the Larcrowe and powered across the clearing, entering the giant forest, weaving between huge trunks and disappearing into the shade beneath the canopy of foliage.

This forest was different from the one Sunburst had led him through. The trees were enormous and the spaces between them were much wider and easier to navigate. He would have been able to compete with Sunburst through this forest as there was much more space for him to manoeuvre.

Looking behind to make sure the Larcrowe weren't too close, he changed course, flying sharply to the left. He peered back through the tree trunks, checking to see his evasive tactics hadn't been seen. Below the leafy canopy the forest floor was shaded and dark, perfect camouflage for a black dragon.

Nightstar aimed himself for a wide space between two large trunks and spread his wings wide, pulling himself up short and stopping in the air. Leaves and twigs flew out in front of the black dragon as he came to a spectacular halt, sharp talons ploughing grooves in the earth as he landed. Twisting his long neck past the two concealing tree trunks, he glanced back the way he had come for any signs of pursuit, but for the moment, he was alone.

Alduce reached for the magic that allowed him to hold the form of Nightstar. He was so used to being in dragon form that it took him no effort to remain that way now and he had to consciously choose to change back to a human. As the hold on the transformation spell slipped away and he willed himself to change, a wave of heat washed through him, burning from the inside. Nightstar's scales shimmered, each scale surrounded by white light as the magical metamorphosis took place. The black dragon shrank and changed shape, like melting ice, reducing until the man was all that remained.

Alduce stepped from the giant grooves Nightstar's talons had left, naked except for the pendant he wore around his neck. The small silver coloured dragon was warm against his skin and tingled with the residue of sorcery from the transformation spell. Alduce could feel Nightstar's presence with him, the strength of the dragon within making his return to human form much more bearable than the first time. He rubbed his hand across the new skin on his chest, the damage from the lighting strike almost fully healed. The only sign of the wound was a circle of pink new skin where the charred black mess had been.

The dull ache that had throbbed in agony when he awoke in the cave, was gone. His fingers probed the new skin but no pain remained, just the annoying itch of healing tissue. The blood, warm and alive, Sunburst dripped into his wound, had saved his life and generated a magical healing. Alduce now believed that it was also helping him separate his thoughts from Nightstar's. Since his incident with the lightning he had a clearer understanding of where his persona and the dragon's met. No longer were they a mixed jumble of thoughts from both human and dragon. Now he was able to better separate the two conflicting entities contained in one consciousness. Why this had happened was a mystery to him, at present, but the scholar would not let this phenomenon pass him by without investigation. When the time was right. Whether it was the lightning or the dragon's blood, or a combination of the two, he didn't know. Research would need to wait until he returned to his laboratory.

The soft loam of the forest floor felt strange against his bare feet, just as walking on two legs in his true form took a few minutes to get used to.

Caltus had once told him of a man who had lost a leg and come to his former master after the wound had healed, asking for help. The man told the sorcerer he could still feel the limb, painful and itching, even though it wasn't there. He wanted to know if Caltus could help with the phantom feeling. Alduce wasn't in pain, but as he walked, he could feel where his wings and tail should be, ghost limbs that were a just a memory and no longer physical anymore.

He shivered in the shade and shook off the feeling. As he stepped out into the clearing the sun warmed his thin human skin. Hundreds of Larcrowe perched in trees, flying in the air, and settled on the ground, turned their heads as he strolled into view. Their chatter increased as the naked man advanced to the centre of the clearing, steadier now and a little more confident on his two human legs. His dramatic entrance created a stir with the large birds, squawking and crowing to each other, no longer afraid, as they had been at Nightstar's presence. Now they were excited. And to his surprise, Alduce understood the word they spoke in awe.

Man!

The Flaire artefact had the ability to translate words from languages he didn't speak and allowed him to converse in foreign tongues. Somehow, now he was able to translate the caws of the Larcrowe and understand their meaning. The silver dragon around his neck hadn't done this before and he had never been able to understand birds previously. He wondered if the transformation spell and the changes his body had undertaken, coupled with the blood from Sunburst, had contributed to this new ability. Another question he didn't have an answer to.

Man. The voices repeated.

The Larcrowe, inhabitants of a continent populated only by dragons, were actually familiar with humans. They knew him for what he was and revered him. He believed he was in no danger from these strange and wonderful creatures. He could change back to Nightstar in an instant, should he desire to, but he knew that wouldn't be necessary. The chattering voices of so many huge birds, with larger voices than their smaller counterparts, was deafening. Alduce, used to being obeyed, held up his hand and the Larcrowe gradually quietened, watching intently, waiting for his next move.

Alduce spoke and the power within the Flaire artefact shaped his voice into one the Larcrowe could understand.

Greetings, he said, *I mean you no harm.* As the words left his mouth, he understood them, but to his ears, the sounds he made were the caws and crows of the birds around him.

The cacophony that answered him was one of surprise, as hundreds of Larcrowe voices, spoke a new word.

Listener! Listener! If birds could whisper, this is what they would sound like. They named him Listener, it sounded like a title, rather than a description of his ability to listen. There was more mystery to the Larcrowe than he knew.

He could understand them and they him. These birds were considerably more intelligent than he originally thought. Alduce wished he had time to spend with them, but he needed to find Sunburst and there was a sense of urgency connected to that feeling that he couldn't ignore.

The chattering of the Larcrowe subsided and from their midst, one of their flock approached. The bird stood taller than most of the others and carried itself with a proud, almost regal manner. The other birds deferred to it, pulling back and dipping their heads. A sea of black feathers parted creating a pathway through the crowd of gathered Larcrowe, making way for their leader.

The huge bird stopped before Alduce and cocked its head, a dark beady eye examined him, black and unfathomable. The sorcerer met the bird's gaze, trying to read its mood. Then, the Larcrowe squatted low and bowed its head to him and spoke.

Welcome Listener, it cawed, holding its pose.

I am honoured to meet you, Alduce crowed back in the bird's strange language, unsure of how one should address a huge crow.

You come from the forest where the black firedrake vanished, is it now safe? The Larcrowe asked, looking beyond Alduce and into the forest behind him.

The black dragon has gone, Alduce cawed. *It will not bother you again.*

Safe! Safe! The flock behind their speaker murmured.

You have saved us from the drake, Listener. The colony is grateful.

Alduce could use this to his advantage if the Larcrowe believed he had rescued them from the black dragon. He decided to play his hand while he held good cards.

This Listener is interested in these firedrakes, these dragons. I wish to know if you have seen more.

The bird cocked its head, eying him before it spoke.

Another passed before. A dra-gon the colour of the sun. Not the black of the Larcrowe or the drake the Listener chased away.

Sunburst! He had passed this way and the Larcrowe had seen him. Alduce was sure the yellow dragon would not have bothered the Larcrowe, he knew Sunburst thought them stupid and uninteresting. He needed to find out when they had spotted him and where he had gone.

When did you see this sun coloured drake? He crowed.

Many days have passed, but it has gone. We are safe. The leader of the Larcrowe said.

Many days, it could only be four or five at most. Rather than push the Larcrowe about how long it had been he changed tact.

Where did this sun coloured drake go?

It flew over our forest, higher than the black drake. It did not come close, our scouts watched for danger. It flew out over the great water, out beyond our shores. We watched until it grew small and the morning sun rose to obscure it.

Sunburst had flown into the morning sun. East! Across the ocean. But to where? The Larcrowe usually wouldn't see dragons this far to the east. Sunburst had told him dragons didn't usually venture this way, there was nothing here for them. So where would he go?

Had he flown out over the great eastern ocean for a reason? Why would he fly into the unknown without telling Rose where he was going? Alduce knew the only way to find out was to follow him.

This Listener is sure no more firedrakes will disturb you, he said.

Tipa thanks the Listener, the Larcrowe said, *and the colony thank the Listener.*

Tipa can call me Alduce. That is my name.

The Larcrowe repeated his name, the word sounded strange coming from a bird's beak. The flock joined in and Alduce heard his name like a chant as the birds spoke it.

Why does Al-duce visit the Larcrowe? Tipa asked.

The sorcerer thought about his answer, he was done lying and he wanted to be honest with these fantastic birds.

I did not know that your colony was here and would like to learn more about the Larcrowe. Chatter rose from the flock and the Larcrowe were pleased with his words.

The Larcrowe were in awe of him, the title of Listener they bestowed upon him, he sensed, was one of great honour. These birds were a lot more than just giant crows. Sunburst had been wrong when he called them stupid and Alduce wished he could stay and learn more.

I have urgent business that I must attend to, he said, *but I would hope to return one day, if I am welcome.*

Welcome, the flock responded. *Always welcome.*

Even though Alduce stood in the direct sunlight, he felt his skin prickle with gooseflesh. He was overwhelmed with the acceptance of the flock for what he was. He had tried so hard to be accepted by the White Mountain dragons, a human hiding behind the scales of a black dragon. Here, in the presence of the Larcrowe, he felt like a dragon, hiding beneath the skin of a man. This time though, he wasn't lying, he was a man. A man who knew it would be best not to tell the Larcrowe of the dragon within.

I will return to the forest, Alduce announced, *and when I am able, I will return to the colony and speak with Tipa again.*

Tipa nodded to Alduce and backed away, joining the flock of Larcrowe gathered on the clearing floor. The sorcerer walked backed to the treeline and turned around, taking in the assembled colony of Larcrowe, a host of black eyes followed him as he returned to the forest. He raised one hand in final salute to these intelligent creatures. Tipa, head tilted back and beak pointing to the sky, cawed a single note. The colony responded as their leader had, open beaks lifted skyward and cawing, bidding an earie farewell to their visitor.

Alduce walked back into the shadows beneath the trees, the hairs on his neck standing up as he withdrew from the Larcrowe host. He was pleased they hadn't seen him change from Nightstar to Alduce and he would like to keep it that way when he changed back. Only Sunburst knew his secret and he needed to protect it as best he could. If the Larcrowe had known, they may not have spoken with him or revealed to him where Sunburst had went. He now knew that Sunburst had flown east and Nightstar would follow him.

Once more Alduce would journey into the unknown, but this time, with Nightstar to help him, he was confident he would be better prepared for the unexpected when it undoubtedly arrived.

* * *

The sun moved west, slowly sinking in the evening sky. Pink tinged clouds darkened to red. The tranquil evening was illuminated by a flash of lightning as it streaked down from above the forest. The forked bolt penetrated the treetops, spearing downward through the leaves, singed twigs and the smell of ozone drifted on the breeze.

A black shape burst forth from the canopy of foliage, a horned head followed by a long neck cleared the fragile leaves. Powerful wings propelling the body of the black dragon up and out of the forest, the treetops swaying in their downdraught. As Nightstar cleared the forest canopy, disturbed twigs and branches rattled and bounced from his body, raining down on the treetops below.

Leaving the colony of the Larcrowe behind, the black dragon flew east in pursuit of his friend.

Chapter 2

Sunburst opened his eyes, the pain in his head severe, a sorcerous hangover hammering the inside of his skull in an attempt to break free. He studied his surroundings in the dim light, stone walls and iron bars suffused with human magic made up his prison. His legs and neck were shackled with huge bands of iron, attached to chains which were secured to metal rings, fixed into the solid rock floor. His cell was roughly twice his size, a deep hole cut into the rock with heavy iron bars blocking any exit. The rigid bars sank into the floor and disappeared into the rock above and a huge gate was fashioned into the metalwork.

Sunburst shook his head and instantly regretted it, the iron collar jerked sharply, the chain limiting his movement, reminding him of the pounding in his skull. He roared in anger and attempted to free himself, throwing his weight against the chains that held him captive, his aching head the least of his concerns. He fell just short of the iron bars, the chains pulling tight, hampering his effort. Even if he hadn't been tethered, he doubted it would have made any difference. And if he had managed to reach the bars he didn't think he would be able to break free in his weakened state.

Sunburst felt helpless for the first time in his life, the strength he usually possessed was gone.

Human magic ran through the metal of the bars and chains and Sunburst felt himself weaken as it drained his strength. He was a captive, held in a magical prison, powerless to escape. Not yet willing to concede defeat, he reached for his own dragon magic, hoping to counter the spells that held him in this depressing dungeon. There was nothing there, the magic, along with the strength he once possessed, had left him.

How had he ended up like this? After he found out the truth about Nightstar he'd thought things couldn't get any worse. His best friend had turned out to be something he wasn't. He'd shared his blood with a human and he couldn't shake the torment of his own inner conflict. His head hurt the more he thought about it. He left his home and family, unsure where to go or what to do, only to end up a helpless prisoner. He had been a fool, a stupid yellow dragon who had acted rashly and only had himself to blame. He needed to get away, he was confused and upset. Flying east on impulse, a stupid yellow's impulse, was another bad decision. Blinded by a turmoil of conflicting emotions, he had flown out over the sea to escape them, only to end up trapped once more. This time it was a cage of iron bars that held him. Freedom beyond his reach.

A gate creaked, the sound coming from somewhere along the dark corridor outside his prison cell. He pushed his head forward against the cold metal collar, ignoring the irritating human magic and peered into the gloom. A faint light appeared at the end of the dark passageway accompanied by footsteps. The bobbing light grew brighter and the footsteps louder as a human figure strolled towards his cell. He held a tall wooden staff with a bright orb on top.

White light radiated from the orb above the figure's head making it difficult to distinguish any features. His faceless enemy stopped and the light he carried revealed many cages similar to his own, lining the passageway. Most of them occupied by dragons!

The dark human shape approached the bars of the cage diagonally opposite Sunburst's and the light revealed a small green dragon. It did not look well. Not only was it small, it appeared frail and sick, a look of defeat in its dead eyes. It shrank back from view as the figure neared, chains rattling. The dark figure shrugged, removed something from his robes then bent down and marked the floor, scoring a white cross on the ground outside the cell. He rose and continued his approach until he stood directly outside Sunburst's cell.

He peered into the cell and studied the yellow dragon. Sunburst met the man's eyes and tried to bring him under his hypnotic spell, but his magic failed him. A wave of anger and frustration washed over him and he launched himself at the bars once more, knowing it was hopeless. The impact jarred his whole body, chains biting into his shackled limbs as he thrashed against his constraints.

The man never even flinched, standing just on the other side of the bars that separated them, his gaze unbroken as he glowered at Sunburst. The yellow dragon could feel himself weaken as he strained defiantly against the chains in an effort to break free, unwilling to stop trying even though he knew it was useless. He felt like a newly hatched dragonet, spent and exhausted after breaking out of the shell. He stopped his futile pushing, slumping onto the stone floor as much as the chains would allow. Hate burned in his stare, refusing to break eye contact with the man.

Shaking his head the man turned and walked away, the light fading with him as he went. Sunburst watched his back as he departed, the light from the staff reflecting in the eyes of the other imprisoned dragons as he passed their cages.

When he escaped from this prison, this man would be held accountable, he was responsible for this dank dungeon, for all the dragons held captive here, and he would pay. In blood.

The gate groaned far along the passageway and then clanged shut with a depressing finality. He wished he had never met Nightstar, never found out about Alduce and had stayed at home with Rose. But he was too curious, he was a yellow dragon and it was in his nature, always sticking his snout where he shouldn't. This time it had landed him in more trouble than he could handle. His future looked bleak.

Why had this man taken him prisoner? Why were the sorry looking dragons in the other cells here? Would he end up like those pitiful creatures?

He closed his eyes and rested his head on his front legs, trying desperately to ignore the biting chains, and thought of Rose.

* * *

Nightstar soared above the eastern ocean, his wings outstretched as he caught the warm thermals rising from the water's surface. He gorged himself on the scraggly goats after leaving the forest of the Larcrowe, taking as much sustenance as he could before embarking on his journey. He had flown for two days and could see no land behind him and nothing in front. The energy he used was minimal, gliding as much as possible to conserve his strength.

With no other distractions and only the ocean below to keep him company, he had more than enough time for contemplation. Nightstar's will was stronger than before and Alduce rarely influenced his decisions. Alduce was still there, part of everything Nightstar had become, but the dragon and the man were more at peace with each other now. It had taken some time for both entities to come to terms with their shared consciousness, but after the accident with the lightning strike and receiving Sunburst's blood, something had changed. Something both Nightstar and Alduce agreed was for the better.

Now there was a clear understanding that without Alduce, Nightstar could not exist, but the dragon was no longer a cloak to be worn, he possessed a mind of his own. Subconsciously, Nightstar wouldn't do anything that would result in putting Alduce in danger. Alduce decided to stop fighting the dragon's mind and embrace the change, trusting the black dragon he'd created, as he would trust himself, as they were the same. Alduce felt the decisions Nightstar made were reflections of his own, he was both halves of the one mind and the choices he made, whether it be man or dragon, were for the best.

He was still a sorcerer and a scientist, but he was also a student, learning something new, learning to listen to Nightstar, allowing him the freedom to evolve.

There was still the conflict of two minds, but both Alduce and Nightstar had come to accept that this would always be, but there was room enough for both personalities, and, Alduce discovered, when it came to making decisions that impacted on dragons, it was best to let Nightstar's persona take the lead.

Alduce wanted to run back to his laboratory, take the easy way out, but Nightstar had taught him that the easy option wasn't always the best one. Sunburst had been a true friend to him and it was wrong to abandon that friendship when things grew tough. Sunburst had shown him how to behave like a dragon, had taught him all about his culture and his home and he had repaid him with betrayal and lies.

Nightstar no longer blamed Alduce, it was what it was. It had happened and he regretted it. Simple dragon logic. He discovered that there was more to his human life than submerging himself in his studies and experiments. He could still have these things, they were still important to him, but friendship and acceptance had also become something he wanted. And now needed.

Sunburst had given him a taste of something new, something he had never experienced before, shown him there was something missing that he hadn't even realised he wanted. It had taken a yellow dragon to show him the empty space he once had in his life, then fill it full of a desire to live and enjoy it.

Alduce was smart enough to understand this was what Winterfang meant when he said there was something missing, something lost that he needed to find. Sunburst's blood was helping him find a small part of what was missing, his dragon self. It was the unknown missing ingredient he didn't know he needed until now. It had shown him what he desired from his dragon life, and also his human one.

It wasn't only the fear of his secret being uncovered that made him feel empty inside, it was fear of living. He no longer needed to impress anyone, he had risen from the ashes and trauma of his past life, become a man, learned sorcery and excelled at it. But all he had to show for his labours was a lonely life in an empty laboratory. Nightstar had opened his eyes to a new world, new passions that invigorated his soul. Alduce would still be the man he had always been, but he believed now, with the help of Sunburst and Nightstar, he would be more than a sorcerer and a scientist, he would be able to be live his life as a man and understand how to enjoy it. The White Mountain dragons had shown him how. He would have Nightstar to guide him and show him how to employ these new attributes he had discovered. This would also help him become a better man.

Nightstar's thoughts returned to the present as movement in the waves below caught his keen dragon eye. The ocean had been peaceful and calm for the last two days, nothing but rolling waves, constant and unchanging. But now there was a new pattern disturbing the crests and troughs, a growing movement below the ocean's surface, breaking through the waves and disturbing the sunlight that reflected upon the water.

Nightstar descended from the high altitude he maintained, casually dropping from the sky until he was closer to the ocean's surface and the unusual activity. It was an unnecessary waste of his strength, but after two uneventful days of flying, anything that broke the monotony was a welcome distraction.

Huge underwater creatures swam beneath the waves, and at first Nightstar thought they were whales. As he studied the creatures, he realised that their shape was not one of a whale, but more like a dragon without wings. Long graceful bodies with huge flippers instead of legs, wide powerful tails and long thick necks, raced through the water beneath him. The underwater leviathans surfaced, breaching the waves, giant dorsal ridges cut through the water, leaving wakes of white spindrift that sparkled in the sunlight.

Alduce watched through Nightstar's eyes and believed these creatures to be distant relatives to the sea dragons, evolution changing their appearance and adapting them to the most efficient form for their environment. If creatures like these swam in the oceans of his own world, they would surely be named sea serpents by the sailors that navigated them.

A streamlined head breached the waves, long trails of seawater ran from its sleek skin. The beast looked up with deep intelligent eyes at Nightstar. Two small nubs sat either side of the head, like worn down horns and behind them, gills flapped, opening and closing as the creature's neck rose higher out of the water. Smooth turquoise skin glistened in the sunlight, appearing blue then green, as the giant sea creature's body rose above the surface.

It opened its mouth and exposed a pink tongue surrounded by rows of small pointed teeth, then it produced a high pitched sound somewhere between squeaking and screaming. Nightstar was unable to fathom if this was a greeting or an attempt at communication. The Flaire artefact that made up his silver scales no help in translating this voice.

He responded to the sea creature with a trumpeting roar and was rewarded with more heads popping up from below the waves. Each creature emitted a sound, similar to the first, but each noise was a different pitch, some high, some low. He counted nine heads in total as they cut through the waves, taking turns to sound off, creating an eerie song that drifted across the ocean. A song only for the black dragon to hear. The strange singing continued for a few minutes, then just as quickly as they had appeared, one by one, the heads of the sea creatures disappeared below the waves, until only the original one remained. It tipped its head to the side once and Nightstar nodded his in return. The creature slowly descended back into the water, dorsal crest and head nubs the only thing breaking through the waves. It sped along for a few moments more, then vanished underneath the surface and Nightstar watched the graceful sea creatures as they disappeared into the ocean depths.

Alduce would have to catalogue this in his journals when he returned to his laboratory, singing sea serpents were just one more wonderful occurrence witnessed through Nightstar's eyes.

He beat his wings, pushing upward and catching the warm currents of air rising from the ocean's surface. He climbed back into the sky, checking his position with the sun after the welcome distraction. He knew which direction he travelled, using his dragon sense instinctually like an internal compass. Trusting to this new ability, positive he flew due east, he wondered how far off the shores of the eastern continent lay.

* * *

Sunburst awoke again to the sound of the creaking gateway and observed the faint light as it crept down the passageway towards his cell. The dark figure that had visited him previously was missing from the group of humans that appeared out of the gloom. As they came closer, Sunburst counted five men, carrying lamps and burdened with an assortment of strange devices. The men stopped outside the cage of the small green dragon, examining the ground where the dark figure had made the mark. They offloaded their burdens and hung their lamps from the ceiling of the passageway, illuminating the area in front of the poorly green dragon's cage.

One of the men unlocked the cage and pulled open the heavy iron bars, standing aside as two of his companions stepped inside. They took hold of a circular device and heaved together, grunting as they rotated it. Chains rattled as the small green dragon hissed and was pulled back, away from the intruders, the chains tightening and pinning the defenceless beast tightly against the cave wall. The man that had unlocked the cage picked a long pole from the pile of equipment and stepped into the cell's doorway, raised the pole to his shoulder, pointing it at the helpless dragon.

He turned his head and looked at Sunburst, a wicked smile spreading over his lips, then he focused his attention on the green dragon within the cage.

Sunburst flinched as the deafening sound of thunder roared within the tunnel, a blinding flash of red flame leapt from the end of the pole. Smoke curled in the lamplight, the smell reaching his nostrils. The two men inside the cage released the circular device and stepped back into the passage. The confining chains rattled free and the device spun, the head of the green dragon slumped forward, its weight pulling it free to rest on the cell floor.

A black hole at the base of the dragon's neck dripped blood onto the cold stone floor and dying eyes stared at Sunburst as its spirt departed and its life ended.

Painful tears rolled down his yellow scales, unstoppable and filled with shame even though he could do nothing to help the condemned green. Sunburst was in no position to do anything but bear witness to the murder of one of his kind and it filled him with strong emotions of hate for these cruel humans. He pushed forward against his own chains, the metal collar tightened against his neck as he attempted to summon his fiery breath and send vengeful flames at the murderer who stood so close, yet so completely out of reach. Nothing came. The charm of incarceration and the human magic within his bonds prevented any attempt at breathing fire.

Frustration and anger filled him as he opened his jaws and roared, he was thankful he still had his voice, but took little pleasure as the five men raised their hands and covered their ears. He might not be able to flame them, but his defiance was clear.

The man that had released the thunder walked slowly to the bars of Sunburst's cage and set a large key in the lock, all the time holding the yellow dragon's gaze. He showed no fear at meeting the stare, arrogant in his movements and confident the dragon was unable to do him harm. He must be aware that the confines of Sunburst's cell were not only physical, but also magically enhanced, inhibiting any attempt of attack.

Sharp words spilled from his cruel mouth, high pitched and harsh, and Sunburst didn't understand them, but the meaning they conveyed needed no translation. The man then turned his back on the yellow dragon, showing not only his earlier arrogance, but a contempt. An enemy of a dragon, ordinarily would never turn his back on his foe, but this man deliberately demonstrated that he didn't fear Sunburst in the slightest.

The yellow dragon pushed forward against the chains and roared again and was rewarded as the man jumped, the sound loud and unexpected behind his head. He left the cage and closed the gate, locking it behind him and walked back to his comrades without a backward glance. He spoke again and the four men laughed and looked in Sunburst's direction. He barked what could only be a command at the four subordinates and they scurried into action like busy rodents. They gathered their equipment and entered into the cage then proceeded to butcher the unfortunate green dragon.

Sunburst watched as the men systematically reduced the dragon to a pile of parts, cutting and dismembering the poor creature's body until nothing remained. Only blades enhanced by sorcery would be able to cut through the armour of a dragon. Limbs, scales, wings, claws and a lifeless head were stacked without any respect. The spilled blood was scraped up and gathered, nothing of the dragon wasted.

If the humans of the east treated dragons this way, the old stories must be true. Sunburst understood the men of this land were powerful enough to disable a dragon and its magic and could kill one without any remorse. No wonder his ancestors had taken flight and journeyed across the vast ocean in search of a new home. He was unaware he was keening quietly until another voice joined his, adding to the sad sound. The men continued with their grizzly task, oblivious to the sad lament of the dragon's death knell. More sorrow filled voices joined Sunburst's dirge, slowly at first, growing louder and with more intensity. As he peered from behind his bars, he saw the reflection of many dragon eyes, incarcerated in their own cells, imitating his own actions.

He wasn't alone in this terrible place, but after seeing more trapped souls than he wanted to, he wished he was.

Chapter 3

The morning sun appeared on the horizon, a red slither of light rising above the grey ocean, painting the distant sky a warm pink. Nightstar flew ever east using his instinct and the internal compass, confident in the knowledge his dragon sense, his *perception*, knew the way. It was nice to see the sunrise, knowing he flew unerringly in the right direction. This was his fifth sunrise since leaving the shores of the west, his wound was fully healed and he felt as strong as he ever had, confident he could travel as long as he needed to.

As the morning brightened, a dark shape was visible on the horizon. A small black stain on the otherwise unmarred grey of the constant ocean. As the sun climbed higher and turned from red to orange, then to bright yellow, the grey of the ocean gave way to blue and the black mark in the distance was easier to see.

After five days of flying, gliding and flapping, flapping and gliding, following the same unending pattern, hope sprang forth and Nightstar's excitement grew. As he neared what could only be land, he longed to feel the ground beneath his claws, to rest his wings, to sleep soundly instead of the flying slumber he had adopted. As the dark shape on the ocean grew closer, he realised he'd discovered an island and was disappointed that it wasn't the eastern continent he searched for. But, it was an extremely large landmass and he would be able to land and take a well-earned rest. The distance to the island was a lot farther than he anticipated and the sun was almost at its zenith before green foliage replaced the waves beneath his wings.

The island was dominated by high mountain peaks at its centre, surrounded by densely populated forests and steep hillsides. The hills gave way to flatter lands, eventually becoming shores and beaches. Alduce concluded that the island had been birthed from a volcano rising from the ocean floor, the molten lava that had shaped the lofty peaks, now dormant. He would have liked to have witnessed that event as Nightstar, flying safely above the smoke, gases and newly formed rock, being present for the creation of a new land.

Green seas surrounded most of the island, the colour of the blue sky and the yellow sand changing the shallow waters from the normal blue-grey that the deeper ocean wore. The new colours were welcome to his eyes after days of the same unchanging hues.

He glided over treetops circling back towards a sandy bay, picking a wide stretch of golden sand to land on. As he descended, he spotted huge blunt nosed fish swimming in the shallows, their silver bodies easily seen in the clear water. Grumbling hunger pangs reminded Nightstar that it had been five days since he had eaten the stringy tasteless goats. The thought of fish for breakfast made him change direction and swoop back out over the ocean he had longed to be rid of.

Talons opened wide and extended forward, Nightstar plunged into the sea and grasped a wriggling fish in each claw. Water ran from their silver scales as he plucked them from the safety of the ocean. The two captured fish unsuccessful as they writhed in an attempt to free themselves from the dragon's grip. Nightstar was amazed at how fat the fish were as he carried them towards the beach. The remainder of the shoal, scattered when the dragon had disturbed them, grouped back together now the danger was gone. The shadow of the dragon scudded over the calm waves of the bay, gliding over the sand beneath the water's surface until Nightstar dropped to the beach, dragon and shadow becoming one.

He folded his wings, sighing in exaggerated relief and tucked them to his sides, relaxing as the heat of the sun warmed his scales. He hadn't noticed the difference in temperature as he had flown and had become accustomed to the cooler heights and continuous breeze.

He tore into the first fish, the taste of sweet flesh, succulent and warm, exploded in his mouth as he gulped down his first food in five days. It was true that dragons could gorge on food and it would sustain them for weeks at a time, but the human part of him missed regular meals and delighted in his feast. After he devoured the second fish, Nightstar helped himself to seconds, then thirds. Dragons made excellent fishers and as he finished his meal, Nightstar shared a memory that Alduce recalled, another saying that Caltus favoured.

Give a man a fish, he would eat for a day. Teach a man to fish and he would eat every day.

Nightstar's forked tongue flicked between his teeth cleaning the remnants of his meal from his mouth. He licked his snout next and when he was satisfied that every last morsel of fish was gone, he curled up on the sand. He wondered if master Caltus would be able to teach a dragon how to fish, after he got over the shock of meeting one. His old master, or rather the master of a younger Alduce, would probably have tried. A small puff of smoke snorted from his nostrils as Nightstar laughed and Alduce understood and appreciated the dragon's humour. Nightstar had never known Caltus, but he knew how the old sorcerer behaved and he'd made a joke, based on how the old man would have reacted. Caltus would have attempted to teach a fish to fish and the irony would have been lost on his old mentor, but not on the dragon that shared his former pupil's mind.

Now sated after the six large fish he had consumed, Nightstar wanted to sleep, but Alduce was eager to explore the temporary haven of the island. The dragon stretched out on the warm sand, drowsy with the heat and the meal, but also weary after five days flying. Sleep won and Nightstar closed his eyes and let himself drift peacefully into slumber. His last thoughts were of Caltus and of Sunburst and as dreams rose to fill his tired mind, he imagined the old man with a fishing rod, sitting on the shores of Sunburst's favourite lake, explaining the finer points of fishing to an enthusiastic yellow dragon.

* * *

Nightstar opened his eyes, the afternoon sun had lost its midday intensity as it travelled west towards the horizon. The black dragon felt refreshed after his sleep, his belly full and his wings rested. Flying such a long distance was possible for a dragon, but stopping to recuperate made it easier.

Nightstar was conscious he shouldn't delay his search for Sunburst unnecessarily, but he was intrigued to learn more about the island. He could spend a few hours exploring the green forests, the sandy shores, and mountainous crags and still depart in the darkness, as he could fly with or without light. He felt a growing urgency to find the yellow dragon, Winterfang had sensed he was in danger and Nightstar did not want to waste too much time.

He pushed upwards from his sandy beach and beat his wings, creating small sandstorms as he flapped. He banked out over the empty sea, the shoals of blunt nose fish no longer filled the bay. Lazily turning, he gained height and flew back over the beach, the marks of his time spent on the sand visible above the high tide line. Following the contours of the ground, he climbed, gaining height until he rose above the dense trees and was crossing the rocky slopes of the inland mountain peaks. Higher and higher he climbed until at last he was circling the crater mouth of the extinct volcano, the once deep depression had been shallowed by centuries of erosion.

Nightstar flew above the crater and saw he wasn't the first to have explored it. The volcanic sand that made up the crater floor had been disturbed and dark claw prints stood out against the sun bleached surface.

Nightstar dropped into the crater mouth and spiralled down, following the lip of the crater rim. He wanted to observe the disturbance before landing and adding his own claw marks to the existing ones. He circled the inside of the crater a few more times, taking a good look before landing, claw prints weren't the only trace the previous visitor had left behind.

A half-eaten carcass, host now to buzzing insects, lay on the volcanic sand. Nightstar was reminded of the partially eaten curly buck Sunburst had left for the scavenging Larcrowe. The yellow dragon consumed his favourite parts of the beast, leaving the legs and head. The bloated remains of the animal, swarming with flies, a perfect match for Sunburst's left overs. Examining the claw marks in the sand and the depression where a smaller yellow dragon might have rested or slept, he was convinced his quarry had stopped here.

Nightstar was delighted at his find and eager now to continue his search, confident his friend had come this way and he was heading in the right direction. Having seen the evidence, he was sure that it could only have been Sunburst that had spent time in the volcano's crater. His enthusiasm was renewed. Days of flying over the eastern ocean with no land marks or traces of Sunburst's passing were difficult to accept. No longer did he doubt himself, no longer did he doubt his direction. He was Nightstar the Black, confident now he was closer to finding Sunburst, both physically and mentally.

He leapt from the sandy crater floor, disturbing a million angry insects from their fetid feast, the powerful downdraught of his wings dashing the black buzzing cloud in all directions. Beating his wings harder and faster, he cleared the rim of the crater and set his wings to glide down over the opposite mountainside, leaving the centre of the island and the dormant volcano behind. Gathering speed as he descended, he cleared the dense jungles and sandy beaches, leaving behind the shallow bays of the shoreline and replacing them with the cool blue depths of the ocean.

A few hours later, with the sun sinking behind him, Nightstar travelled through the night sky. A vacuum of darkness surrounded the black dragon and the memory of the tropical island with its golden beaches and lush green forest felt like a distant dream.

Nightstar felt closer to his goal now and was confident he would find Sunburst and return him home to the White Mountains. With a renewed vigour, he looked to the horizon. The sunrise was still a long way off, but he looked forward to the new day with anticipation, sure that his long journey east was almost over.

Chapter 4

"I am known as Sunburst," the yellow dragon addressed the dark, "my yellow scales are the colour of the sun. When I take flight I burn across the sky like a celestial fire."

Silence greeted his words, the other captive dragons shuffled in their cages, but none responded. If he were to escape this dungeon, he would need help and the only allies he could call on would be the other caged dragons that shared this dismal place with him.

"Are any of you able to speak?" Sunburst asked.

"Yellow scales?" A small voice asked from somewhere beyond his metal bars.

"There are no yellows left!" A gruffer sounding voice scoffed. "There is no sky to burn across down here. Be quiet. The Extractor will hear your empty rumblings and the less we see of him the better."

"Skin and scales! I'm stuck down here with Galvon's distant cousin," Sunburst said. "I *am* yellow, as yellow as the sun. Who dares to dispute it?" Silence once more filled the darkness. "Tell me of the Extractor. Please. I've come a long way to end up stuck in this cell and I need some answers."

"Well, celestial Sunburst with the yellow scales, if you don't already know, you are a captive of the humans, held in an underground dungeon. Your blood will be drained from your body, extracted and used by humans to fuel their dark magic. When your blood grows weak from constant draining, when you tire and you are exhausted and useless to him, you'll end up like Elvor. Chopped into pieces and your magic will be extracted from your *yellow* scales, your skin, your wings, and your very bones. Nothing is wasted, the Extractor consumes it all."

Elvor must have been the unfortunate dragon Sunburst had witnessed being horribly dismembered. He was sure the Extractor was the evil human who had stood outside his bars taunting him with cruel words. He didn't understand the language, but the message was clear enough

"The Extractor will pay for his crimes," Sunburst said. "When I escape I will char his flesh, all he will extract will be his own ash!" This human should be punished.

"Brave words," the gruff dragon replied. "How is it you plan on escaping? You are chained by iron strengthened with human sorcery, it weakens the strongest of us, supressing our magic. It is impossible to fight back. Once you are taken, that's it. There is no escape."

"I'll think of something," Sunburst said, determined not to let the gruff voice dampen his fighting spirit. "I'm not giving up."

"Brave words won't help you down here. We were all defiant when we were first captured, but after a while, the darkness and the draining wear you down. The Extractor may be cruel, but he is also cunning. He knows dragons and how to best them with sorcery and slow torture."

Sunburst put aside the notion of escape for the time being, that problem needed some more thought. For now this gruff dragon was talking to him. If he could find out more, it might help him come up with a plan.

"Will you tell me your name, cousin captive?"

"You ask a lot of questions," the gruff voice said, then after a pause, it continued. "I am Fentor the Green, of the forest, if you must know."

Sunburst was reminded of Nightstar and the questions he continually asked. He thought the black dragon asked many questions. It was strange that he now found himself in a similar role, looking for answers rather than providing them.

"I am pleased to make your acquaintance," Fentor added, "though I wish it were not in this dungeon. I would like to look upon your yellow scales and see them shine in the sun. This dank hovel depresses me, it is no place for a dragon."

A forest green, just like Galvon, no wonder he was reminded of the grumpy dragon from the White Mountain Moot.

"I am pleased, too, cousin Fentor, my line is also descended from forest dragons. We are well met." He would prefer if he could befriend these dragons, rather than upset them, as he often did with Galvon when he talked with him. Forest greens could be cranky and suspicious at the best of times.

"I'm Serth," the small voice piped up, "I too would like to see your yellow scales, Sunburst."

"You don't have any yellow dragons here?" Sunburst asked in an attempt to engage the timid female voice.

"Mostly greens," Serth said, her young voice more confident now.

"And a few reds and blues." Fentor added.

"Do you have any blacks?" Sunburst asked.

"Blacks! Bah!" Fentor grumbled. "They are a myth, everyone knows that."

"I have a friend who's a black, with silver scales emblazoned on his chest," Sunburst needed to tell the dragons something to lift their spirits. "He's larger than any dragon you've ever seen."

He wished Nightstar were here now, he would know what to do. He had left his home and travelled across the eastern ocean, too distressed to think, upset at the realisation his friend wasn't what he seemed. He had tried to forget Nightstar and Alduce, but he couldn't. It was strange, even after everything that had happened, he looked to Nightstar for answers.

Stuck here now, facing the same fate as poor Elvor, he began to question his decision. He was in a worse position than he had been when he left Nightstar. Was he wrong to let Alduce live? Being held captive and waiting to be tortured, his blood drained, with only death and dismemberment in his future, what he had given to Alduce didn't seem so bad now. The three drops of his blood he willingly gave to save the life of the sorcerer was a small thing compared to what the Extractor was doing. He was sure even Alduce would be appalled. Nightstar had lived as a dragon for months and he was as much a dragon as any other dragon Sunburst had known.

"Tell us about your friend," Serth asked. "What is he called?"

"And why is he not here with you?" Fentor sneered. "Myth I tell you, he's not here as he doesn't exist."

"Nightstar the Black is no myth. In some places dragons are believed to be myth by those who have never seen us, but we are real, we are all very real. Just because you haven't seen a black doesn't mean they are myth." Nightstar may be many other things, but these dragons didn't need to know that. "When darkness fills the night sky, the star on his chest blazes silver, a beacon of hope in the blackest hour."

Sunburst remembered his first meeting with Nightstar and the joy of his friendship, before uncovering his terrible secret. He instantly liked the black dragon and enjoyed his company. Flying free with Nightstar was better that being a prisoner in these miserable dungeons. Even if he was part sorcerer.

"He *is* real," Sunburst said, almost to himself. He may also be a man, but the black dragon was real. He couldn't be anything else. He had flown and hunted with Nightstar, he was more than just a man in another shape and he had the spirit of a true dragon.

"I believe you," Serth said. "I would like to have met your friend."

"I believe he would like to have met you too, all of you," Sunburst told them. It was true, Nightstar loved all dragons. He even liked Galvon!

"He should think himself lucky he wasn't stupid enough to get caught and end up down here with us. He wouldn't like that!" Fentor said.

"He is one of the largest dragons you will ever meet, he wouldn't fit in these cages. And he is more powerful that you could know." Sunburst wasn't sure why he was defending Nightstar. He was still angry at his betrayal, but anger was a wasted emotion when you were waiting to die.

"Tell us more about Nightstar."

"Where do you come from?"

"How did you get taken?"

New voices spoke, sad and forlorn, sounding like faint reflections of once free dragons. Sunburst hoped the captives would forget their plight for a little while and he could lift their spirits. If he could get them talking perhaps he could uncover something that would help them all to escape.

And so it began, one by one, dragons spoke their names in the darkness, twelve in total, introducing themselves to the newest inmate in the Extractor's prison. Sunburst could feel a difference in the atmosphere as each captured dragon spoke their name and expressed a wish to see his yellow scales and met the black dragon who was his friend. He provided his fellow captives with a respite from their inevitable doom as he told them where he had come from. He shared the story of his crossing of the eastern ocean. He told them how he had been captured, trapped in a sorcerous net he couldn't break free from.

The other dragons told of their own demise and shared their stories with Sunburst, slowly at first, then more confidently as Sunburst engaged them, realising that he was gently questioning, gathering information, as Nightstar had done with him.

They discussed the Great Exodus, the eastern dragons amazed as he told of them of his home and the lands to the west. They could hardly believe the land that lay beyond the vast ocean was free from humans.

The dragons that were left behind all those years ago, were smaller and weaker. The captives held in the dungeon of the Extractor were their descendants. If these survivors were all like poor Elvor, and his *perception*—his dragon sense—told him this was true, the years had been cruel to them. For five hundred years, the remaining dragons bred smaller and less powerful individuals, their colours less vibrant. Their magic had faded over time and even in his own weakened state, he could sense this.

He told them what they needed to hear, what they wanted to know. As he spoke, he wondered about his friendship with Nightstar, about the time they had spent together. The more he spoke about the black dragon the more he wondered what he could have done differently, if he had known what his future held.

He wasn't yet ready to admit that there was nothing he could do, even though things looked hopeless. He remembered his visions of Alduce and how, no matter what, the stubborn human never gave up. He would stay strong, not only for himself, but for the poor persecuted dragons that shared their fate with him.

He would wait, try and find out about the Extractor. He was larger and stronger than these eastern dragons. The Extractor hadn't faced a White Mountain dragon before.

Sunburst would show him he was a different breed from the victims he had previously picked on.

Chapter 5

The eastern continent of Eusavus drifted by below Nightstar's wings. Finally crossing the ocean and arriving in the east, the vast sea replaced with dark countryside. It was still night and the morning's sunrise would herald the seventh day of travel for the black dragon.

As he flew, he scanned the land, occasionally spotting the isolated lights of human habitation. As the morning sun rose and daylight crept above the horizon, Nightstar identified small settlements and villages. He descended from his cruising altitude, conscious that as the morning sky grew lighter, he would be easily seen from below. The structures he observed so far were similar to rural residences from his homeland; farms and hamlets devoid of any signs of life this early in the day.

This was a new land and he wasn't familiar with the people who inhabited it, so he thought it best to remain hidden from the population until he learned more. He imagined that if dragons departed these shores over five hundred years ago, he would stand out and his appearance would be highly unusual. Something he wished to avoid, especially as the circumstances leading up the Great Exodus were less than favourable for dragon kind.

In the distance a large city spread out across the land, as good a place as any to seek answers, but not as a dragon. Nightstar changed direction, veering away from the man made place, circling the countryside and using the forests and hills as a natural shield, mindful that even though it was early, if he wasn't careful, he may attract unwanted attention.

Spotting a remote farmstead, he looked for somewhere to land, far enough from the ramshackle buildings to stay hidden. Silently gliding until he found a sheltered spot behind a small copse, he dropped quickly to the ground, closing his wings and remaining alert for any signs of alarm. None came.

Nightstar withdrew, consciously letting the dragon form slip. Alduce had become comfortable holding the transformation spell. Remaining as Nightstar was effortless to him now. Only when he wanted to change back, did he need to think about it.

The awareness of Alduce came forward as the human part of his mind became more prevalent. The black dragon's body shimmered, soft white light surrounding each scale as he shrank, reducing his dragon's body and changing the black scales to pink skin, leaving a naked man where the giant dragon had stood.

Alduce shivered in the cool morning air, his flesh raised and the small hairs of his human skin standing on end. It was a strange feeling after being almost impervious to the elements and he swayed slightly, finding his balance on two legs. Changing from Nightstar back to Alduce wasn't as painful anymore and the sense of disorientation was shorter. Alduce could still feel the ghost limbs of wings and tail, but that faded as he regressed back into his human body.

Nightstar was buried deep in his subconscious, but the dragon mind was still there, reachable and real. Rubbing hands up and down his arms vigorously to heat them, Alduce started walking in the direction of the old farm building that was close to his landing site. The ground was hard and small stones and sharp twigs dug into his bare feet. Human feet—no longer protected by the tough hide and talons of dragon claws.

Realisation of just how frail human beings really were, more obvious to the sorcerer now, when he compared his human body to the armour and strength of a dragon.

Alduce didn't regret his human form, it was his natural state and there were advantages to being a man too. The dexterity of his fingers was a pleasure to him. He wiggled them unconsciously, bending and clenching the amazing digits. Such a normal action, but wonderful too. It was all down to perspective and if he could maintain the correct mind set when he was in either manifestation, he would be fine.

As he walked, there was less turmoil in his mind and the conflict between himself and Nightstar was now more tolerable. Gradually he was learning to accept his other persona. The worry he felt about Nightstar taking over his identity was replaced with a more comfortable relationship. The change in his physiology, blended with magic, had settled, stabilising as his body and mind adapted to the massive strain he had inflicted upon himself. Another saying Caltus often used came to mind.

What doesn't kill us, makes us stronger.

Alduce hadn't known what to expect when he performed his magic on the lonely hilltop all those months ago. Science and sorcery were never without risk, and the greater that risk, the greater the reward. He could feel the dragon in his blood when he reached for it, knew he could easily call on Nightstar and slide into his mind and his shape. Even the pain of transformation from man to dragon was less of a concern. His achievement with the original spell, while ground-breaking in his field, had lacked one key ingredient, the missing part that made the shape changing perfect.

Sunburst's living blood.

This was what made his transformation complete. The live dragon blood was potent beyond everything he knew. Not only had it saved him from the wound the lightning inflicted, it was the catalyst that he needed to find balance and sanity between his two personas.

If events hadn't transpired in this way, Alduce wasn't sure the long term results of his transformation would be as successful.

He needed to find Sunburst, the feeling of danger for his yellow friend was stronger than ever. Winterfang and the pearl had both sensed something was wrong. Nightstar knew it instinctively, his *perception* was clear. And as a result of the dichotomy between the dragon and the sorcerer, Alduce could feel it too. He couldn't quite understand how. He just knew.

He had been ready to leave this world and return to his own, but now he knew Nightstar was right, he could never abandon Sunburst. Even as Alduce, he was willing to stay and find him. Nightstar had shown him the meaning of true friendship and both man and dragon needed to make things right, as between them, they had ultimately been the cause of Sunburst's troubles. But first, he needed to find the yellow dragon and he already had the beginnings of an idea.

Alduce wished he was able to carry clothes with him when he was Nightstar, changing back to human form and being naked was fine when you had access to your clothing. Another disadvantage of being a man.

Cursing the cold and shivering, he gripped the small silver dragon that hung around his neck, drawing warmth from the metal, letting it heat his body. Hopefully he would find something to wear at the nearby farmstead, which for the moment, was his priority. If he could clothe himself and depart undetected, all the better.

It didn't matter where you were, what world you walked upon, a naked man wearing only a valuable necklace would stand out. Alduce needed to blend in. Once he tackled the problem of his nudity, he would be ready to find Sunburst. He approached the outer buildings of the run down farm, the scholar already thinking about a plan.

* * *

The Extractor drove the sharp wedged blade under one of the scales on Sunburst's belly. Cold metal forced its way into his armour, painful and foreign, burning with human magic. The hammer rang in the confines of the underground dungeon as it struck the head of the wedge repeatedly. With each heavy blow, the wedge prised open a gap, pushing the protective yellow scale away from the skin underneath.

Sunburst flinched each time the Extractor swung the hammer. Unable to resist as chains pulled his body back against the stone wall. The iron links and human magic held him firmly in place, allowing the Extractor and his men to perform their horrific deed unhampered. Sunburst coughed attempting to call forth his dragon flame, gagging loudly instead of releasing the fire he so desperately wished for. The magical bonds restraining his ability to do anything other than endure the invasive attack.

With a final blow, the metal wedge broke through the natural seal, separating the scale from the others, bending it at an angle and exposing the pale yellow flesh it protected. One of the Extractors men forced another piece of metal underneath, holding the scale away from Sunburst's body and preventing him from closing it back in place. The Extractor stood back, tossing the hammer out of the cell, where it landed on the stone floor with a clatter. He reached up and slapped Sunburst's side affectionately, opening his mouth, harsh unintelligible words spilled out. His companions laughed, a crude guttural noise that offended his ears, the vile humans finding humour at his expense.

The Extractor rummaged in a large bag of equipment sitting on the floor and removed a wicked looking device. A long tapered needle protruded from one end, sharp claws surrounding its base. A thick tube exited from the base, with levers fixed to the metal encasing it.

The Extractor checked the device, thumbing the tip as he tested its edge under the lamplight. When he was satisfied with his examination, he placed one hand on Sunburst's side, next to the open scale and drew back the device with the other.

Sunburst followed his actions, angling his head to see what his captors where doing. Straining on already tightened chains, the metal collar bit into his neck, the human magic subduing him. Without warning the Extractors arm lanced forward and the needle point of the device drove under the open scale and into the yellow skin.

Pain exploded through his body as cold metal suffused with foul human magic punctured his unprotected flesh. He threw back his head as far as his constraints would allow and roared. The sharp needle burrowed deep into his flesh, white hot pain causing dizziness and nausea. The human magic of the Extractor sapped his strength, draining his life-force and added to the agony. Low keening drifted from the surrounding cells as the other imprisoned dragons sympathised with their fellow captive's torture.

Sunburst was barely conscious, the agony almost too much to endure. The Extractor and his men scrabbled around the cell, clamping the device in place and attaching a long hose to the open end and rolling an open barrel to catch the flowing life blood spurting from the open end. Steam rose from the inside of the barrel as Sunburst's blood gushed from the open hose. The speed and efficiency of the well-practiced procedure ensured that not one single drop of the precious liquid escaped.

The men laughed and hopped around like insects on rotting flesh, pleased at their success. Sunburst's consciousness drifted as the pain from the restraining magic washed through his body. He hung limply in the chains as they supported his weight, weakness draining his spirit, physically beaten and unable to resist. His anger was all that kept him awake, meeting the eyes of the Extractor, his hateful stare conveyed his defiance. Sunburst forced his eyes to remain open and waited for what felt like hours as the blood drained from his body and into the barrel.

When the men had finished stealing his blood, the Extractor removed the needle, sliding it painfully from his skin, taking care not to lose any precious drops. The men sealed the barrel and removed it from the cell and the Extractor followed them out, their harsh chatter echoing along the passageway.

The gate slammed shut, iron bars clanging into place and the Extractor released the mechanism that pinned Sunburst to the stone wall. Chains slackened and Sunburst slumped to the floor in a heap, exhausted and weak. His belly throbbed and his head swam. Before he finally surrendered to the unconsciousness that swallowed him, he wished, not for the first time, that he had never left the White Mountains and crossed the eastern ocean.

These shores offered nothing the yellow dragon wanted. He longed for the freedom of the skies and to fly high and fly free.

Chapter 6

The old man wandered through the city gates, his back bent, keeping close to the wagon he followed. If he appeared to be travelling with the wagon, the city watch wouldn't give him a second look and he didn't want to be stopped and questioned about his business in the city. Legitimate merchants and farmers were welcome in towns and cities, but ragged beggars would be chased off. There were enough homeless in any large town without adding any more to their number.

Walking with his head down, the old man avoided eye contact. He wore a grey threadbare blanket wrapped over his shoulders, a functional work shirt and a pair of homespun trousers. A small shapeless hat, perched atop his head, completing the disguise. He appeared as a work weary farmhand accompanying his employer, and his produce filled wagon, to market.

The city watch paid him no mind and once he passed under the gateway and entered the city proper, he straightened his back and detached himself from the wagon. He no longer appeared old as he strode along the main thoroughfare, walking with the confidence of someone who belonged, even though he looked like a beggar. He clasped the blanket around his throat, not because it was cold, but because he didn't want the dragon pendant he wore around his neck to be seen. It was an extremely fine piece of workmanship and not something a ragged beggar would usually own. An unseen knife from the shadows would relieve him of his life and his valuable pendant if he didn't take care and keep it out of plain sight.

After walking all morning Alduce chose to enter the city using a stealthy approach. A huge black dragon soaring through the skies would have attracted too much attention. His legs weren't use to the physical exercise as he had relied on his wings over the last few months. However, he enjoyed his walk, slow as it was, meeting strangers on the road as he neared the city known as Hermanton. Questioning the unsuspecting travellers he encountered, he enticed snippets of information from each one, piecing together as much as he could about this continent and its inhabitants.

Dragons were hunted and captured here, prized for their magic. There were regiments of soldiers trained for the task and there was a certain prestige attached to the hunt. They were armed with sorcerous weapons that could weaken a dragon and disable its natural magical defences. Alduce knew now why the Great Exodus was so important. This powerful race, strong in body and magic, had hunted dragons to near extinction.

He followed the main road into the heart of the city, careful to remain unobtrusive, favouring the adjacent streets and parallel avenues when possible. As he made his way deeper into human territory, he was surprised to feel like an outsider. His life over the past few years had been that of a recluse, hidden away in his laboratory, studying, learning and experimenting, happy in his solitude. After spending time at the White Mountain, he could appreciate the benefits of community. The dragons had welcomed him and shown him what it meant to be a part of their world.

Maybe it was because this was a foreign city and he was a stranger that his experience felt more alien than human. He didn't know these people, although from what he learned from the ones he had spoken with, he wasn't sure he wanted to. When he returned to his own world, he would spend some time getting to know his own species, visit his acquaintances in the city of Learning. But first he would need to record his experiences in the dragon bound journals, *always a scholar first*, as Caltus said.

On the periphery of the market square, the poor gathered, seeking charity from the rich merchants and the townspeople who came to buy and trade. Ragged dirty people, dressed as he was, staked out their place along the wall surrounding the market. Crude shelters and piles of rags populated by the dregs of the city, the poor and homeless, the unworthy, criminals and beggars.

Alduce joined them, sliding his back down the wall into the space between an old woman and a boy with one leg. Both had their begging bowls sitting in front of them, a few meagre coins in each. They eyed him suspiciously as he sat down and removed his hat, turning it upside down and dropping it on the ground in direct competition with their own source of income.

A passing woman, dressed in expensive clothes dropped four small coins into Alduce's empty hat. He touched his forehead in deference to his betters and mumbled thanks, playing the role of a homeless bedraggled beggar to perfection. The woman walked on and the boy and old woman to either side glowered at him.

He reached into his hat scooping up two of the four small coins and tossed one into each of the beggar's bowls to his left and right, gaining a nod from the old woman and a suspicious look from the one legged boy. The old woman hesitantly reached her hand towards to the two remaining coins in his hat and waited, meeting his eyes. Alduce nodded and she deftly lifted the two remaining coins and tucked them under his own blanket, leaving his hat empty.

Leaning back on the wall, Alduce listened to the world around him, eavesdropping snippets of conversations from the passers-by, learning all he could about Hermanton. Over the next few hours, he sat and pretended to be one of the invisible people who lived on the street, relying on the generosity of others to survive. Always listening, always learning. Each time he collected enough coins in his hat, he followed the old woman's lead. He would keep a few for himself and pass one to either side, one to the woman and one to the boy.

They kept their own bowls almost empty, hiding away the extra coins Alduce passed them. Human nature was something he had studied and being a scholar he was eager to learn how people acted. If he kept his own hat free from coins, while the beggars to either side of him had a few, the charitable donors were more likely to drop their offerings in his empty hat, rather than add to the beggars who had already received something.

His reaction from the woman and the boy changed as he kept them sweet, sharing his growing wealth. They may be ragged and down on their luck, but they weren't stupid. They worked together as a team, making sure the extra coins they received were hidden away safely, keeping the amount displayed in their begging bowls the same, a few paltry coins in each. If you were to survive on the street, you needed to adapt and Alduce was a quick study.

When he first joined them, he was as welcome as a fox in a henhouse, encroaching on their turf, taking potential earnings from their pockets. Now, adding extra coins to their daily income, the old woman treated him to toothless smiles and even the boy grudgingly nodded to him each time he received a bonus coin. Alduce believed they both realised their new arrangement was a joint effort, they wouldn't get as many coins if they didn't all play their part and keep their bowls as they were.

After ensuring that his new companions were well looked after, building a little trust, he started to engage them in conversation, slowly learning as much about Hermanton as he could. The information he received wasn't what he hoped for. Where to find a reasonably sheltered place to sleep, what inn keepers would pass out stale food, things that would be helpful for someone like his companions, but not the information he was looking for.

The jingle of coins alerted him to a new donation and he caught the last part of the conversation from the man who had provided it as he departed.

"...biggest one I ever saw, and yellow! I thought all the yellow dragons were gone."

Alduce sat up at word of the yellow dragon, straining to hear what else the stranger said, his patience eventually paying off.

"Saw it too," the old woman said. She spoke for the first time, noticing his interest in the conversation. Reaching into his hat, Alduce fished out the coins the man deposited. He flipped a single one to the boy and turned back to the old woman. Adding a few more coins from the pile stashed under his ragged blanket, he held his hand out, three coins flat on his palm.

"Tell me about the yellow dragon, madam," he prompted.

She snatched for the offered coins and Alduce drew his hand back out of reach.

"Madam!" The old woman cackled with a toothless laugh. "I seen 'em bring it in, netted and chained, massive it was, biggest ever, I'd wager." Alduce dropped the coins into her hand and they disappeared with the skill of a conjuror.

"When was this?"

"Four or five days ago, maybe a little more, week at most." the boy added, keen to earn more coins. "I seen it too! Passed right by old Aggie and me. Trussed up like a hog, it was!" He held out his hand and Alduce took a few more coins from his pile and passed them to the boy

"Do you know where the dragon is now?" Alduce asked.

"Where *he* takes them all. The Sanguinorium." The boy answered, as if stating the obvious.

"Who's *he*?"

"The Extractor of course, the most powerful sorcerer and most feared dragon hunter in history, that's who," the old woman said.

"And how would one find this Extractor do you know? And where would you find the Sanguinorium?"

The boy and the old woman looked up, beyond the canvas roofs of the market stalls and Alduce followed their gaze. A large building resembling a palace dominated the city skyline.

"There," the boy pointed. "There's where you'd find them both. But the likes of us aren't welcome up there."

For the next hour Alduce quizzed his comrades about the Extractor and the Sanguinorium. He found out everything he could about when Sunburst arrived and how he had been captured. The boy and the woman liked to gossip, especially as their benevolent acquaintance made it worth their while.

When he had gleaned all he could, Alduce thanked them both stood up and pocketed what was left in his hat, then placed it back on his head. He had accumulated enough money to get a meal and a beer. Where better than a local tavern to buy something to eat, sit and nurse a tankard or two and listen to the local gossip. Where alcohol was involved, people were more likely to have loose tongues.

Performing a small bow to his fellow beggars, the one legged boy touched his hand to his forehead and smiled, patting his pockets. "Best day I've had in months."

The old woman grinned, nodding her agreement and gave him an unexpected wink. He winked back.

Alduce headed in the direction of the large palace known as the Sanguinorium, in search of a tavern or inn. He would gather some more information and when he learned as much as he could, he would look for a way inside. The stories the beggars told him about dragons and what happened to them after the Extractor took them, filled him with dread.

If Sunburst had been taken there, he needed to find a way in before it was too late.

Chapter 7

Sunburst opened tired eyes, helpless to resist the ministrations of the Extractor and his subordinates. He felt the blood drain from his body, weakening his mind and his spirit. He floated, semi-conscious as the parasites stole his life, drop by drop.

Fentor had been right, there was nothing he could do to escape the dungeon, and the longer he was held captive, the harder it was to resist. The other dragons were left alone while the Extractor focused solely on his blood. Being larger and stronger, his blood was of higher value to the men that coveted it. More potent than that of his new friends. As a result, Fentor, Serth and the other caged dragons were given a respite from the draining, but Sunburst suspected this would only be temporary. When the Extractor had used him up, just as he had with poor Elvor, he would continue with his cruel torture of the smaller and weaker dragons.

They all received food and water, dead animals, functional but far from appetising. The Extractor would not allow his assets to die from thirst or starvation. The longer they were kept alive, the longer they could produce live blood. As a result of being left alone the other dragons had recovered some of their strength, engaging him in conversation in an attempt to keep up his morale. They spoke about what they would do to the Extractor if they ever escaped, but Sunburst admitted to himself that their fate would be the same as his. Draining and dismemberment.

He had arrived in the dungeon, bringing with him hope, determined to help these weak pathetic prisoners who had resigned themselves to their fate. Now it was he who had given up and the dragons of the eastern shores, smaller and weaker than himself, had strengthened their own resolve.

The Extractor ushered his men from Sunburst's cell, removing the contraption from under his violated scale. He leaned his hand on the yellow dragon's side, looking into his eyes. Sunburst glowered back, the hate that had once shown in his eyes replaced with defeat. The Extractor was taunting him, standing close, touching him without fear, unafraid he was inside the reach of the chains, confident the yellow dragon was beaten and unable to react.

Sunburst focused, willing the floating sensation to pass just enough for him to bite his tormentor's head off. It would probably taste worse than the fetid remains of the meat he was fed, but it would be sweeter that the tastiest curly buck as he crushed the man's skull between his jaws. He lunged forward, jaws wide, attempting to sink his teeth into his foul tormentor's head, only to fall short as he crashed to the floor, pain exploding inside his head.

The Extractor swung his leg, his booted foot connecting with his snout, delivering another shock to his skull. His vision swam and his eyes rolled. He felt so weak. He could easily close his eyes and drift away, embracing death and escaping this horrible place for ever. His vision slowly cleared and when his eyes focused, he was being observed by the Extractor, who squatted in front of him. He patted Sunburst's head and the cell filled with his disgusting laughter.

Powerful hatred flared anew and Sunburst's thoughts of death vanished, no longer wishing to die. This man, this butcher of dragons, defiler of all that was good, did not deserve to live. As long as one drop of blood remained in his body, Sunburst would resist, he would fight back in any way he could. He met the Extractor's gaze, his sight clearer than before, his defiance rekindled.

The Extractor stood and departed the cell, slamming the gate closed, the clanging jarred inside Sunburst's already fragile head. Resistance was the only victory he could reach for, small as it was, he held on to it and fantasised about grinding the Extractor's bones between his teeth. As he slid into blackness, he cursed his bad luck and his last waking thoughts returned to how he had been captured.

* * *

Sunburst flew across the forests of the eastern continent, feasting his eyes on the colours below, happy to have finally crossed the vast ocean. He travelled inland, exploring the terrain, searching for food and a place to rest. Fat animals, hooved and horned, roamed the open lands, areas with artificial boundaries of straight lines that didn't occur in nature. Plucking a beast from the scattering herd, the animals bleated and brayed in panic as they fled from the winged menace.

As he dined on his prey, men appeared and he sensed a strong human magic from them. He left his half eaten meal and climbed into the air, circling the area and watching the small men on the ground, scrabbling frantically and making more noise than the panicked beasts.

They launched magical blasts from long staffs and he evaded them, dodging and swerving as they streaked by, feeling heat on his scales and the power of the magic they contained. He climbed higher, hoping to move far enough away from the potential danger, aware that if the bolts of magic were to hit him, he would be in trouble.

Images of the storm and the lightning striking Nightstar flashed through his mind, the disaster that had befallen the black dragon and the aftermath that followed. Harsh reminders of why he had fled from the west. He wouldn't become a human if the magical attacks struck him, but they could cause him to fall, as Alduce had. There would be no kindly yellow dragon to rescue his falling body from the hard ground and a dead drop mid-flight was not something he wanted to experience.

Undulating and swerving, he continued east, away from the men and their magic. He should have followed the coast and found somewhere to rest, still tired from the long crossing. If he had been smarter and taken some time to recuperate he would have been ready for the next attack when it came.

Bolts of blue shot up from the ground as he skimmed over the tree tops, flitting and weaving until one magical bolt glanced his wingtip. Paralyzing pain lanced along the entire length of his wing, a combination of a freezing and burning at the same time. It was all he could do to stay in the sky, stretching out his wing as agony wracked the appendage, fearful if he didn't hold it there, he would plummet to the ground. It was impossible to flap the disabled wing, it remained stiff and stubborn and wouldn't do as he wanted.

Gliding was his only option, holding the wing straight, he tipped his body weight forward and angled away from his attackers, knowing that if he flapped the wing that wasn't frozen, he would spin in a circle, presenting an easy target. He had two choices. Land now while he had some control or risk the slow gliding and attempt to escape. If he chose the latter, relying only on blind luck to avoid another strike, and was hit again, he would crash into the ground uncontrolled.

Diving towards the ground was the better of the two options and if he landed quickly, surprising his attackers, he might have a chance to fight back. Tipping his head forward and shifting his body weight, he dropped like a stone. The ground rushed up to meet him as he braced his talons, grabbing at the soft soil, claws ploughing dark furrows as he slowed to a jarring halt.

His frozen wing trailed along the ground after him, adding to the uncontrolled landing and acted like an anchor. Dirt and dust exploded and debris filled the air as he tumbled snout over tail, grinding to a stop.

Dazed and confused, he righted himself, his trailing wing refusing to behave as it should. Before he could shake the dirt from his scales, men appeared, some on foot, others riding large four legged beasts that looked and smelled appetising. Only a yellow could think of his stomach at a time like this! Cursing his nature, anger and frustration overwhelmed him as he darted his neck forward to the nearest human and missed, the small annoying enemy dodged quickly away from his snapping jaws. He felt a jolt of pain as a bolt of magic hit from behind. Pivoting round, he whipped his tail with all the force he could muster, the bladed appendage, unique to yellow dragons, clove into his attacker like a giant axe, severing him in half. But it was already too late, the attack sapped his strength, weaking him.

Men, fearless and fast, danced round his disabled body, jabbing long spears that stung with magic as they made contact with his scales. His attackers circled, striking from all directions, shouting and screaming, arms waving. He turned to face one attacker and was struck from behind. As fast as he spun to defend himself, another tiny invader launched an attack from a new angle.

The more they struck, the weaker he became, their long staffs depleting his strength. Sunburst's anger grew and a rumbling in his throat sounded as he called forth his flame. He would show these men that a White Mountain yellow was not to be trifled with. Extending his neck and opening his jaws, dragon fire spewed from his mouth, hot and deathly satisfying. A semi-circle of flame blasted through the men and their mounts and the stench of roasting flesh assailed his nostrils.

Burning figures screamed as the intense flames consumed them.

Sunburst twisted back to treat the remaining attackers to more of the same and opened his jaws for a second time. Pain criss-crossed his body and a heavy net landed atop him, neutralising his magic in an instant. An empty rumble escaped his belly but no flames came this time, only the feeling of paralysing emptiness and defeat. The net immobilised him, rendering any attempt at using his magic useless. The strong strands of netting stung his body where they touched, sapping his strength and constricting his movement.

He had been so distracted by the scrabbling men he failed to notice the crew that launched the net. Struggle as he might, he couldn't break free and he could no longer rely on his fiery breath, the net's magical constraints rendering flame impossible.

Flying east was his way of dealing with the betrayal of Nightstar. He didn't know what to do and had flown from his problems. It was only now, when he thought of Rose and the dragonets that he wished he could return. He was too impulsive, a true yellow's nature. He should never have left his own shores, but blind rage had marred his already confused state. He regretted his rash actions and now it was too late.

Sunburst's efforts at evading escape over, order was restored to his captors. They quickly trussed him with chains, the metal links smothered in human magic, suppressing his strength. All the yellow dragon could do now was suffer the indignity of being bested by these small annoying men as they bound and contained his proud dragon body with their foul magic. The net and chains restrained him and the magic they held subdued any attempt to cast his dragon magic. He was winched on to a mobile platform, pulled by many four legged creatures.

He suffered the shame of being captured by humans and then transported through their city to his dungeon. The arrogant captors displayed their newly acquired prize as they dragged him deep into their maze of structures. Unpleasant and ugly, a mar on the landscape and a defilement of nature, this city of man, stinking of humanity as its occupants scurried like rats and cheered on his escort.

The memory was still painful, even though he had lost track of how long he had been held captive. His mind was weak and confused from the constant draining. His new home of blackness and despair replacing the daylight and the warmth of the sun he longed for.

* * *

He awoke to Serth's voice calling his name, his neck was stiff and his mouth dry. Cracking open one eyelid, he stared blankly at the floor of his cell.

"Sunburst!" Serth hissed. "Can you hear me?"

"I think that last draining has ended him," Fentor said.

Sunburst moved his head, lifting it from the floor, the weight of the chains like a mountain pushing down on his skull.

"Quiet Fentor, I think I can hear him moving."

"Quiet would be nice," Sunburst croaked. "My head doesn't feel too good." Each word an effort, he wished they would shut up. He longed to drift back into the blackness, away from the pain and exhaustion that wouldn't leave.

"Don't sleep, Sunburst," Serth said. "I fear you will never wake if you leave us now. The Extractor takes more from you than from all of us combined. He hasn't touched us in days. You grow weaker with every drop of blood he takes. I know you feel like sleeping the long sleep, but if you go there, only death waits behind closed eyes."

"Good advice, Serth," Fentor said, "but how much longer can he take it? Any other dragon would have long since faded and died. He is strong, very strong, but eventually he won't be able to withstand it."

"I would have liked to see the White Mountains of his home," Serth said. "The dragons there sound wonderful, the Grand Moot and the aurora. It gives me peace to think there are places where dragons can live without men to hunt us."

Sunburst could hear the respect in Fentor's voice and the longing in Serth's. He would have gone mad down here without their voices to keep him sane. He wondered what they looked like, it was difficult to get a good look inside the cells outside his own, due to the layout of the dungeon. Any dragons, however weak or small would be a welcome vision to him right now. He was sick of seeing the Extractor and his men, ugly humans, cruel and vulgar.

The eastern dragons had asked him all about his home, questioned him even more than Nightstar. How he longed for Nightstar's inquisitive words, he would happy spend days explaining things to the black dragon, even now he knew the truth about him. A dragon was a dragon, skin and scales! Nightstar had been his friend. He regretted their parting had been as difficult.

"I'm right here," Sunburst said. "I haven't gone anywhere yet."

"Sunburst the strong," Fentor said. "You inspire us with your resolve. Hold to life, yellow cousin, it is more precious with each day that passes in this bleak place."

Sunburst chuckled, Fentor's words made him think about the friendships he had forged in adversity, these dragons of the eastern continent were a hardy breed. They might be smaller and weaker on this side of the vast ocean, but what they lacked in strength, they made up for in spirit. They survived in this land against all odds. It was true, since his arrival, they had latched on to their newest inmate, stood by him as he suffered the torture of the Extractor. Talked to him, kept him sane, embraced him as part of their community and they hadn't had the chance to meet him properly or seen the colour of his fabulous scales.

"Sunburst the stupid," he replied, "captured by men and held against my will. I would flame them all, these men of the east, crush them in my jaws and rip them apart with my talons!" His anger returned, hatred for the Extractor and his men greater than any other emotion he felt. He no longer hated Nightstar or Alduce. Nightstar was a dragon and dungeons such as these and what these humans had done to their kind would disgust him. Somehow, Sunburst knew the same to be true of Alduce. Alduce loved dragons, even before he was Nightstar, his father's story was only the start of his passion. He had seen inside the man's mind and knew it to be true. Even the sorcerer would find this place vile and repulsive. He had looked deep into the heart of Alduce and he was nothing like these humans of the east.

Tiredness and exhaustion still plagued him, but he was determined to stay strong. He needed to for the sake of all the dragons held in the dungeons. Maybe he was unable to escape, but if he could offer his fellow captors even the smallest respite, give them the feeling of freedom and make things just a little more bearable, he would.

"Now," he cleared his throat, "who wants to hear about a cool mountain lake full of delicious silver fish?"

Chapter 8

Alduce left the tavern, his head buzzing with everything he had heard. It hadn't been too difficult to find out about recent events. All the inhabitants of this tavern could talk about was the capture of a giant yellow dragon. Tales of bravery about the dragon hunters were now standard fare for the minstrels and troubadours that plied their trade in the city.

The giant yellow dragon could only be Sunburst. Alduce learned that most dragons in the east were green or red, yellow being thought extinct. Added to that, according to the talk, the normal size of dragons here was half the size of the huge beast they'd captured.

The story the minstrel regaled the tavern common room held the drunken revellers enthralled. The man was a talented bard and was rewarded with a hat full of coins for his troubles.

His listeners were treated to a story about a huge yellow dragon that terrorised the countryside. The beast was of unnatural size and strength and yellow of his scales, yes, yellow, rare and unusual. Yellow dragons were known for the fierce and violent nature. The worst dragons to encounter. The residents of the tavern hung on the storyteller's words and Alduce wondered how they would feel if they came face to face with a black dragon. Woe betide these eastern men if they thought the amiable Sunburst was fierce.

The minstrel told of the yellow dragon's rampage, stealing cattle and burning everything in his path. Alduce struggled to hold his tongue, wanting to leap to Sunburst's defence and set the record straight. The minstrel embellished and exaggerated the facts, spinning a meatier tale would earn him a better reward.

He horrified his audience as he told of the heroic battle with the Extractor and his men as they rushed to the countryside's defence. Luckily they were alerted to dragon activity in the area and arrived in time to face the terrible creature. There ensued a gallant fight, where many of the heroes died, burned alive by the savage dragon. But in the end, the Extractor saved the day, trapping the fire breathing monster with a magical net, bravely putting himself in harm's way, no regard for anything but the safety of the people.

Victorious in their conquest, the Extractor's crew restrained the massive yellow beast, trussing it with nets and chains and loading it onto a huge flat wagon. Ten horses were needed to pull the heavy prize back to the city, parading the rare yellow dragon through the streets for everyone to see, before taking it to the Extractor's dungeon.

The minstrel proclaimed that as long as the Extractor ruled, they would remain safe under his protection. The spoils of his fight, the pure blood of the yellow dragon, more potent with its magic than any other dragon captured in the last twenty years.

Listening to the words of the minstrel, Alduce separated fact from the fiction. He found it hard to believe his friend would wreak such havoc amongst humans, it was not in his nature. Sunburst was unable to kill *him*, the only human ever to set foot on the shores of Aurentania. Even though the dragons of the west instinctually loathed humans, this yellow dragon couldn't bring himself to destroy the man that had deceived him. Giving his blood to save a human life was against everything he believed and he wouldn't kill men for the sake of it.

Dragons residing on the eastern continent of Eusavus were perceived in a bad light by the humans who lived here. They were everything the story teller's tales made them out to be. He had lived with the community of the White Mountain dragons and he didn't think the descendants that remained in the east after the Great Exodus, would be any different from the ones he knew.

If Sunburst used his flame, he would only have done so as a means of defence. If he had battled the Extractor and his men and been subdued by their magic, it was only natural he would try to fight for his freedom. Dragons should not be held captive, they were creatures of the sky, free of spirt and of mind. Sunburst had taught him this, opened his mind to what a dragon really was. Once he would have believed the minstrel's tale, even though his love of dragons was strong, he only knew about dragons through human eyes. Nightstar had changed that preconception and shown him what dragons truly were. The eyes of the black dragon within saw more than any human ever could.

He needed to get inside the palace of the Extractor and find Sunburst. He didn't want to contemplate the stories of blood draining and the use of their parts for magic. If his friend was subjected to this treatment as a result of his actions, then he must do everything he could to save him.

It was true, he had stolen an egg and performed similar acts on the embryo inside, but he would never have dreamed of harvesting what he needed from a live dragon.

He had thought long and hard about his actions, from a human perspective and also when he was Nightstar. He wouldn't be the black dragon, would not exist, if he hadn't done what he needed to complete the transformation. But he regretted it, even though it was necessary. Being Nightstar, he could agree with Sunburst that what he had done was abhorrent, but although his actions were detestable, there would be no Nightstar if he hadn't stolen the egg.

He justified his actions by telling himself the unborn dragon had been dead, had no chance at a life and it would have decomposed, its vital resources going to waste. But what of the unborn spirit? After studying the dragons and living with them, he had come to realise it was their belief the dragon spirit was immortal. Creatures born of magic, reincarnated back to the egg. Alduce could neither prove nor disprove this, but as a student of all things, be they scientific or supernatural, he couldn't ignore the dragon's beliefs. Nightstar believed without question and it was hard to disagree with the strength of his conviction.

Alduce would never have intentionally performed his metamorphosis, had he known about the dragon spirit, and he would never have known about it, if he hadn't. A paradox. One thing was clear to him, the persona that had grown to be Nightstar wasn't all Alduce. The black dragon was not just a man dressed in scales, he was more than a transformation spell. He was an entity with his own self, part Alduce and part something or someone else. The embryo that he cut from the unhatched egg, not only contributed its blood and scales, it provided an unknown ingredient into the mix. Unknown at the time, but Alduce now realised part of the fading spirit of the unborn dragonet had been incorporated into Nightstar's being. Merged with his mind, Nightstar was greater than the sum of his parts, more than a man and more than a dragon.

It was best not to dwell on this just now, he had larger concerns to address.

There would be ample time to reflect when he returned to his laboratory and recorded everything in his journals. If he ever returned.

Focusing on finding Sunburst, he followed the side streets, heading uphill towards the dominant structure of the Sanguinorium. Even the name of the place turned his stomach. These humans were not like the people of his home world. From everything he had learned, he would not want to live as a man on this continent. No wonder the dragons had left the east in search of a new home.

The Sanguinorium and the palace of the Extractor were not a place you could approach unnoticed. The buildings were surrounded with open grounds, providing nowhere to hide for a potential sneak thief. Alduce observed from the shadows of an alley, far enough away to remain safely inconspicuous, but too far to perceive any useful information for his infiltration.

Frustration welled inside as he attempted to formulate a plan. He couldn't cross the open expanse without being spotted, guards were posted at the entrance to both palace and Sanguinorium. If he changed into Nightstar and stormed the place, he would alert the Extractor's men. They were practiced at fighting dragons and Alduce knew that rushing headlong at the problem would only result in disaster. Nightstar might be able to defeat the men, might even be able to resist their magic better than the other dragons, but ultimately he didn't stand any reasonable chance of breaking in and freeing Sunburst if he engaged the enemy in battle first.

He needed to think things through, come up with a better plan. Caltus had often told him to think before he acted, good advice if you had time to spare. Alduce was concerned that he needed to act sooner, rather than later. Sunburst was in danger, Winterfang told him, and the pearl had made it clear. He was convinced if he waited too long, Sunburst would not survive.

The burden of responsibility weighed heavy on his human heart, hopelessness and self-doubt ate at his resolve as daylight faded and the darkness of night crept into the alley. He wished he was able to use the chameleon spell Nightstar learned from the pearl of wisdom, but that was dragon magic and impossible for a human to learn. As Nightstar, he promised Winterfang he wouldn't use his knowledge and the black dragon intended to keep his word. He wanted to make amends with the moot leader. Winterfang had expressed his disappointment at Nightstar when he discovered he had touched the pearl and stolen its forbidden secrets. But the frost drake offered Nightstar the opportunity of redemption and

Alduce not only wanted that redemption, he needed it. Not just for Nightstar but for himself.

A memory from the pearl surfaced in his mind and Nightstar joined it. Alduce was no longer aware of his physical surrounding, the alley he hid in, forgotten. His vision transported him back to the night of the aurora. He swam in the silver threads of wisdom and secrets the pearl had revealed to the black dragon. Heat prickled his skin and sweat ran down his face as he recalled the pearl, the chamber of the moot and the forbidden spells it protected. A surge of energy pulsed though his human body and his mind reached out, unbidden, connecting with Nightstar's. His body shuddered as the heat subsided, tendrils of mist rose from his exposed flesh, like hot breath on a frosty morning, creating a shimmering vapour cloud. The steamy cloud swirled around his form, slowly at first then with greater speed, cooling human skin with dragon magic.

Alduce couldn't believe what was happening, humans couldn't access dragon magic just as dragons couldn't access human magic. With the help of the dragon within him, something unheard of was happening. He could feel the dragon magic as it ran across his skin, he could reach out and touch it, bend it to his human will. He knew it as Nightstar did, could control it and shape it as he could his own human sorcery. He bathed himself in its strength and employed it as a dragon would.

Lifting his hands to his face, he peered in amazement.

They had become invisible! He embraced the chameleon spell as it came to him now, through necessity, just as it had for Nightstar in the chamber of the moot.

Alduce, a human, had used dragon magic! If he was all but invisible to his own eye, he could use that to his advantage. Nightstar had agreed with Winterfang that he wouldn't use the pearl's secrets, but Alduce hadn't made any such promises about using the spell himself. He hadn't broken his word with the frost drake, Nightstar would not call on the wisdom of the pearl. Alduce, however, was not the black dragon and he wasn't using the same spell... not exactly. He would honour the promise he made as Nightstar. He really didn't want to betray the frost drake's trust. He had learned that lesson and understood when Winterfang explained it to him. As Alduce, he reasoned the necessity of finding Sunburst before it was too late, outweighed the luxury of doing what was right.

Wasting no time to ponder the implications of this newly discovered phenomenon, Alduce stepped from the shadows and quietly strode into the open. He may be difficult for the human eye to see, but he still made noise when he moved. Employing a stealthy walk, carefully placing one foot forward, heel first, he crept towards the perimeter of the Sanguinorium.

Alduce wasn't just holding the chameleon spell, he was holding his breath and his chest ached. He silently expelled the air from his lungs and breathed normally, terrified the miracle of controlling dragon magic would vanish, but it didn't. He was a ghost, unseen as he slipped through the evening dusk, the chameleon spell and the fading light shielding him from discovery.

After what felt like hours of sneaking and creeping, he arrived at the walls of the huge building, pressing his back to the stone, becoming part of the brickwork.

Less than fifty feet away stood the huge double doors of the Sanguinorium. They were made from thick wood and the image of a dragon's head was carved into their surface, half a face on each door. The wooden dragon's face stared out, blind eyes seeing as much of Alduce as the two guards that stood either side of the giant entranceway. This must be where they had taken Sunburst, the oversized doors would only be made this size for one reason, to accommodate the entry of a dragon.

Alduce needed a plan to get past the guards, he needed to lure them away from their post and sneak inside the building. He was unsure how long the chameleon spell would hold, dragon magic used by a human was new territory for him. He stuck to the wall, edging closer to the carved wooden doors, taking care to do so as quietly as possible.

He was contemplating what to do next when a group of the Extractor's men rolled up in a wagon stacked with animal carcasses. The stench of rotting meat filled his nostrils, accompanied by the buzzing of insects. The entrance to the Sanguinorium became a hive of activity as the men started to unload and transport their grisly cargo inside. There would be no better opportunity to infiltrate the building than this, risky as it was. Alduce peeled himself from the wall and crept towards the wagon, taking care to give the men a wide berth. A collision with an invisible entity was the last thing these men needed to experience.

He waited until the last man approached the wooden doors, then fell in behind his unsuspecting escort, matching his footsteps as he entered the realm of the Extractor.

Detaching himself from the man once they were inside, he hunkered down, seeking out the relative safety of shadows behind the main door as the man disappeared down a huge corridor. There were no guards inside, it was obvious the Extractor did not expect anyone to infiltrate his dragon prison. His arrogance was Alduce's good fortune.

He waited patiently, limbs stiffening up as he crouched in his shadowy corner, hesitant to let go of the chameleon spell. His magic wasn't unlimited and he didn't want to waste it unnecessarily. Listening for the return of the men, he released his hold on the spell, his skin tensing with the cold wave that followed, the hairs on his arms and neck standing up. His physical form returned to normal, but the corner he had chosen to hide in was nearly as good as the invisibility that had cloaked him. Confident he could call back the spell if he needed to use it, he settled down, stretching his legs. As he sat waiting for the men to return, his eyes adjusted to the dim corridor, wide as any town thoroughfare and large enough for a medium sized dragon to walk down comfortably.

Before too long creaking hinges and a metallic clang echoed along the corridor, followed by the scuffing of footsteps, accompanied by the bobbing of torchlight. Alduce reached for the chameleon spell and faded from sight, invisible and quiet, holding his breath as the men departed through the huge wooden doors, slamming them closed as they left. He waited, making sure the men had gone, then stood and released the spell.

He kept close to the wall as he padded down the corridor, his senses on full alert. He hadn't seen anybody else come or go since he'd been observing the building, but there was no reason to take chances, not now he had made it this far. Eventually he arrived at a huge metal gate spanning the entire corridor like an internal portcullis. It was locked but the spaces between the bars were large enough for him to slip through. This wasn't to keep men from passing, this was to prevent dragons from escaping. As he squeezed through the gaps in the bars, the metal brushed his skin and he could feel the protection spell infused within. Strong human magic ran through the steel bars, a warding spell against the magic of dragons, designed to leach their strength.

Was this how the Extractor subdued his captors? If Sunburst was held behind powerful wards like this, he wouldn't have the strength to break free. Normal steel wouldn't hold a dragon for long, but steel steeped in this magic would make an impenetrable barrier. Alduce remembered the tale the minstrel had told, of the chains and nets the Extractor had used. No wonder Sunburst had been captured, this type of magic would render him defenceless.

Following the wide corridor deeper inside the building, the floor angled downward and the brickwork walls changed to natural rock. The farther he travelled, the lower he descended, the path leading him underground.

The corridor widened, giving way to huge cells tunnelled from solid rock and fronted with metal bars infused with sapping magic. He could hear heavy breathing from the darkness of the recesses behind the bars. The cells were occupied!

He called once more on the chameleon spell, remembering he was human and fearful that the dungeon residents would see him as one of the Extractors men. He didn't want to reveal his human self to the unknown captives, he was here to find Sunburst. Quietly he paced along the middle of the corridor, peering into each cell he passed. Most of the cells housed smaller green dragons, sometimes a red and they were half the size of Sunburst, similar in build to Little Wing, the smallest adult dragon of the White Mountain.

The dragons were in poor shape, frail and weak. Confined inside the Sanguinorium and suffering at the hands of the Extractor, they reeked of despair. Each cell was positioned in such a way that the dragon that occupied it only had a limited view. They would be able to see the wall directly opposite their bars and if they strained, the cage fronts to either side. The cells had been designed to restrict the field of vision of the residents inside. It was bad enough that the captured dragons were imprisoned in this way and he was convinced that depriving them of seeing much of their fellow inmates, wasn't just coincidence, but was deliberate. The Extractor didn't just torture and drain these pitiful dragons physically, he used a cruel form of mental torture, depriving them of the ability to see very little of who they shared their fate with.

Alduce continued down the corridor, invisible and silent, searching each cell he passed until he caught a glimpse of a pale shape, larger than the previous occupants. It was huddled as far back as the wall of the cell would allow. He pushed against the bars, staring into the darkness, the magic in the metal pulsed as it touched his skin. The constant power of the restraining magic would keep the occupants docile and subdued. Living with this sapping force each day would slowly kill the imprisoned dragons. How could the Extractor treat these once magnificent creatures this way? He must realise what he was doing and his barbaric practice made Alduce ashamed to be called human.

He slipped between the bars, narrow enough to let a man pass through and focussed on the unmoving, faded yellow scales, of the dragon within.

Sunburst lay on the dirty cell floor, exhausted and dying. Alduce stood in shock, this limp yellow shape, beaten and broken was all that was left of his friend. Alduce wished the pearl had been wrong, but it had foretold the truth. Sunburst was in danger, mortal danger for an almost immortal creature.

He remembered their first meeting and the words the yellow dragon had spoken. *I am known as Sunburst, my yellow scales are the colour of the sun. When I take flight I burn across the sky like a celestial fire.* The memory of Sunburst's words caused tears to wet his cheeks. There was no golden glow from the dragon's scales, his colour faded and pallid, the fire extinguished.

This was all his fault! He was responsible for Sunburst leaving the west. The Extractor may be guilty of many atrocities, but Alduce was equally to blame for his friend's suffering.

He slowly approached the dying yellow dragon, horrified at how terrible his friend looked. Crouching down beside Sunburst's head, he released the chameleon spell, shimmering back into existence and tentatively reached out his hand, gently stroking his snout.

Sunburst eye's opened in surprise and his nostrils flared. He jerked his head back, pulling away from Alduce's hand, chains rattling as they jerked tight. Terror filled his sad green eyes as he stared at Alduce, shrinking as far from the man as his restraints would allow.

Alduce withdrew his hands, holding them palm up, indicating he posed no threat and hoping Sunburst recognised he was no danger. He was unable to offer the yellow dragon any words of comfort, the lump in his throat preventing speech. He swallowed and tried again.

"Sunburst," he whispered, afraid the dragon had lost his mind. "It is Alduce. I mean you no harm. Do you remember me?"

"Nightstar?" The yellow dragon answered, his voice barely audible. "Where is

Nightstar?" A pitiful sound escaped Sunburst's throat, half way between a sob and a moan. Alduce had never heard anything so sad. The pained look in the dragon's eyes spoke more than words ever could and what they said wasn't what Alduce wanted to hear. Shame consumed him and hot tears blurred his vision, obscuring the ruined dragon before him.

The Extractor had succeeded in draining the life from Sunburst, the constant syphoning of living blood weakening his body and spirit. The wrongness of everything this vile man had subjected Sunburst to, and every other eastern dragon before him, pierced his heart like white hot iron. He must stop this, now and forever, he would never let this happen to another dragon as long as he drew breath. He wiped his eyes, brushing tears from his face.

"Nightstar is with me," he told Sunburst, reaching out once more and gently stroking the bruised yellow snout. "He is closer than you think, old friend." Sunburst didn't pull away this time, making a soft crooning sound deep in his chest, which was somehow sadder than the sobbing.

"Old friend?" He asked, barely above a whisper.

"Always," Alduce said, "if you will have him."

"We have been fools, you and I," Sunburst rasped, each word an effort. "Nightstar should know I missed him. I have had time to reflect on what is important." He coughed and spasms wracked his body. Alduce patted the dry faded scales on Sunburst neck. The scales on his chest no longer blazed with their natural golden sheen and were dirty and dull. One scale was out of place, bent away from Sunburst's body, the unprotected skin underneath scared and scabbed, exposing a raw and bloody wound. This must be where the Extractor had breached the dragon's armour and was extracting the precious blood he coveted so much.

"I would see the sky one last time, sorcerer. The darkness is no place for a dragon to die."

Alduce remembered Galdor, trapped underground, confined to the darkness for over a century. The sadness and sorrow of the green dragon was bad enough, but at least he hadn't been physically tortured. Galdor's spirit had been strong enough to survive the mental hardship. Sunburst's blood had been drained continually and in his weakened physical state, it was little wonder it was killing him. The knowledge that each visit from the Extractor would result in the pain of draining, the taking of his life blood, with no ability to resist, must have been extremely difficult for Sunburst to endure.

With no hope of escaping, a bleak future to look forward to, Sunburst held on remarkably well, but Alduce could see he was near his end.

"Return to Rose and the dragonets, tell them I am sorry," Sunburst choked back a harsh sounding cough. "Fly high and fly free, friend Nightstar." The yellow dragon's head slumped, as if holding his own weight were too much effort. His green eyes fixed in a glassy stare as the life faded from them, his eyelids slowly drooping closed, anticipating his impending death like welcome sleep. One last snort fluttered wheezily from the dying dragon's nostrils and then he was still.

Chapter 9

Alduce dropped to his knees, cradling the lifeless head of Sunburst in his arms, silently weeping. A soft crooning filled the dungeon as the captive dragons, sensing Sunburst's demise, paid respect to their fallen comrade.

The needless loss of Sunburst's passing was too much for the sorcerer to bear. A crippling pain exploded in his chest, more painful than the lightning strike he had suffered. Emotions boiled inside, his blood pulsed through his body, his face flushed, hot tears mixing with sweat. His heart felt like it would burst from his chest and his head swam, nausea rising as dizziness and uncertainty assaulted him.

He attempted to stand, the soft crooning of the dragon's dirge roaring in his ears, the peaceful sound deafening him like a raging ocean, crashing onto the shores of his mind. Staggering backwards from Sunburst's fallen body, the metal bars held him upright when his legs failed him. He stumbled through the spaces, landing outside the cell and sprawled on his back. His mind swirled as a thick fog constricted his human brain and Alduce was powerless to resist.

Visions of the pearl floated through his human mind, flashing memories from Nightstar's consciousness writhed inside his skull, accompanied by blinding pain. He was back in the cavern of the moot, once more experiencing the wisdom of the pearl, but this time, not as the black dragon, this time he saw it with his human mind, impossible, yet it was happening.

A black scale was forced into his vision, black as the darkest night, one scale among the many. A hard and unyielding armour. A strong sense of reliving a previous moment in time surfaced as he jumped to another thread, weaving and spinning through his consciousness.

The memories of the pearl revealed more, a talon lifted the black scale, exposing the skin below, vulnerable and unprotected as the armour that shielded it slid aside.

He remembered now, he had seen these images before but he didn't know why. He hadn't understood them and he dismissed them as parts of the pearl's confusing, swirling mix of images. When he touched the pearl, it revealed its secrets. It had shown him the secret of the chameleon spell, it had revealed the long sleep, filled his mind with the Great Exodus and exposed how to the use the hypnotic stare. He now realised it had taught him more—so much more. Information subconsciously hidden in the patterns and swirls, barely perceived and only half remembered.

Until now.

A sharp talon opened the skin beneath the scale and drops of blood pooled from the cut to gather on it, blood red on midnight black. Blood, precious drops mixed and whirled through the haze of his memory.

The final part of the vision faded and Alduce opened his eyes, staring up at the cavern roof, the coppery taste of his own blood in his mouth. He knew what he must do now, and how to do it.

The dragon pendant around his neck glowed brightly, casting an eerie light in the darkness. The pendant hot on his skin, tingling with faint traces of electrical energy. The magic of the ancient artefact, acquired all those years ago from the unknown dead sorcerer in Galdor's underground prison, took on a life of its own. Alduce was scared to move, the cold stone on his back a strange contrast to the heat from the artefact.

He had worked out how to tap into the artefact's magic when he was an apprentice, and was able to use it to call forth the vast reserves of energy it stored within. But even after all these years, he had barely scratched the surface of its potential. He knew it was there but hadn't been able to discover everything it was capable of.

The artefact had activated by itself, Alduce hadn't called on its magic. The artefact and its abilities were still a mystery to him and this was something new. The walls of the cavern crackled and small streaks of blue sparks leapt over the stone, their ethereal light merging with the glow from the pendant. The crooning of the mourning dragons had fallen silent, the only noise now the thrum of magic, tense and expectant.

The electrical sparks danced and jumped, leaping towards the dragon pendant and activating the artefact without the need of natural lightning. Alduce rolled over as the transformation began, hands and knees splayed out on the cold stone floor, his back arched as light consumed his human form. His limbs stretched and grew, his clothes ripped from his body as the glowing light radiated from the gaps between his black scales.

Nightstar returned.

A huge black dragon with a silver star on his chest took the place of the tiny human, barely fitting in the confines of the corridor.

The Extractor built this terrible place to restrain the eastern dragons he captured. Sunburst managed to fit inside, being a yellow he was naturally smaller. Nightstar was a much larger specimen. The Extractor wrongly believed Sunburst the largest of the dragon's he'd captured.

Nightstar was ready to prove to the deluded human how mistaken he was.

The Extractor could wait, Nightstar had more pressing issues. He turned around, the cave wall restricted his movement, dust and dirt showered from the disturbed roof where his wings and shoulders touched. He faced the cell of his friend, metal bars separating them.

Huge talons wrapped around the magic infused steel, the pulse of human magic flowed through the metal, magic any dragon should not be able to resist, However, Nightstar wasn't just any dragon. He was an amalgam of both human and dragon, both sides of the sorcery and magic.

Just as Alduce had reached the chameleon spell, Nightstar was able to mimic his human counterpart. His talons gripped the metal bars, feeling the magic within the metal, magic designed by the Extractor to weaken and sap dragon strength.

The catalyst that assisted Alduce was his frustration and helplessness, it had made it possible for him to reach and use the chameleon spell, a spell only a dragon could perform. Nightstar reacted to a similar combination of anger and frustration. He pushed past the barriers and reached for the human magic, feeling its flow, touching its power, shaping it to his dragon will.

He bent the bars with his massive talons, rendering the human magic within useless, extracting it from the metal and into his body. It was neither foreign to him, nor foul. He embraced the power and used it against itself. His scales tingled with human magic, it ran from his claws, surging through his body to the tip of his tail. He understood it and knew instinctually how to manipulate it for his own purpose.

Metal groaned and creaked as he ripped it from the stone, bending and breaking apart, the entranceway to Sunburst's cell cleared of its obstruction. He tossed the twisted remains of the metal into the darkness of the long corridor, clattering bars rattled as they struck stone.

Nightstar pushed into the recess, cramming as close to Sunburst as he could in the confined space. Pushing his snout right up to his still form, he sniffed his friend, nostrils flaring. There was still a tiny spark of life within the tormented yellow body chained to the cave wall. Nightstar forced his claws between the cruel metal and the scales of Sunburst's neck. He forced open the collar that restrained him, using the new human magic he'd learned, turning it to his own use. The collar shattered, dropping from Sunburst's neck. The magic within the metal no longer draining what remained of the yellow dragon's life-force. Nightstar ripped the chains from the wall and removed all the restraints, freeing the yellow dragon's limp body.

Sunburst slumped forward, rolling onto his side exposing his pale chest and belly. The battered and bruised dragon deathly pale, his yellow no longer bright. A broken scale protruded from his flank, the raw wound underneath, red and weeping.

The visions of the pearl flashed once more, this time through his dragon mind. A subliminal message planted like a seed, grew, showing him the way. He saw the black scales, the sharp talon, the dripping blood and it was clear what he must do.

He flicked out a long sharp talon, like a huge pointing finger, probing his scales until he found the right spot. Pushing hard, the needle thin point found its way between two scales. He used his dragon magic, coaxing the scale free from the rest, instinctually knowing where to probe, guided by the wisdom imprinted by the pearl. The scale lifted, tilting and twisting, opening a space in his armour.

Pushing the talon into the soft skin underneath the scale, Nightstar dragged his razor sharp claw quickly over the exposed flesh. Dragon skin may be softer than the scales that protected it, but it was still leathery and tough. Once the skin was punctured, Nightstar wiggled the claw, digging into the black flesh until he was rewarded with the trickling of blood.

Wisps of steam rose from the gash and the hot blood hissed, alive with potent magic. Nightstar dipped his claw into the red liquid that the Extractor so vehemently desired. He gently flicked his tongue across the raw wound beneath Sunburst bent scale, cleaning the crust of dried blood away, opening it up and revealing the soft flesh below. The yellow scale broke away from Sunburst's body rattling to the floor like a spinning coin.

After he cleaned the skin surrounding the wound, he plunged his talon deep into the open puncture, forcing his blood inside Sunburst's body. Withdrawing the talon, he quickly licked it clean, then caught more drips from his own bleeding wound. Holding his claw above the hole in Sunburst's flesh, he dripped more of his hot sizzling blood into the yellow dragon.

Nothing happened.

The broken yellow scale lay on the cell floor, devoid of dragon magic, damaged and useless after the Extractor's continued abuse. Nightstar knew this missing part of his friend was the final piece of the puzzle. He needed to cover the wound and seal it, in order for his own healing magic to work. The tarnished yellow scale would take too long to heal and Sunburst was too weak to lend any of his body's own depleted magic. The pearl's influence swirled in his mind and showed him what he must do.

Nightstar gripped his own bent scale tightly between his talons, still amazed at the dexterity of his dragon claws. He ripped the scale from his body, the self-inflicted pain causing him to wince, but he was Nightstar, strong and fierce. He would bear it. The agony was a small price to pay. Blood flowed from the root where the scale had been torn, pooling in a puddle on the cell floor. Nightstar covered his detached scale with the warm sticky liquid—a wellspring of magic and life.

Wasting no time, he jammed his own scale over the wound on Sunburst's side, his blood like glue, allowing the scale to stick to the flank of the yellow dragon. Once more Nightstar reached for his dragon magic, pushing it into the lone black scale, using his talon to hold it in place. Pulsing white light glowed from the flesh under the black piece of armour he had donated to his friend and this time he was rewarded with a reaction. The yellow scales surrounding his black one withdrew, shrinking back to allow the larger scale space. Nightstar pushed harder, both with his claw and the magic. The black scale rocked from side to side, moving on its own, sliding into the space and shrinking to fit. A burning sensation travelled up his claw and Nightstar pulled it back as the yellow scales moved back into their former positions, embracing the black replacement and locking it safely in place. This was the final step. The pearl had demanded a sacrifice from the black dragon, not only was his blood required, part of his body was needed too. The pearl of wisdom had guided his path and shown him the way.

Nightstar licked his self-inflicted wound, attempting to stem the flow, but the torn flesh still bled. Then, seeing the broken yellow scale from Sunburst's body, lying discarded on the floor, he grabbed it and forced it into the bleeding space where he'd torn free his own scale. He pushed his magic into the dead yellow scale, as he had done with his own and fused it to his black hide. The flow of blood slowed and gradually, the yellow scale, darker now, expanded to fill the larger gap left by the original.

A sound from the cell floor brought his attention back to Sunburst, the yellow dragon moved, his limbs twitching like a newly hatched bird, feeble and weak. A low gurgling sound escaped his throat and a tiny curl of smoke rolled from his nostrils.

Huge dragon tears spilled from Nightstar's eyes, relief and joy overwhelming him. Sunburst was alive!

Before he had time to contemplate it, he was swallowed up in the fevered dream of the yellow dragon, as their minds connected with the joining of the blood magic. Sunburst started thrashing on the cell floor, his legs flailing as strength and life returned to him.

Nightstar's role was reversed, once Alduce had been the receiver of blood, had been healed by his friend. Now it was his turn to pay back the favour and save Sunburst's life. The yellow dragon had shared Alduce's own dreams and nightmares, now Nightstar would share those of the yellow dragon.

He relived Sunburst's hatching, the exhilaration of breaking free of his shell.

Something Nightstar had never experienced, until now, another gift that Sunburst had unintentionally given him.

He knew Sunburst's mother, his clutch mates, he saw the young dragon grow to maturity, shared moments from his life as his blood mixed and flowed through Sunburst's veins.

Nightstar may not have been hatched from the egg naturally, but the fevered recollections of the yellow dragon, as his blood repaired him, allowed him to know what it was like to be reborn a dragon.

Sunburst finally stopped writhing and opened his eyes, green globes rekindled with life. It had taken Alduce days to recuperate after the lighting strike when Sunburst had used his blood on him. It had taken Sunburst a few minutes, a few minutes that condensed a lifetime of memories, emotions and experiences that he shared with Nightstar, and ultimately Alduce.

"Thank you, Nightstar the Black," Sunburst said. His voice stronger and clearer, the fog of confusion driven from his mind, now the constricting magic had been lifted.

"You are most welcome," Nightstar managed, emotion betraying his voice. "How do you feel?"

"I feel better than I have in weeks, the dull pounding of my head has lessened and my mind is clearer," he sniffed and blew a little smoke, "I can feel my magic! I'm almost a dragon again!"

Nightstar understood the irony. Almost a dragon! Sunburst had a way with words that made him laugh. There was no anger from the yellow dragon, no confusion, he had returned from near death, back to his old self.

"I'm sorry, Sunburst." He was afraid to say anymore for fear of the hatred returning, the lie and the betrayal that stood between them, heavy in his heart.

"I know you now, Nightstar. I know Alduce, and I would call you both friend. You have given me back hope and life. You have come unasked and unexpected into this dangerous place when I was ready to die. Sunburst the Yellow holds no grudge, he has decided that Alduce has the heart of a dragon. Nightstar would not exist without the sorcerer. What you have done to get there, what you did with the egg was wrong. I know you understand, no words are needed, I have seen it all, our blood and bodies have shared much. We are brothers of that blood, now and always, we are connected by a bond stronger than kin. It is a dragon thing, something Nightstar knows and Alduce will learn, given time." He paused, expelling breath that sounded like a sigh. "My words are easier to say in the dark. I am pleased you have given me a chance to say them aloud."

Alduce didn't know what to say or how to respond to Sunburst's words. Anything he could say, any attempt at justification to what he had done, the lies he told and secrets he had kept, would be too soon and he would surely risk damaging their friendship again.

The articulate way in which the yellow dragon had filled the quiet void with his heartfelt words, were reflections of his own thoughts.

"We have much to discuss," Sunburst continued, "and many comprises to make, you and I, but not now and not here. Not in this foul place, it isn't the time. I hope we can work it out, fly once more together as friends."

"Your words are wise, Sunburst. And you are right." A calm relief filled Nightstar, now Sunburst had spoken. "We need to escape this place. I doubt we will be able to leave in the same manner I entered."

"And just how did you manage that?"

"That," Nightstar said, "is a tale for another time, as I don't fully understand it myself." He stepped back into the corridor. "Are you well enough to fly?"

"I could fly all the way to the White Mountain, all I need is the sky! But I fear for the others, they are smaller and have less stamina."

"Others?"

"I'm not leaving without them. All twelve of them!" He stepped around the puddle of blood in his cell, squeezing past Nightstar and into the corridor. "Serth! Fentor!" he called out into the darkness. "Where are you? Speak out, I need to find your cells."

Nightstar followed Sunburst, the yellow dragon certainly didn't make things easy for him and it was something he was still trying to get used to. If this was the price of their renewed friendship, then he would willingly pay it.

Sunburst was right, the wisdom of dragons was something he would have to work harder at, if he wanted to live as one. Sunburst was many things, but most of all, he was a hero amongst dragons. Even if most of them didn't know it.

Twelve more prisoners to rescue and escape with. Twelve lives to save. Twelve more tortured souls who deserved to see the sky. To once more fly high and fly free.

Chapter 10

Sunburst scrambled along the corridor in search of the other incarcerated dragons. He was free at last, free from the chains and the foul metal that sapped his strength. It was good to walk, unrestricted, even if it was within the confines of the prison.

"I'm in here," Serth's voice echoed from inside her cell. "How are you free? What was all that noise? I can't see anything from my cell."

"It's another of his games," Fentor said. "How could he be free? He's restrained like us. The Extractor would never risk his source of prize blood escaping. I can't see anything either because there's nothing to see. Nothing but metal bars and rock walls!" Trust Fentor to doubt him, forest greens could be so annoying.

"The Extractor," Sunburst spat, "didn't count on one thing." He pressed his head to the bars of Fentor's cell, the human magic causing him to jerk back in pain.

"Serth?" Fentor said, "There's a yellow dragon with green eyes standing outside my bars! I think I've finally succumbed to madness, this place has driven me to hallucinations!"

"Help us!"

"Save us!"

"Free us!"

Cries filled the corridor as the captured dragons pleaded for rescue.

"I'm looking at a yellow dragon!" Fentor exclaimed.

"I'm no hallucination, Fentor," Sunburst chuckled. "But you are still a mad forest green, that I can't help you with!"

"What's going on?" Serth called out. The dark corridor filled with excited voices, each one asking to be saved, to be set free. They had remained silent as Nightstar freed Sunburst. Unsure in the darkness, not knowing what the noises were, they had cowered in their cells as Nightstar rescued him. An air of expectant hope replaced the tension, their mundane and unchangeable routine of imprisonment shattered.

"Sunburst, can you ask your friends to stay calm? The quicker and quieter we do this, they better for us all." Nightstar's powerful voice echoed off the cave walls, rumbling down the dark corridor.

The questioning stopped and the dragons fell silent at the commanding voice.

All except Fentor. "Who is that? And what is this one amazing thing the Extractor didn't count on?" Fentor demanded.

"That," Sunburst said, a smugness in his tone, "would be the friend I told you about. The mighty Nightstar. He is the one dragon the Extractor didn't count on." He stepped aside and Nightstar took his place.

"Serth?" Fentor whispered, "He's... black! Black as night! And huge!"

"I told you he was real," Serth said, "you didn't believe. I want to see him."

"All in good time," Nightstar said, gripping the bars of Fentor's cage and ripping them from the stone. Fentor flinched and Sunburst soothed him. "He is real," he said looking at Nightstar, "as real a dragon as you will meet and he's our salvation. Let him free you, his magic is stronger than that which binds us." He wasn't sure how Nightstar's magic could break the bonds the Extractor used, he suspected it had something to do with the human element that was part of the black dragon, but he didn't care. Not anymore.

The black dragon had come, he was here now and that was all that mattered. That's what friends do, help each other. He had helped Alduce when he was dying because instinct, his *perception*, told him it was the right thing to do. He saved the dying man so he could find out what had happened to Nightstar. If he hadn't used his blood, Nightstar would have died along with the sorcerer that had given him life. A life of his own, not just an illusion or a spell, he knew now, beyond any doubt, Nightstar, as Fentor had discovered, was real.

The black dragon unshackled the quivering Fentor, tearing lose the chains and bursting the metal collar from his neck. The unbelieving forest green's eyes bulged, staring at the huge black dragon that had just released him.

"I thought you were a myth! Another one of Sunburst's tales, but you really are black," he said. "Thank you mighty Nightstar." He tried to stand, his legs weak after his prolonged incarceration and his exposure to the human magic.

Sunburst studied Fentor, he was small and frail, weakened at the hands of the Extractor. Even had he been in perfect condition, he would never be as strong as the smallest White Mountain dragon. How could they expect to break free when the dragons were so fragile?

He had an idea. "Fentor, can you walk?"

"I can, although my legs are a little unsteady. I feel better now I'm free of the chains."

"I know how you feel, believe me." Sunburst said.

"I should have believed you before... before all of this—whatever this is—happened."

"You didn't know, how could you? I could show you so much more that these shores have to offer, a better life for you all."

"Better listen to him," Nightstar said, "he's the wisest dragon I know." He winked at the dumbfounded green.

"Do you trust me?" Sunburst asked Fentor, "Will you follow my lead?"

"I will follow you, Sunburst the Yellow, you have my trust, you have the trust of us all, I believe."

"Good! If we want to escape, we're going to have to work together. Nightstar, if you can free everybody, I think I have a plan that will help."

"You have my trust too, Sunburst and I would welcome any ideas you have."

The huge black dragon hunched his way along the corridor to the next set of bars. Metal groaned as he set about releasing the next of the captives.

Fentor watched Nightstar, mesmerised and Sunburst understood why. The huge black dragon was a magnificent sight. He remembered his first meeting with him by the lakeside. The eastern dragons had doubted his stories, had never seen a yellow or a black. Dragons here were mostly green or red and small compared to their western counterparts. It was no surprise Fentor was in awe.

"Follow me," Sunburst said to Fentor. He led the small green dragon back to his own cell. "Nightstar has brought more than his strength with him. He has magic more potent than you can know." He dipped his talon in the congealing puddle of blood that had leaked from Nightstar's side.

"Open your mouth, Fentor. Taste what it is to be free!" He held his talon aloft and the green dragon sniffed at it, smelling Nightstar's elixir of strength. Cautiously he extended his tongue, licking the blood from the outstretched talon.

Sunburst watched as the green dragon consumed Nightstar's blood. Licking clean his talon and swallowing the red liquid, absorbing it into his stomach. It was cold now, not as powerful as it had been when the black dragon had administered it into his own dying body. It no longer sizzled and steamed with a life of its own, but it was still filled with the black dragon's unique magic, a mix of human and dragon, sorcerer and serpent. With Fentor the blood was consumed, with Sunburst it had been added directly into his own blood. Drinking it down wasn't as effective as adding it to another bloodstream, wasn't nearly as strong, but it still did what Sunburst hoped.

Fentor's eye's blazed, his small frame appeared to fill out and he looked greener, even in the darkness of the dungeon. He could see the change in Fentor as the magic worked, restoring him, revitalising him, giving him strength and feeding him what he needed.

"More!" Fentor growled, "I want more."

"No, friend Fentor," Sunburst soothed, "you have had enough. I understand you want more, but we need to make sure everybody gets a little, we all need its strength." He didn't want to give the eastern dragons too much of Nightstar's blood as he didn't know what might happen. He knew it wouldn't have the same effect as it had on him, but these were desperate times and all would be lost if he didn't try something.

Fentor shook his head, dispelling his compulsion for more. "I'm sorry, it's just... it feels so good after... after being trapped in here." Sunburst watched him carefully until the surge of adrenalin had peaked and the craving for more of the life giving blood passed.

"You'll be fine, I know how it feels. I experienced the rush, as you have, but stronger. Nightstar healed my wound with his live blood."

"Nightstar gave you his blood? Mixed it with your own? Not the cold spilled blood I tasted, he gave you it straight from his veins, hot and alive? No wonder you recovered so quickly." He lowered his head. "I'm ashamed. I thought you were dead. I didn't think any dragon could survive the draining you suffered. The Extractor came each day, taking more and more. The dragons from the White Mountain are made of strong stuff, Sunburst the Yellow."

Sunburst was proud of his heritage, but the forest green standing with him was proud too. He had survived in a harsh land, filled with fearful enemies, he was strong in his own way.

"I am proud to call you friend, Fentor the Green, the dragons of the eastern shores may be smaller than my kin, but they have huge hearts."

Fentor dropped to one knee, his wobbly legs steady now as he bowed his head. "How do the dragons of the west feel about the Extractor? Do you have enemies like him in the west?"

"This dragon feels the Extractor is long overdue answering for his horrific deeds, but we need to escape his clutches. I know you want to exact vengeance for what he has put us through, but sometimes we must settle for what we can get." He thought of Nightstar and everything that had passed between them, his words a lesson for himself as much as Fentor.

"We don't have enemies in the west, only dragons. Let's help Nightstar with the others, they'll need calming and reassurance and you're just the level head we need."

"Me? I'm not convinced you... "

"Well I am, don't argue with me! Are you sure you aren't descended from the same line as a forest green called Galvon?"

"I think there was a Galvon, far back in my lineage. We forest greens are known for remembering our history." Fentor looked at him, cocking his head and Sunburst was sorry he'd snapped. It wasn't impossible Fentor could be distantly related to Galvon. They were so alike.

"Look, you just need to be there for them. Nightstar is a little overwhelming when you first meet him. I can only imagine what it's like for you, never seeing anything like him before. I need you Fentor, keep them calm, while I make sure they all receive some blood. Then we'll all be better prepared to leave this dungeon behind."

"I can see why Nightstar defers to you, he is correct when he says you are wise."

"Nightstar and I are equals," Sunburst said, "we are both dragons of the White Mountain and we will do everything we can to help our distant cousins."

"Fentor! Sunburst!" Serth called, "You are a yellow! See Fentor, you were wrong!" The little dragon tiredly trudged towards them. "Did you see Nightstar? He is so big... and black!"

"For once," Fentor said, "I'm glad I was wrong. Go with Sunburst, he has something for you, something that will give you strength and hope." He squeezed by them both and headed for the sound of creaking metal.

"Where are you going?" Serth asked.

"To help," he replied.

Serth stared after the green then faced Sunburst, "What's gotten into him?"

"I'm glad you asked, friend Serth, why don't I show you?"

* * *

Nightstar freed every dragon imprisoned in the Extractor's dungeon, bending the metal bars and using the magic infused within against itself. Reaching the human spell and using it as no other dragon could, breaking the chains that restrained them and removing their collars. He destroyed thirteen cells, freeing seven greens, four reds, one blue and of course, a yellow.

The captives were all in poor condition, weakened by torture, their strength sapped by the Extractor's leaching magic. But, there was an inner strength among them, forged hard by desperate times. Now they had something to believe in, no longer resigned to their dismal fate. Sunburst had given them hope. Nightstar listened to their quiet conversations as he freed them, heard how Sunburst rallied their dwindling spirits and told stories, preventing them from giving up.

Even though Sunburst had known his situation was dire and he was near death himself, he had persevered, raising their spirits and giving them hope.

Sunburst won their hearts and now Nightstar was here to free them. Sunburst took the opportunity to use the spilled blood on his cell floor. His blood. It would seem that he had changed his opinion of what Nightstar was and didn't mind that the blood contained more than the magic of dragons, if it would save them.

If they survived, he would need to have a long difficult discussion with his yellow friend, there was so much they needed to straighten out, but now, he had hope too. Hope to mend his friendship and repair the broken trust between them.

He gently pushed his way through the throng of dragons, taking care for such a large creature, aware of his size compared to his smaller kin. They looked like juveniles, small alongside Sunburst, tiny beside him.

Now everyone was liberated from their cells, they needed to break free from this miserable dungeon.

"Does anyone know," he asked the assembled escapees, "if there's another way out of here?" His question was met with silence, the dragons still a little awestruck by his presence.

"Sunburst? How did you get in here?"

"I was flying over the forest... " Sunburst began.

"I know how you were captured, I meant when you were brought inside the dungeon."

"Ah, well," Sunburst began, sounding a little disappointed at not being able to tell his story, "as far as I know, and my experience is limited, those cells don't have the best view... "

"Sunburst, think." Nightstar cut him off, "Did you enter through huge wooden doors?"

"It's not the only way in for dragons," said the small blue.

"What do you know Breeze?" Serth asked the lone blue dragon.

"There are gates at the end of this row, it is how most of us smaller dragons were brought here. I've been here for months. I think the Extractor keeps me alive, as I'm a blue and less common than the others." He looked around nervously then carried on, "My cell was the last one and I was able to see any new captives being brought in."

"Thank you, Breeze the Blue," Nightstar said. "Sunburst, take Breeze and investigate, see if you are able to find another way out."

He tore away the bars that formed a gateway across the far end of the passageway, just beyond the cell Breeze had occupied. This would give Sunburst access to the far end of the corridor and allow him to search for an alternative exit.

"If we try and leave the way I came in, we'll alert the Extractor and his men. I might be able to withstand his magic, but I fear his human sorcery would be no match for you and the others."

"We would be struck from the sky with his fire lances. Once you've been hit, you don't stand a chance." Fentor said.

"And they sting!" Serth said.

"And render you powerless, once I was hit, my wing was paralysed," Sunburst added.

"How did you get in, Nightstar? You are too large to slip in unnoticed." Serth asked.

"Nightstar's right, we need to hurry," Sunburst interrupted. Nightstar silently thanked the yellow dragon, he hadn't shared with him just how he managed to sneak in undetected, but he would know it wasn't all just the black dragon's doing.

A creaking of metal sounded along the corridor and Nightstar froze, thirteen heads turned towards him, eyes of all colours looking for his guidance.

"Quickly, someone's coming!" He hissed at Sunburst. "Go! See if there's a way out behind us." Breeze followed the yellow dragon as he retreated into the darkness.

"Stay here," Nightstar said to the others, crouching low to the stone floor and advancing stealthily back towards the huge wooden doors he had sneaked through earlier.

Along the passageway the metal gate clanged in the darkness. Lamplight flickered off the walls, chasing the back shadows, as four men carrying swaying lanterns came into view. They were dragging flat barrows stacked with barrels and behind them strode a tall man filled with an air of importance, obvious by the way he held himself.

The Extractor.

Nightstar's rage devoured him as he realised this man, this sorcerer, had come to steal more blood from his friend. His arrogant demeanour brought forth a deep rumbling growl from his chest.

The men transporting the barrels stopped short, looking up into the face of an angry black dragon. He was almost invisible in the darkness, their lamplight highlighting the silver scales on his chest.

Panicking men scrabbled backwards, tripping over each other in their haste to retreat, the last thing they expected to see was a huge black dragon filling the corridor and blocking their way.

Nightstar opened his jaws and called on his dragon's fire, feeling the heat rise from deep within his throat, rushing from his mouth with an intense fierceness that surprised him. The action was pure instinct, he didn't have to think about how to breathe fire. Dragon nature took over.

Flames filled the passage, curling up walls and rolling along the ceiling, engulfing the first two men and igniting them like small suns. The two men behind managed to avoid the main blast, one fell in his rush to escape, dropping to the floor and the flames missed him completely. The other wasn't as fortunate. Dragon fire consumed his clothes, setting his hair ablaze and he ran screaming until he collided with the cave wall and fell, lying still. The stench of burning men, smouldering piles that had once been living humans, assaulted Nightstar's nostrils.

The Extractor stood his ground, unperturbed by the devastation, burning bodies and wooden barrels aflame with Nightstar's vengeance. Arm outstretched, he gripped a long staff emanating blue light. It surrounded him in a see-through bubble, protecting him from the flames in a cocoon of magic.

Nightstar met his eyes, the Extractor was calm and unruffled as he peered back through the blue haze of his magic. A sneer curled his mouth, part cruel smile, part challenge.

The lone survivor of the flames, scuttled like a crab, flailing arms and legs moving in a blur and he sought the safest place he knew, behind the Extractor's shield. From his belt he pulled a shorter shaft than the Extractor carried, leaned out from behind his master's shelter and released a bolt of blue-white energy from the magical weapon. The Extractor dropped his magical shield and used his staff in the same way. Two bolts flew towards Nightstar, one hitting his throat, the other his wing. Small jolts of pain, a pinprick of magic, attacking his scales. If the Extractor and his man through that these would disable or paralyse him, as they had the eastern dragons, they were sorely mistaken.

The mix of human and dragon within him absorbed the magic, drawing the power from the spell. His human blood, or what was left of the mix of human blood, counteracted the effect, rendering it useless.

The Extractor let fly once more, pointing the staff and releasing bolt after bolt in rapid succession. Nightstar had the measure of his magic and had already deactivated the spell, letting the bolts harmlessly bounce from his scales, reversing the energy and consuming its power. A fantastical magical light crackled and danced over his black scales, lighting the corridor in a celestial glow, surrounding him in a corona of sparkling magic, neither human or dragon, something new and more powerful than both.

Nightstar reached again for his flame, but it was slower to come this time. The first blast had expelled an incredible amount from deep within his chest, and magic or not, it needed time to recuperate.

The Extractor and his only remaining man, realising that their weapons were no match for this dragon, withdrew down the corridor, retreating from danger as fast as they could.

Nightstar's chest rumbled as he desperately tried to hurry the flame from deep within, chasing after his quarry, pushing his bulk along the passageway in pursuit. The Extractor reached the metal gate, turned and spun his staff, whipping it through the air and cracking the skull of his remaining lackey. The man wobbled, dazed by the unexpected blow. The Extractor leapt up and kicked out, planting his boot squarely on the man's chest and propelled him back along the corridor towards the advancing dragon. He leapt through the open gateway they had brought the barrels through earlier, slamming it closed with a clang. Pointing his staff at the lock he released a blast of energy and fused it closed.

Nightstar let loose his second volley of dragon fire as the confused man stumbled forward and was engulfed in the deadly fire, bursting into flame, absorbing the brunt of the blast. The Extractor faced the dragon, his expression one of anger and bewilderment. He swiftly spun on his heal and dashed for the huge wooden doors. Nightstar batted the burning man from his path and rushed towards the closed gate.

The magically sealed lock was of no concern as he gripped the bars with his talons and performed his own magic. As with the cell doors, he countered the spell contained in the metal, bending it to his will as he tore it from the stone that had held it for unknown years, tossing the twisted bars aside.

The Extractor turned at the sound of Nightstar's demolition, surprise now plain on his face. He muttered something, a curse or an oath, Nightstar wasn't sure, before slipping through the wicket in one of the wooden doors and escaping.

Nightstar roared in anger, the noise exploding from huge dragon lungs, his neck stretched forth and his jaws wide as frustration screamed out along the empty corridor, his body shaking with rage. He turned and withdrew down the corridor as fast as his bulk would allow. They would have to act fast now, if they wanted to break free. The Extractor was alerted and Nightstar was sure he would do everything in his power to stop his prize possessions from escaping. He was able to withstand the human magic, but he knew Sunburst and the eastern dragons didn't have his unique resistance.

Even if they all managed to break free of the dungeon, the staffs of the Extractor and his soldiers would knock his friends from the sky. He had better find Sunburst and see if there was another way out, a safer path for them all to take.

* * *

Sunburst charged back along the passageway, Nightstar's deafening roar ringing in the close confines of the dungeon.

"That sounds more like anger than pain," he said to Breeze, more to reassure himself than the little blue. "Hurry now, we need to get everyone to safety." Breeze followed, struggling to keep up with Sunburst, his legs smaller than the yellow's.

They arrived back in time to meet Nightstar as he returned to the group of waiting dragons.

"Breeze, lead the way! Show them the way out," Sunburst instructed the blue dragon. "There's a gateway at the end of the passage," he said to Nightstar, "but," he hesitated, "a word, Nightstar," and he pushed past the black, sniffing the air. "Dragon fire?" he asked.

"Yes," Nightstar croaked, "it's like vomiting lava."

"First time?"

Nightstar nodded, hacking, the sound like waves on a gravel beach. He spat, saliva sizzled and hissed as it hit the cold stone floor and evaporated. He quickly told Sunburst of his encounter with the Extractor and his men.

"I wish he died in your flames," Sunburst said. "He is wicked and cruel, an enemy of all dragons, east or west."

"I wish I had ended him. You are right, he's cunning and powerful. Men like him have a knack for evading justice and bending the world to their whims."

"I would see him bent and broken for the suffering he has inflicted," Sunburst growled.

"You said there was a gateway, but?" Nightstar said, prompting Sunburst to finish what he had started before he became distracted.

"But you won't fit through... unless... " He didn't want to say it out loud.

"No, I have an idea," Nightstar said.

"How *did* you get in, undetected?"

"I had a little help from... "

"Our friend," Sunburst finished, not mentioning Alduce and keeping his voice low.

"Yes, the very same. He is smaller and less obvious than a dragon. Look, we don't have time to discuss this now, I will tell you all about it, you have my word, but once we are safely away from here." He stared at Sunburst and the yellow dragon nodded in agreement.

Sunburst wanted to reassure Nightstar he had changed his mind about Alduce and their friendship. He had discovered more about how he really felt about Nightstar and his secret, as he slowly waited for death at the hands of the Extractor. Having nothing other to do than reflect on everything that had passed, he had decided that Nightstar was a real dragon. Alduce was part of that, but he wasn't either. It was confusing, but somehow, he felt he was right. He didn't know why, he couldn't explain it, even after the endless hours of contemplation in his miserable cell.

Alduce had come to rescue him, Alduce and Nightstar. The man must have risked everything to sneak into the dungeon, but still he had come. And Nightstar, immune to the human magic that crippled the other dragons, had come too. He would accept them both for what they were, dragon and human, both part of one presence, but both strangely separate. One would not have existed without the other, but Sunburst suspected, no, he knew, that Nightstar was so much more than Alduce's creation. And, he thought, *he is my friend.*

"I look forward to that conversation, friend Nightstar. I too, have things I would say. But I will hold you to your word, when we are safe." He met the black dragons gaze and saw the turmoil in his eyes, words were difficult for him too.

"What is your idea? Can you not leave the way you came in, the humans won't be expecting a man after encountering Nightstar."

"No, if I disappear, they will hunt you down, pick you off and disable you with their staffs. The magic they use is strong."

"Indeed it is. I was caught once by it, never again!"

"Then you will need time to escape. I can create a distraction, occupy them while you lead the others to safety. The Extractor has faced me and I have bloodied his nose, so to speak. He will be furious and will not wish to lose face. Anger will cloud his judgement. It is best to act now, take advantage while he's vulnerable. He will hunger to even the score, prove he is better than a dragon. Hopefully, if he's busy with me, that will be enough to let you escape unnoticed."

"You don't have to do this," Sunburst said, "we could leave together."

"I think this is the only way. Go to your friends, see them safely away from this place. Wait until I've distracted the humans."

Distracted the humans, Sunburst thought. Nightstar thought like a dragon, even with Alduce in there somewhere. All the more reason to trust his plan. A dragon's plan.

"How will I know when to go?" he asked.

"You'll know," Nightstar said, a hint of humour in his voice. "Everyone will know."

"Be careful. I don't want to be the one telling Amethyst or Winterfang you're not coming back."

The black dragon reared up as much as the corridor would allow.

"I am Nightstar the mighty, scourge of the Extractor, blood brother to Sunburst the brave. I am strong, my magic is powerful. I am a dragon of the White Mountain. The time for careful has long passed. Now is the time for freedom and redemption. Go Sunburst, ready our kin. When you escape the city of the Extractor, turn west, fly from these shores and wait for me at the island of the volcano."

313

Sunburst stepped forward and rested his triangular yellow head against Nightstar's. He looked down at the black dragon's scales and saw a yellow scale, bright against the dark.

"Fly high and fly free," Sunburst spoke the traditional words. They meant more to him now than they ever had.

Nightstar nodded once. "Higher than you know," he whispered.

Sunburst turned and hurried after Breeze and the others, he had a feeling things were going to get interesting.

Chapter 11

Nightstar watched Sunburst depart, the eastern dragons couldn't have had a better chaperone. Sunburst would lead them to safety, he was sure, as long as he created enough of a distraction and kept the Extractor and his men occupied. He was a powerful sorcerer, he knew that when he had faced him—and the man had been unprepared. If Nightstar waited too long he would give the man time enough to regroup, he needed to act now before that happened.

He advanced towards the huge wooden doors, wondering what to expect when he exited the dungeon. The twisted metal of the gate lay where he had tossed it earlier. Picking up what was left of the bars, he crushed the metal into a rounded shape, drew back his talon and launched the makeshift projectile at the entranceway as hard as he could.

The twisted metal bars struck the door with the speed and power of a cannonball, wood shattered with an almighty crash and the doors splintered, their hinges ripping free.

Through the hole where the door had been, Nightstar watched his missile fly out across the courtyard, followed by what was left of the shattered door, wood and metal scattering far and wide, right into the heart of the Extractor's hastily assembled troops.

Hundreds of soldiers scattered as the debris tore into their ranks, but for each man who fell, there were many more to take his place. The soldiers were in mixed states of readiness, obviously mustered by the Extractor after his unexpected encounter with the black dragon. The majority of his men were heavily armoured and each one carried a staff. They were better prepared than he hoped. Even being caught off guard they appeared professional and disciplined.

Nightstar could feel the thrum of magic in the air, so many men, all armed with staffs of power. He could smell their fear. Even though they stood ready, they had never faced a foe as strong as him before.

These men were used to subduing smaller dragons, dragons who could be disabled by their magic, weaker opponents that they were prepared for.

Nightstar was going to teach them a lesson. They were not prepared for him, for his power, his fierce anger or his unique blend of magic. He would see to their education, but doubted they would be thankful of it.

He tipped his head back and bellowed, his neck strained and his jaws wide as the ear splitting roar exited the passageway, a challenge to every assembled man that stood against him.

He knew what he must do, he needed to engage the Extractor's army and distract them while Sunburst led the escape. He told the yellow dragon he would know when the time was right, all he needed to do now, was give him a sign.

Nightstar charged along the passageway towards the broken doorway, four legs fuelled by adrenaline and rage. He burst from the dungeon, the remains of the smashed doors scattering as his body forced itself through the gap.

Bounding forward, half leaping, half gliding, he landed in the centre of the courtyard, trampling bodies and swatting soldiers. He looked for the Extractor, but there was no sign of him in the ranks of his army. The men surrounding him pointed their staffs and struck back, the air filled with hundreds of blue bolts, crackling and sparking from their weapons.

Nightstar was bombarded with wave upon wave of needle sharp bolts, tiny points of agony, burrowing into his hide and jolting his scales. The magic was strong and he fought to resist it, withstanding the pain and absorbing the energy. He writhed, every strike hurting, the intensity multiplied each time another blue bolt hit. He could withstand one or two of these magical attacks, shrug them off with ease and combat the spell, but being assaulted with hundreds at one time was more than he could take.

A man could be stung by one or two angry wasps and suffer little, but step on a wasp's nest and have them all sting you, was a different story. Nightstar had stood on that wasp's nest today.

Slowly he fought back, taking each bolt and breaking down the energy, counteracting the spell, one by one, piece by piece, he managed to fight past the pain and steal the magic for his own. The more he was hit, the more he gathered the magic inside, each sting lessened, each bolt a little less painful than the last, until his body reacted instinctually, his scales taking the human magic and changing it, mixing it with his own unique power.

He stood, wings outstretched, catching the bolts like wind in a sail, filling his being with the magic that should have killed him. He pulsed with its power, overfilled with magical energy, his scales alive, crackling and sparking.

Enough.

Bending his legs and crouching low, he sprang from the ground, leaping high as the strength of his jump thrust him skyward. The men below continued to send staff blasts after him, but now they bounced harmlessly from his scales. His body overflowed with the magic he had absorbed, creating a protective shield. Small wisps of smoke drifted from him where each blue bolt struck, reminding him of something just out of his memory's reach. It was similar to the vision of the black smoke the pearl shared with him. Unknown, yet important. He didn't know why, but he trusted his dragon sense.

Nightstar beat down once, his wings lifting him higher, small blue bolts followed him up, dragging in his wake.

He stroked again, powerful wings lifting him another full length of his body, hanging momentarily at the apex, the downward position of his wings parallel with his body.

Pushing his wings above his head, reaching as far as he could, he stretched the tips and grasped for every inch of sky he could take, his body hanging, his tail trailing low, his full length exposed, poised and ready.

With every ounce of power he could muster, he pulled his wings down, faster and harder than ever before, gaining speed as they passed his neck, a blur of motion, faster still as they thrust downward reaching the bottom of his stroke. This time, he didn't relax and pull them back to the apex for another wingbeat, this time he kept going, following through to the limits of his wingspan. There was no end to this stroke, no holding back, he pushed with every fibre of his being, forcing the power of his muscles, the physical strength of his limbs and the stored magic absorbed from the staffs.

His wings met beneath his body, colliding with such a force and speed that the came together with a thunderous crack that split the air. A thunder clap louder than the fiercest storm boomed from the coming together of wings and hundreds of men dropped to their knees, staffs forgotten as they covered their ears from the deafening sound.

Thick black fog rolled from between his wings as he pulled them apart, flapping once more. The dense cloud of black mist dropped like a stone. A mist created by the magic stolen from the human attacks and infused with the knowledge of Alduce and the power of Nightstar. The black fog trailed from his wingtips, like smoke from a dying fire, the swirling dense smoke the pearl had shown him.

He rose higher, a long dark cloud of potent deadly magic rolling down and settling on the ground, thick and dark, swirling and alive.

The army below pulled back from the black fog, unharmed. It sat like a huge cloud that had fallen from the sky, thick and menacing.

Nightstar climbed higher, the last of the swirling black mist dissipating from his wings. Higher and higher he climbed, no longer in range of the half-hearted thinning blue bolts from the soldiers below.

Up and up he rose until at last he stopped, high enough. Closing his wings and shifting his body weight forward, he dropped into a dive. Tucking his wings tightly to his flanks, pushing his snout forward and straightening his tail behind, he plummeted back towards the courtyard, the soldiers, and the black cloud.

As he gathered speed, he thought back to the first day he had flown with Sunburst and the dive he made, almost crashing into the ground. He needed to time this dive to perfection or all would be lost.

The ground rushed up to meet him and at the last second he opened his wings, two huge anchors ripped through the air, spread wide to halt his breakneck descent. He pushed magic along his forewings, strengthening them as they caught the wind and were forced sharply backwards.

The downdraught blasted into the black cloud, exploding it outward, spreading it over the entire courtyard like a wave crashing over a sandy beach, engulfing everything in its path.

Nightstar braced for impact and his talons ripped into the ground, bending his legs and absorbing the shock, wings dragged behind, two black battle standards declaring his claim to the courtyard.

He stood in a clear circle, untouched by the spreading black fog as it blanketed the entire courtyard. The muted coughing and spluttering of the Extractor's army the only sign he wasn't alone.

Nightstar rose up, standing on his hind legs and unfurled his wings, disturbing the black mist with his movements. With head raised to the sky, he took a huge breath of clean clear air, sucking in as much as he could, filling his lungs to their capacity. Then, he shot his neck forward, plunging his head into the black fog that surrounded him and expelled his dragon fire, holding the flame, pushing everything he had into the cloud. He spun, facing the opposite way and repeated his action, turning his head through the swirling black fog and spraying flames into the dense mist.

Leaping skyward, he climbed from the courtyard as the chain reaction accelerated. Orange flame crawled, slowly at first, through the black fog, bright lines creating a pattern like marble, stretching and growing, gathering speed as they wove through the fog. Crackling and sparking, leaping and jumping.

The voices from within, the men trapped inside the fog, changed. Coughing and confusion was replaced with wailing and screaming.

Nightstar rose higher, he could feel the intense heat from below on his belly, could see the writhing flames creeping through the dense cloud, spreading and stretching, veins of colour changing the black fog, making it brighter. Reds and oranges glowed and pulsed, turning lighter until the courtyard below was covered in a bright yellow spider's web of fire and fog.

The cauldron of magic, fog and dragon fire reached ignition point, exploding in huge waves of flame that engulfed the courtyard, turning the black fog to intense fire, consuming the enemy caught within.

Black smoke billowed up from the ground, a swirling ball chased by bright flames, filling the air with a column of cleansing fire.

Nightstar flew over the palace, spewing flame as he went, scorching the rooftops and igniting the stronghold of the Extractor. The occasional blue bolt of magic struck him as he flew, but resistance from the Extractor's men had lessened.

He flew east, destroying buildings randomly, crashing through high towers, flaming roofs and sowing the seeds of mayhem wherever he passed. With so much fire and destruction, the humans would be fully occupied and this would allow Sunburst the opportunity he needed.

Let these men of the east believe in the tales of fire breathing dragons, creatures that terrorised and destroyed for no reason. He no longer cared what these humans believed, he knew the truth and that was all he needed.

Chapter 12

Excerpt from Alduce's Atlas of Dragons.

The Forest Green Dragon: draconis vertus arbor.

Forest greens are darker than the common green dragons and are slightly smaller in size. They are known for their distrustful and argumentative nature and can be deliberately annoying and obtuse.

They question everything, believing little at face value and rarely take another dragon's word or explanation for anything remotely disputed, demanding proof or evidence.

They make ideal candidates for positons of authority, especially when involved in Dragon Moots, record keepers and other similar roles. They have exceedingly good memories and are seldom wrong when it comes to statistics or historical events.

However, for all their social shortcomings, the forest green, when befriended is extremely loyal.

Notable forest greens: Galvon, member of the White Mountain Moot and Fentor from the continent of Eusavus. These two dragons are so alike they could be related.

* * *

Sunburst waited anxiously at the gateway to the rear of the dungeon corridor, peering out through the crack between the doors and listening to the crashing of metal and the splintering of wood. Behind him were assembled the twelve eastern dragons. It was up to him to lead them all to safety, far from the dungeon and the torturing grasp of the Extractor. No more would these dragons be subjected to his foul deeds, these dragons would escape and be free.

"What do you think he's doing?" Breeze asked.

A deafening roar of defiance was followed by the sound of smashing wood.

"Creating a distraction," Sunburst answered.

"Should we leave now?" Serth asked.

"The humans have all gone," Fentor added.

"They were in a hurry," Breeze said.

"Getting ready to fight," Sunburst said. "Nightstar is drawing them to himself, clearing us a path." They had observed the scrabbling rushing men through the gap in the door as they hurried to join the battle with Nightstar.

"Will he escape?" Serth said. "He must come with us, we can't leave him behind."

"He does what he needs to do, what a true friend must." Sunburst said, knowing that Serth was right, he shouldn't be left behind, but there was no other way. "He is Nightstar, black scales and silver starlight, he will prevail." He would trust his friend, put his faith in the black dragon, it was what had to be done.

The crackling of magic prickled his scales and he could hear the voices of men. The sound of energy bolts filled the air like angry bees, making him shiver. He hoped Nightstar's magic was a match for the Extractor. Silence descended and Sunburst worried that it was all over before it had started.

"What is he doing?" Fentor said. "It's too... "

A thunderous crack split the air and even though it was far enough away, Sunburst's ears rang.

"Get ready." He could feel more magic in the air, not the human magic of the Extractor, this was dragon magic, Nightstar's magic, powerful and alive, causing the membranes of his wings to tingle.

They waited, poised on the brink of freedom, only a black dragon and his sacrifice between them and their escape. Sunburst believed it was enough.

An explosion filled the void of expectation, ripping through the air and giving Sunburst the sign he had been waiting for.

"Now!" he roared above the din, "Follow me!" He flung open the double doorway and leapt out into daylight. His eyes slowly adjusted after weeks of darkness, to see the sun once again, to look up and see the sky, it was more than he had hoped for.

"West! Fly west, to the great ocean!" He beat wings, closed for too long, enjoying the simple freedom of flight. Rising higher, he led the dragons away from the city of men, away from the hated dungeons of their imprisonment. Twelve smaller shapes rose into the sky, strengthened by the blood from the black dragon, the higher they climbed, the less chance they would be struck by the soldier's staffs.

Looking over his shoulder, behind the flight of dragons that followed, he watched the black cloud rise, bright flames leaping and rolling after it, Nightstar's magic, fire and retribution. There was no sign of the black dragon, only the destruction he left in his wake. He contemplated letting the dragons carry on themselves and turning back to look for his friend. They wouldn't let him go alone, they would follow him, fight with him, and die for him.

He wished it were different, but somehow, he had become their hero, even though it was Nightstar who freed them. Sunburst the Yellow had arrived in their midst and been the main focus of the Extractor. While the vile human drained him of his lifeblood, he had left the others alone. They had regained their strength and recovered their pride and given them something they had lost.

Hope. He had helped them to remain strong and never give up, taught them how a White Mountain dragon behaved.

When Alduce appeared in his cell he was broken and beaten, he hadn't believed he was real. He was delirious and near death, ready to lie down and die, but the man he had saved returned the favour, saving him. The sorcerer had given him his own hope back, but it had been a friend who had given him his blood.

He was a brother of blood, not only with a dragon, with a man too. He had seen inside this man's soul, knew his human heart and shared visions of his life. How could he not change his mind about Nightstar, about Alduce, after everything he had experienced? Their roles had been reversed when Nightstar had given him his blood. They had seen inside each other, been revived and repaired by the blood that flowed through them both, blood created from an ancient magic, a sorcerer's spell and a living dragon.

There were a lot of questions he wanted to ask Nightstar and he wanted to learn more about Alduce. But it wasn't what was important. What mattered was that he was free, regardless of who had freed him, be it man or dragon, he was thankful. He could accept Nightstar for what he was, he didn't need to question *who* he was anymore. He was a black dragon and a sorcerer, but more than that, he was his friend.

As much as he wished to return, he knew he must leave Nightstar to do what he must, to let them all escape.

As they cleared the city and flew over the countryside, he began to relax, the danger of the Extractor and his men behind them now. He looked back at his entourage and his heart lurched, there were no longer twelve dragons following him, one of their number had gone.

He counted again, eleven! Someone was missing.

* * *

Nightstar raged through the city and destruction followed in his wake. With each building he flamed, with every roof he smashed, he focused the attention of the soldiers on himself. The Extractor had more men than were assembled at the palace courtyard. Patrols of staff bearing troops trailed behind the rampaging dragon, using everything in their magical arsenal in an attempt to bring him down.

After igniting the black fog, he saw Sunburst and the other dragons rise from the palace grounds, exiting the dungeon and fly west. Small dragon shapes taking to the sky, following the yellow lead dragon.

Nightstar still marvelled at the exceptional eyesight that dragons were graced with. He was even able to pick out the colours of each dragon as they followed Sunburst away from the city.

He drew the defenders away from the escaping dragons, heading east, but the fight was out of them. Once he evaded the Extractor and his men, he would circle back around and join Sunburst. Risking a quick look back, he could see the familiar yellow shape, sunlight catching his yellow scales. He appeared revitalised after the infusion of blood and some of his usual colour had returned. He hoped that he wouldn't be spotted, as he stood out, a target for anyone caring to look in that direction.

A few random bolts streaked up from bellow the line of escaping dragons, most of them falling short. Just as they cleared the city walls, a lone bolt of energy shot from the battlements, clipping the last dragon in the line. The small blue dragon faltered in the air and dropped, wavering as it descended, out past the city and into the open fields below.

The flight of dragons, led by Sunburst, didn't see Breeze fall. He was the last in line and with no-one behind him to see him go down, he dropped from sight, separated from the others.

Nightstar banked west and headed after Sunburst and the escaping dragons. He had wreaked enough havoc to allow them the time they needed to exit the city.

He pushed through the air, adrenalin surging through his body, spurring him on. He was larger and stronger than the eastern dragons and he hadn't been tortured or drained, so he was in better shape. It didn't take him long to catch up to Sunburst's escape party.

"We've lost someone," Sunburst said, as he drew abreast with him.

"I know. Keep going, I'll find Breeze," he called back, "I saw him fall. Don't stop until you reach the island."

"I should help!" Sunburst said.

"You need to get everyone to safety, trust me, I'll find him." The look in the yellow dragon's eyes was one of pain and Nightstar knew how he felt at losing a friend. Sunburst gave a quick nod of agreement and Nightstar peeled away from the formation, turning back to where he had last seen the blue dragon. Scanning the fields and surrounding trees he spotted him, surrounded by soldiers.

Breeze was pinned down by a net, the strands light and thin, but strengthened by human magic. The Extractor's troops, some on foot, some mounted, were attempting to harness the struggling dragon with chains and ropes. Nightstar could feel the Extractor's powerful magic as it worked to weaken Breeze, sapping his strength, restricting his movement and weakening his resistance.

Descending rapidly from above, the black dragon swept down over the fight and grabbed the net that pinned Breeze down. He wrapped his talons around the ropes, his claws tingling as the magic attacked him, and pulled, tearing the net from the back of the blue dragon. He reversed the spell and absorbed the magic, drawing it from the net and making it his own.

Breeze wriggled and twisted, free but unable to coordinate his movements, the energy bolts had temporarily stunned him and Nightstar remembered what Sunburst had said about being paralysed when he had been hit.

Men shouted, high pitched and full of panic, as a larger foe entered the struggle. Nightstar tossed the net at a group of riders, horses and men going down in a tangle of limbs.

He pivoted back towards Breeze, dropping down beside him on the soft grass and asked, "Can you fly?"

"I c... can't feel my l... left wing," the little blue stammered. "I've been hit by a st... staff."

Nightstar gathered his wings around them both, as Winterfang had done symbolically with the moot, sheltering them both and protecting the blue dragon from any further energy strikes. With Breeze wrapped inside the safety of his wings, he used his dragon magic, creating a shield around them both, his dragon sense instinctually guiding him. Keeping the men's attacks at bay, he searched inwards, probing Breeze, feeling for the human magic that disabled the blue dragon, repairing the damage and removing the spell.

"When I open my wings," he told the terrified blue, "I want you to stand behind me. I've disabled the spell that trapped you. I'm going to hold off these men, while you fly west. Sunburst isn't that far ahead, catch up to him if you're able. If you can't, wait for me on the shores of the vast ocean, find somewhere to hide." He pushed his own head against the head of Breeze. "Are you ready?"

"I'm ready, Nightstar, and thank you," the gratitude obvious in Breeze's words.

"Now!" he roared, opening his wings and spreading them wide, putting a black barrier between Breeze and their attackers. He pushed a protection spell from his wingtips, sending up a curtain of translucent red light, high and wide.

Breeze didn't need any further encouragement, leaping into the air and using Nightstar as a protective barrier between himself and the barrage of staff bolts. They sparked and fizzled as they struck the shimmering curtain, unable to reach their intended target.

Nightstar watched Breeze as he flew west, keeping low and cleverly using the shimmering red curtain to his advantage. When the blue dragon was far enough away, he dropped the barrier and the curtain dissipated, fading from sight.

Nightstar was exhausted, he needed rest, he had used more magic today than he had for months and was physically drained. He turned to follow Breeze and pain lanced into his side as potent magic assaulted his tired body.

The Extractor rode into the fight upon a jet black warhorse, clad from head to foot in gleaming green dragon scale armour. He sported a huge helm, fashioned in the image of a dragons head, horns protruded from either side, the visor a dragon's snout. Nightstar wondered how many dragons had died to make such a suit.

He held aloft a staff, this one different from the one he had used in the dungeon passageway. This staff was crowned with a huge red jewel set in a Flaire wrought cage. He pointed the staff at Nightstar and released a second blast. The metal surrounding the jewel sparked with electricity and the red stone glowed, fed by the Flaire energy.

This was a magic to match his own and he understood the power of the Flaire. In his depleted state, any confrontation with the Extractor would be dangerous.

He drew his wings around him and cast another protection spell, this time he wove an explosive reaction into the surface of the barrier.

The Extractor's bolt struck the shield and Nightstar released his hold on the spell. The magic gave way as the bolt collided with the protective curtain of red and the explosive barrier erupted in a blinding flash of light. Nightstar released his dragon self and became Alduce, shrinking from the huge black dragon to the man. He embraced the chameleon spell and used the exploding shield to disguise the transformation.

When the noise faded and the after effect of the blinding light disappeared, where once a huge black dragon had stood, there was nothing except a few fallen soldiers, who had been caught in the blast.

The Extractor's men gave a ragged cheer at the perceived destruction of the black dragon, the armour clad Extractor stood up in the stirrups of his warhorse, scouring the area in front of him where Nightstar had been, then held aloft his staff, inspiring another cheer, more hearty this time.

Alduce remained a statue, naked and exposed. He felt vulnerable and unprotected, feeling the loss of protection from dragon scales and wings, his preferred armour, compared to that of his soft pink human skin.

He was counting on the dragon magic being used in such a small scale, that the Extractor wouldn't be able to sense the chameleon spell. After all, this was a secret from the pearl of wisdom and no human should be able to feel it, let alone master it.

The Extractor looked skyward at the departing blue dragon, then shouted at his men, rallying them as he rode west, chasing after Blaze. The soldiers gathered themselves and followed their leader, leaving their fallen comrades behind. Alduce waited, letting them leave, powerless in his present form to stop them.

Red bolts of energy burst from the Extractor's staff, chasing through the air after the blue dragon. Blaze weaved and swerved, dodging the missiles that would bring him down. The blue dragon had spirit and a will to survive, but even if one of the energy bolts hit their target, his chasers would be on him again.

The soldiers, their vigour renewed by the Extractor's actions, joined the attack, raising their own staffs and sending blue blots to accompany the larger red ones from their commander.

Blaze managed to keep one step ahead of his pursuers, his aerial prowess impressive after his incarceration, but Alduce knew the odds were stacked against the brave blue.

Raising his arms high, he called on the power of the artefact, drawing the lightning from a clear sky and invoking the transformation. It was so much easier, almost instinctual, from the first time he had made the change, standing alone on his starry mountain top. There was less agony this time as his body stretched, pink flesh growing into black scales, long neck and tail sprouting from the small human form as wings grew. The pain of the metamorphosis was less intense, it was still uncomfortable, but now it was more bearable. It seemed that each time he transformed, it was less difficult than before. He stored his thoughts away, a subject to ponder another time, more to record in his journals when he eventually returned to his laboratory. It was bizarre to think of his research at a time like this. As Caltus often liked to remind him, he was always a scholar.

Nightstar rose from the ground, lifting into the sky, huge black wings propelling him after the Extractor and his men. The time for definite action was now, as a clarity of mind settled over him. His magic was nearly depleted and he was thankful that holding the dragon form only required the smallest spell.

The Flaire artefact was filled with an almost inexhaustible supply of power, stored within the rare metal of its manufacture, but a sorcerer needed his own magic to access and control that energy.

Nightstar would count on his strength now, the physical prowess of a dragon, powerful wings and strong muscles, tough scales and sharp talons were the weapons at his disposal.

He cut through the air with an impossible silence, his huge bulk should have made some sound, but was unnaturally quiet.

The black warhorse thundered across the grasslands, huge hooves drumming as the Extractor stood in the stirrups with his back to Nightstar's stealthy approach. He remained unnoticed by the Extractor or his men, as they continued to launch energy bolts, intent on bringing down the blue dragon they chased.

Nightstar tilted forward, angling his trajectory at the men on horseback as they galloped after the escaping dragon, oblivious to his presence.

Black and deadly, he scythed through the air, an ebony blade of vengeance, intent on the human that had tortured and destroyed an unknown number of dragons.

The time of reckoning was here at last, pent up anger and rage pulsed through his body. An immense hatred for the Extractor and all he stood for burned in his blood, igniting his desire to eliminate this enemy of dragon kind, once and for all.

Faster and faster his descent thrust him towards his goal, air rushed over his sleek scales, wind tore at his eyes. Blurry tears formed, not from the draught, but tears of anger and pain for all his fallen kin.

His wings streamed behind him, shedding air silently as he plummeted downwards like a spear, then he pulled them back, opening them wide and creating a rush of intense air pressure, buffeting every fibre of his being.

He opened his jaws and roared, releasing the pent up emotion he held inside. Anger at the Extractor, the fear of his discovery, the loss of friendship, the frustration of helplessness and the pain of the all the stupid lies and deceit.

The Extractor turned in his saddle as Nightstar's talons closed around his armour encased body, his own scream joining the dragon's as the crushing grip tore him from the saddle.

The chasing soldiers scattered, horses fell and men were thrown from their mounts as a violent tidal wave of air crashed into them.

Nightstar squeezed the dragon scaled armour of the Extractor, crushing the shell he was encased in. The armour was strong, a protection against most attacks, but against Nightstar's forceful grip it was a poor second. He felt the scales give as his claws pierced and cracked the green armour, sinking with an unexpected satisfaction into the man encased within.

The Extractor went limp and the red glow from the jewelled staff faded, but it remained tightly grasped in the man's death grip.

Nightstar rose once more, the Extractor's limp corpse hung lifelessly below him, impaled on his talons. He could feel the man's blood seep from his crushed body, dripping through his claws as it leaked from the holes of his ruined armour. It was his blood that ran now, not that of the dragons he had harvested, an ironic justice and a fitting end to his existence.

Alduce surfaced in Nightstar's consciousness, his human half thankful of the dragon spirit, a guiding strength that had steered him away from a similar path taken by the Extractor.

He roared again, scattering the remains of the Extractor's soldiers, no longer a threat, beaten and bested by the creatures they had, for too long, butchered and killed.

He carried the broken body with him, following after the tiny blue speck that was flying west. In search of the vast ocean, Sunburst and the dragons of Eusavus.

Chapter 13

The black and blue shapes of Nightstar and Breeze glided into the crater of the extinct volcano. Sunburst had reached the island with eleven free dragons. He refused to feast on the plentiful wildlife with the other dragons, instead pacing along the rocky crater ridge, watching and waiting. Searching the eastern horizon for his absent friends.

Stepping back, he gave the approaching pair space to land. Nightstar and Breeze dropped onto the black volcanic sand, side by side, blue and black scales vibrant in the warmth of the evening sun.

A chorus of calls greeted the retuning pair as voices rose from the thick trees below, trumpeting in triumph, dragons greeting their own, happy and free.

"Are you hungry?" Sunburst asked Breeze, cocking his head towards the other dragons. "They've been feasting on beasts that look a lot like curly bucks."

"Like the ones you told us about when you hunted with Nightstar?" Breeze asked.

Nightstar looked over at Sunburst and he nodded his head. "Yes," he said, "they look very like them. And on this island, there's not much chance of them running too far away."

"It will be good to hunt freely again." He looked at Nightstar and then back to Sunburst. "If you'll both excuse me, I believe I'll join my cousins in the feast." The little blue was perceptive, recognising the yellow and black dragon would want to speak alone.

He dropped one foreleg to the volcanic sand and bowed to Nightstar, showing respect to the giant black before him.

"Thank you Nightstar, my life is yours, not once, but twice." He hopped over the ridge and dropped down into the trees, trumpeting to the dragons that were waiting below.

"It is good to see you, Nightstar," Sunburst said. "I'm happy you brought Breeze back with you. I suspect there's a tale to tell about his rescue."

"It is good to be here," Nightstar paused, "among friends," it was almost a question. He dipped his head, avoiding eye contact.

"Old and new friends, brother Nightstar," Sunburst reassured him. "Tell me what happened?"

"Anything for a story, eh?" Nightstar said, sounding more like the black dragon he had known before everything changed. Sunburst listened as Nightstar told of finding Breeze and his encounter with the Extractor. These were the actions of a true dragon, not the human within.

"And what of the Extractor's body?" he asked.

"The Extractor's body and his red jewelled staff will never be found, I dropped them into the ocean, in the deepest darkest waters I could find. No-one will have his power or wield that magic again."

"Did you... Alduce, not desire the staff?" It was still strange, knowing the sorcerer was a part of the dragon before him, but it didn't bother him anymore.

"No. Let it lie on the ocean floor, far from any temptation or further corruption. We *both* made that decision," Nightstar said, putting an emphasis on the word. Sunburst understood that it wasn't just the choice of the black dragon. "It is a magic best lost. Even the scholar in me knows the price is too high."

"And it would look odd carrying it home to the White Mountains," Sunburst said. Nightstar didn't answer when he mentioned home. "You are coming back?"

"I'll accompany you home, Sunburst, but I cannot stay."

"Why not? You're a hero! You set everyone free! Winterfang must be told of what you have accomplished."

Winterfang. Sunburst recalled his fevered memories when Nightstar had shared his living blood with him. The moot leader told Nightstar he would be banished for a year and a day. He had tasked the black dragon with finding him and bringing him home, but he would still have to leave, his punishment for touching the pearl. Nightstar must realise that he knew he had touched the pearl, but Sunburst believed that without its influence, none of the dragons would have survived. Perhaps the pearl had intentionally shared its wisdom with Nightstar. Maybe it wasn't his fault, it could have compelled him, chosen the black to be their liberator. He supposed that was something else they would need to discuss, but for now, it could wait.

"I'm no hero, Sunburst. I might have freed the dragons from the dungeon, but it was you who truly freed them. You freed their minds and their spirits. You told them of a better life, of the White Mountains and all that is good there. You won their hearts and gave them hope, even when you were dying, you put them first. That's heroic and that is why they will follow *you* home, not me." He paused, as if searching for the right words to continue, but said no more.

"And you still carry the guilt of your... secret." finally, the subject that neither wished to discuss, but must be addressed before it grew and drove a wedge between them again. The words were difficult to say, but if he didn't tell Nightstar, the black dragon would be consumed forever, lost in his own turmoil.

"It is my secret too and it will remain so. We have shared too much for this to come between friends. I have had time to think and we have shared blood, not once but twice. I gave freely of my own, as you did. It's not just the mixing of our blood and the insight it gives us both, I understand you now, as you surely must me." It was said, out in the open, his decision made. "We will face Winterfang together, as brothers."

Nightstar's lifted his head, "After all I have done? You would stand with me? I don't know what to say."

"Then say nothing more, it will be between us only. You have two sides to you, dragon and man. I have seen evil men, and I know that Alduce is not one of them. I admit to having prejudice, but I see things more clearly now. Life isn't as easy as right and wrong, I should know that!" he snorted, "I am a yellow after all."

"You will keep my secret, even though you know what I am?" Nightstar whispered, doubt in his voice.

"You are a dragon first... to me at least. You might have a bit more to learn about your kin, but I will teach you, if you wish. Your banishment isn't forever and there are others at the White Mountain who will be pleased to see you again."

"I would like that," Nightstar said. "It is more than I could have hoped for, after everything that has happened. You have already taught me more than you could ever know."

"Then let us put our differences behind us, brother black, a new beginning for us both."

"Agreed, a new beginning," Nightstar replied. "Not just for us but for the dragons we saved. Do you think they will be able to cross the ocean with us? They are much smaller and less resilient than the dragons of the west."

"They have tasted the blood of the mighty Nightstar. Now they could cross over and back again, I'm sure of it. They may have been weak, but they are changed, like me. They are stronger now and will fly where we lead. Look at them Nightstar, they are reborn. We've given them a second chance. They are dragons and I'm taking them home." *Home* Sunburst thought, nothing more to say than that.

He leapt up onto the rim of the crater, turning back to face Nightstar. "My yellow scale has turned black on you, look at it." He looked down at his own chest to the black scale Nightstar used to heal his wound. It had changed too, no longer black, but faded and turning yellow.

The black dragon looked at both swapped scales. "And my scale is taking on your colour."

"Everything is as it should be," Sunburst chuckled. "Back to normal."

"Normal?" Nightstar said.

"Accept it brother. Now let's feast. I am ravenous!" He stepped from the ridge and set his wings to glide, dropping down into the trees in search of food, hoping the eastern dragons hadn't eaten all the best bucks. Nightstar's deep voice reached his ears, following him down.

"Somethings never change."

*   *   *

Eight days later, fourteen dragons arrived at the White Mountains on the western continent of Aurentania. Their party was led by the returning yellow dragon named Sunburst, followed by seven greens, four reds, and one blue. All natives of the eastern shores, newly liberated from across the vast ocean. A giant black, Nightstar by name, brought up the rear, carefully avoiding the attention of the native dragons.

Their arrival was later to be known at the Second Exodus and Sunburst the Yellow, basked in the glory that was bestowed upon him, as he told the tale of his adventure in the east.

The Moot Leader, Winterfang the frost drake, welcomed the new dragons to their community and a celebration was held for the safe return of one of their own and the new friends he brought with him.

Sunburst and Nightstar were summoned to a closed moot with Winterfang and what transpired inside the cavern was never made common knowledge. Shortly after the celebration, Nightstar departed on his own and flew south. He informed his friends that there was something that he must attend to, but he would return in a year and a day. Much mystery surrounded the disappearance of Sunburst, his return and Nightstar's part in his adventure, but such is the nature of rumours and speculation.

Perhaps, one day, the full story would be revealed, but until that day, the version Sunburst told, and retold, would have to suffice.

Epilogue

Excerpt from the private journals of Alduce.

The differences between man and dragon are vast, like the difference in their size, but their minds, their hearts, their values, their morality and basic needs are closer than I would ever have guessed.

The persona of my dragon self is an individual in his own right and I am Nightstar as much as he is Alduce. We both exist as separate entities and as one. We have learned to co-exist and I cannot write on a page, why or what that is. I only know what I feel and can finally accept it for what it is.

Even now, I feel the dragon inside, part of my being and so much more of my soul, bound together forever, two sides of the same coin.

The voyage I started so many months before, standing naked and alone on the mountainside, calling down the lightning and working the spell of transformation, has been filled with many emotions. Some I welcome and others I despise.

I have felt physical pain, unbearable agony as my limbs stretched and changed as the fire in my blood burned. The strange feeling of loss when I am in my human form, small and insignificant.

The joy of flying, free and unburdened, the exhilaration of flight. I have known true friendship, freely given, and unexpectedly welcomed.

The weight of deep guilt and selfish betrayal and the web of lies that can pull one's very soul into the dark abyss of no return.

But I have also found forgiveness and compassion where none were expected, acceptance and understanding, and also redemption.

I never truly understood what it was to be human until I was a dragon, with dragons to teach and guide me. I am much more than a scholar and a sorcerer, more than any scientist or mage, yet I realise now just how humble I am.

However much I strive for more answers, reach for the knowledge that drives me, I know now that I must stop on that journey and look around at the little things that are equally as important.

Alduce.

* * *

Alduce lay down his quill, leaving the pages of the book open, allowing the ink to dry. It was a habit he had adopted as he couldn't stand to see smudged ink on his precious scale bound pages. He had made many journals from the gift Galdor the Green had given him. Just books, but transformed into something special by the rarity of the beautiful green dragonhide they were bound in.

The bookshelves in his living quarters, deep inside his laboratory, were crammed with his work of the last eleven months, since his return from the White Mountains. He had written each day, recording his findings and thoughts, using the sorcery of a recall spell to aid him in remembering the smallest of details with accuracy, filling page after page, volume after volume. He had laughed and cried as he wrote, so vivid were the memories, the dragon's blood in his veins enhancing them and the emotions each one brought.

He didn't care if anyone would ever read them, they were personal to him, but educational as well. His discoveries would read like fairy tales to those that didn't know, didn't understand, but it was his journey, his story, his life that was immortalised in ink, and that was enough.

The Atlas of Dragons was the work he was most pleased with, it was a factual record of the many different dragons he had encountered, their lore and their lives. The pages were crammed with everything he had learned, but more importantly, there was no record of who Nightstar really was. He had remained objective, distanced his dragon self from this book, to provide an unbiased volume that scholars could learn from, should they ever read it.

Furthermore, he had kept that secret, only himself and a particular yellow dragon shared that knowledge, and that was how they intended it to remain. His private writings would remain inside this laboratory, his eyes the only ones that would read them.

He stood and stretched, surveying his tiny room, taking a last quick look around now his writing was complete. Opening the door, he stepped into the laboratory and flicked the light switch, plunging his living quarters into darkness. He picked his way through the many benches and machines until he reached the table where the sets of Flaire rods lay.

Gathering up eight of the rods, he left the laboratory, palming the orb set beside the doorframe. The room behind him went dark and the metal door closed, the central panel briefly glowing with a faint light, then the lock clicked into position.

The outer cave had been expanded and Alduce walked to the far wall and placed the Flaire rods in the eight holes, hollowed from the rock and arranged like the points of a compass.

He turned from his work as a loud scuffling from behind alerted him to someone entering the inner cavern.

Sunburst pushed his bulk through the entranceway from outside. It was a tight squeeze for the yellow dragon, but Alduce hadn't wanted to enlarge the cave entrance too much, for fear of his private laboratory being discovered.

"Are you finished at last, sorcerer?" The yellow dragon grumbled, shaking the dust and debris deposited on his back from squeezing through the narrow cave mouth.

"I am. And can you please stop calling me sorcerer, dragon! You know I don't like it."

The yellow dragon chuffed, amused with himself and Alduce couldn't help smiling at the infectious sound.

"Why do you think I do it?" Sunburst said. "You humans are so touchy. Are we ready to leave?"

"Humans are not touchy, I think... " He paused. "Am I really touchy?"

"You've spent months shut up in that cave. You need to stretch your wings."

"I need Nightstar. You're right. Tell me, how does a mere *yellow* get to be so wise?" Alduce said, getting his own back.

"Enough *sorcerer,* or I'll eat that mangy pony of yours and terrorise the villagers."

"Don't bother my pony, he's a loyal friend... "

"That you don't need, now you have wings," Sunburst chuckled. "Relax, the pony is safe, there are much tastier bucks north of here. A dragon has to eat, you know."

"Are you ready then?" Alduce asked.

"To meet the legendary Galdor the Green? To fly free through new skies? Alduce, I am more than ready. This little cave and your mountain are pleasant enough, but a yellow needs adventure in his life."

"Adventure? Remember that when *you* have to explain to Rose and Amethyst why we've been away for so long."

Sunburst puffed a little smoke from his nostrils. A gesture Alduce associated with his yellow friend when he was being dismissive.

"I'll just tell them I was off rescuing more dragons in need of my help."

"Sunburst, my friend, you are by far the most magnanimous dragon I've met."

"My charitable spirit and forgiving nature shine like my yellow scales, allowing me to ignore your sarcasm," the yellow dragon retorted.

Alduce clipped the Flairestaff together, inserting his artefact into one end and pointing it at the circle of rods and thumbed the switch. Lightning crackled from the staff jumping to the rods set in the cave wall, sparks of energy leaping from rod to rod and completing the circle.

The rock inside the circle shimmered and a hazy view of a world beyond appeared, out of focus at first, then slowly becoming clear. Galdor's world.

Removing the Flaire pendant, he propped the staff against the cave wall. He dropped the chain over his neck, the silver of the tiny elegant dragon, catching the light beyond the portal.

He removed his clothes, tossing them on the cave floor beside the staff, looking down to the yellow shape on his skin, remarkably like dragon scale. He ran his human hand across the unusual mark and his fingers tingled at the dragon magic that was now a familiar part of him.

Alduce stepped from the shadows of the cave into the warm sunlight of an unknown summer sun. He turned back and looked at the golden yellow of Sunburst, his name mimicking the light from this side of the portal.

Grinning at the yellow dragon he said, "Let's Fly!"